EASTERN LIGHTS

BRITTAINY C. CHERRY

To those who are alone:

May you find a love so strong within yourself that even when you're alone, you are far from lonely.

"The most terrible poverty is loneliness,
and the feeling of being unloved."
—*Mother Teresa*

PROLOGUE

Connor

Eight years ago
Seventeen years old

Every grand story began with once upon a time. It didn't even have to be a grand story. The mediocre ones began the same way, too. At least that was how mine began.

Once upon a time, a young boy was scared shitless about losing the person he cared about most.

I once had a teacher who taught me that there are two things in life a person can never prepare for, no matter how hard they try. Those two things are love and death.

I'd never been in a romantic type of love, but I knew the love between a kid and his parent. It was due to that love that I'd experienced the fear of death. For the past few years, it seemed I'd been swimming in a pool of sorrow that'd appeared out of nowhere. I wasn't prepared for it at all. For the past few years of my life, my search engine was filled with thoughts no kid should ever have to consider.

What happens if your only parent passes away?

What is the likelihood of a person surviving stage 3 cancer?

How much money do you need to make to pay for experimental treatment?
Why don't all people get the same treatment for cancer?

Not to mention the number of jobs I tried to apply for to help my mom with the bills. I even started up a few of my own companies just to help make ends meet. Mom hated that I worked so much. I hated that she had cancer. We'd call that an even deal of hatred.

I put on a brave face for the rest of the world, being the charmer I'd always been. Everyone in my small town knew if they needed a decent laugh, a good friend, or a great worker, they could come to me. I took pride in being the hardworking class clown of sorts. Hell, I needed it because if I wasn't being goofy or a workaholic, I was overthinking. And if I overthought, I'd drown.

I never revealed my pain to anyone. I figured if they knew how bad I hurt, they'd worry about me. I didn't need anyone worrying about me at all—especially my mother. She had enough on her plate as it was, and the last thing she needed was to be concerned about me being concerned about her. Still, that didn't keep her from worrying about me. That was what mothers did when it came to their children, I supposed. They worried.

Our relationship was a forever loop of us checking in on one another. Mom was my partner in crime in that way—we worried about each other's worries. Wash, rinse, repeat.

"You can come in with me," Mom said as we waited in the lobby of the doctor's office. "You've been with me through every step of this both times, so I want you in the office with me, no matter what."

I swallowed hard and nodded my head. Even if I didn't want to go in, I'd never leave her alone.

I hated how the waiting area smelled, like mothballs and peppermint patty candies. Years back when Mom was first diagnosed with cancer, I'd stuff my pockets with those candies when I came with her to the doctor's office. Now, just the smell of them made me want to heave.

We were waiting to see Dr. Bern to get the results of Mom's last round of testing to see if the chemotherapy had worked or if the cancer had spread throughout her body. Needless to say, my stress level was through the roof.

"Mrs. Roe? You can come back now," a nurse said, smiling toward us. Even though my mom had divorced my lowlife father years before, she'd held on to his last name. I'd told her to change it, but she told me she had received the best thing from having that last name—me. Plus, she loved how we were still tied together with our last names matching.

Mom was a softy like that.

As we walked into the office, I hated how familiar everything felt to me. No one should ever have to become familiar with a doctor's office. I hated how I'd sat in that waiting room when I was ten, eleven, and twelve. I hated how I was forced to do the same thing again when I was fifteen, sixteen, and seventeen.

I called ages thirteen and fourteen the wonder years—when my happy was really happy and my sad hardly visited me at night. All I wanted for my future, for Mom's future, was more wonder years.

I hated the nerves that built up within me from the memories that led us to that office. I hated everything about that building, from the crappy chairs to the harsh lighting. The carpet had stains that had probably been there from the nineties, and there was a good chance Dr. Bern was over two hundred years old. The dude didn't look a day over one hundred, though. I had to give him props for that.

Mom never complained about it, though. She never complained about anything really. She was just thankful she had a doctor who looked out for her even when the insurance companies didn't. I wondered what it was like for rich people. Did their hospital waiting rooms have cappuccino machines? Were there mini fridges with chilled drinks? Did they get asked for their insurance card before they received treatment?

Did the receptionist look them up and down when they learned they were on government assistance?

Did the cancer leave their bodies faster than it left the bodies of the poor?

How different would Mom's life have been if we came from money?

We sat down.

I felt nauseous.

"Think positive thoughts," Mom said, squeezing my kneecap as if she knew I was slipping into my place of doubt and anger. I didn't know how she did that. I didn't know how she knew when my mind floated away from me, but she always did. A mother's gift, I guessed.

"I'm good. Are you good?" I asked.

"I'm good."

The thing about my mother—even if she wasn't good, she'd lie and say she was because she didn't want to put any stress on me. I never understood that. That woman was going through her second round of cancer, and she was still more worried about my well-being than her own.

I supposed moms are kind of like that—superwomen even when they are the ones in need of being saved.

The clock ticked abusively loudly as we waited for Dr. Bern to join us in his office. My fingernails couldn't have been any shorter with the way I was chewing at them, but I didn't care. I couldn't focus on a damn thing until I knew the results of Mom's labs.

"Are you getting excited for your birthday carnival?" Mom asked, nudging me in the arm. She was talking about my eighteenth birthday festival that was going to be over the top and ridiculous, but truthfully? No, I wasn't excited. I wouldn't be until those results came back, and I knew she was going to be okay.

Anyway, I lied. I pushed out a smile because I knew she needed it. "Yup, so excited. It's going to be amazing. Everyone in town is coming. I even think I convinced Jax to stop by."

Jax was my boss, and I was his pain in the ass, also known as his bestie. Most people in town didn't understand the grumpy dude, but I did. He'd been dealt a shitty hand in life, but he had a better heart.

The thing about Jax was he didn't exactly know we were besties because he was a bit slow on the arrival of truths, but he'd come around to the idea. I was like a fantastic fungus—I grew on people.

"Of course he'll come. He loves you," Mom agreed, because even through Jax's annoyed expression around me, she saw how much he liked me.

That, or we were both insanely in denial.

Dr. Bern came into the room, and I tried my best to assess his thoughts based on how he moved. Was he coming to deliver bad news or good? Was there a heaviness that sat on his chest or not? Was he going to be the devil or an angel that afternoon?

I couldn't read him.

My stomach was twisted up, and all I wanted was to know what was written on the papers he held gripped in his hands.

"Hello there. Sorry for the delay." Dr. Bern's brows were knitted closely together, and his forever grim expression weighed heavily on his features. His shoulders were always hunched, and I knew exactly what that meant.

He had bad news.

The cancer wasn't gone.

Had it remained the same? Had it spread to different locations in Mom's body? Was she dying? How long did she have to live? How many more days would I be able to spend with her? Would she see me graduate college, would she see me find success, would she—

I glanced over at Mom, and tears were rolling down her cheeks. I blinked a few times, wondering why she was crying already, why she was falling apart. I looked at Dr. Bern, realizing I'd zoned out for a bit, contemplating the amount of time I had left in the world with my mother, my person, my best friend.

Yeah, I was a seventeen-year-old kid and my best friend was my mother. I'd bet a lot of other jerks would feel the same way had they almost lost their mothers twice to painful cancer battles.

Pain.

My chest.

It felt as if a semitruck was pressing down on me, blocking my airwaves from allowing air to flow through my lungs. I couldn't breathe. Mom was crying.

I couldn't breathe, and Mom was crying.

I wanted to cry, too.

I felt the tears sitting at the backs of my eyes as I swallowed hard and tried to be the strong one. I had to be the strong one; that was what being the man of the house meant—it meant being solid even when you felt as if your heart was being liquified into a puddle of pain.

"Did you hear that, Connor?" Mom said, her shaky hands in a prayer position.

I looked up to meet her eyes, and for a second, I thought I saw a flash of hope. Her lips were curved up as the tears kept falling. My stare shot to Dr. Bern, and I sat back in my chair the minute I locked my eyes with his.

He had the same splashes of hope in his stare as Mom had—and he was smiling. I hadn't even known Dr. Bern knew how to curve his mouth in that direction. Everything I'd received from him in the past had been doom and gloom, and now, he was freaking smiling.

"I'm sorry, can you repeat that?" I muttered, feeling too cautious to dive into the land of hope before I heard the words leave the doctor's mouth.

He removed his glasses before leaning forward on his desk, giving me that smile I hadn't known existed, and said, "We got it all, Connor. Your mother is in remission."

I collapsed back into my chair, feeling every good emotion crash into my chest all at once. An overwhelming feeling of bliss overtook every single part of me.

The cancer was gone, Mom was okay, and after the worst years of my life, I was finally able to breathe again.

"Mom?"

"Yes, Connor?"

"I'm taking you to fucking Disney World."

"Language, Connor."

"Sorry, Mom."

ONE

Aaliyah
Present day

"A
LL RIGHT, THAT'S A WRAP ON THE DEPRESSED, EMO GIRL
vibes. Aaliyah. Look at you. You look awful from head
to toe. You've been eating like shit to the point that even
your ankles are getting fat," Sofia said, shaking her head in complete
disgust. Nothing like a roommate telling you how shitty you looked to
make you feel better about yourself.

I grumbled in response.

She rolled her eyes. "See? This is what happens when you lay
around for weeks, crying over a dude who cheated on you. You're literally mourning a cheater. That's embarrassing. Now, get your ass up. It's
Halloween. We're getting drunk."

That conversation got me off the couch and into a Little Red Riding
Hood costume. Sofia and I weren't really even friends. We'd been living
together for a few months, and we were complete opposites. She was a
party girl, while I'd rather be home reading comic books. Over the past
few weeks, I hadn't been able to read as clearly, though, due to the tears
wetting the pages.

Sofia pitied me. I knew because she said the words, "Damn. I really pity your sad ass." She was very straightforward that way.

That night she dragged me out for a girls' night before she ditched me within ten minutes of finding some guy to make out with in a bathroom stall.

I shouldn't have expected anything else from her. She was pretty much a stranger to me yet still my closest friend.

Talk about a sad life story, Aaliyah.

After uncomfortably standing around, feeling oddly alone in a very crowded room, I'd stepped outside of Oscar's Bar for some fresh air. I tried to call Sofia, who hadn't been answering her phone for the past twenty or so minutes. The infamous Sofia disappearing act. I probably wouldn't see her for a few days, but she'd randomly reappear at the apartment with a pack of cigarettes, a stockpile of crazy stories, and a request for twenty bucks to buy lottery tickets.

The October breeze brushed against my skin as I witnessed Thor deck Captain America square in his chiseled jaw. If that wasn't some kind of civil war, I didn't know what was.

I watched the whole situation unfold before my eyes. I always felt awkward going outside alone for air because I had nothing to keep me distracted. I never stood on the streets of New York with my cell phone in my face when I was alone because I didn't like the idea of some random psychopath coming up and killing me.

That was where my mind always went, at least. If I were on my phone at night, I'd be murdered—end of story. I knew I suffered from an overactive imagination, but I couldn't help it. Probably watching too many episodes of *Criminal Minds* could be blamed for that.

Whenever I stepped outside, I wished I was a smoker. Not for the enjoyment of it, plus I doubted my heart and lungs could handle a smoking habit, but I would've preferred having something to do with my hands when outside. Smokers always seemed comfortable being outside on their own because they were busy doing something. Me, on the other hand, all I could do was people watch, and boy, oh boy, did I stumble onto a gem watching Thor slam his fist into Captain's face.

Wonder Woman was there, too—though nothing was wonderful about this woman. Captain came out of the bar after me, and he seemed unafraid to make a phone call on the streets of New York, probably because a guy was less likely to be harassed and attacked than a woman. *Count your blessings, Cap.*

He pulled out his cell phone but got distracted when he heard Thor hollering, cussing Wonder Woman out. And by cussing out, I meant he was using every foul term that came to his mind. Whore. Slut. Bitch. Tramp.

Wonder Woman's back was against the building as Thor spat his words at her, hovering over her body in the most intimidating way. She was already a small woman, but the way he surrounded her made her look even tinier. Her shoulders were rounded forward as her knees buckled, and she took in the disgusting words being thrown at her.

I hated some men and the way they thought they could treat women.

Captain slowly lowered his cell phone from his ear, becoming more aware of the situation that I, too, had become oddly invested in. I felt the nerves forming in my gut before anything even happened.

Thor shoved Wonder Woman against the brick wall.

"Hey!" I shouted. I stood straight, alarmed as Wonder Woman began sobbing. She shoved him back, and before she could speak, he slammed his fist into her face. A wave of nausea twisted in my stomach. He didn't tap her. He didn't slap her. No, he tightened his hand into a fist and swung it straight into her face.

I'd never seen anyone punched before, and that night I'd seen two people get hit. It was nothing like the movies, and it affected me a lot more than I thought it would. As she gripped her face and cried out, I felt an aching along my own jawline.

I parted my lips to speak up again as I started in her direction, but before I could insert myself into their storyline, Captain America was on the scene.

"Get the hell away from her!" he barked, marching toward the pair. He had a Southern accent. I didn't know why that surprised me, but it did. A deep, smoky voice with a Southern twang to it.

"How about you mind your own business?" Thor slurred, obviously drunk and belligerent.

"It becomes my business when you put your hands on a woman,"

Captain argued back. He wasn't backing down, getting chest to chest with Thor.

You tell him, Cap! I cheered in my mind.

"She's my property. I can do whatever the fuck I want to her," Thor said.

Your *property*? What a fucking troll. I mean, who talked like that? What kind of messed-up planet was that superhero from where he thought that was okay? He was acting a lot more like Loki than the hero of Asgard.

"Are you okay?" Captain asked Wonder Woman, disregarding the ignorant man talking to him.

"Don't get near her," Thor hissed, gripping the woman's wrist tightly and swinging her whole body behind him. She tripped and fell, hitting the concrete sidewalk with a hard thump. Her hands went to stop her fall, scraping against the ground, probably slicing her skin raw. A sickened chill hit me at the idea of her skin being ripped open.

Her boyfriend didn't even look toward her to make sure she was okay, but Captain did. He moved in to help her up but was stopped when Thor's fist slammed into his face.

My stomach knotted again. Watching a second person get punched wasn't any easier than the first. My chest felt as if it was on fire watching everything unfold in front of me. What amazed me the most was how so many other people walked past without even noticing the intense moment.

Captain stumbled a bit before standing up straight. He went to help the girl stand, but instead of taking his hand, she reacted in a completely deranged way.

"Get the hell away from me and my boyfriend, asshole!" she hissed, rising to her feet and whipping him with her lasso. She hit him repeatedly as if he wasn't trying to save her from her abusive asshole of a mate.

How ironic.

The whipping sound felt so aggressively intense I forced myself into the picture, grabbing the whip from the woman's hand and tossing it to the side of the road.

"He was trying to help you!" I barked, disgusted by everything happening.

She looked at me with her bloodshot eyes and rolled them so hard I was surprised her vision wasn't impaired from the dramatics of it.

"Shut up, will you? Come on, Ronnie. Let's go," Wonder Woman said, taking Thor's hand into hers. He wrapped an arm around the woman and kissed her temple as if they weren't in an insanely toxic relationship. I swore they even had a bit of bounce in their step as they walked away.

Halloween was weird.

I wished Mario were there to witness all of it with me. I wondered how he would've handled the situation. *I bet he would've stepped in to help. I bet he would've been his own kind of superhero. I bet—*

Wait, no. Screw him.

Why was I thinking about my ex-boyfriend Mario at that very moment? Was I drunk? No, just sad. Funny how my sad and drunk thoughts sometimes were interchangeable.

"Shit," Captain groaned, rubbing the side of his head. America's sweetheart had really taken a beating. He started walking back toward the bar entrance, and I did something completely out of character for me—I inserted myself into someone else's world for the second time in the span of a minute.

"Hey, you dropped this," I called out, bending down to the ground where he'd dropped his cell phone and shield. I picked up his items and walked over to him as he kept massaging his jawline. It was a nice jawline, too, the kind you'd imagine Captain America would have: chiseled to a godly point of perfection.

He turned to me, and my breath caught in my throat. He was beautiful. I knew men probably didn't want to be considered beautiful, but that was the only way I could describe him. He had the bluest eyes I'd ever seen in my life, almost as if the ocean had decided to reside right inside his spirit. His lips were full with a small Cupid's bow, and his facial hair was groomed to a T. Unfortunately, his left eye was already swelling from the punch, but that did nothing to take away from his good looks. If he wasn't a superhero, I was almost certain he could land a Calvin Klein ad.

"I must look like I feel." He chuckled, shaking his head as he took his items from me.

"I'm sorry, what?"

"The way you're looking at me makes it clear that I look like I got my ass kicked, which is…well, accurate. Did you see that?"

"Every second." I wrapped my arms around my body and tried to ignore the slight chill that hit me. I needed to head inside before I got too cold. "For the record, Thor was a dick, and what you did was noble."

He held his arms out and smirked. "Comes with the suit." His smile disappeared for a moment as he lightly touched around his eye. "Though, in my mind, that situation was going to end differently."

"Let me guess: in your mind, the woman was thankful for you saving her from an abusive man?"

"Yeah, something along those lines."

I arched an eyebrow. "You aren't from around these parts, are you?"

He laughed. "Does the accent give it away?"

"No, the fact that you tried to help in that situation did. Most New Yorkers keep their heads down and stay in their own lane."

"I never was any good at that staying in my own lane thing. Plus, my mama would kill me if she knew I saw something as shitty as that and kept walking."

I didn't know why, but I liked the way he said mama. He really was a Southern boy.

"Well, I'm sorry that moment didn't turn out like the comic books."

"It's okay." He smiled. "Maybe next time it will." His smile somehow seemed to make his eyes brighter than before. He brushed his thumb against his nose and nodded in my direction. "Thanks, Red."

"Red?"

He gestured toward me. I glanced down at myself and rolled my eyes at my slowness. Right… Red, as in Little Red Riding Hood.

"Oh, right. Thanks to you, Cap, doer of good." *Doer of good? Could you sound any more lame, Aaliyah?*

He kept smiling as his eyes traveled up and down my body, not in an invasive way, but as if he was simply taking note of me overall. It happened quickly, and I didn't feel an ounce of disrespect because my eyes had done the same thing to him.

Then his blues locked with my browns. "You think I can buy you a drink?" he asked, bruised eye and all. The amount of confidence it took for him to offer me a drink after I watched him get his butt kicked was inspiring. If it were the other way around, I'd be on the subway, licking my wounds and avoiding human interaction for the remainder of my life. Perhaps that was how my villain origin story would've begun—beaten up by Wonder Woman and Thor outside a New York bar.

But Captain? Nope. He still seemed as confident as ever.

I hesitated on the drink invitation for a moment. On one hand, interacting with the opposite sex was at the bottom of the barrel as far as things I wanted to do. On the other hand, my other option was going home, drinking wine, and crying as I played Taylor Swift and looked at old photographs of Mario and me while reading old text messages.

"Oh, Cap." I walked over to him and patted him on the back. "Let me buy you a drink. You need it more than I do."

TWO

Aaliyah

HIS DRINK OF CHOICE WAS WHISKEY, WHICH MADE ME THINK HE was a lot older than he looked. What guy my age drank straight whiskey? Most guys I knew were drinking beer or the cheapest shots they could find. My drink was a Long Island because I was a wild child. When I reached into my purse to pay for said drink, he'd somehow already had the bartender put it on his tab.

"Hey!" I argued, shooting him a stern look.

He shrugged. "Sorry. Where I come from, the man pays for the pretty lady's drink."

He called me pretty, and I pretended not to notice. "You came from like 1918, sir. Times have changed."

"So you know your Captain America trivia."

"I'm a comic book nerd. On top of that, I went through a Chris Evans phase—which, honestly, I'm still in."

"I can't blame you. Have you ever seen that man's butt?"

"That's America's ass," I joked, lifting my drink. "Thanks for this, but just so you know, just because you bought me a drink doesn't mean I owe you anything. Not my time, not my attention, and not my body."

He laughed and nodded. "Thank you for making that clear. Would that go both ways if you bought me a drink?"

"Oh, no." I shook my head. "You would have to give me your time, your attention, and your body."

"That seems ass-backward."

I shrugged. "I don't make the rules. I just follow them. By the way, how old are you?"

"Twenty-five. You?"

"Twenty-two. I could tell you were old because you're drinking straight whiskey."

He laughed. "I'm only three years older than you."

"A lot can change in a person's life in three years."

"You're not wrong there. Three years ago, I probably wasn't drinking whiskey, but somewhere along the way, I started making business deals with older gentlemen who poured me expensive glasses. So, I've adapted."

"Do you actually enjoy the whiskey, or is it just something you were told to enjoy?"

"Ah, the old question of what's truly a person's choice, and what was chosen for them based on their surroundings." He tapped his pointer finger against his chin. "I think I like it because I like it."

"I guess it's possible to grow into things society introduced you to, too."

His eyes narrowed, and he looked at me as if trying to uncover some secret about me. He blinked and turned away to lift his drink, then his stare came back to me. For a moment, it felt as if we were the only two standing in the middle of the packed bar. I lost myself in his eyes for a moment—up until Big Bird bumped into me, bringing me back to reality.

"You want to find a table to drink these together?" he asked, very attentive. Even when the bird bumped me, he didn't look away. He stayed focused on me, making it easy for me to return my attention to him.

"If you're able to find a table in this packed place, I'll have two drinks with you," I joked, knowing it was damn near impossible to find a vacant table in any bar on Halloween night.

He cocked a brow and gave me a mirthful grin. "Challenge accepted. Follow me."

I did as he said, and we circled the bar not once, not twice, but three times. Each lap was unsuccessful. We ended up standing by a staircase that led upstairs to where the bar kept their inventory. Captain clapped his hands together, walked over to the staircase, and took a seat. He patted the step below him as a clear invitation for me to join him.

"This isn't exactly a table," I said, sipping at my Long Island. "Which means you failed the challenge."

"What makes a table a table exactly?" he urged. "It's a made-up concept that some man or woman created in their mind, and then they told everyone about it."

I laughed. "If you look at it that way, everything is just a made-up concept."

"'There are no facts, only interpretations.' Nietzsche said that." He gestured for me to sit, and I did because honestly, I found this guy amusing. I hadn't felt amused in weeks. All I'd really felt was sad and lonely. It felt good to feel something different for a short period.

"Are you big on philosophers?" I asked. He seemed surprised that I knew he was referring to Friedrich Nietzsche, but he didn't say it out loud.

"I took a philosophy class before I dropped out of college. It changed my life, and I fell into a deep pool of seeking truths by following the greats. You know, Plato, Nietzsche, Aristotle, Socrates. I could nerd out on any one of them."

Something was sexy about a man who was nerdy. It seemed as though the two concepts should've canceled one another out, but alas, the sexy nerd was something that was here to stay.

"Okay. Nerd out about Aristotle," I urged, tipping my glass in his direction before I took a sip. "Give me one of your favorite quotes from him."

He sat up a bit straighter, pleased with the challenge. "'Hope is a waking dream.'"

I liked the way words left his mouth. It wasn't just his words, but the way he connected to them, to the person he was delivering them to. Captain spoke to me as if I were the only person who existed at that very moment, and that fact sent chills down my spine.

Hope is a waking dream.

"Do you have any waking dreams?" I asked.

He smiled and sipped his drink. "I hope so." He scratched at the side of his facial hair and wiggled his nose slightly. "Speaking in philosopher quotes kind of makes me sound like a pretentious asshole, though. So, I think this is the proper time to inform you that I am also trained in bad jokes."

I laughed. "I'll need proof."

He leaned in toward me, and those eyes of his made my heart skip a few beats. "Why did the ketchup blush?"

"I don't know. Why?"

"He saw the salad dressing."

I laughed out loud, shaking my head in disbelief. "You're right—that is a bad joke."

"Why did the mermaid wear seashells?"

"Do tell."

"She outgrew her b-shells."

It took a moment for me to connect the dots on that one, but when I did, I burst out laughing. "You really just have these random quotes and bad jokes in your head, don't you?"

He tapped his temple. "It's a very scary place inside this noggin. The number of useless facts I have up here is terrifying, but I think I have a lot of good information, too, so it's a balanced place."

"I can see that already."

"Did the bad jokes make me less of a pretentious asshole?"

"Yeah, they just made you kind of dorky, but I hear dorks are in this year."

He wiped his head in relief. "Good because otherwise I'd be fucked."

I smiled at him, and he smiled back effortlessly. For a few moments, all we did was grin at one another, but the silence didn't feel uncomfortable. It felt satisfying as if being silent with him was normal.

Then, we fell back into conversation, and that felt normal, too.

We talked about a lot of things, but what shocked me the most was that I was laughing so much. Gosh, I couldn't remember the last time I'd laughed so freely and openly.

"Uh, can you two not sit on these steps?" an employee said, standing in front of us with a tray of dirty dishes.

We instantly stood with our now empty glasses and moved out of the way. The employee muttered something under her breath about how annoying people were, and I couldn't blame her. The Halloween crowd had to be a handful.

"Well, our drinks are gone," Captain observed, waving his glass in the air.

"That's a shame. I was having a good time talking to you."

"If only there was a way to get another drink," he said, shaking his head.

I smirked. "If we have another drink, I'm paying for it. No ifs, ands, or buts."

"If the only way you'll let me continue talking to you is if you buy the drink, I surrender my wallet and leave it all up to you."

Good boy.

I could feel the cocktail I'd had making my body feel a bit relaxed in a good way, but I knew my drink of choice would be a water this time around. I had a very solid rule about drinking water after every alcoholic beverage. I never went out to get wasted. My idea of a good time was to have a nice buzz that hovered over me. It left me still feeling like myself, but a heightened version of me.

We walked over to the bar, and I ordered the drinks. I noticed Captain's disappointment about not being able to pay, but he didn't complain or fight me on the subject. A part of me couldn't understand why he wanted to talk to me so badly. Another part figured maybe it was as easy for him to talk to me as it was for me to talk to him.

Maybe he enjoyed the effortlessness of it all too.

"I just realized...we've spent the past thirty minutes talking, and I don't even know your name, Red."

My chest tightened a bit. I'd realized the same, but it made it kind of fun for me. "Don't tell me your name, and I won't tell you mine. I think once we do that, the magic of our conversation will fade. It will make it...real, and honestly, at this point in my life, I can't do much real."

He arched an eyebrow but didn't push for me to give my name. "Okay, I'll call you Red."

"And you're Captain for me. Cap, for short, obviously. I—"

"Holy shit!" Captain barked. Breaking his stare away from me, he grabbed our drinks and dashed off to the left of the room, leaving me standing there dazed and confused. As I followed his movements, the situation became clearer as he slid into a booth being vacated by two Tinker Bells and a Peter Pan. The way Captain claimed that spot made me smile. A certain amount of pride flooded his face as he puffed out his chest and patted the seat beside him.

I walked over and slid into the booth, leaving a bit of space between us even though an odd part of me wanted to move in closer.

"Based on us not learning each other's names, I get the feeling I'm not going to get your number at the end of the night."

I shook my head. "Probably not, no."

"Okay. So that means whatever we say tonight is probably the last things we'll ever say to one another."

"Yes."

"So…" He leaned in closer to me and swiped his thumb against his bottom lip as his eyes sparkled with intrigue. "What was the happiest thing that happened to you this year?"

I laughed. "That's a big question."

"I need to ask the big questions now because I won't get to ask them ever again. I think it's important in life to ask the big questions when you get a chance."

My stomach fluttered with nerves as I shifted a bit in my seat. He was asking me to be an open book to him for the evening, and most of the time, my thoughts were like a locked diary. Only I had the key, and I never shared it with anyone else. Honestly, no one seemed interested enough to read said thoughts.

But still, I told him. I didn't know if it was due to my buzz or the intrigue of him, but I opened up and shared.

"I got an internship at my dream job. It's a very underpaid and underappreciated internship, but I figured now that I have my foot in the door, I can maybe move my way up to be a junior editor at the magazine."

"A junior editor? So you're a writer?"

"A wannabe writer. I'm getting my degree in journalism and hope to someday get myself to a senior editor position."

"You will."

He said the two words with such certainty that I almost believed him.

"I don't know. It's a very competitive industry, especially in New York."

"Do you love it? Writing?"

"Yes."

"Then the competitive nature doesn't matter. If you have a dream, fight for it."

"Other people are fighting for the same dream, too, though."

He leaned back against the seat and lay his arm across the top of it. "If you think about others trying to get your dream, you're wasting your energy on the things that don't matter. The only real estate in your mind should be you and your dream. Life is short. We don't have the time to look at what other people are doing. That sidetracks us from our destiny."

I smiled. "You must have a dream of your own."

He glanced around the bar and shook his head. "Have you been on the rooftop of this building?"

"No, never."

"It has one of the best views. I come here at least once a week just to breathe up there and clear my mind." He stood, lifting his drink, and held his hand out toward me.

I raised a brow. "You just bulldozed through the crowd to get this booth, and you're telling me you're willing to give it up to go stand on the roof?"

"Sometimes you have to move when your soul tells you to move," he replied.

"Which philosopher said that?"

He bit the corner of his bottom lip and shrugged. "I did."

Impressive.

He held his hand out toward me again. "Come on. Do you trust me?"

"When people ask 'Do you trust me?', it instantly makes me trust them a lot less."

"Good, as you should. I'm a complete damn stranger. Trust is earned, and I haven't earned it. Still, I want to show you the rooftop."

I knew it was idiotic, but I wanted to go.

I prayed the pepper spray in my bra wouldn't have to be pulled out that night as I took his hand with mine. The moment our palms met, a wave of warmth shot through my system, as if holding his hand was the most natural thing I'd done in quite a while.

He pulled me through the crowded space, and every now and again, I'd look down at our connected hands. After being broken up with, you missed the small things: laughing with your other half, cuddling, holding hands.

It was funny how holding hands felt like such a small feat in the relationship, yet you missed it more than words when it was gone.

We reached a door at the back of the bar, and my red flag alert went off as I dropped my hand from his. He opened the door and we looked up at a staircase that seemed to keep going for days.

"After you," he said, nodding toward the steps.

"Oh, no." I shook my head. "There's no way in hell I'm going up that staircase with my back to you. If I'm honest, that idea gives me big serial killer vibes."

He narrowed his eyes. "Do you trust me?"

"No."

"Good." He smiled, and hell, I was an idiot because a part of me trusted that smile. I supposed that was how Ted Bundy had succeeded.

What a twisted thought, Aaliyah. What was even more twisted was the fact that I knew I would go up that freaking staircase.

"I'll go first, and I'll get a few steps ahead of you, so you feel safer," he said. His eyes looked at me with concern. "If you're comfortable with that. Otherwise, we can go back and try to track down a table."

Let me make one thing clear—I wasn't a rebel. I didn't break laws, I didn't speak back to individuals who held authority, and I always offered my seat to the elderly on the subway. Yet for some reason, going up this staircase felt forbidden.

"Are we allowed to go up there?" I asked, noticing that no one else was even eyeing the staircase that seemed a bit hidden.

"Well, I am. You'll just be my plus-one."

"Why are you allowed to go up there?"

"I work with the man who owns this building."

"What kind of work do you do?"

He smirked and held his hands up. "Red, if you're uncomfortable, we don't have to go up here. Or I can try to grab Tommy and have him reassure you."

"Who's Tommy?"

"The owner of the bar."

"You work with him?"

"No. Tommy doesn't own the building, but he works with the investor, who works with me."

I narrowed my eyes and softly chewed on the tip of my thumb—a nervous habit. His eyes followed my finger before meeting my gaze again.

I cleared my throat. "How annoyed would you be if we asked Tommy?"

He laughed and shook his head. "I got beat up in front of the building earlier, and you offered me a drink and made me smile after the most humiliating moment of my life. I doubt you can do anything to annoy me tonight, Red. Come on."

He held his hand back out to move me toward the office in the back of the bar, and I took his hand in mine once again.

I didn't even know I missed his touch until it was given back to me.

We moved to the office, where a man sat behind his desk and was about to stand when he noticed us.

His stare met Captain's, and he began to speak. "Hey there—"

"Don't say my name!" Captain shouted, waving his hands in panic.

Tommy cocked a confused eyebrow. "Okay…uh…what's up, man? I gotta get back out there to help with the crowd."

"Yeah, of course. Just a quick question—can I go up to the rooftop?"

Tommy chuckled. "Since when do you ask permission?"

"I want to take a friend up there," Captain said, gesturing toward me.

"I swear to God, if you fuck Little Red Riding Hood on the top of this building, I'm going to murder you."

My cheeks blushed, but not as much as Captain's, which turned a strong shade of red. "Dude, that's not it. I want to show her the view."

"The view where you daydream like a little bitch," Tommy joked, making Captain turn an even brighter color. My worry began to subside as I watched the two interact. "Go ahead and take her. That space is more yours than mine." He looked at me. "My apologies if he nerds out up there. The guy's a loser."

Captain laughed and patted Tommy on the back. "I love you, too, Tom." Captain turned to me and gave me a questioning look as if waiting for my next move.

I nodded and smiled. "Let's go."

Walking up that spiral staircase was a workout for my heart. By the time we reached the top, which took a good while, I was breathing as if I'd run a marathon. Captain didn't seem winded at all, which must've been due to his superpowers.

"I should really do the StairMaster more at the gym," I said as my breaths weaved in and out heavily.

"That machine is a devil child," he explained as he placed his hand on the doorknob that led to the rooftop. "Are you ready?"

"Yes."

He opened the door, and a gasp left my system as we stepped outside.

"Oh my goodness," I exclaimed as I breathed out, looking out into the night. We were up so high that I was shocked by how many steps we'd actually taken to make it to the top. You could see everything from the viewpoint we stood at. All of New York City was lit up with the night sky as the backdrop.

It was breathtaking. Everything looked so stunning from up so high.

"Wow," I whispered.

"Exactly," Captain replied, taking my hand into his. Every time he did that, I liked his touch a little more.

We moved to the edge of the rooftop and he pointed out at the busy city, eyes widened with passion.

"This is it, this is what I want to do. While I'm in the real estate world, that's not my biggest dream. My biggest dream is to create. I want to create, and I want to build. I want to buy buildings like that one right there and flip them into luxury condominiums for the lower class. Just think, Red. How crazy would it be to create something of luxury for people who are so far overlooked?"

"That's an amazing idea, but wouldn't that cost a lot of money?"

"Yes." He clapped his hands together and was smiling bigger than he had all night. "That's why I'm on a mission to make a shit ton of money. I don't care if I lose some if I have a crap ton. I want to give back to people who grow up without a lot. Then on top of the buildings, we can have greenhouses so the community has their own gardens to pick from throughout the summer and fall seasons. Community gardens could change and save so many lives. It would be great. The facilities could have activities for kids whose parents are working two or three jobs, to keep them out of trouble. Plus, the units could have deep soaking tubs for the single parents who need a few moments of solitude to themselves." He stared out at the city lights and placed his hands against the back of his head. "I want this so bad. I just want to help people."

His passion sat right there behind his eyes. Every word he was delivering my way was coming straight from the depths of his soul. When he spoke about his dream, I could feel it increasing my heartbeats.

It made me think I wasn't thinking big enough for my own goals in life.

"I think that's a beautiful dream," I commented, standing next to him. I didn't think he noticed, but I'd inched closer to him because I liked the warmth he gave off.

"It's going to happen," he said, nodding in pure bliss. "And it's going to be beautiful."

"What made you have this dream?"

He looked my way and then took a seat on the pebbled ground. I sat right beside him. He bent his knees and wrapped his arms around them. "I grew up poor. My mom was a single parent, and we had pretty much nothing to our name. It got even worse when she learned of her cancer."

"Oh my gosh, I'm so sorry."

"It's okay," he said, nudging my knee slightly with his. "She's okay. She's been in remission for years, thank God. But, growing up struggling without much comfort in our home, in our lives, made me passionate about this. At a young age, I learned how to hustle, how to move in a way that enabled me to get what I needed for myself and my mom. But I understand I was luckier than most. I lived in a small town where people helped each other, and I think a lot of people felt bad for me, so they gave to my random entrepreneurial endeavors. Where I grew up, people took care of each other."

"So the complete opposite of New York City."

He laughed. "The complete opposite."

"I think that's noble. I grew up on these streets without a lot, so I know how hard it can be to struggle to keep stable physically and mentally. I couldn't imagine doing it with a kid."

"A lot of times, I don't know how my mom did it, honestly. Superhero, I guess."

"Must run in the family. I can't help but wonder what Captain America's mother would be like," I said, wrapping my arms around my legs.

"I would say she's like Wonder Woman, but since I just got my ass handed to me by said woman, I'm not much of a fan anymore."

I smiled. "You're close to your mom."

"Not to sound like a punk, but she's my best friend."

That made my heart grin. A mama's boy. "And your dad?"

His energy shifted to a more somber tone. He shook his head. "Deadbeat. Ran off after cheating on my mom when I was a kid."

"Have you ever tried to find him?"

"No. I figured if he was a real man, he would try to find me. I spent eighteen years of my life sitting in the same place. He knew where I was and still didn't come." He began fidgeting with his fingers, seemingly a nervous habit or something he did when uncomfortable.

I kind of liked that about him—how I'd seen so many of his different layers within such a short period. I'd seen him happy, I'd seen him passionate, and I'd seen him somber. Somehow that made him more human than the superhero persona he was putting on that evening.

"What about you? How's your relationship with your parents?"

I'd known the question was coming, but I still wasn't fully prepared for it. I'd been around for twenty-two years, and I still was never ready for when people asked me about my family. It wasn't due to my discomfort with the subject. Long ago, I'd come to terms with what had happened to me and how I grew up. What bothered me the most, though, when I told others was the pitying looks they'd give me. It always seemed as if they were filled with guilt, as if they were the reason I didn't have a family.

"I grew up in the foster care system. I never knew my parents."

"Oh." He paused for a moment and looked down at his hands. When he looked back up at me, he didn't radiate that pity I was so used to seeing in others' eyes after said discovery. Instead, he asked, "How did that affect you?"

I was so taken aback by his comment. No one had ever asked me that before after finding out I grew up in the foster system. Most people gave me the cliché apologies then told me I deserved the biggest kind of love. They'd mention that we create our own families in life, and the beginning doesn't equate with the ending. All good and fair responses. They never bothered me any.

Captain's words hit me a bit differently. It felt like a heavy question, but at the same time a very honest one. I wasn't certain if I liked it or not.

"The truth or the nice lie?" I asked.

He looked out toward the city lights before turning back to me. "The truth. Always the truth."

"It gave me trust issues, sprinkled with a dash of codependency. I hate to admit it, but I think I dream of love more than most people. Not even a romantic kind of love, but any kind of love. Love from my friends, love and admiration from my professors, from my boss. I want people to like me...to love me. Because somewhere in my head, I connected the idea that the number of people who love you is what makes you a worthy person."

"You're a people-pleaser."

"To the extreme. In my freshman year of college, I failed my first history test, and I cried the whole weekend. The following Monday, I took the professor blueberry muffins during his office hours because he'd mentioned once that they were his favorite. I apologized for failing, and I'll never forget what he said to me. He looked at me and said that failing the exam was in no way an indication of me being a failure. I still struggle with that, the idea that one life failure doesn't make me a failure."

"You're too hard on yourself, Red."

"How can you tell? You just met me about an hour ago."

"I think you can know a person based on the first few minutes you meet them if you look closely enough."

"Is that what you do? You read people?"

"Yeah. It comes in handy for the industry I'm in. I have to get a quick grip on who my clients are when it comes to real estate, so I know which persona I should present to them."

"You put on a different mask with everyone? That sounds exhausting."

He shrugged. "Not really. Everyone wears different masks on a regular basis. Some people simply aren't aware of it. Also, I like to think of the masks as different versions of the same person. Humans are complex, complicated. We are so much more than just one mask."

The more he spoke, the more I dreaded the fact I wouldn't get any more of his words after tonight.

He brushed his thumb across the bridge of his nose. "What was the nice lie? To my question about how being in the foster system affected you?"

"Oh." I sat up a bit straighter and gave him a big, fake smile. "My upbringing had no effect on my life. I believe we create our own life stories. The past doesn't define us."

"I see that it's a lie in your eyes."

I turned to look out into the night. "That probably means you're looking too closely."

"Can't help it. Looking at you feels like the best choice I've made in a while."

I laughed, trying to play off the butterflies he was sending through me. "Is that a line you use on all the girls?"

"Nah, but seeing how it made you blush, I might start," he teased.

"Well, you're going to have to try harder. I'm not blushing—my cheeks are just cold."

He raised an alarmed brow. "We can go inside. It is a bit—"

"I'm not complaining. I'm just trying to find a lie to cover up the fact that I'm blushing."

"You're beautiful."

I rolled my eyes and laughed at his abrupt statement. "Shut up. You already got me to blush. No need to dig deeper."

"No, I mean it. You're beautiful. I don't even mean your looks, but those are spot-on, too. I mean your spirit. That's beautiful."

A wave of shyness found me as I shifted myself and crossed my legs like a pretzel. "You don't even know me."

"As I said, I'm good at reading people."

"You aren't the only one gifted at that. I grew up a solid introvert who prided herself on being a people watcher. I learned to read people at a young age."

"Is that so?"

"It is. That paired with the knowledge I've picked up from watching *Criminal Minds*, and well, I'm pretty much a professional people reader."

"Okay, Red." He turned to face me directly and crossed his legs in front of him. Our knees brushed against one another as he raised a brow in intrigue. "Read me."

I rubbed my hands together. "Game on. Okay." My eyes moved across his body, taking in his entire being. His shoulders were relaxed. He was fit, as made clear by the bicep muscles showing through his costume. He had a nice-sized—

Don't look at his package, Aaliyah. Stop staring at Captain's America.

I quickly redirected my eyes from his lower region back up to his face, the face that had a smug smirk and eyes filled with mirth. He'd definitely caught me looking at what he was packing, and the embarrassment building inside me was enough to make me want to crawl into a cave and die.

But still, I couldn't turn down the challenge of reading him.

"You work out a lot. Not to stay built, but as a form of escapism. Your day-to-day life is hectic, which you don't mind. You like being busy because it keeps you from overthinking. But then, when you get alone time, you get lonely, so you hit the gym to focus on something else. You're a workaholic, and your mother probably tells you to take breaks. You're driven and passionate, though sometimes you fear you might not achieve everything you dream of. You will, though. That's not me reading you. It's just me knowing."

He smiled.

I liked it.

I continued. "You're a people person. People like you instantly due to your charm and charisma. When you engage with someone, you really focus on them. You listen not to respond, but to really hear what is being said to you. You're a student of life, and you do your homework on the regular. And you miss your mother. I can tell that because when you speak about her, there's a momentary break where your smile falls when she comes to your mind. Sometimes, you consider moving back home to care for her and be close again. Then you realize you can't change the world by sitting in the same pond of life." I clapped my hands together. "Oh! And you're a Leo."

He narrowed his eyes at me for a second before pointing a stern finger at me. "Turns out, I don't like being read."

"Don't worry—most people probably won't read you. I'm just gifted."

"How did you know I was a Leo?"

"Oh, that was the easiest—from your driven personality and easy-to-approach persona. Plus, your good hair was a dead giveaway."

He raked his fingers through his sandy brown locks and smirked. "You think I'm Captain with the good hair?"

"Don't let it go to your head, sir."

"Too late—ego already inflated. Do I get to read you now?"

"Like a book."

He rubbed his hands together and nodded in enjoyment. "All right. You didn't fully want to come out tonight, but the idea of being alone was a sadder thought. You recently went through something heavy—a breakup maybe. The way your mouth just twitched in the corner makes me think I'm right. You struggle with abandonment issues, which is why you try to hold on so tight to those in your life. Though, the people in your life are few and far between. It takes a lot of trust for you to allow someone into your world, let alone into your heart. But when you let them in, you pray they'll never leave."

The discomfort began to buzz throughout my system at how spot-on he was, but I didn't want to make it obvious because I wanted him to continue. I didn't know why it was important to know what he saw when he looked at me, but I needed to know.

He continued. "When you decide to love, you consider it a forever thing. Even people from your past that left your side still hold a place in your heart, no matter how hard you've tried to get rid of them. You're afraid of letting people down, but you also undersell your own talents. You think you don't deserve the success you dream of because someone else might be more worthy. You love animals. I don't know if that's actually true, but I definitely get that vibe from you. You hate seeing people struggle or hurt and want to make the world better, but you're not exactly sure how to go about doing that. You like scary movies, but you hide under a blanket." That one made me smile. "You're too hard on yourself. You keep your deepest hurting to yourself. You worry about your friends worrying about you, so you don't let them deep into your pain because you don't want to be a burden. Oh"—he placed his hands against my kneecaps and leaned in toward me—"and you're a Gemini. I just say that because it's the only other zodiac sign I know. I don't know anything about astrology."

I laughed. "Pisces over here."

"Ah, they must be known for beautiful eyes."

"Stop dropping compliments in."

"Stop deserving them." His hands were still on my knees, and he had no clue the sparks he was igniting with the seemingly gentle touch. "How did I do?"

"You did good, but you were wrong about one thing."

"Oh?"

"I hide under a pillow *and* a blanket when watching a scary movie, not just a blanket."

"Close enough." His playful look shifted a bit as he looked my way and nibbled on his bottom lip. "So there was a recent breakup."

"He broke up with me about five weeks ago."

"What an ass."

"Yeah, but I love him. I wish I could say past tense, but here we are. My roommate Sofia said the best way to get over a man is to get under another one, but I can't even consider that right now. The last thing I want to do is sleep with someone else."

"Plus, sex wouldn't fix a broken heart and—*holy shit!*" He clapped his hands together and hopped up from the ground to a standing position. The grin on his face was so big, but I didn't understand what caused his sudden shift. "I got it, Red! I know what we can do to help you."

I arched an eyebrow and stood. "I'm confused."

"I know, I know, and you're going to think I'm crazy—which, maybe I am—but here's the deal: You can't bang your way out of a heartbreak. That's not how love works. Love isn't a physical connection; it's an emotional one. Plus, after breakups, people replay the good memories over the bad in their minds and start thinking they somehow failed, when, in reality, the bad probably always outweighed the good. You simply held the good tight in your grip because it was few and far between in the end. Otherwise, the good would've been enough to keep you together."

I hated that he was speaking facts. Over the past weeks, all I'd done was replay all the good times Mario and I had together. My mind was stuck on a loop of moments that meant the world to me in my past relationship.

There were only a handful of good memories, yet I simply played them on repeat, making them feel bigger than they already were. Mario was a master at doing the bare minimum, and I celebrated that fact as if he was a god. It wasn't his fault he gave me mediocre love. It was my fault for accepting it.

"So what's your point?" I asked.

"Do you believe in destiny?"

I chuckled. "Don't tell me you do."

"I think everything happens for a reason, even if the reasoning isn't clear as day right away. Maybe that's why we met tonight, Red because we were meant to. Maybe I had to get socked in the eye and whipped with a lasso because we were supposed to cross paths so I could help you get over your ex."

"How?"

"The best way to get over a love is to find a stronger connection with another person. So, I present to you, your Halloween love story." He took a bow as if he was making any sense at all.

I stood still, confused as ever. "Am I missing something?"

"Clearly because you're looking at me as if I'm having a mental breakdown—which, I mean, is probably accurate." He cleared his throat and stood taller as he smoothed his hands over his chest. "I'm asking you to fall in love with me."

I snickered. "I'm sorry, what?"

"Give me the chance to make you fall in love with me before the sun comes up in the next"—he glanced down at his phone—"five hours or so. It's just past midnight. Give me those hours to make you fall in love with me. Then we'll end the love story on a good note. No tragic heartbreak, no hard moments or relationship struggles. No cheating or scandals. Just two people who fell in love, then life or, in our case, morning made them say their goodbyes."

"You really think two people can fall in love within five hours?"

"I don't know." He shrugged and held his hand out toward me. "Want to try?"

I should've said no. I should've laughed off his crazy idea and ended the night right there on the rooftop, but I didn't want to go home. I didn't want to be alone. But most of all, I wanted more time with Captain, even if only a few more hours. Even if there wasn't a real chance of me falling in love with him but just a chance of more time to feel happy.

Happy.

I felt happy.

I hadn't even known how much I'd missed happiness until it found me that night.

So, I did what any insane girl would've done. I took his hand and agreed to the idea of falling in love within the next five hours.

He clasped my fingers with his and pulled me in close to him. It was the closest we'd stood since meeting, and the way he looked down into my eyes caused the butterflies to intensify. He had to be well over six-foot-two as he hovered over my five-foot-eight frame—and that was with heels. The way he looked at me made me feel important, as if he was going to give this crazy plan of his all that he had.

"Knock, knock," he said, with the goofiest grin known to mankind.

"Who's there?"

"Will you fall in love with?"

"Will you fall in love with who?"

"Me."

THREE

Aaliyah

I wasn't completely sure I wasn't suffering from a mental breakdown seeing how I agreed to fall in love with a superhero for the remainder of the night. The whole situation seemed bizarre in the best kind of way. Potentially falling in love with someone in such a short timeframe sent a certain excitement coursing through me.

It seemed almost unrealistic, which made the concept that much more intriguing. It had taken me over ten months before I told Mario I loved him. I didn't give love so freely. Captain knew that about me because he'd mentioned it when he read me. I found it interesting that he believed he could make me fall in love with him in so little time.

Thank goodness we lived in the city that never slept because even though it was past midnight, we had so many adventures we could take part in.

"Okay, so how about we do it this way: we each pick two places to take one another. One is a place we love, and the other is a place we think the other would love. We share these moments with each other as we dive deeper to get to know one another," Captain suggested.

"Ladies first."

"Ah yes, that Southern hospitality thing."

"I stand by it when it comes to respecting females." He rubbed his hands together. "So, what's up first?"

I wanted to take time to figure out a place I thought he'd love, so I figured it was best to start with a personal favorite of mine. Plus, my rumbling stomach was a clear indication that the first trip should include food of some sort.

"Are you hungry?" I asked.

"Could always eat."

I grinned, excited to take him to my favorite spot in town for my favorite food. "Have you ever heard of Grant's Wings?"

"Never."

"Well, my friend, you're in for a treat. Let's get on the subway and go." Even though I had my own Metro pass, Captain made sure to swipe his for me. Being on the subway on a regular day was one thing, but riding it on Halloween night was a completely different experience.

We were lucky enough to score a pair of seats beside one another, and the people watching was beyond compare. There were so many different costumes, so many expressions of creativity that it was almost impossible to look away. Most of the time, I was a professional at minding my own business, but that night, I wanted to take everyone in.

"I think the one-night stand is the winner for me," Captain whispered, leaning into me. I looked to my left to see a man wearing a box shaped like a nightstand, with a lamp shade on his head. The words 'one-night stand' were written across the fabric covering the box, and condoms were tossed over it.

I snickered. "I don't know, the cereal killer is kind of calling out to me." I gestured to my right, where a man was wearing a T-shirt covered in red stains, mini boxes of cereal attached with plastic knives going through said boxes.

"Oh, okay, a good contender. But I think we can both agree that cat ears is a bit lazy, no?"

"Absolutely, but she's wearing them with pride. Can't fault her for that." As we came to a stop, an older woman dressed as a slice of pizza climbed onto the subway. Without hesitation, Captain stood to give her his seat, taking hold of the standing pole in front of us.

She sat down beside me and heard the rumbling of my stomach. I placed my hands against my angry belly and smiled at her, silently apologizing for the noise.

Her stern look pierced into me as she pointed a finger. "Don't you dare try to eat me, you psychopath," she warned. At first I thought she was joking but she dramatically turned her back toward me and huffed in irritation. Then she went on mumbling to herself nonstop.

I looked up just in time to find Captain holding in his laughter that was about to burst out of him.

"Shut up," I mouthed, and he turned away and released his loud chuckles, unable to control himself. I couldn't even be annoyed by the random rude lady who was offered a seat. Captain's laughter made me forget about anything else in the world.

I loved the way he laughed, as if he was tickled to his core. His laughter was the kind that made you want to snicker, too.

When we got to our stop, he gave me his hand to help me up from my seat. Then he turned to pizza lady. "Sorry she was going to eat you," he stated, making me swat his arm.

Pizza lady replied, "It's because she's a psychopath." Then she went back to her mindless muttering.

Only in New York.

Once we were off the subway, he dropped my hand and looked at me with so much concern. "Why were you going to eat that woman, Red? Is it because you hung out with the bad wolf a little too much? Eating people seems more of his avenue of choice. Also, if you are thinking of taking me to your favorite spot to eat right now just as a way to fatten me up, I need you to know I'm pretty lean on fat. All muscle."

He flexed like a nerd, and I blushed like a schoolgirl.

Sure, he was being silly and dramatic, but my gosh, his biceps on biceps pretty much proved his point about him being all muscle.

I rolled my eyes. "If I were going to eat a Marvel character, it definitely wouldn't be you."

His eyes narrowed. "Wait, what? You wouldn't pick me?" he asked, seemingly offended.

"You're upset that I wouldn't eat you?"

He grimaced a bit and nodded as we walked down the street. "Well, kind of. I mean, what the hell? Who would you eat first?"

"Are we really having a conversation about me being a cannibal?"

"We absolutely are. Now, come on, fess up—who would you be eating?"

I shrugged. "I don't know. Thanos, probably."

"*Thanos?!*" he shouted, causing a few bystanders to look our way. Of course, they quickly looked away because New York.

"Don't shout. People are looking!" I whispered, nudging him in the side.

"They should be looking!" he kept hollering. "You just said you would eat Thanos!"

"I did, and I stand by that. Sure, he's a super villain who tried to kill half of the planet, but he's a bigger guy, which means more meat to consume. Plus, I like darker meat."

"He's not dark meat, Red. He's freaking purple."

"I'm just saying he's my choice. I don't have to explain my cannibalism to you."

He released a hot breath of air, shaking his head back and forth. "It disgusts me that you would choose the world's most hated villain over the best superhero."

I laughed out loud. "The world's best hero? Don't flatter yourself."

"What?!" He gasped again, still loud as day. "Are you kidding me? I'm Captain America! Doer of good!"

"Yeah, but that doesn't make you the best. Your moral compass often gets in your way. You can't be good all the time. But don't worry—you are at least in the top ten of best superheroes."

"I hear what you're saying, but it doesn't soothe my bruised heart."

"I'm sorry if I hurt your feelings by claiming I wouldn't eat you."

"It's okay. I forgive you. Not everyone in life makes good choices, but I just want you to know one thing before we continue this walk." He placed his hands on my shoulders, pausing my steps, locking his beautiful blue eyes with mine as he gave me the most serious tone he'd delivered all evening. "I would eat the hell out of you."

A pool of heat filled me up as his words simmered in my head and in my lower region. "Is that a sexual reference?"

"What? No. All I'm saying is that I would willingly eat you." He cocked a brow with a smug smirk. "I would eat you…all…night…long."

I shoved him away from me and continued walking. "You're annoying."

"Maybe you should eat me to shut me up."

"No, I'm going to feed you to shut you up," I explained right as we stopped in front of Grant's Wings. "Welcome to Grant's. This, my friend, is where all dreams come true." I gestured toward the small restaurant as if we'd just found our way to Disney World.

Captain got a goofy look on his face, and I was learning fast that whenever he got a goofy stare, his mind was thinking something ridiculous.

I sighed. "What is it?"

"Nothing, nothing. It's just that you called me friend."

"Oh gosh. Don't let it go to your head."

"I'm not. I mean, I am, but I'm not. All I'm saying is that we've already progressed from perfect strangers to friends." He wrapped his arm around my shoulders and gave me a tight squeeze. "And everyone knows every great love story begins with friendship. Ask Harry and Sally."

He ordered three different types of wings, and I was deeply offended when he got boneless. 'Boneless wings' was just a code word for chicken nuggets. He watched me as I taught him how to successfully remove all the meat from the bone of a wing, and then I sucked it down, cleaning the bone completely with one swipe.

Captain's eyes were wide with amazement as he witnessed me taking care of the bone. "I know that wasn't supposed to be a sexual experience for me, but holy shit, that was quite the sexual experience."

I smirked and shrugged, grabbing another wing and pushing the meat down the bones. "What can I say? I'm good with my mouth."

His eyes widened with intrigue. "Is that a sexual reference?" he asked, using the question I'd asked him before we walked into the restaurant.

"What? No. All I'm saying is I'm good at sucking." After my words, I sucked the chicken wing clean then slowly licked my fingertips, one at a time, very, very slowly because I knew he was watching.

"You're a damn tease," he said, shaking his head in disbelief.

"Says the man who talked about eating me all night long."

"Touché, Red. Touché."

He slightly readjusted his superhero suit below his waist, and I couldn't help but think that my small actions might've actually awakened something in him. I didn't know why, but that idea kind of made me smile. I liked the idea I was able to turn him on, even if it was from just eating a freaking chicken wing.

He went back to eating his wings, clearly not wanting to push the sexual comments too far, and asked, "When did you find this place?"

"Oh gosh, it's been years. I think I was like fifteen years old when I ran away and came here."

"I'm sorry, what? Ran away?"

"Yeah. I was placed in a bad home for a while. I wasn't the easiest kid to deal with, but they were cruel. So after a night of them belittling me, I ran away. I didn't want to go back to a group home, either. I didn't know where I was going and I didn't know what I was doing, but I packed up the few belongings I had in a backpack, and I left. I wandered the streets for a while. I spent one night sleeping under a fire escape behind a building.

"The following day, I walked up and down this street, feeling scared and alone. Then I ran into Grant, who was standing outside the shop. He asked me if I was hungry. I was starving, so he took me in and fed me. He did the same the following week, and he allowed me to sleep in that booth right over there. He brought me blankets, pillows, and everything. He never even talked to me after the first night I showed up for food. It was like an unspoken connection."

"That's amazing."

I nodded. "He was amazing. He's the one who bought me my first comic books, actually. After the first week passed, he spoke to me again, sat right beside me after making me chocolate chip pancakes—my favorite. As I was shoving the food into my mouth, he said, 'It's time to go home.' I told him I didn't have a home. He told me I needed to go back to the group home. If I did that, he'd give me a job and send me to college. I laughed because I'd never thought I would ever go to college. My grades weren't impressive, and I never really felt as if I had anything worth being driven about. I told him I didn't believe in myself."

"What did he say?"

I laughed lightly, looking down at the glass of water both of my hands were wrapped around. My fingers were wet from the condensation, cooling off my system as I thought about Grant. "He said it didn't matter if I believed in myself. He'd believe in me until I learned how to do it myself."

"And he followed through?"

"Yup. I graduate next spring because of that man. I owe him my life."

He smiled, but then it faded a bit. "You said he was amazing...past tense."

"Last year, he was in a bad car accident. He didn't survive it."

"I'm sorry to hear that. I couldn't imagine."

"He was my almost..." My voice cracked a little as I thought about Grant. "My almost family."

"No—he was your family. He will always be your family."

I smiled. "Thank you for saying that. Each week, I go to his grave and read him comics. It's a weird tradition, but he's the one who got me into comic books, and we'd always read them together. So, I just still need to hold on to him that way and have conversations with him, even if he can't hear me."

"He probably can."

"I hope so. It's also weird how you can randomly meet people who just so happen to change your life forever."

He leaned forward and placed his hands on top of my hands around the glass. "You're going to change my life, Red." His words weren't said in a joking manner. No, he said them so sincerely that somehow his touch was more chilled than the glass I held.

"What makes you think that?"

"You ever just get a feeling in your gut?"

"Mostly after I eat these wings. I just call it gas."

He laughed, and the sound made me melt inside. A part of me couldn't believe I'd spoken about gas in front of him. The other half felt as if it was completely natural. What was it about this guy? Why did it feel so easy to be myself when I sat across from him?

Without asking, he reached across to grab one of my bone-in wings, and I smacked his hand.

"What are you doing?" I yelped in horror.

"I wanted to try a wing with the bone in."

"Well, you should've ordered a bone-in wing. Honestly, I silently judged you when you ordered boneless wings. In my expert experience, they aren't wings. They are big chicken nuggets."

"You're a professional wing eater?"

"Yes, and don't mock it. I wear that title with pride."

He held his hands up in defeat. "Okay, okay. Sorry. I never mean to offend a woman and her food."

I sat back in my chair, smiling in pleasure that he knew when to let up. At least I thought he had. Right when I got too comfortable with his defeat, he leaned forward and swiped one of my wings from my basket. After waving it in the air with pride, he licked it as a way to indicate I wasn't going to get it back.

"You're a jerk," I said, glaring his way with the death stare.

"A jerk you're going to love soon enough."

"Don't hold your breath."

"I wouldn't dare. I'd end up choking on my chicken wing."

I rolled my eyes and sighed. "At least eat it like a champ. Use my technique, and I swear to the heavens above if you leave any meat on that bone, I am coming for you."

"But no pressure, right?" He laughed. Then he looked up at me. "Dare or dare?" he asked.

"Don't you mean truth or dare?"

"Yeah, but I don't want to give you the chance to back out and choose truth. So, dare or dare?"

I snickered under my breath. "Hmm…I think I'll go with dare."

"All right. I dare you to hold eye contact with me as I strip this chicken wing."

"You're insane."

"Yes, but you agreed to the dare, so here we are."

He shimmied his Captain America pecs a bit before locking his stare with mine. Gosh, his eyes. The universe shouldn't have ever created eyes like his. They had more power behind them than anyone should've ever possessed.

"I'm going to do it exactly like you did," he warned.

"I wouldn't expect anything less."

He started by standing the wing straight up on his napkin and then slowly, slowly, slowly pushing the meat down the bones to capture it all at the bottom. He then lifted the wing to his mouth and lapped up the buffalo sauce with his tongue before lowering it into the pool of ranch sitting in front of him. He brought it back up to his mouth, cocking an eyebrow with a wicked smirk that made my thighs quiver involuntarily. He parted his lips and slid the meat into his mouth, sucking it all off, his tongue licking the bones clean of any sauce that might've missed the initial entry into his mouth.

Then he placed the bones down and dipped his index finger fully into the container of ranch. Pulling it out, he allowed it to drip all over before he brought it to his mouth and sucked it slowly, sexually—and oh my goodness, I instantly became pregnant with twins.

All I wanted to do was look away and hide my schoolgirl blushing, but a dare was a dare, and I maintained that eye contact the whole time as he made my thighs quiver from eating a freaking chicken wing.

"You're ridiculous," I said, breaking our stare after he finished sucking the wing clean. I took a big gulp of my water, trying to cool my insides from the dramatics that had taken place.

He laughed. "I think you like that about me."

It's true. I like that about you.

I shifted in my seat, trying to take the conversation away from the oddly sexual yet not sexual situation that had occurred. "So..." My voice cracked. "Where's our next stop?"

He grabbed a wet nap and started cleaning his hands. "Oh, it's a good one—a great one, actually—and it's one-hundred-percent solely for you."

FOUR

Connor

I HAD AN UNEXPLAINABLE NEED TO TRY TO MAKE PEOPLE HAPPY. DID I understand that a person's happiness was their own responsibility? Yes. Did that ever stop me from trying to nudge people in the right direction of said happiness? Not at all.

I prided myself on being an overall happy-go-lucky guy. Sure, I wasn't always in a good mood, and I had crappy days and nights—I was still human, after all—but at the end of the day, I knew my happiness was something to keep at the forefront of my life. If I felt myself slipping too far down the other road, I did things that made me feel good to find my footing.

It just so happened that what made me feel good was making others feel good. I got my happiness high from seeing others smile. Something was so rewarding about knowing someone might have a better tomorrow because they crossed paths with me today.

What I didn't expect was the fact that Little Red Riding Hood would be the reason for my happiness tomorrow because of the experience she'd given me that evening. I'd already come to terms with the fact that she'd cross my mind repeatedly in the upcoming days.

Man…that woman.

I'm in love, I'm in love, and I don't care who knows it!

Okay, it wasn't love. But dang, I liked this girl. I'd met a lot of cool people since moving to New York from Kentucky. I prided myself on being a people person. Being involved with others was where I shined. Truth be told, I didn't do so well by myself. When I was alone, my thoughts got lonely and traveled to places I didn't want to deal with. Some called it anxiety, but I called it 'get the fuck out of my head'. Therefore, I spent a lot of time surrounded by people. If there was a gathering, I wanted to be a part of it. Look up the word extrovert in the dictionary, and there would be a cheesy-ass photo of me grinning ear to ear.

I felt as if Red was different. When I first saw her outside the bar, I could tell she'd stepped outside to get a breath of air, a break from the crowd inside. Every time we moved through it, she cringed a little, even squeezing my hand a bit tighter as I guided her. She wasn't the same level of extroverted as I was, and I liked that. I liked how calm she was, how deep she seemed without even trying.

As I said, I liked her.

Plus, outside all the parts of her I'd discovered from conversation, she was beautiful. Her black hair was long with bouncy tight coils, her lips were full, and when she smiled, it highlighted the golden-brown glow of her cheeks. Her body had curves in all the places I loved, and goodness, did I mention her smile? Yeah, I did—but it was worth another mention. She smiled in a way that could make the saddest person feel happy for a few moments. It pulled me in and made it almost impossible for me to look away.

A part of me was shocked when she agreed to my crazy idea of falling in love before sunrise, but something within me didn't really want to face the possibility of never seeing her again after the bar closed. If we were dealing with limited time, I wanted to fill it up with experiences outside of drinking in some bar.

Did I hope by morning she'd give me her number? Yes.

Did I also hope she wouldn't? Also yes. I knew what my current life situation was—I was a workaholic, trying to make the craziest dreams come to life. The amount of success I'd found in the past few years had come from me making sacrifices to build the empire that lived in my mind. That meant personal relationships weren't really on my radar. I wasn't boyfriend material, and if I couldn't give Red the time and attention she deserved, I wasn't going to waste her time.

But damn…tonight was turning out to be one of my favorites. Had you ever lived in a moment you knew was going to be one of your favorite memories? That was exactly what Halloween night was becoming for me. I was almost certain no Halloween night could ever live up to the situation I was experiencing that night.

The craziest part of it all?

I still didn't know her name.

"Are you going to give me any clues about where we're going?" she asked as we walked down the streets. We'd taken a subway to Queens, and I could tell she was confused about what was going on. I had to thank my first New York roommate for putting me onto the location I was taking her to, and I prayed she would like it.

"Don't worry, we're almost there. It's right around the corner." I saw as she shivered a bit, and I placed a hand on her lower back, pulling her in closer to me to try to help keep her warm. Before the night was over, I needed to search out a store that might have a coat for her to wear. She didn't complain about being cold, but it was clear her small frame was freezing.

To my surprise, she leaned into me, allowing me to wrap my arm around her. She fit against me as if she was always supposed to be there, too, as if she was a missing puzzle piece I hadn't known belonged to my world.

At least temporarily.

"No way," she said breathlessly as we stood in front of a gaming arcade. She raised an eyebrow. "How did you know I love arcades?"

"I didn't until you just said so, but that's not exactly what I was going to show you, so that makes this a double win. Come on, let's go inside."

UpDown was a bar arcade where people were able to drink and nerd out all at once. The place was packed that night, not surprisingly. Even on a non-holiday night, UpDown always had a line to get inside.

We hopped in line, and her puzzle piece stayed connected to mine as we talked about our favorite video games growing up. Small talk with her came so effortlessly, yet it felt so big. I took in every word she gave me and listened closely. I also took in her small mannerisms. The way she wrinkled her nose when displeased, how she shimmied her shoulders when excited. The way her two dimples deepened when she smiled, how she unconsciously swayed her hips whenever music began to play.

Once we finally made it inside the arcade, I couldn't help but smile when I saw Red's eyes widen, and she did her little shimmy. Then those brown eyes turned to me, still gleaming.

"Can we play anything?"

"Anything you want, darlin'. Let me get some tokens."

We played games for an hour, all types of games, from pinball machines to old-school *Simpsons*. She laughed and cussed when she messed up. She'd jump up and down with excitement and twirl and curtsey every time she kicked my ass at a game—which was often. I'd like to say I let her win, but that would be a lie. She was just that damn good.

What amazed me most about that girl was that she somehow managed to be sexy and cute all at once. There was something so damn attractive about her and the way she moved, yet it was adorable, too.

What's the word to describe someone who is sexy and cute—sute? Cexy? Hell, I didn't know what to call it, but she encompassed it completely.

I glanced down at my watch then leaned in behind her as she stood at the pinball machine. "It's almost three thirty in the morning," I told her, feeling a bit sick to my stomach. I had this plan to spend the night doing all these different activities, but with the subway travel time and the city being busier than ever, time wasn't on our side. The closer it grew to morning, the more I wanted to freeze time. I wanted more of her, more of us, whatever it was that we were.

"I wanted to show you the other part of this location before we head out," I explained. As I leaned in, my body pressed against her back, and for a second, I thought she leaned into me, allowing her body to mold into mine. As the night went on, our bodies found ways of being closer to one another, as if a magnetic pull was forcing us together.

I didn't mind. I liked it when she was close to me.

"It's already three-thirty?" she asked, turning my way and frowning. It was good to know we were both displeased with that reality.

"Yeah. Come on, let me take you to the best part of this." I took her hand and began leading us through the space. There was a door with a large glowing C over it.

"What's this?" she asked.

"This is the part that reminds me of you." I grabbed the handle of the door and pushed it open. At that moment, I felt as if I were Santa Claus and I'd just unlocked Red's wildest dreams. Behind said door was a huge room with shelves and tables filled with comics. Special collector's editions were even set behind glass at the cashier's table.

"Oh my gosh." She was stunned by what she was seeing. "Are those...?"

"Yes."

"Can I...?"

I smiled. "Yes."

She pushed past me and dived into the room, bum-rushing the Marvel section. The room glowed from the vintage club lighting, and it felt tacky in a cool way, if that made any sense. Carpet covered one of the walls and against it were giant posters of superheroes from all different universes.

I crossed my arms in pleasure with how it seemed I'd tapped into something she loved. I liked how she smiled as she paged through the stacks of comics. I walked across the aisle she stood in front of and began thumbing through them, too. The only thing separating us was the bin with the comics, and honestly, that was more space than I liked.

"Truth or truth?" she asked me.

I arched a brow. "Truth."

"What was the happiest day of your life?"

"The second time I learned my mom's cancer was gone for good."

"That's the best pick."

I couldn't have agreed more.

"Truth or truth?" I inquired.

"Truth."

"Why did your last relationship end?"

She paused a moment from paging through the comics, and I saw the split second of hurt flash before her. She shook her head a bit before replying. "I walked in on him cheating on me. Then he broke up with me because he was in love with her."

"Again, asshole."

"Yeah. But still…he broke up with me. I can't believe I stood there while he was naked and allowed him to break up with me. I always thought I'd go into badass-strong-woman mode and snap during those kinds of moments. Break a lamp or two and kick him in his privates— but instead, I just stood there and took it. Then I cried for five weeks." She stood straighter. "Actually, today's the first day I haven't cried."

"We celebrate growth," I said, applauding.

"I'm sure it has something to do with you distracting me from my heartache, so I thank you for that."

"You're still sad."

She nodded. "Yes. Less sad today, though."

"Which means you could be even less sad tomorrow, too."

"Yeah. It's just that breakups make you doubt everything about yourself. I keep thinking about how I could've been better for him, how I could've been his heroine instead of Monica." She made a gagging face. "Gosh, Monica—what a stupid name. Can you believe it? He fell in love with Monica, and he talked about her as if she was his happily ever after. She was his heroine this whole time, and there I was thinking I was the leading lady in his story. All along, I was really just the basic barista, the side character no one remembers. I don't know, maybe that's my role in life. Maybe I am destined to be nothing more than a background character in people's main stories. I'm just the girl who gives the hero and heroine their coffee."

"You can't really believe that."

Her shoulders shrugged, and she said nothing else.

She went back to paging through her comics, and her eyes lit up with joy when she found something she loved. Her whole mood shifted when she held it to her chest and hugged it. "Do you see this?!" she excitedly asked.

"I can't exactly see it because you're squeezing it to death."

She turned it around to reveal it to me, and there I was—well, not me, but my alter ego. "Captain America—a 1950 edition. This is a gem."

"Get it. I'll buy it for you."

"No. You don't have to do that."

"I know. I want to. While you're at it, build a collection for yourself to take."

"Captain—"

"Please, Red." I sounded as if I was begging. I was pleading because the way her eyes lit with joy looking at those comics was something I wanted to keep her feeling. "I know it's a different time from 1918 when I was around, but I just want to do this for you."

"Why?"

"Because it's you."

"What's so special about me?"

I walked around to her so we stood face-to-face, and I slowly moved a piece of hair that was dangling by her cheek and placed it behind her ear. "Everything's special about you."

"What scares you?" she asked, throwing me off, clearly changing the subject from her to me.

"Oh, a lot of things. Snakes. Turbulence on airplanes. Being late for important meetings. Kangaroos."

"Kangaroos?"

"Have you ever seen a kangaroo fight? Thor has nothing compared to a kangaroo."

"Fair enough, but I was hoping for less surface-level fears. So I'll ask again. What scares you?"

My brows knitted together. I didn't talk about my fears out loud often. I believed that once you put words to something, once you gave voice to the monsters you kept locked away in your head, they were uncaged and able to be brought to life.

Even so, Red had been open with me, so she deserved the same respect. Maybe if I whispered it, my fears would stay only against her eardrums.

"Letting people down," I confessed. "My mom's cancer coming back and her dying from it. Losing people I care about. Leaving this life without making an impact."

She smiled. It was small but felt massive in my chest. Her big smiles were amazing, don't get me wrong, but those small, almost secret grins made me want the sun to stay down a few more hours.

"What about you?"

"I'm afraid of never having a family…of dying alone."

"It seems we both fear the idea of death, huh?"

Her brown eyes gleamed with a bit of mirth. "You got a philosophical quote for that?"

"Hmm. 'What worries you, masters you.' John Locke. Which is why," I explained, flipping through the bins some more. "I don't speak about my fears very often. The more you feed them, the more they grow. Yeah, I have my fears and my worries, but I have more hope than that, too."

She paused for a second and stared at me. Her eyes searched mine as if she were trying to decode something within me.

Just ask me, Red, and I'll tell you my secrets.

Her body straightened as she stood taller with her comics pressed to her chest. "I know where I want to take you next for the place I think you'll love."

I arched an eyebrow and glanced down at my watch. "We're inching closer to sunlight."

"Well…" She walked around and held her free hand out toward me. "We better hurry."

"Wish Alley?" I asked, raising an eyebrow as we stood at the end of a very well-lit alleyway.

People in costumes were standing around the alleyway, chatting, talking, and writing on Post-it Notes. The smoke from the sewer drains intermixed with the people's cigarettes, creating an unmatched vibe. The laughter that filled the space was powerful, but then I'd look around and notice one or two individuals who were alone, who looked more somber, more heartbroken than the others surrounding them. They stared at the walls of Post-its before writing out their own and walking away.

"People come here to write down their wishes and stick them to the wall. I figured we could write down our hopes and leave them here to put them out into the world. You said you don't like speaking of your fears, which I get, but speaking about your wishes…" She paused and wrinkled her nose. "Is this lame? Feel free to tell me if this is lame."

I laughed. "This is the opposite of lame. This is amazing." I walked up to the wall and crossed my arms, reading some of the wishes left against the bricks.

Some wishes were material things: expensive cars, expensive games, purses.

Others' wishes were a bit deeper.

I wish for my ex to love me again.

I wish to get out of toxic relationships.

I wish for a home.

I wish for a cure for cancer.

I felt that one deep in my bones.

I looked over at Red, who was reading the words, too. I loved the way she took them in, holding her hands over her heart as if she were connecting personally to each word written upon the pieces of paper.

"Ready?" I asked her, walking over to the stack of unused Post-it Notes and grabbing a pad and a pen for us to use.

She took a deep breath, stepped away from the wall, and nodded. "Ready."

"How many do we get to write?"

"Three seems like a magical number to me."

Three wishes. If I had three wishes, how would I use them?

Number one: I wish my mother's cancer would never come back.

Number two: I wish no kid would ever go hungry or be without shelter or love.

Number three:

I turned to Red, who was in deep thought as she bit her bottom lip and scribbled on the Post-it. Every now and again, she'd pause and nibble that lip. I couldn't stop watching her stop-and-go writing process. Everything about her, I found so damn attractive.

I went back to my last Post-it and scribbled down my last wish.

Number three: More nights like this. More nights with Red.

We put the notes up on the brick wall. I knew they'd probably blow away at some point in time. I knew they would roll up and tear at some point. But, at that moment, it felt powerful to put our wishes into the atmosphere.

Red walked over to my notes, and I walked over to hers. She wished for longevity, she wished for love, and she wished for more time.

I couldn't help but wish for more time, too. Each second I spent with her that evening felt like something important was slowly evaporating from my life. There I was, hoping to make her fall in love with me as a way to help her get over her ex, and there I was, falling quickly for a girl who wasn't going to stick around after sunrise.

Oh, the situations we put ourselves in, Con.

"More nights with Red," she said out loud before turning to me. "You wished for more nights with me?"

"Yes. More nights with you."

She laughed a little and fiddled with her hands. "That's funny," she said, pointing toward the wall. "Because I cheated a bit and wrote a fourth note." She revealed the sticky note in her palm, then handed it over to me. "I wished for you, too."

I read the words: *More Captain America.*

I smirked and brushed my hand against the back of my neck. "More of me?"

"More of you."

Fuck.

My heart.

I'd always known it was there, but I hadn't known it could beat like that, like a million fireworks all exploding at once into a damn masterpiece.

I held my hand out toward her. "Dance with me."

"What?" She giggled. And my gosh, I loved her giggle. "There's no music."

"Don't care. Just dance with me."

She gave me her hand, and I pulled her toward me. Our bodies swayed slowly as she wrapped her arms around my neck and rested her head against my chest.

"I can feel your heartbeats," she told me.

Now, don't get me wrong, I was a corny guy. When it came to being the cornmaster, I was the leader of the pack. But I didn't want to go full-blown corn and tell her that heart she was feeling was beating for her.

But let's be honest…that heart was beating for her.

"Mario never danced with me. He said it was stupid," she told me. Everything she told me about that man made me hate him that much more.

"Do you like dancing?" I asked.

"Yeah. I love it."

"Can you make me a promise, Red?"

"Yes."

"Never again fall in love with a man who won't dance with you."

She looked up at me for a second before laying her head against my chest. "How many times have you been in love?"

"In the normal sense of the word? Never."

"What do you mean by that? 'In the normal sense'?"

I smirked. "I've never had a girlfriend. Therefore, I've never had that normal boy meets girl, boy and girl see each other nonstop and talk nonstop and fall madly in love kind of love story."

"If you've never loved a woman, then you've never been in love. Easy as that."

I smiled. "I disagree with you on that. If only it were that easy. But I feel love all the time. I call it flashes of love, small or big moments of connection with a person. It's the small moments of love that I like the best. Like when a person rushes to open the door for you when your hands are full. Or when a little kid falls into a laughing fit and can't stop giggling. When an older couple walks by holding hands. Those are moments when I feel love. Those are the moments I fall head over heels. I love the flashes of love."

"See, I hear what you're saying, but can I be honest for a second?"

"I thrive on honesty."

She pulled away a bit, bringing our dancing to a stop, and she scrunched up her face. "When you say all of that, 99% of me believes you, but the other one percent is like, *That sounds like some major fuck-boy stuff*," she joked.

I laughed and nodded. "Yeah, I guess you could see it that way. Honestly, that's why I wanted this night to be only tonight. Do I want more time with you? Absolutely. But am I aware that I'm not in a place to give you the love and time you deserve? Yes. I'm too focused on my career to respectfully take up real estate in a woman's life when I am not equipped to give her the fair equity she deserves."

She arched an eyebrow. "So basically, you're trying not to waste people's time."

"We're on this earth with limited time. It would be a shame if I wasted someone's."

"That's really un-fuckboy of you to say."

I snickered. "I'm trying to be as un-fuckboy as possible."

"Captain?"

"Yes?"

"Can we dance again?"

Within seconds, we're swaying again to our own kind of music.

"So this would be one, wouldn't it?" she asked.

"Be one what?"

"A flash of love."

I rested my chin on the top of her head as we moved back and forth. "This whole evening with you has been nothing but flashes of love."

After our time in Wish Alley, dancing to our own music, we both realized time was running out, and it was my turn to take her to a place I loved.

"So, here's the thing. I love a lot of places in the city, but I kind of want to go back to the beginning of the night where you and I began. I was hoping maybe we could watch the sunrise over the city on the rooftop of the bar," I offered.

"I feel bad. I feel as if I took up too much time in the comic bookstore geeking out. Now, you don't have enough time to take me to a place you love," she explained.

"The places I've loved tonight were the ones I went with you. Wherever you were tonight, I loved it."

She blushed, and if that wasn't a small sample of what love felt like, I didn't want to know what love truly was. Because the feeling in my chest was so overwhelmingly packed with joy that I thought my heart was going to explode.

"You're such a smooth talker, Cap."

"I think you like it, Red."

"I do," she confessed. "I've liked every single moment of the night. Well, minus the one when you got a black eye," she said, gently touching the space around my eye. I'd almost forgotten I got my ass kicked.

Funny how she didn't think she was the heroine of her story when she literally made me forget about my pain. Only a leading lady could do that.

"Won't the bar be closed by the time we get there?" she asked.

"Don't worry about that. I have a few connections, remember? Unless you want to do something else to help ensure you fall in love with me. I can book us a quick trip to Bora Bora or something," I joked.

"No." She laughed and shook her head. "I think the best way for me to fall in love with you is just being around you."

This time it was my turn to blush like the schoolboy I had been.

"You're a smooth talker, Red."

"It's only because I want you to fall in love with me."

Dammit, Red...it's working.

FIVE

Aaliyah

WE STOPPED FOR COFFEE BEFORE ARRIVING AT THE BAR where we'd begun. The club was already closed, and the only people left inside were the workers cleaning up. My heart dropped a bit the moment I realized we were locked out, but it began skipping again when Captain pulled out his cell phone and made a call.

"Hey, Tommy! It's me. Yeah, I'm outside the bar. I left my keys inside. Can you let me in?" He paused, then bit his bottom lip. He got a little shy, and that was adorable. "No, Tommy. I'm not going to have sex on the rooftop." *Pause.* "I know! Okay, what about this: I'll give you those season tickets for next season we were talking about two weeks ago." *Pause.* "Yes, okay. Fine—but only if you promise to let me go to one game with you." *Pause.* "Thank you kindly, sir. We have a deal."

Within seconds, Tommy stood in front of the door, unlocking it for us to get in. "I can't believe you left your keys here," he said. "You should be letting yourself in."

Captain leaned in and kissed his cheek repeatedly before smacking his bum. "I know. Stupid mistake. Thanks, Tommy!"

"Yeah, yeah. I'll probably be gone before you tonight, so will you lock up?"

"You got it."

Captain took my hand and pulled me through the now empty space. As we moved forward, it felt odd having no one around us after being in a packed room before. It was just another example of how our time that night was running out; our clock fading to black.

He took me to the office where I'd met Tommy earlier and grabbed his keys from the desk. He also grabbed the jacket hanging on the back of the door and placed it over my shoulders.

"Ready?" he asked.

"Time-out—why would you have keys to this place? And why would he let you lock up? What am I missing?"

"Oh." He rubbed the back of his neck and shrugged. "I own the building."

"I'm sorry, what?!"

He smirked, and his dimple deepened as he took my hand. "Come on, let's go."

We began our hike up the staircase, and my chest felt tight halfway up the stairs. I hated how winded I got. I knew I wasn't in the best shape, but I felt as if my heart was racing faster than normal. I took more breaks than I was proud of, but Captain didn't judge me. When I stopped my steps, he stopped his, too.

"I need to get back to the gym," I joked three-fourths of the way up the stairs. I rested my hand against my chest, feeling my heartbeats intensifying. Each breath was deeper than the one before. He stayed patient with me. He even slowed his steps when we moved up the stairs.

As we reached the top, we found a spot to sit, facing the sunrise, waiting for the beginning of the end of us. I tried to control my inhalations to bring them back to a normal speed. I wanted to speak, but I knew I wouldn't be able to until I gathered myself.

When that time came, I looked over at Captain. "So…you own this building?"

"Yeah, this one and a few others," he said nonchalantly as if it was a normal thing for a twenty-five-year-old to say.

"I'm sorry, what? You own buildings plural? What exactly do you do for a living?"

"Oh…a lot of different things."

And there goes my heart rate increasing again.

"That sounds like something someone in the mafia would say, and if I just spent the evening with someone in the mafia, I'm truly going to rethink all of my life choices. Oh my goodness, have you killed someone before? Are you a murderer?"

He cocked an eyebrow. "If I were, do you think I would tell someone I'd just met?"

Fair enough.

He must've noted my low level of fear because he laughed. "I run my own real estate company and am an investor. I've been working my ass off since I moved to New York when I turned eighteen, and let's just say it paid off."

"Holy crap. Are you rich?"

He snickered. "Being rich is such a hard thing to claim. What makes someone rich, anyway?"

"Do you have over a million dollars in your bank account?" I asked bluntly. His hesitation was enough of a response for me. "Holy crap! You're rich!"

"It's not a big deal."

"Says the rich guy. Oh, my gosh, I can't believe you had me buy your drinks tonight! And your chicken wings!"

"Hey now! I offered to pay!"

"You should've told me you were a millionaire, then I would've allowed you to pay," I joked. "I should've asked you to buy me that extremely rare comic behind the counter."

He started to stand. "I mean, maybe we can head back that way and—"

"Shut up." I laughed as I grabbed his arm and pulled him back down. "I'm just kidding."

"Next time, I'll get it for you."

"I wish there was a next time," I said without thought. He stared my way for a moment before looking out at the sky.

"You know what's weird, Red? You're still here, and I already miss you."

I smiled, he smiled, and I loved the way we smiled together.

He pulled out a comic book and began to read to me. His thumb brushed against his upper lip before turning the pages, and I became fixated on watching his every move. At that moment, my heart decided it would beat for him for the remainder of the night. Probably into the next morning, too.

Unfortunately, the sun began to rise, and I hated that the good was coming to an end.

I hated the sun. I hated how it couldn't shift its schedule for one day to allow me a few more hours with him. I should've felt tired, but if anything, all I felt was sad. The lighter it grew, the sadder I became.

How had a stranger become so important in such a short period?

"Remind me again why we aren't allowing ourselves to fall for one another tomorrow and the day after that, too," he said, his voice low and shaky. He was becoming more anxious about the impending end of whatever connection we'd formed, too.

I sighed. "Because you're too busy building an empire, and I'm a girl who hasn't unpacked the past baggage and insecurities from my previous relationship enough to truly engage in a new one this fast."

"Ah, yes. Reality."

"I hate it here," I joked, biting back the emotions sitting behind my eyes. Did I desire more nights like the one we'd shared together? Yes. Did I understand that we both weren't truly ready for more? Also yes. I had never believed you could meet the right person at the wrong time until this very night.

"We have to make a few promises," Captain said as he placed the comic book down. He turned to sit face-to-face with me and took my hands in his. "This night was special, and I don't want to jinx it in any way, shape, or form. I like the idea of us crossing paths again, with destiny tossing a coin into that chance encounter. So we have to avoid the places we've gone to tonight. We can't force the universe to push us together. We gotta trust the stars that somehow we'll cross paths again."

"And if we don't?"

He turned my palm up. "Well then, Red"—he kissed my palm, causing a wave of butterflies to flutter through my system—"thank you for the happiest night of my life."

My eyes felt like watering because he'd done the same—given me the happiest experience, which I needed more than words.

He kept holding my hands and stared down at our fingers, which were now intertwined. "I have a confession to make."

"A confession?"

"Yes. I knew you wouldn't fall in love with me in five hours."

I raised an eyebrow. "You don't think I love you?" I asked. We hadn't even discussed the challenge we'd created about falling in love. We'd simply spent the past five hours laughing, diving deep, and connecting. Honestly, I'd forgotten all about it until he brought it up.

"No, I don't." He shrugged. "And I'm okay with that because I might have had an ulterior motive."

"And what was that?"

"All I wanted to do was make you happy, remind you that no matter how bad your heart can hurt, you can find happiness again. You can love yourself enough to find joy in life. You can get back up again after feeling defeated. I knew it would be impossible to make you fall in love with me—I mean, I'm just some guy from Kentucky—but I also knew it was possible to make you fall in love with yourself again. Because that kind of love never strays too far."

"I don't think you know how much I needed you tonight."

"The feeling goes both ways, Red. But just in case you forget again tomorrow, here's a list I compiled tonight of things about you that are worth loving." He cleared his throat and pretended to pull out a piece of paper from his invisible pocket, which he read from. "The way you wrinkle your nose when displeased. The way you dance when no one is looking. The way you nerd out about comics is worth every second of loving you. The way you feel things deeply—that's a gift. So many people in the world are closed off and disconnected from their feelings. Your emotions live loudly inside you—the good ones and the bad— which makes you balanced. You should love the way you smile. That smile is worthy of all the love. And your eyes, the way they drink people in and are filled with kindness. The way you love others who probably don't deserve your love. The way you live. The way you breathe. The way that outside of all those things, you deserve to be loved because you exist. Your mere existence is reason enough for you to be loved."

And just like that, I fell.

I loved him—at least for that single moment.

That night I learned it was possible to love individuals in singular moments. I learned there could be seconds of time when the world aligned perfectly to create a moment that caused your body to be overwhelmed with love for a complete stranger. I'd discovered flashes of love.

We were close now, so close I was almost sitting on his lap as our foreheads rested against one another. He wrapped his arms around me and pulled me against him, allowing me to fall into his body. I liked the way that felt. I already missed the way that felt.

"I feel bad for whoever it is that gets to love you next," he whispered, his lips almost brushing against mine. "They will never be worthy of the magnitude of love you'll give to them."

I closed my eyes. As he inhaled, I exhaled. Our breaths intermixed as our bodies did the same. I didn't want to let him go because that meant waking up from the dream I'd been living that night and going back to reality.

I wasn't certain I wanted to live in a reality where he didn't exist.

"The sun is up," he said softly.

"Yeah."

"It's time to let go."

"I know."

Still, we stayed frozen together for a little bit longer. We allowed the sun to kiss our skin as we both worked hard not to kiss one another. Our lips were close enough, but I knew if I gave in, I wouldn't walk away.

As we stood, I felt like crying, but I also felt an overwhelming amount of peace.

"For the record, Red, you aren't the barista," he said as the sun kept rising behind us. "You're not the quirky best friend, and you're not some random woman on page forty-five. You're the main character. Day in and day out, you are the leading lady. And for me, you're the one who got away."

I hugged him. I rushed into him and held on tight because after that moment, I knew I wouldn't be able to hold the stranger who didn't feel so strange to me anymore. I held on and felt my eyes filling with tears as he held on tighter. He held me as if he cared for me more than any other person ever had, as if he'd given me his all, and my goodness, his all was enough.

I'd never known I could need someone I didn't even know to re-mind me what it meant to fall in love with myself again.

"Thank you," I whispered as I lay my head against his chest. He leaned down and kissed the top of my head.

"Thank you," he replied. "Can you make me a promise?"

"Yes."

"Next time you get into a relationship, don't settle for less than you deserve."

I smiled. "I promise."

"I got this weird feeling we're gonna meet again. Mark my words," he said, seeming hopeful about the possibility of us crossing paths again.

"You believe that much in fate?"

"No." He shook his head. "I just believe in us."

"How about we bet on it. If we meet again, I'll pay you a dollar. If we don't...well, I won't pay you a dollar," I joked.

"All right. Deal. Each year that passes, though, you add a dollar onto the tab."

"Spoken like a true businessman."

"If anything, I'm consistent."

We parted ways, and the broken parts of my heart were temporar-ily healed by his kind words. He emptied my sad soul and filled it back up with love.

I took the subway home, holding my hands against my chest to feel my heartbeats. The heart that seemed so deeply broken was begin-ning to beat again, and for the first time in a long time, I felt as if I'd be okay. When I emerged from the subway, I breathed in deeply and ex-haled the chilled air as the thoughts of the stranger who'd made me the main character for one night kept crossing my mind.

I knew it seemed ridiculous, and the next morning, I'd likely awaken to reality, but I was almost certain the thought floating around in my head was somewhat true. I'd fallen in love with a man that night, and I hadn't even known his name. But I knew his touch. His laughter. His heart.

I'd remember the feeling he'd given me as I moved on through life from that day forth.

I'd never forget his flashes of love.

The following week, he stayed on my mind. I moved through my internship with more smiles on my face, and each day I worked at the coffee shop, I felt as if I were floating as I brewed coffee for individuals.

"Excuse me, can I get a few extra sugar cubes for my coffee? And maybe a cinnamon roll, too," a woman asked me as I stood at the counter of C&C Café. She broke me away from my thoughts of Halloween night, forcing me back to reality.

I smiled at the warm grin she was giving me. She'd been a regular for the past few weeks, a beautiful Black woman who had the most striking brown eyes I'd ever seen. When those eyes looked at me, they seemed so welcoming, as if one of the best moments of her day was looking my way—almost the same way Captain had stared at me. It blew my mind that some people were born with such gentle, caring eyes.

"Of course! Let me ring you up, and I'll bring it right over to your table," I told her, punching numbers into the keyboard.

"Thank you, uh"—she looked down at my name tag then back up at me—"Aaliyah. That's a pretty name."

I smiled. "Thanks."

She moved back to her corner table and sat down, pulling out a novel. She'd been reading the same book for the past week, *The Rule of Magic* by Alice Hoffman. Each week, she'd bring in a new book, falling deep into the pages.

As I brought over her chai tea and cinnamon roll, she didn't tear her eyes away from the page. Sometimes, she seemed somewhat invested in her novels, but she was more than intrigued with this go-around. She was melting into each word that came to her, flipping the pages with speed.

"It must be a good one," I said, placing her order on the table.

She looked up and laid the book down. "Oh my goodness, it's such a good one. I'm part of a book club, and this is our current read."

"Oh, that's fun! I'm a big reader, too."

"Are you?" She raised an eyebrow. "What kind of books are you into?"

"Personally, comic books, but I do dive into thrillers from time to time."

"Comic books?" she asked, surprised. "That's fun."

"Well, you know me. I have good taste," I joked. "Enjoy yourself, and if you need anything—"

I paused as my chest tightened a bit. Everything came to a rushing stop as my knees began to buckle. My hands flew to my chest as I began gasping for air. My heart was pounding at an irrational speed, and as I fell to the ground, I was quickly surrounded by my coworkers.

Their lips were moving fast, and I saw the fear in their eyes as I tried to control my labored breaths. I shut my eyes and knew nothing good was going on. My heart felt as if it were on fire. As if it were shattering right inside my chest and trying to pound its way to freedom from the chains that seemed to be suffocating it.

I passed out at some point, wanting nothing more than the pain in my chest to disappear.

I awakened to bright lights shining down on me. My arms were hooked up to machines, and a nurse stood with her back to me as she was filling out something in her hand.

"What happened?" I asked, dazed and confused with cotton mouth. Nothing was making any kind of sense as I tried to get a grip on the situation. Everything seemed so fuzzy in my mind as I tried to connect the dots.

Flashes.

I remembered flashes that took place before my arrival at the hospital, yet none of them were flashes of love. No…

I had flashes of pain, flashes of fear, flashes of death.

The nurse turned my way with a big, bright smile. "There you are. It's good to hear you talking. You're at St. Peter's Hospital. Do you have any family you'd like me to call?"

I shook my head. "No. It's just me. What happened?"

She smiled, walked over to me, and took my hand in hers, squeezing it lightly. "You're going to be okay. You had complications with your heart and—"

"Complications?!" I asked, panicked about her word choice, and the worry that hit her eyes made it clear she wasn't the right one to deliver the news.

"Let me go get your doctor so he can explain everything to you, okay? I'll be back with answers for you."

"How long have I been here?" I asked, moving only slightly but feeling intense pain shoot down my spine.

"About twelve hours."

"What?!" I spat out, sitting up straighter, terrified. Had I been out for that long? What was happening?

"The doctor will be in shortly."

She left me to sit by myself, scared about what was happening to me. I looked at the numbers on the screen, my vitals. My hands were clammy, and my mind spun as I tried to figure out what exactly was going on. The last thing I recalled was being at work, and then everything went black.

It took over forty-five minutes for the doctor to arrive, leaving me with nothing but anxiety-packed thoughts.

"Hi, Aaliyah. I'm Dr. Brown. It's nice to meet you." The doctor walked in with a half-grin, and a few others followed, including the nurse who greeted me before. "I hear you are a bit confused about everything going on."

I wrapped my arms around my body in a protective stance because I felt emotionally exposed and needed the tight hug I'd given myself. "Yes. I don't understand why I'm here."

"Do you recall what happened?"

"I remember being at work and then blacking out. I woke up here. That's all I know."

He pulled up a chair next to my bedside and clasped his hands. The somber look on his face worried me.

"What is it?" I asked, panic clenching my insides.

"It's your heart."

"What do you mean? What do you mean it's my heart?"

He grimaced and nodded once as if he was preparing for his next words. "Your heart is failing at this time. Your blood has backed up in the pulmonary veins, which transports the oxygenated blood from your lungs to your heart. This means your heart cannot keep up with the supply, causing fluid to leak into your lungs. This is diagnosed as congestive heart failure."

"Oh, my goodness." I placed my hands against my chest, terrified of what he was saying. My mind began to spin as he spoke those words to me. Had he said my heart was failing? "What does that mean? How do we fix it? I'm only twenty-two. This doesn't make any sense. I'm healthy. I've always been healthy. Oh, my goodness, am I dying? What do I do? How do I—"

"Calm down…it's okay," the doctor told me, placing a comforting hand on my forearm.

I ripped my arm out of his grip as tears formed in my eyes. "You can't say calm down after telling me my heart is failing! Oh, my gosh. This can't be happening. What do we do? What do I do?"

"I understand this can be a scary diagnosis, but we will come up with a plan to help manage your condition. There are different medications we can—"

"Manage or reverse?" I cut in.

His eyes looked heavier than his frown, and I knew nothing good was coming next. "With the stage you are at, managing the condition and making sure it doesn't worsen are our best bets."

Which meant there was no reversing what'd happened to me.

It was all adding up.

The swollen ankles. The exhaustion. The shortness of breath…

How long had my heart been struggling to beat?

The doctor kept speaking, using words I couldn't understand and also tossing in words I should've comprehended. But none of it was sticking because I was stuck on one main fact: my heart, the heart I'd carried inside my chest since the day I was born, the one that moved me through life and made it possible for me to exist, was breaking.

My heart was breaking, and I feared there was no way to put it back together.

One moment.

It only took one moment for my whole world to change. A diagnosis that would live with me for the remainder of my life. How long was that? How much time was left for me? And would I be able to achieve all the things I wanted to achieve now that I had this impending doomsday clock ticking in my chest?

I went home, and I pulled out my laptop and began searching for more information on heart failure. I dived deep, and by the end of my searches, I felt a level of fear I wasn't certain how to face.

Five years.

Only half of the individuals who'd been diagnosed with congestive heart failure survived past five years. Ten percent made it ten years.

Ten years.

I'd only be thirty-two in ten years.

Time.

It would have been almost comical how time worked if it hadn't been so tragic.

Six weeks earlier, I had been heartbroken over a man who never truly loved me. One week earlier, a stranger had reminded me how to love myself. Then that afternoon, I'd found out my heart was truly broken.

Funny how a real broken heart hurts more than any pain a boy could cause me.

I grieved that night. I grieved for all the life I'd miss out on. I grieved the loss of my future goals and dreams. I grieved the idea that I might never celebrate my thirtieth birthday. I allowed myself all the time I needed to truly sit with my grief, and I let it swallow me whole for a bit.

I stayed sad and depressed for a good while. Sofia couldn't stand my mood, she said I was bringing down her energy, so shortly after I found out about my heart, she moved out. Never in my life had I felt more alone. During the silence, my anxiety hit new heights. Still, each day I woke up. If only I could've realized what a blessing that had been.

After some terrible nights and harsher days, I pulled myself together the best I could. I took a deep breath and tried to find a way to be grateful for the sunlight that poured onto my skin to wake me up each day. I returned to a place I'd told Captain I wouldn't visit to avoid us crossing paths, but I needed to go back to Wish Alley to write down another wish upon a Post-it. This time my wish was simple.

I wished for more time.

SIX

Aaliyah

Two years later

I COULD COUNT THE NUMBER OF FACTS I KNEW ABOUT MY MOTHER on one hand. Two fingers, as a matter of fact: I knew she gave birth to me, and I knew she gave me my name. That was the extent of my knowledge about the woman who brought me into the world. Everything else, I made up in my mind, millions of fictional stories I told myself throughout the years. For example, maybe I'd gotten my eyes from her, or perhaps my nose. Maybe she had named me after the gone-too-soon musician Aaliyah, which was why I listened to her soundtracks throughout my teenage years, wondering if my mother would've dedicated a certain song to me.

My fictional mother loved brunch, which was why I found a new brunch spot each week, and she loved to travel, too. I didn't have much time or money to travel the way I wished I could've, but I had a vision board with photographs of Greece, Spain, and Bora Bora hanging over my desk at home. Fake Mom must've hated spicy things, she couldn't stand Brussels sprouts, and the way she loved? She probably loved so much it hurt her. She loved me so much she let me go.

At least those were the lies I told myself.

In my thoughts, she had tight coils of hair dipped in black ink. Her laughter was infectious, the kind that made others chuckle just from the enjoyment of her sounds. She danced, too—poorly, like me, but oh, how her body swayed. Sometimes, I pretended she was African royalty and was forced to give me up after an affair with some B-list Hollywood actor. They'd met on a Roman holiday and fallen in lust within days. Then he'd left her behind to pursue his dreams of becoming an A-list star.

At least those were the stories I'd tell myself throughout my adolescence. I didn't create many stories about her now that I was in my early twenties. Most of the time, I only thought about her whenever a big life event happened, during which I wished to have a mother by my side. I wondered how she would've felt about how my life was shaping up recently. I wondered if she would've been proud of the choices I was making that afternoon.

Get out of your head, Aaliyah, and pull yourself together.

"You can't be serious," Maiv said, staring at me as if I were the most idiotic woman to ever exist in the world. "You're quitting your job here, at *Passion Magazine*, a position any sane human would kill for, in order to—I'm sorry, explain your reason again," she said as she waved her hand toward her head as if trying to recollect my words.

"To get married to my fiancé. I recently learned we'll be moving to California full-time, and since we're getting married, I figured it would be best to be in the same location as newlyweds," I explained as my stomach twisted in knots.

The disapproval of my answer and the way her lips turned upside down made me want to vomit. With one look, she made me feel like a child who'd misbehaved. In reality, the only misbehaving I'd done was falling in love.

Maiv Khang was terrifying. She was one of the most successful women in all of New York, but completely coldhearted and a hard one to read—which was ironic because she ran a magazine about following one's passion in life. We covered athletes, scientists, politicians, social businesses, restaurants, etc. Anything that had a passion behind it, we were writing top-of-the-line articles on the subject. You would think someone who ran such a business would, oh, I don't know, be a bit passionate themselves.

Not Maiv, though. She always appeared empty. Bored of life. She did a fantastic job with the magazine, but her people skills were yikes.

Maiv's hair was gray and always pulled back into a perfect bun. She wore her most expensive jewels on a daily basis, and although she was in her seventies, everyone who worked for *Passion* assumed she would never step down from her CEO position to pass the company on to her daughter, Jessica. She was more than willing to hold on as tight as she could, like Queen Elizabeth, while Jessica was a solid Prince Charles.

"So you're quitting your job at the top magazine line in the world to go be a housewife for some guy?" she asked, but it came off as more of a disdainful statement.

"Not just for some guy—for Jason, my fiancé."

"You're young. What is this, your third fiancé? Fourth?"

I snickered until I saw the seriousness in her stare. I cleared my throat and moved around in my seat. "Um, my first actually."

She rolled her eyes again and waved her hand in dismissal—again. "Never quit a job for the first man who proposes to you. Not the second or third either. Seventh maybe, but that depends on his status."

I smiled an uncertain grin and shrugged. "Well, I think I'm going to take this chance with Jason."

She laughed.

Yup. Maiv laughed out loud—a sound I hadn't known she was able to create. "How long have you been in a relationship?" she questioned.

"We are going on a year and a half."

The way she burst into a laughing fit almost made me want to cry. Tact wasn't her strong suit.

Please go back to the nonlaughing boss I know and fear.

"Well, it's your life. You're free to make all the mistakes you want, but remember, each mistake turns into a forehead wrinkle, and Botox is expensive." She waved me away and went back to reading whatever it was that sat in front of her.

"Um, okay...but I do have one more thing to say." She looked up from her paperwork and arched an uninterested brow. "I won't be becoming a housewife when I move out to California in a few weeks. I am in search of another journalist position. I am hoping to ask if you could maybe write me a letter of recommendation?"

"You should probably leave my office now."

"Okay, right." I stood swiftly from the chair I'd obviously stayed in a second too long. As I was walking away, I turned back to face her. "I hope you know, Maiv, that I am so honored and thankful for you giving me the opportunity to work for your company. This has been the best job I've ever had and the experience of a lifetime, and—"

She held her hand up to silence me, took off her glasses, and pinched the bridge of her nose. "You don't get it, do you?"

"Get what?"

"You told me when you came to work here that working at *Passion* was your biggest life dream, and you are throwing that away for probably an average-sized dick of a man you've known for less than two years. Did he ask you how you'd feel about giving up your dream for him?"

"No."

"Then don't expect your dreams to go any further when you're married to a man who doesn't even try to come up with a way for both of your dreams to come true."

I stood there, completely quiet and baffled by her words.

She looked back down at her paperwork and cleared her throat. "I'm also assuming my invitation got lost in the mail."

"Your invitation…uh, right. Yes, of course. Your invitation definitely got lost in the mail."

"Then you better make sure I have a seat at a table. Send the information to my assistant. I don't require a plus-one, but I'll be in attendance."

"Why?"

She looked up eerily slow and cocked an eyebrow at me, forcing me to speak again.

"*Why* that is wonderful news," I said, trying to shift the why that left my mouth.

"Why are you still in my office?"

"Right. Of course. Goodbye."

I left a bit stunned, uncertain of what to say, and unsure how I should've felt. Had Maiv just invited herself to my wedding? Had she said she was coming? Oh gosh, the seating chart was already done. I'd have to call to get that shifted around. Luckily, right after work, I was on the way to my soon-to-be mother-in-law's home, where she'd help me fit Maiv into the chart without issue.

If I'd ever gotten a shot at having my own mother, I'd have wanted her to be just like Marie Rollsfield. When I first met her, she talked about her son a lot, about how she and her husband adopted him when he was five years old. I told her about how lucky he was to be adopted by a great woman, and I'd never forget how that comment made her eyes fill with tears.

"I'm not a great woman, but I try to be a good mother," she explained, wiping the emotions away from her eyes.

I disagreed, though. Anyone kind, filled with love, and willing to take in a child who wasn't biologically their own was a hero in my mind. I would've killed to be adopted by parents as loving as Walter and Marie.

Mr. and Mrs. Rollsfield were my favorite kind of love story. They'd just celebrated thirty years of marriage the summer before, but if you looked at them, you'd think they were still squarely in the honeymoon stage. I'd never seen two people who loved so loudly at all times. From the handholding to the forehead kisses, Marie and Walter were relationship dreams come true.

It wasn't until Marie invited me over for Christmas dinner that I was introduced to Jason. Marie recalled it better than either of us did, but I remembered being in the Rollsfields' home and feeling as if I belonged.

Sometimes I wondered if I loved Jason's parents more than I loved him. Especially his mother, Marie. She was the definition of motherly love, and she welcomed me into their family with arms wide open. When I still worked at the coffee shop, she was the one who actually called 911 for me when I had the episode, and from that moment on, she had a special place in my heart. After that, to keep myself distracted from my health situation, I joined Marie's book club, and we grew closer and closer.

The best part of Jason's and my love story? Not only did I find a fiancé but I also received two dedicated future in-laws who made me feel like I had always been a part of their family. Being welcomed with arms wide open was the dream I'd always wished for—to have a family, to be a part of a strong unit, to create traditions we could share with one another. For example, Marie and I still had our weekly coffee dates. I always looked forward to them, too. If I could've grown up with a mother, I would've dreamed of one like Marie.

"I cannot believe it's really happening!" Marie squeaked as we stood in her living room while I got my last fitting done for my wedding dress. Every detail of the wedding had been handled by Marie and the wedding planning team she'd hired. She was hands-on in walking me through all the details I didn't really care about.

All I wanted, all I'd ever wanted was to walk down the aisle and say the only two words that mattered—I do.

I didn't care about all the ins and outs of the wedding day. I cared about the happily ever after that came afterward.

I smiled at the overzealous Marie. For the past few days, she'd been jumping up and down over the excitement of Saturday. "I can't believe it either." I stared in the mirror, feeling every butterfly form as I stared at the white gown custom designed for me.

Marie and Walter had covered the cost of the gown. They'd covered the cost of the whole ceremony and reception. If it had been up to me and my wallet, I'd have gone down to the courthouse with a dress from a thrift shop.

"I can't thank you enough for everything you and Walter have done for this wedding, Marie—and for me. I don't deserve all of this."

She walked over to me as the seamstress finished working on the hem of my dress. Marie placed her palms against my cheeks and smiled that bright smile she always shared with me. "You deserve the world, Aaliyah. You will never understand what you coming into our family has done to my heart. You are nothing less than the light we Rollsfields needed, and soon enough, we'll share the same last name."

I fell into her arms and hugged her tightly. When she pulled away from me, I laughed at the tears flooding her eyes. "You can't start crying yet. We still have to make it to the wedding day."

She waved a dismissive hand my way. "I think we'll just have to realize I'm going to be a hot mess that whole weekend. Thank goodness for waterproof makeup and a makeup artist on staff for the entire evening."

As I gazed at myself in the large mirror in the living room, I took a deep breath. A million emotions rushed through my mind, but only one was sitting at the forefront. And that was the fact that after all these years, I was finally going to be a part of something bigger than me.

I was finally going to have a family.

That alone made me want to tear up, too.

"Hello?" a voice called out, breaking me from my stare. "Mom! Where's Dad? I've been calling him for—"

I shouted as I turned around to see Jason staring at me with a tuxedo in his grip. "Oh my gosh! Get out of here! You can't see me in the dress before the wedding!" I ordered, darting behind the couch to try to hide.

"You don't really believe in those silly traditions, do you?" Jason said, brushing his thumb against his nose. "Just get up, Aaliyah. I already saw it."

"No!" I said, feeling silly for hiding but not wanting him to get another peek at the gown. I wasn't extremely superstitious or anything, but one thing I did believe in was that it was bad luck to see the bride before the wedding day.

Thankfully, Marie was on the same page as me. "She's right! What are you doing, Jason? I told you to call before you stopped by."

"I did. Dad's and your phones are on silent. Plus, Aaliyah's went to voicemail. Listen, I'm just here to drop off Dad's tux for Saturday."

"Put it in the foyer and then leave. We'll see you tomorrow for the rehearsal," Marie told him.

I could almost feel Jason rolling his eyes at the thought of it all. When it came to superstitions, he believed in none of them.

"Whatever. I'm leaving." He began to walk away and then glanced over his shoulder toward me. "Aaliyah?"

"Yes?"

He smirked widely. "Your ass looks fat in that dress."

"Take that language elsewhere," Marie said as she threw a couch pillow at her son, who hurried away, slamming the door behind him.

Marie looked at me as I stood straight, and the warmth of her smile made me grin. "He's right, you know. You look to die for."

SEVEN

Connor

HADN'T HAD A GOOD NIGHT'S SLEEP IN WEEKS, AND MY OVERPROTECTIVE mother was concerned.

I didn't even tell her I hadn't been sleeping, but she always seemed to be able to tell.

"You really need more sleep, Connor Ethan, and a girlfriend," she'd always say. I didn't know how, but she somehow managed to toss the word girlfriend into almost every conversation. She was gifted in that way.

My mother was convinced I was going to die alone. She called me weekly to remind me. On the days she had too much wine, she'd cry about it over FaceTime. She often reminded me that I was a workaholic and didn't take enough personal days. She wasn't wrong about that. Day in and day out, I worked myself to exhaustion.

At times, my days felt more like years. I was proud of many parts of my life, but being a workaholic wasn't one of them. Sometimes I wondered what would've come of me if I hadn't pushed so hard to make a name for myself in the world. Then again, if I hadn't pushed myself, I wouldn't have been able to give back to the world in the ways I'd been able to give. Every sacrifice comes with its own set of negatives.

I'd take long days and nights if it meant I helped make someone else's life a bit easier. Still, a few large coffees were needed to get me through the long days.

"I have the afternoon reports and coffee for you, Mr. Roe—I mean, if you aren't busy. Because if you are busy, I can come back when you aren't busy, and I mean—if you're not busy, I can update you now on the calls that came in and the emails that, um, I mean—"

"Slow down, Rose," I said, looking up toward the nervous girl who stood in the doorway of my office, pretty much shivering in her heels. "Right now is a perfect time for the updates."

Rose was pretty much a kid. It seemed odd to say because she was nineteen, and I was twenty-eight, so there were only nine years between us, but I knew for certain I wasn't the same man I'd been nine years before.

She was the new intern at Roe Real Estate, and the poor girl's nerves got in her way more often than not. I didn't mind, though. We all had to start somewhere, and I was willing to put up with her slipups and mishaps. Everyone deserved a chance in life.

Plus, she only came in twice a week in the afternoon, so she couldn't do too much damage.

Rose took a breath and walked into the room, tripping a bit over her own two feet before catching herself by gripping the back of one of my office chairs. She stood straight and cleared her throat before setting the coffee on the edge of my desk. Thankfully she didn't spill that since I was in desperate need of a caffeine kick.

She looked down at her paperwork and began speaking. Even though she was still nervous about working for the company, I could tell she was becoming more comfortable week by week because her voice didn't shake as much as it had before. Progress.

"Well, four magazines reached out with massive offers for you to do interviews with them," she explained.

"I don't do interviews."

"Yes. Right. But they are offering hefty amounts of money for an exclusive cover and—"

"I don't do interviews," I repeated. I also smiled so she wouldn't feel intimidated.

She gave me a half-smile too and continued. "I, uh, your mom called and said you need to stop working so much."

"Noted. Next message?"

"Your suits are done at the dry cleaner, and I will pick them up this afternoon and bring them back to the office tonight. I know I was supposed to get them before I showed up today, but they got backed up, and well, I'm really sorry. I'll definitely work later to make sure they are here tonight."

"Don't worry about getting them back tonight. I can pick them up on my way home."

She frowned. "No, really. It's okay. I just…" She paused before letting out a big sigh. "I don't want to disappoint you."

"Rose."

"Yes?"

"You're doing a great job, every single day. Don't be so hard on yourself."

"It's just…this opportunity is a big one for me, Mr. Roe. I know I'm young and nervous, and you could've probably hired someone better for the position. So, I want to give it my all."

"Which you are. Keep doing what you're doing, and you'll be fine."

Her shoulders dropped a bit as relaxation hit her. Good. I didn't like the idea that my employees were nervous around me. I wasn't some big bad wolf. If anything, I wanted everyone who worked for me to feel at home as though we were a big family.

Hopefully, she'd come around. Earning trust goes both ways.

"Okay, well, thank you." She paused for a moment and nibbled her bottom lip.

I arched an eyebrow. "Is there something else?"

"Well, it's just that one of the magazines offered you a lot of money. And I mean a lot. Like over one hundred thousand dollars a lot."

I could see the dollar signs in her eyes as she spoke about the amount. Not to sound like a jerk, but I could have easily made that amount of money in my sleep. And even if I hadn't been able to, I still wouldn't have wanted to do some magazine article.

I'd seen what being in the spotlight could do to a person's mental health and their actual businesses. Nothing good came from giving the world a view into your life. They'd love you at first, maybe, yeah, but the moment they needed a reason to turn on you, they'd twist your words and call you the devil.

Life was easier with me being a bit of a mystery. All they could do was assume, and anyone who had time to assume about someone else's life was clearly not living their own to the fullest. I wasn't into that world—the gossiping scene. Since I'd moved to New York, I'd learned that the gossiping habit didn't stay in high school. I'd crossed paths with individuals in their sixties still shit-talking about people. Whenever it happened, I'd exit stage left.

The less drama, the happier life was to me.

Rose's mouth twitched once, and I smirked.

"What else did they offer me, Rose?"

"The cover of *People* magazine for sexiest man alive! And oh my gosh, Mr. Roe, they only do that for celebrities! Like real celebrities! Like Ryan Reynolds and Idris Elba! It's so cool. Like that's the dream."

I laughed. "Is that it?"

"Absolutely."

"So what do these guys get from holding the title of sexiest man alive?"

She looked at me as if I were idiotic for not understanding what an honor said opportunity was. "Uh, the sexiest man alive title! You literally hold that title for life."

"Wow. Well, as wonderful as that sounds, I think I'll pass this one up. But thank you, and please let each outlet know I am honored but kindly turn down the offers."

"Well, okay, Mr. Roe." She paused and arched an eyebrow. "Are you sure you don't want me to pick up the suits tonight?"

"Positive. Thank you, Rose."

She left my office, and just as she exited, Damian walked in with a grimace on his face.

"Good afternoon, Damian," Rose stated.

He moved past her as if he hadn't even noticed her existence. Not a hello, not a hey, nothing. A completely and utterly silent response.

Rose was a very attractive girl, and Damian was her same age, just a year younger. I would've thought he'd develop an attraction to her just as the rest of the guys in the office were, but he seemed far from interested.

Then again, that was Damian's norm for the most part. He was extremely good at not caring about pretty much any other human being. He and I were the complete opposite. He was cold as ice, and I was known for my warmth.

Still, to me, he was family. I'd met Damian two years earlier when I was looking for a kid to help mentor through a program, and I was paired with him—the grumpiest sixteen-year-old I'd ever seen in my life. For a long time, I took his bad attitude personally, but then I realized it was a defense mechanism. He'd grown up in the foster system being tossed around from home to home, never really finding a stable life, so he closed himself off to everyone around him. He had trust issues that ran deep. He tried his hardest to push me away because so many people had pushed him away in his lifetime.

Too bad for him that I was an annoying motherfucker who didn't give up when something was challenging.

I'd stayed in his life for the past two years, and I had no plans of exiting anytime soon. When he told me he didn't see himself going to college, I made sure to get him a position working for me. I didn't believe everyone was meant for the college life track, but I knew Damian was smart as hell and could do amazing things if given the opportunity.

It turned out, he was one of my best employees—grumpy self and all.

"You didn't say good afternoon to Rose," I mentioned as he moved to sit in the chair across from my desk. Unlike Rose, there was nothing nervous about his entrance into my office. He moved with confidence.

"Why would I say hi to her?"

"Because she greeted you first."

"She's a fake, shitty employee. I don't like her."

"To be fair, you don't like anyone."

He parted his lips to respond but then shut it when he realized there was nothing but the truth in my words.

"What makes you think she's fake?" I asked.

"The whole clumsy, stuttering, innocent girl act. She only puts it on around you. When you're not around, she's busy flirting it up and pushing her tits in the face of any person who will look."

"No way. She's a good worker."

He sighed. "Must be hard believing everyone in the world is a good person."

"I don't think Jason Rollsfield is a good person."

"Congratulations, Connor. You don't like one person out of seven billion on this planet," he sarcastically remarked. "Then again, you hate him and still gave him a job. Shocking. If you knew about Rose's past—"

"No!" I hollered, tossing my hands up. "Don't tell me. Every time you tell me about a person's past, it changes how I view them."

"As it should."

I called Damian the grave digger. He had an ability I'd never seen before in a person—the ability to dig up dirt on anyone. He'd been able to unlock secrets people thought were buried deep. The only secrets he was unable to uncover were probably the ones he craved the most—the story behind his biological parents. No matter how hard he tried, he'd never been able to track them down. I knew it ate at him every single day.

When he and I met, I made him promise not to dig up dirt on people I knew before he came into my life. I didn't need to know the skeletons of my business partners. Rich people did a lot of weird shit.

Damian was dressed in black from head to toe, as always. Black suit, black tie, black shoes. Every day, he showed up wearing all black and had ever since I met him. He said it was his favorite color and matched his soul.

I couldn't help but smirk at his emo tendencies.

At the same time, he was built like a linebacker. He stood at over six feet four with muscle on muscle. I wasn't too close-minded to state he was a good-looking guy. Women would've been all over him if he wasn't grimacing all the time. If it wasn't for his cold personality, he'd have women throwing themselves at him on the regular.

"Anyway, got bad news," he said, brushing his thumb against his nose.

"First, I didn't get to tell you the joke of the day."

He gave me a blank stare. "Are you serious right now?"

"I've told you a joke every day for the past two years. Of course I'm serious."

"You won't be in a joking mood after I tell you the bad news."

I stood from my desk and slid my hands into my pockets. "Which is exactly why I should tell you the joke now."

He sighed and shrugged. "Okay, whatever. Go."

"Did you hear about the new restaurant called Karma? There's no menu—you get what you deserve." I snickered, smacking the side of my leg. "Get it? Karma? You get what you—"

"I get it. It's just far from funny."

"I'll get you laughing one of these times. Mark my words."

"Don't hold your breath. Now, can I tell you the shit news?"

I nodded.

His brow furrowed, and I could tell whatever he was about to say was going to be bad. Whenever Damian's brows got closer during our meetings, nothing good was coming from him.

"The Brooklyn property fell through."

I moved toward the edge of my desk, feeling as if I'd been sucker punched. Every inch of mirth evaporated from my body. "What do you mean it fell through? We had that in our grip. It was all but a done deal. Besides, no one even knew about it except us."

"I know. Don't know how it happened, but they decided to sell the building to another buyer."

"Who?"

"They wouldn't say."

Dammit. Damian was right. After that news, I was far from in a good mood.

"I'm going to find out, though," Damian said, resolute and sure.

"Yeah, thanks."

He grimaced, of course, and stood from his chair. His gray eyes locked with mine as he shrugged again. "Your joke was kind of funny," he dryly stated, trying to make me feel better.

"You don't gotta lie, Damian."

"All right. It wasn't funny at all."

I rubbed my hands over my face and sighed. "When you find out who bought the property, let me know." I moved back around to my desk and plopped down. "You coming to the dinner party on Friday night?"

"Am I coming to a dinner party for an asshole I hate to the depths of my core to celebrate him getting a job he doesn't deserve? I think I'll pass. I don't even know why you hired someone as incompetent as that douche to run the West Coast division. I could do a better job than he ever could. He's a joke."

Was he wrong about my new business partner Jason? No. He was the only person I truly couldn't stand in my life. Everything about the spoiled jerk rubbed me the wrong way. But was I giving Jason the opportunity because his father offered to partner with me on my dream of building luxury low-income properties if I hired his son? Yes.

Jason would be taking over Roe Real Estate West Coast in the coming weeks, and my anxiety about it all was through the roof. That Friday night, we were having a celebration dinner for Jason where I'd do some kind of passing of the keys to him. It was a photo opportunity to paint Jason in a good light and probably his parents' idea, seeing how most of the time, Jason was in the press for being a trust fund idiot.

Over the past two years or so, he'd seemed to tame his party-animal ways, but that didn't mean I put any trust in him running a part of my business. Still, I respected his dad enough to give it a shot.

Walter Rollsfield was one of the richest men in the world, and he was the first person who ever invested in me at a young age. Since then, he'd been like a father figure to me. His son, on the other hand? A hot damn mess who left a disaster everywhere he went. I had my fears about hiring Jason, but my hope was that he would get bored with the job over time—just like he got bored with everything else—and I'd be able to hire a real leader for the position. Plus, I'd have both Walter's and my wallet to build my dream properties.

It was a risk to take Jason on, but the bigger risk was losing Walter's backing for my next business endeavor—which reminded me how perturbed I was that I'd lost the property that afternoon. If only I knew who'd gotten in the way of my Brooklyn dream. The moment I found out, I was going to raise some hell.

♡

What a shitastic day.

I was in a mood. I'd been in a mood since Damian informed me about the lost property. A mood bad enough that I doubted any of my favorite things would've been able to pull me from my grump-fest. Whenever I was in a mood, I needed two things: Mom and Cheetos.

After stuffing my face with Cheetos Puffs, I picked up my cell phone and called the only woman willing to have heart-to-hearts with me when I was cranky. My number one spot on speed dial.

"Hey, sweetheart. How's it going?" Mom asked when she answered my call.

I sat back in my chair and groaned.

She knew exactly what that groan meant, too.

"Oh, honey, I'm so sorry. Do you want me to fly out to New York to make you some chicken and dumplings? You shouldn't be alone right now."

I almost took her up on the offer. What could I say? I was a mama's boy and talking to her always made the failures seem less harsh.

"I'm good, Mom. Just wanted to feel a piece of home tonight."

"How about you come home for a quick visit?" she urged. "Kentucky is missing you."

I'd been in NYC since I was eighteen years old, and just last month, I turned twenty-eight. With each day that passed, New York felt more like home base. The only thing missing was Mom's love and cooking.

"I'll be down there in a few weeks for a visit. Until then, I have a lot of work to do."

It was her turn to groan, and I knew exactly what that groan meant, too.

"Work, work, work," she complained. "Don't you ever make time for play?"

"Play doesn't bring you income," I said.

"But it brings you the important things. Don't you think it's time you settled down with someone? Maybe give me a few grandbabies. Or, heck, I'll take a grand fur baby at this point. You can't stay cooped up in your house and office all the time, Connor. You have to put yourself out there to experience real life."

You know how I said Mom was almost always in my number one

spot? She only slipped a little when she'd scold me for not having a life outside of work.

I wasn't built to be the family man. I decided that a long time ago when I chose to give myself to my work. I was only twenty-eight years old, but I had the income of an eighty-year-old man who'd worked his life to death. I'd spent the past decade of my life hustling hard to build my empire. With that gift, I had to let go of some other things, like relationships and family. I didn't have the time for it. It would be selfish for me to bring a woman into my life and not give her my all. At least that was the bullshit reason I gave people. The truth of the matter was relationships terrified me. Giving someone your all to only have it taken away someday? No, thank you. Not interested.

"I hear you, Mom." I lied to get her to pull back on the topic.

"Don't say that to get me to shut up, Connor Ethan. I mean it. Make time for the important stuff. After beating cancer twice, I know how much that important stuff means. Money isn't everything."

"But it's enough," I joked. "Really, Mom. I hear you. I'll work on putting myself out there."

"Liar."

What could I say? She knew me well.

"Listen to your mother, Connor. What's the point of having an empire if you have no one to pass it down to once your time comes to an end?"

"I already have charities lined up to give everything to, so we're all set there." She sighed, and I felt bad.

"Connor Ethan, don't upset your mother. Promise me you'll do at least one thing that isn't work-related. You'll find a hobby over the next few weeks."

"Mom—"

"Promise me! On my life!"

I hated when she did that. I hated when she made me promise on her life because I knew I could never break that promise. After you'd watched your mother battle cancer twice, after you'd shaved your head multiple times with her in a small bathroom with a cheap electric razor, you realized how important said mom's life was.

I'd never make a promise on her life if I had no drive to keep that word. The desperation in her voice was almost too painful to bear. She worried about me being lonely.

I worried about that sometimes, too. To combat my loneliness, I stayed later at work some nights, spent hours in the gym, or played *Call of Duty* with people from around the world. You hadn't lived a worthy life until a fifteen-year-old in Canada called you a fucking cock-sucking little prick bitch after midnight.

I hoped they didn't kiss their mothers with those filthy mouths.

"I promise," I swore. "Fuck, I shouldn't have called you."

"Language, Connor," she scolded.

I downed my whiskey. "Sorry, Mom."

"I have to go, sweetie. Danny is picking me up for a late date."

I sat up straighter in my chair. "Wait. Danny? Who's Danny?!"

"Oh honey, I can't talk now. I love you. We'll talk soon! I'll call you tomorrow. Kisses!" And with that, she hung up.

Who the hell was Danny?

Within seconds, I was shooting off a text to Jax down in Kentucky. Even though I'd moved to New York, he was one of my closest friends in the whole world. I knew he'd be able to help me figure out what was going on.

Connor: Who the hell is Danny?

Jax: Good to hear from you, too.

Connor: Sorry. Hi, Jax. How's Kennedy? How are the kids? How's the weather? Who the fuck is Danny?!

Jax: Language, Connor.

Connor: Yeah, yeah, yeah. My mom said she has a date with Danny. Who is this guy?

Jax: Unlike every other person in this small town, I stay out of other people's business.

Connor: My mom can't be out there dating jerks.

Jax: Danny isn't a jerk.

Connor: So you do know him! Tell me everything. I'm gonna call you.

Jax: Don't call me, Connor. I hate talking on the phone.

Connor: Even with your bestie?

Jax: You're not my bestie.

Connor: Your sense of humor doesn't come off as well as it should via text.

Jax: ...Right.

Connor: Tell me one detail about this Danny guy, and I'll leave you alone.

Jax: Swear?

Connor: On my mother.

Jax: Fine. He's a hardworking employee.

Connor: What?! This guy works for you?! What in the land of betrayal is that?!

Jax: Listen, it's not my fault he met your mom when she brought some of her baked goods to me at a landscaping job. It just so happened Danny was there with me, and he liked her baked goods.

Connor: I hope to God you're talking about her lemon bars and not her personal baked goods.

Jax: Definitely talking about her personal baked goods. It seems Danny's really into her cinnabuns.

Connor: You think this is funny, but it's not. Now you have to think about my sweet innocent mother having sexual relations with some random guy named Danny!

Jax: You want me to think about your mom having sex?

Connor: What? No. Stop. Don't do that.

Jax: It's too late. The images are already in my head.

Connor: I hope Kennedy divorces you.

Jax: Do you think sweet Rebecca is a top or bottom?

Connor: This conversation is over.

Jax: I wonder if she's into role-playing.

Connor: Shut up.

Jax: It's like those bad knock-knock jokes you've always told. Rebecca's like knock-knock, and Danny asks who's there, and bam! It's her sitting on his face.

Connor: I hope you burn in hell.

Jax: I could use the tan. Night, kid.

After a conversation with Jax that only gave me more stress than I had before, I was left wondering how my sweet mother ended up getting tangled up with some dude named Danny.

EIGHT

Aaliyah

NOTHING SAID ANXIETY LIKE ENTERING A ROOM FILLED WITH complete strangers. If I were ever in those old *Saw* movies where I was put into a deadly situation that terrified me, it would've been me in a room surrounded by people I didn't know. What were they thinking when they looked at me? What were their first impressions? Did they like me? Did I come off as weird?

Then I had the fun habit after said gathering, where I went home and overthought every conversation, wondering if someone took my words the wrong way or if I said something idiotic. I'd only been standing around for about an hour, and my palms were already sweaty from the pressure of it all.

Why did an hour feel like ten when you were in a place you didn't want to be?

"Say cheese!" a photographer remarked before flashing a camera in my eyes and hurrying off to his next victim. I blinked a few times to try to recover my sight and thought of his words.

What I wouldn't have given to have some deep-fried, bad-for-my-hips-good-for-my-soul cheese in my mouth right at that moment. I daydreamed about cheese oozing out of a mozzarella stick as I placed a tiny slice of sweet potato into my mouth. It was topped with some weird smelly cheese, pecans, and cranberries. The waitress told me the green sprinkled on top was rosemary, but I was pretty sure it was grass.

Sweet potato crostini bites, she'd called them, but I knew I was actually just eating fancy trash.

I wasn't a very fancy girl. Never had been, never would be. I never really needed more than some good wings and french fries. At least, that had been the case before my diagnosis. Alcohol had been completely cut out of my life ever since I was placed on the heart transplant list the previous summer, and it'd been two years since I had anything deep-fried because of my condition. I'd been forced to give my whole life a complete makeover.

"Would you like another?" the waitress asked, and I cringed, making her hurry away with an annoyed sigh.

I didn't mean to make a face. I simply hadn't ever been one to have a solid poker face. All my true emotions and feelings shined through my eyes and the curves of my lips. If I was mad, annoyed, or disgusted, everyone around me could tell.

I wondered if I'd gotten that trait from my mother. I wondered if her displeasure sat on the bridge of her nose as it wrinkled up. If she was happy, did her eyes shine in such a special way?

I shook the thought of her away before letting it settle in my heart. The last thing I wanted to do was make myself sad during an event meant to be a happy occasion. Therefore, heavy thoughts were strictly off-limits.

With a deep breath, I surveyed the room before me.

Over one hundred people had shown up to a dinner to celebrate my fiancé's new position running Roe Real Estate West Coast. It was the first work event I'd been to with him, and I was terrified. I didn't know a soul outside of Jason's parents.

The dinner was extremely fancy. Or, more so, it was a gala. Everything was so over-the-top for truly no reason at all except Jason could afford it.

We could afford it.

Jason hated when I called it his money, but at the end of the day, it was his. He was the extremely successful businessman, and I was the junior editor his mother had met two years earlier, then introduced to her son.

A whirlwind romance set up by Marie.

True, we'd only been dating for a year and a half, but it felt longer.

"Cucumber bites?" a woman asked, shoving a tray in my face with literally just pieces of cucumber sprinkled with paprika.

My nose obviously wrinkled up. "No, I'm good."

The problem with galas was the lack of food and the abundance of liquor. Everyone around me was drinking, except for me. But I was a big believer in using carbohydrates to soak up the alcohol sitting in my gut, and I was sure some of those individuals could've benefited from a bread bowl or two.

Cocktails and truffle fries.

Whiskey and pizza.

Beer and cheese fries.

Oh, my gosh…

Did I mention fries? What I wouldn't have given for a big plate of french fries right then, but none of that was on the menu at The Lily that night. There was hardly any food to be found, just overpriced bite-sized appetizers.

Maybe that was how rich people stayed rich—they didn't eat, so no need to spend money on food.

Two hands landed on my hips, and my body melted into the touch. I knew it was him before he even spoke. Jason always smelled like smoky rosewood dipped in sex appeal. I turned to face him, and my heart skipped a few beats when I found his frown, which in turn made me frown.

"What is it?" I asked.

"Your hermit crab vibes are strong tonight," he whispered, leaning into me. "People are talking, saying you seem uppity."

"Sorry. My brain's shutting down. I can't survive on air." I placed my hands against his chest and gave him my best puppy dog eyes. "Can we just ditch and find some real food?"

Before he could reply, a woman with a tray of some kind of raw meat walked over to us. "Would you like one?" she asked.

"Sure, after you cook it," I replied.

Jason laughed, but it wasn't his amused laughter. It was his annoyed laugh. He said, "No, thank you," to the person before turning back to me. "You're so extreme, Aaliyah."

He wasn't wrong. At times, I could be dramatic. "Other than the lack of food, everything else is pretty great, yeah? The event turned out well. I'm so proud of you."

Jason smiled. "Yeah, if only you'd actually talk to some people other than me."

"I've talked to your parents all night long!"

"I think we both know that doesn't count as putting yourself out there. Aaliyah…you have to talk to people." Jason sighed, pinching the bridge of his nose. He was tired. How could he not be? Lately, Jason's default mode was tired. He'd been working nonstop for the past few months trying to get the real estate company running in Los Angeles. He was beyond stressed, and I wasn't certain I'd fully understand the answer if I asked him what all his job entailed. All I knew was that he was always busy. Therefore, that meant early mornings and late nights. Early-bird flights and redeyes. Intensely brewed coffee and painfully strong whiskey.

I worried about him sometimes. I worried about the burnout all great businessmen experienced. Still, he always told me he was fine, even on the days it was clear he wasn't.

Fun, free-spirited Jason hardly came out to play lately, and I was somewhat kicking myself for not latching on tighter when I felt it slipping away. When we had first started dating, he'd been so energized and full of life. Yet after we moved in together, it felt as if I was living with a stranger. He was short with me a lot, but then he would apologize, saying it was due to his workload.

"You know how I feel about socializing," I explained, fiddling with my fingers.

He nodded. "Yes, only with your friends."

"Exactly. Ross, Rachel, Phoebe…"

"Aaliyah." Jason stated my name as if I were a misbehaving child, and I nodded, knowing from his slight undertone that he was feeling the pressure. "A lot of people who are important to me are here tonight, and I think it's important for them to interact with the most important person in my life."

"Okay, okay. I need ten minutes of fresh air. Then I'll come back and be the perfect bride-to-be."

"Sounds good."

"Before I go, can you make me a promise?"

"Anything."

"After we're done here tonight, can we go get some real food? Maybe a place with a bread basket?"

He laughed his real laugh, and that made me happy. "Oh, Liyah." His mouth grazed over mine before he moved his lips to my forehead, where he planted a kiss. His voice was low, full of a sweetness that didn't exactly match the words he spoke. "You know you shouldn't be eating carbohydrates."

"What's that supposed to mean?" I asked, stunned by his comment.

"God, don't do that," he groaned.

"Don't do what?"

"Get all emotional."

"What are you talking about? You said that weird thing about me eating and—"

"Not now, Aaliyah," he whispered with sternness to his tone. "I'm not going to have one of our pointless arguments at my event. This is supposed to be a happy occasion. Don't ruin it with your emotions."

"I'm just saying...that was a rude comment."

"Rude or honest? I mentioned the other day that your ass looked fat in your dress."

I frowned, feeling extremely self-conscious. I thought that was a compliment.

The smell of liquor fell from every exhalation he had. I loved Jason, but I didn't like the man he was when he drank. Some nights, I wondered if I even knew him. I wondered if the alcohol made him speak his truths or transition into someone who only spoke lies. I stared at him as if he were a complete stranger. I'd been noticing his belittling behavior more and more during the past few weeks.

We'd been together for over a year, yet we moved in with one another only six weeks ago, and since then, I'd crawled into bed with a stranger. Our love story began with rainbows and butterflies. I was obsessed with Jason Rollsfield, and he was obsessed with me. That was, until I gave up my apartment and moved in with him. After the move, it was as if my Prince Charming had turned into the Beast.

Everything I did annoyed him. Every time he belittled me, he'd flip it around and say I'd somehow taken his words out of context. He didn't hug me as often; he didn't caress me as he had before. With each day that passed, I felt more of a disconnect, and it worried me to my core.

He drank more than he ever told me he did. He stayed out later than he'd ever mentioned before we moved in with one another. His mother told me he was overwhelmed with his new work commitments and the upcoming move to California, which I understood. I'd only wished he would've told me if he felt that way—not his mother.

Before I could reply to his rude comments, he looked past me. "You haven't met my business partner yet. Connor, come here," Jason said, waving someone over.

I looked up to see who he was calling out to, and my heart skipped before crashing to a full-blown stop as I met the bluest eyes I'd ever witnessed in my life.

Captain America.

In a suit.

My breaths evaporated the second our eyes locked. For a moment, I thought his eyes widened with realization, too, but when he blinked, it disappeared. His gaze softened, and he extended his hand toward me.

"Hi, Aaliyah, is it? I'm Connor. Nice to meet you."

My chest ached as our hands shook. His eyes were still as blue as I remembered, yet his smile seemed a little more broken.

I parted my lips to speak, but at first, no sounds came out...not until Jason awkwardly cleared his throat and nudged me.

I pushed out a smile. "Hi, yeah. It's nice to meet you, Connor."

Connor.

I loved that name a lot—even if it wasn't Steve Rogers.

He looked like a Connor. Sweet, gentle, kind.

Jason downed his drink and gestured toward Connor. "It's because of this guy that we're off to California in a few weeks. Can you believe it? I'll be running my own real estate company."

"Not exactly your own," Connor said with a small smirk. "More of a team thing."

"Yeah—for now, big boy. I'm pretty sure after you see how well I run it, you'll be handing the business over to me in no time," he joked. "Besides, you're already busy with your other investments. I'd gladly take it off your hands."

Connor laughed, but it felt cold. I hadn't known his laughter could feel so chilled. "Roe Real Estate is my firstborn. I'd never give it away," he said, and it was clear he meant it.

I had no clue why Jason was even pushing the idea. He should've been grateful for the opportunity he'd been given, but then again, he had been drinking. Whenever Jason drank a lot, his personality shifted a bit. I loved him a little bit more when he was sober.

I couldn't stop staring at Captain—*Connor*. It appeared the past two years had been good to him. He seemed even more built, his hair was groomed perfectly, and he had a very nice beard. He wore a designer suit ten times better than most of the individuals in attendance that night, and his eyes...

His eyes were still glued on me.

It appeared neither of us could look away, and I didn't know what to think about it at all.

My heart began to race, pounding against my rib cage, and I forced my stare away from Connor to avoid Jason picking up on any of my awkwardness. "Well, um, it was nice to meet you, Connor. But I was actually on my way to get some fresh air. So if you'll excuse me."

I gave Jason a tight smile before hurrying off, tripping over my own feet and almost falling face-first in my high heels. Within seconds, a pair of arms caught me, and I looked up to see those blue eyes once more. Every hair on my body stood up straight as Connor stopped me from falling. I felt the heat in my cheeks as he held me.

"Sorry," I muttered, still flustered like no other.

He pulled me up to a standing position and smiled. That one felt more real, the kind of smile I remembered from him in the past. "Not a problem."

"She's a bit clumsy sometimes," Jason commented, walking over to us. "Just watch your step a bit more, will you, Aaliyah? I don't want to have to make a trip to the emergency room," he joked before turning to Connor. "How about I get you a drink, and we go over some details about a few things?"

That was my sign to keep walking away before Connor could see how humiliated I was.

Unfortunately for me, before I could make my way out of the room, I was ambushed by Jason's associates, and I was cussing at myself for not keeping my head down more.

It was the first night I'd been around anyone who Jason knew on a work level, and they all overwhelmed me. I felt out of place, the black sheep in a way. They looked at me differently and spoke to me as if I were the most naïve person alive. Not only that but they also had a way of being catty with smiles plastered across their faces.

"So, Amanda," one woman stated, giving me a smug smile.

"Aaliyah," I corrected, returning their fake smile.

"Oh, yes, sorry, that was the last girl. So, Aaliyah, it's nice to see Jason with someone who has a normal body type. One can only date so many supermodels." She pursed her lips, and her evil partner in crime joined in.

He nodded once. "Here's hoping this marriage lasts longer than the last two!"

Cringeworthy laughter ensued from all involved.

"I think it's good he's finally thinking of settling down. Though, it does seem a bit rushed, don't you think?" another woman questioned.

The man leaped back in. "Well, you know what they say, the only thing Jason jumps into faster than weddings is divorce."

They all laughed again, having the time of their lives as they mocked me.

"I'm sorry, I was just going to head—" I tried to cut in, but they weren't having it.

"How old did you say you were again, Alice?" the first woman asked me.

"*Aaliyah*," I hissed, annoyance filling me up inside. "And I'm twenty-four."

"Oh, so young! I swear, Jason makes them younger and younger each time," she commented. I parted my lips to defend myself, but the guy dived into the conversation before I could.

"Well, good for you, Aaliyah. You're living the new American dream. With Jason, money is no longer an issue, and I know you gen Z kids don't want to work. You ever think of starting a blog? Maybe a YouTube channel?" Insert mocking laughter here.

"Actually, she's an employee at one of the biggest magazine lines in the world, Wayne, unlike you, who still lives with your parents," a familiar voice said, joining the conversation.

The amount of comfort that hit me as I turned to see Marie was astronomical.

She gave me a wink before turning back to the judgmental crowd. "And Ruby, isn't it true that your husband just filed for bankruptcy? Perhaps you shouldn't cast stones when you already have rocks in your own garden."

Ruby huffed and puffed but didn't say anything in response to Marie. It was clear who the queen bee was, and Marie Rollsfield sat on top of the throne. She stood like royalty, and the bullies retreated as if they were unworthy to take in the same air as her.

"A word of advice, love," Marie said, turning to me with the brightest smile. "Don't ever let peasants intimidate you. You are more than they could ever dream of becoming."

"I'm quickly learning that I don't think I really fit in with this business side of Jason's world."

"Good," she agreed. "These people are animals. You don't need or want to fit in with this world." She gave me a sideways hug. "But you do fit in with our family, and that's all that matters. I always wanted a daughter."

If she knew how much I'd always wanted a mother, too...

"What about Jason's business partner, Connor? Is he one of the good ones?" I asked, trying to seem nonchalant about it but curious about what kind of business person he was.

"One of the most genuine human beings in this world. He's a good person—which isn't common to come across in our world. I'm a bit shocked that the dark side of the business hasn't crushed him yet, but he always seems to make mountains out of molehills. It seems he has angels in his corner. I'm glad Jason is working with him. Even though Jason is older, Walter and I hope Connor can be a bit of a mentor to him. He has a good head on his shoulders. With his help, Jason can do big things."

I smiled, pleased with the knowledge that Connor was just as good of a person as he had been when I crossed paths with him two years earlier.

Marie lightly nudged my arm and whispered, "Now, go get your breath of fresh air before the hyenas come in and attack again."

I smiled. "How did you know I was running to get some air?"

"Oh, sweetheart, don't forget, I was you once upon a time—the outsider brought into a world unknown where people judged me for my looks, for my skin tone, for my lack of finances. I remember needing a few quick escapes from time to time. If you go to the left, take the elevator to the rooftop. The view is beautiful. Just remember, when you take those breaks, strengthen that invisible crown of yours and remember who you are, and remember you have a whole team in your corner now."

NINE

Connor

IF YOU LOOKED UP THE DEFINITION OF A PEOPLE PERSON, YOU WOULD find a picture of me smiling ear to ear. I prided myself on my extrovert ways and how I loved meeting people of all types. One of my superpowers was my ability to find common ground with anyone and everyone—except for Jason fucking Rollsfield. When it came to my disdain for an individual, he was at the top of my list. He was the only one on the list, honestly.

The unstable hothead had recently been placed in charge of running our West Coast division by yours truly. Thankfully, now he wouldn't be in New York, and I wouldn't have to cross paths with him as often as I had over the past few months, but knowing he was taking her with him to California sent a silent rage through my whole system.

How in the world had an asshole like him landed a woman like her?

Her.

Red.

My Red.

Not mine, but still.

My thoughts began to flood with anguish as the realization that

Aaliyah was his settled inside me. Even worse, I thought about how he hadn't even flinched when she tripped. He had stood there glaring like the disappointment he thought she was and then passive-aggressively put her down instead of asking if she was all right.

How did she think that kind of treatment was okay? Surely, she knew she deserved more than someone like Jason out of life. I stood at the bar with him as we waited for our drinks, and like a creep, my eyes darted across the room, looking for her. She stood with a group of wealthy individuals, ones Aaliyah was too good for. I knew each one of them. They were all snakes, but Aaliyah appeared too nice to walk away from their trap.

I noticed the hesitant discomfort weighing heavily on her shoulders as she engaged with them, and my sudden sense of protection shot through the roof. I took a step in her direction but I stopped the moment I saw Marie move into the situation. The moment that happened, Aaliyah's shoulders relaxed, and an authentic smile spread across her lips.

Good. She seemed more at ease. Unlike her dick of a son, Marie was a good person. I knew she was standing up for Aaliyah based on how the rats scurried away. Once they were all gone, it was as if the light came back to Aaliyah's eyes, and she began to shine once more.

Aaliyah.

What a perfect name for her. It was very fitting and beautiful. She was beautiful, even more so than two years before. Her long, now ombre hair was in microbraids and had golden string woven throughout. She wore a skintight black satin dress with a high slit highlighting her long brown legs with her gold high heels. With those heels, we were almost eye to eye with one another.

Her eyes…

Still as powerful as they were back then.

"Did you hear me?" Jason asked, patting me on the back.

I broke my stare away from Aaliyah and turned to take the drink from Jason. The smile I hadn't even known I was wearing as I stared at Aaliyah evaporated once I looked at him.

"Sorry, what were you saying?" I asked even though I didn't care. I wanted my stare to move back to her. I wanted to talk to her. I wanted to ask how she'd been. I wanted to ask her why out of seven billion humans on the planet, she'd chosen him.

"I said did you notice the bombshell to your left wearing the blue dress?" he said, nodding in that direction.

I turned to spot the person he was looking at, and the minute my eyes landed on her, I wanted to claw my eyes out. "That's Rose, my new intern, and she's only nineteen. She's barely of age."

"But she is of age." He smirked and nudged me in the arm. "I gotta tell you, old Jason would've been all over that woman if he had the chance."

"She's a girl, not a woman. A bit young in age, don't you think?"

He shrugged. "I've dated younger." He paused and tossed his hands up in the air. "They were always at least eighteen. I'm not some creep."

Could have fooled me.

"Besides, I wasn't pointing her out for me. I'm a happily taken man. I was pointing her out for you, big guy. Plus, with her being your intern, I bet she'd do anything to please you." He nudged me again, and I wanted to slam my fist into his face.

God, Red. Why him?

I rolled my eyes and looked away from Rose. "That's disgusting, unprofessional, and completely out of line, Jason. And I hope you don't plan on running the company in that manner when you get out west."

"Whoa, whoa, whoa. Easy there, buddy. I was just joking with you. From the rumors, it appears you don't date much. I was just trying to be your wingman."

He was drunk, already stumbling a bit, and I could tell that with a few more drinks in, he'd be his normal mess of a self.

"I'm good, Jason."

He tossed his hands up in surrender. "All right. Suit yourself." He glanced once more in the direction of Rose, and I watched as his eyes moved up and down her figure. What a piece of scum. He caught me watching him, and he smirked. "Just looking, not touching."

He walked away, and the second he turned away from me, my stare moved back to Aaliyah—at least where she had been, but now she was gone. I looked around the space, on a mission to spot her, but she was nowhere to be found.

"Looking for someone?" a voice said, breaking me away from my search. I turned to see Walter approaching me with a smile on his face. Since Walter and Marie had adopted Jason, they shared none of his facial characteristics, which I was thankful for. If Walter had looked like his son, I'd have wanted to punch him on the regular.

"No. Just surveying the event. Seems to be going well."

"I'm just thankful the photographs were taken before Jason got hammered."

I snickered. "You noticed, too, huh?"

"I always do. I don't want you to think this is any representation of how he'll perform once he's in California. After hours, he's a mess at times, but during business, he's levelheaded."

I wasn't sure who Walter was trying to convince—me or himself.

Instead of commenting on how incorrect Walter was about his son, I smiled and lied. "I'm not too worried."

"Good. Plus, after the wedding, I'm sure he'll settle down from his old habits and be the husband Aaliyah deserves."

The wedding.

I still couldn't wrap my head around the fact that Jason, the scum of the earth, had somehow landed Red as his wife-to-be. He didn't deserve her. Honestly, I wasn't certain any guy deserved her. Even though it'd been so long, I hadn't forgotten how she made me feel that night. Hell, after our Halloween night of escapism, I'd had dreams about the girl for weeks.

The one who got away.

Really, though? After our intense soul connection and deep, meaningful conversations, she ended up with Jason? *Jason.* Jason Rollsfield. The man who thought global warming was a myth. The one who'd pissed on the Washington Monument. The one who had spent a few nights in jail for groping a police officer's butt.

Yeah, that was the man she was choosing.

Christ, Red. We taught you better than to settle with Jason.

I couldn't stop trying to figure out how she'd ended up in the position she was in, but hell, there we were.

"Speaking of the wedding…I have a favor to ask you," Walter said. He brushed his hand against his fully gray beard then pushed his round glasses up the bridge of his nose. "Aaliyah and Jason decided not to have groomsmen or bridesmaids of any kind for the ceremony, but there is the issue of the night before—the bride and groom aren't supposed to see one another. Now, normally, I wouldn't think anything of Jason spending the night alone, but I know he gets anxious at times, and I don't want him to freak out the night before his big day. So, I was thinking, perhaps he can stay with you that night? You can have some guy bonding time."

I blinked a few times, trying to comprehend exactly what Walter was asking of me. "You want me to keep him on a leash?"

"To be frank? Yes. I don't want him ruining this one this time around. The last two Vegas crash weddings left a bad mark on his name, but Aaliyah is different. She's a good girl, and she could be really good for Jason. So think about it as an IOU from me to you, Connor. If you do this for me, I'll do something for you."

And he could be very toxic for her.

"I can do that. Not a problem," I agreed, knowing an IOU from a person like Walter would come in handy.

"Also, I heard about the Brooklyn property. It's a shame. We'll get them next time, though."

He nodded once, then walked off, leaving me alone to down my whiskey before venturing off through the crowd. I got stopped a few times for conversation, and I engaged, even though my mind was focused on one thing and one thing only: Red.

I found her on the rooftop.

Her eyes were shut as the late-night breeze swept across her skin. Other people were on the rooftop, but I wasn't paying them any mind. In my head, she was the only one standing anywhere near me.

She looked beautiful. It wasn't that I was looking, but holy shit, I was looking. She could've walked out wearing a trash bag and still been the prettiest woman alive.

The more I thought about it, the more irrationally irritated I grew about the fact that the following week she was going to walk down the aisle and marry Jason. Was I in the twilight zone?

Nothing makes sense anymore.

I hesitated a few moments before building up enough courage to walk in her direction. "If memory serves me right, you owe me two dollars," I said as her back was to me. She jumped, looking startled as she turned to see who was standing behind her. The moment she realized it was me, her eyes grew gentle, and she smiled.

"Hi," she said as she breathed out.

I smiled. "Hi."

I took a few steps in her direction as I began taking off my suit jacket when I witnessed her shivering, then I placed it around her shoulders. She slid her arms into the sleeves, and it hung against her, clearly too big but somehow exactly the right size.

"Thank you," she said. Her voice was sweeter than I remembered, and I remembered it being pretty damn sweet. She wrapped her arms around her small frame and kept smiling. A soft sigh fell from her full lips. "Hi," she repeated.

I chuckled and nodded, taking a few steps closer. "Hi."

"So…" She swayed back and forth in her heels. "This is weird, right?"

"Very." I narrowed my eyes at her. "Did you somehow know that someday I'd partner with Jason in order to cheat the universe and force us to meet again?"

She laughed, and I loved it. "Shockingly, no. This seems to be that fate thing you were going on about all those years ago."

Fate must have a sick sense of humor if it decided to bring Aaliyah back into my life by pairing her with Jason.

"How have—"

"How's life—"

We spoke at the same time then nervously chuckled together.

My hands slid into my pockets, and I couldn't shake the nerves I felt. Why was I nervous around her? Why did my heart feel as if it were going to explode out of my chest at any second?

She nodded my way. "You first."

"Oh no, ladies first always."

"Still a Southern gentleman, I see."

"Some things never change."

"A fact that gives me comfort." She brushed a piece of hair behind her ear, and I watched her moves as if each one gave me my next breath. "How have you been?"

"Good, good. Same ole, same ole."

"All work, no play still?"

I chuckled. "The more things change, the more they stay the same." I walked over to the rooftop railing, placed my hands against it, and stared out into the night. The city lights were vibrant as the hustle and bustle sounds of New York stayed loud. I'd never imagined those sounds would be something I fell in love with. Aaliyah joined me in staring out into the night.

"What about you?" I asked. "How have you been? Have all your dreams come true?"

"Not all, but I'm closer. I was made junior editor at my company. One step closer to senior editor, but..." Her face grew somber as her words trailed off.

"But what?"

She shrugged. "I recently gave my two weeks' notice. With Jason getting the position in California, we'll be moving out that way, so I couldn't keep my job."

"It's your dream job, right? At that company?"

"Yes. But...as a superhero once taught me, you can't have the best of both worlds. So I chose the dream family over the dream career."

She said those words as if she wanted to believe them, but her slight tone made me think she didn't. Or maybe it was just wishful thinking. I didn't know why, but it made my skin crawl when I thought about how she was throwing away her shot at her future for a man like Jason—a man who would, without a doubt, let her down. I knew he would let me down over time, too, but that was a business risk I was willing to take to achieve a future goal.

With Aaliyah, she didn't get any prize from him ruining her life. I had no doubt he'd leave her world in shambles, and he wouldn't even blink twice.

"You think I'm crazy," she said, tilting her head in my direction.

"What? No."

She nodded. "Yeah, you do. You don't have the best poker face. Remember? I'm good at reading people. I get it. Career has always been at the forefront of your dreams, so I completely understand why you think it's insane for me to choose a family life over a job. But in my world, a family has always been my biggest dream."

"I understand completely," I told her, and I did. I had no problem with Aaliyah wanting a family, especially when I knew she'd grown up without one herself. Yet I wished it was with anyone but Jason.

He created more tragedies than happily ever afters.

"I think it's great, Red, that you want a family." I meant that, too. I wanted her to have everything she'd ever wanted from this world. "How did you and Jason meet?"

"It's funny, really. I met him through a matchmaker—also known as his mother." She laughed a little and leaned on the railing. "Marie was a regular at the coffee shop where I worked. Two years ago, not long after I met you, I went through a tough situation, and Marie was there to help me. After that, we grew closer. She had me join her book club, and we started building a good bond. She pushed Jason and me together, and the rest is history."

"Marie and Walter are great people."

"Yeah. Between you and me, I think I fell in love with Jason's parents before him. Some days, I swear I love his mother more than I love him," she joked. "But that's only when he drinks."

I didn't comment on her statement because anything I said would've been negative. I had no positive thoughts about her future husband, so I bit my tongue to avoid making her feel bad.

"How long have you two been together?"

"A year and a half."

I blew out a heavy breath. "That's a quick turnaround."

"Yeah. I understand people thinking that, but honestly, life is short. I don't want to spend however much time I have left waiting for things to happen. I want to embrace every single second."

I placed my hands against my chest and laughed. "As someone who is invested heavily in the stock market for the long-term, the idea of a quick turnaround is terrifying to me."

"I guess that's something different about us, Cap. You're living for tomorrow while I'm living for today."

"I hope today's good for you, Red."

She smiled. "I hope tomorrow's even better for you." She looked down at the statement gold band watch and groaned. "Speaking of living for today, I should probably get back inside."

She was frowning, and that made me sad for her. "You don't want to interact with those people down there, do you?"

"How did you know?"

"Don't forget, you weren't the only one who knew how to read people. Rich people can be a lot sometimes, especially some of the ones in there. Rude, invasive—"

"Total dicks," she added.

I laughed. "Exactly."

"Between you and me, I really don't want to go back in there. It feels like I'm being tossed into the shark tank, and I don't know how to swim. They are just so...so...ugh! Mean. For no reason."

"Oh, there's definitely a reason."

"And what's that?"

"You intimidate them."

She laughed. "What? No way. What's there to be intimidated by? I'm nothing special. Those people in there have it all."

"It's all fake in there. Between you and me, a majority of those individuals likely hate their lives, hate their spouses, or hate themselves. It's probably driving them crazy to see someone like you coming in and showing them something they haven't experienced in a long time."

"And what exactly am I showing them?"

"Your authentic self. They are envious of how real you are, so don't let them get in your head too much."

She sighed and rubbed the back of her neck. "I just wish I had more time to breathe out here to build up the courage not to let them get to me."

"Take more time to breathe up here. I'll cover for you if anyone asks where you are."

"You'll do that for me?"

"Of course. Without question. I'll say you were talking to some big, impressive person."

She reached forward, took my hand in hers, and squeezed it. "Thank you, Connor." She paused. "Connor...I really like your name."

I smirked. "I think I love yours more."

She didn't pull her hand back right away, and I wondered if she felt it, too—the heat that began to race throughout my veins. When she did let go, the chills returned to me.

I gave her a half-smile then nodded in her direction before turning to walk away.

"Connor! Wait!" she called out. I looked back to see her hurrying in my direction. She slid out of my jacket and held it out toward me. "Thank you for keeping me warm."

TEN

Connor

"**H**AVE YOU SEEN AALIYAH?" JASON ASKED, WALKING OVER and patting me on the back.

It was clear that since the last time I saw him, he'd had a few more drinks. If there was anything you could count on with Jason, it was taking everything a step too far.

"Did you see her?" he slurred. He was drunk. When Jason was drunk, he repeated himself and frequently brushed his finger against the side of his nose. I hated that I was learning his small habits because whenever he did them, they irked me.

"I haven't," I replied, lying on Aaliyah's behalf. Jason grimaced, and I couldn't help but notice. "What is it?"

"Nothing. I was talking to Trevor Jacobs, and he mentioned how crazy it is that I'm getting married, which got me thinking…" He rubbed the back of his neck. "Aaliyah is pretty young."

"She's mature, though." Everyone Jason had dated was younger than him. He had that way about him. I had food older than some of his exes in my pantry. If anything, Aaliyah seemed too old for him because she was around our age. He wasn't really robbing the cradle with Aaliyah

"Do you think she's too young, though?"

"No, I don't. Even if she were, it's a bit late to be asking that, don't you think?"

He grimaced.

"You're thinking too much, Jason. You're drunk. Stop thinking so much."

"Yeah…it will be fine." He nodded somberly to himself. "Have you seen Aaliyah lately? She's so damn unsocial." He asked me about her location as if he had already forgotten he'd asked me that question twice.

I parted my lips to lie once more, but I was cut off.

"I'm right here."

Jason and I both turned around to see Aaliyah. She looked refreshed. I assumed a few moments of fresh air had been exactly what she needed to clear her head while spending the night with some of the worst humans on the planet.

"Babe, where were you? I thought you said you'd be back in five minutes, and that was like an hour ago. Where were you that whole time?" Jason repeated, his brows knit with concern.

"Oh, I, uh"—she fumbled with her words—"I was talking to, uh…"

"She was talking to Daniel Price," I told Jason, covering for Aaliyah. Her eyes locked with mine, and she smiled.

"Oh? Is that so?" Jason asked, perking up a bit. "He's one of the people I wanted you to meet. That's great."

"Oh yeah, totally," Aaliyah said, her cheeks turning red. It was so clear she was guilty, though Jason was too wasted to pick up on the clues. "Daniel was very nice."

"Nice?" Jason snickered, stunned. "Never in my life have I heard someone describe him as nice."

He was right. Daniel was a rat.

"Maybe nice wasn't the right word. Maybe, um, intriguing?" she corrected.

Jason laughed even more. "Intriguing? Are we talking about the same Daniel Price?"

"I meant, well…" She started to stumble over her words as she rubbed her hand up and down her arm. Her nerves were getting the best of her.

"Knowledgeable," I spat out. "I'm sure Aaliyah meant he was knowledgeable."

She nodded. "Yes, that's what I meant. He knew a lot about...a lot. Like all things. Daniel knew so much about—"

Clearing my throat loudly, I caught Aaliyah's eyes and shook my head slightly.

Don't push it.

She stopped talking.

Jason didn't notice anything at all.

"Perhaps it's a good time to shut everything down for the night," I mentioned, patting Jason on the back. "We have a few busy weeks ahead of us."

Jason nodded. "Perhaps you're right. I'll go say good night to a few people, and then we can wrap it all up." He hurried off, and Aaliyah moved in closer to me.

"Thank you for that, for covering for me," she said. "I'm a pretty crappy liar. I don't have much practice with it." She laughed, combing her hands through her hair.

"Stay in this room long enough, and you can pick up some tips from anyone here."

"I don't know if that's a good thing. So, um..." Aaliyah rocked back and forth on her heels. She was nervous around me. I felt the same around her. "Before I came over here, I ran into Walter, and he said Jason is staying at your place the night before the wedding?"

My insides cringed. "That's the plan." Not my plan, but alas.

"Perfect because, well, you know the rule—the bride can't see the groom before the wedding and all."

I nodded once.

A part of me wanted to ask her why Jason. A part of me wanted to know how she'd been and if her dreams had come true. Another part wanted to tell her not to marry the man crashing in my guest room in a few days. I wanted her to run, wanted her to find someone she deserved. I wanted her to fall out of love with him.

Instead, I turned to Aaliyah, and said, "You should probably catch up with Jason to say your goodbyes."

"Oh." She stood taller, and I wished I could read her

thoughts. "Yeah, of course. Okay. It was good seeing you again, Ca—Connor."

I smiled at how she almost called me Captain. Hell, I wanted to call her Red.

It wasn't my place, and I shouldn't have said it, but the words left my mouth before I could stop them. "Are you happy?"

She tilted her head, and confusion swirled in her eyes as she tried to comprehend my words. I shouldn't have said anything, but how was I not going to say anything? She was about to tie her life to a loser who didn't deserve her. Sure, I didn't know the state of their relationship, and I didn't know if she was the woman who could magically change a manwhore into a househusband, but the odds were against her on that. No matter how good a woman could be, a bad man would always mistreat her and try to devalue her strengths to make himself feel bigger.

There was nothing big about Jason. He was a small, small man with an unstable mind. There was no way he'd be deserving of Aaliyah's love.

"Am I happy?" She repeated the question as if hearing her own voice would make it clearer. She smoothed her hands over her dress, and I watched as she did it because every time her hands moved across her figure, I wanted to see exactly where they'd go.

"I'm getting married in a few weeks," she said, smiling. That smile…I remembered that smile, the one that made others want to smile along with it. "What's there to be sad about?"

I nodded. If she was happy, then I was ecstatic for her. Okay, maybe not ecstatic. Not in the least.

Run, Red, run!

I pushed out a broken grin as I slid my hands into the pockets of my slacks. "Good. I'm glad. The best of luck with everything."

"Thank you."

I turned to walk away and was surprised when she called out my name. I looked back at her, and her eyes held a bit of worry. Did she know? Did she know she was about to make a big mistake?

"Yes?" I asked.

"Can you, um…it sounds silly, but can you make sure Jason doesn't drink too much the night before the wedding? He doesn't really know his limit at times, and I'd hate for him to be hungover. Ya know, big day and all."

Fuck. She was really going to marry that man.

I gave her that fake smile again. "Of course."

Relief hit her, and at least I was able to give her some comfort. "Thank you, Connor. That means a lot to me."

Are you happy, Red?

I wanted to ask her again, but this time, I wanted to really focus on her eyes because those eyes had a way of telling the stories her lips seemed to refuse to reveal.

As she turned to walk away, I reached out and grabbed her forearm without thought. "Red, wait."

She appeared confused by my sudden action. I was confused by it myself, but I didn't let go. My fingers stayed glued to her arm as my lips parted.

"What is it?" she asked.

"Please don't."

"Please don't what?"

"Marry him."

Her eyes grew dull as the words hit her ears. She stumbled back and pulled her arm away from me, staring as if I'd slapped her right across the face. I didn't want to make her feel that way. I didn't want her to look at me as if I were a complete stranger, but she did. Because I was a stranger.

That hurt more than I could've expected it to.

"Aaliyah, come on, we're leaving," Jason called out with a tone I didn't like. Shit. I hated all of his tones, but I loathed how he used them to order her around.

She kept her stare on me, appearing hurt by my insane but warranted request. Her eyes stayed with me as she spoke to him. "I'm coming."

And with that, she left.

ELEVEN

Connor

I T HAD BEEN TWO WEEKS SINCE I TOLD AALIYAH NOT TO MARRY MY business partner, and I still stood by my request. The day before Jason's wedding, I learned that he was even more of a trash human than I could've imagined. I couldn't stop him from drinking because he showed up at my house already drunk and high. He came five hours later than he was supposed to and crashed in my guest room.

Then came the morning, when I realized how much I truly hated him.

Jason Rollsfield was, without a doubt, a piece of shit. That was nothing new to me. Still, when I woke on his wedding day, I was somewhat shocked at the level of shittiness he'd proven himself to be.

I woke up early in the morning to the sound of something shattering. I sat up straight in my bed, shaken up a bit from the sudden crash, when I heard two voices. That was almost more alarming than the sound of the crash.

"Shh! Don't wake him," Jason said, causing me to wonder exactly who he was speaking to in my house. What kind of person invited others into a home that wasn't theirs? Jason, of course. I couldn't wait until man moved out to California to run the branch there. Sure, I had my fears of him screwing up, but I wanted him as far away from me as possible.

My curiosity pulled me out of bed, and I walked into the living room space, where I found three things that stressed me out. First, my top-of-the-line bottle of whiskey that'd cost me hundreds, the one I was saving for when I closed the deal on my passion project, sat on the kitchen countertop, opened and almost empty. Second, an expensive lamp a client had gifted me for our closing deal on their property was shattered on the floor into a million pieces. Lastly, Rose.

Yep, that was right. My new intern, who was pretty much a day over nineteen, was standing next to the broken lamp in my living room. When she looked up and noticed me noticing her, she froze like a deer in headlights. Her eyes bugged out, and her skin paled. I wasn't sure which looked more damaged—her or the lamp. Her brown hair was tangled and wild. She was wearing Jason's blazer from the night before, and if she was wearing shorts of any kind, they were too short to notice. All I saw was bare legs—bare legs I had no want or need to witness because she was my fucking intern.

Why the hell was my intern in my penthouse with no pants on?

Rose went ahead and did what she had always done so well: she began to ramble.

"Oh my goodness! Mr. Roe, I'm so, so sorry! You can totally take the price of the lamp out of my next paycheck. And, uh, oh gosh, if you'd like, I can pick up the pieces if you tell me where you keep your trash bags in your house. And oh my gosh, what a be-beautiful home you have, and, and—"

"Rose."

She swallowed hard and stood still. "Yes, Mr. Roe?"

"Leave my house."

She blinked a few times. "Of course, Mr. Roe." She began walking toward the front door, and I called out to her.

"Before you exit, please get dressed in whatever it is you wore over here. I don't need people seeing you leave half-naked."

"Right. Of course. Sorry, Mr. Roe. I'll be gone in no time."

I couldn't believe she'd even spent a moment in my home. What had she been thinking? No—what had Jason been thinking?

After Rose slithered out of my house, I stared at Jason as if he were the biggest villain I'd ever crossed paths with.

He held his hands up in surrender. "Hey, don't look at me. She came on to me."

"She's nineteen years old, Jason. Plus, it's your damn wedding day!"

"Don't remind me," he muttered, pinching the bridge of his nose as he walked to my kitchen, swung my fridge door open, and took one of my water bottles. "Shit, my head is pounding."

Not shocking, seeing as how he'd drunk enough for a party of ten.

"What the hell are you going to do? About the wedding?" I asked, hating every piece of him but also thinking about Aaliyah. This was going to crush her.

"I mean, fuck. I don't know, Connor. I fucked up last night—well, and this morning, but maybe that was it. Maybe that was my final bachelor moment, you know? I had to get it out before settling with Aaliyah."

Settling? As if she wasn't the damn prize in their current situation. If anything, she was the one doing the settling.

I brushed my thumb against my chin and sighed. "You should tell Aaliyah."

"Tell her what?"

"About Rose."

He snickered out loud and huffed. "Yeah, okay, Connor. That's how I want to start my wedding day."

"You don't want to start a marriage with that kind of lie."

"If I tell her, there won't be a marriage. She'll hate me."

"Maybe, but if anything, she deserves to know the truth. Just think about it, all right?"

"Yeah, I will."

"Good. Now go take a shower. You smell like whiskey and ass. I'll be back to grab you in a bit. We have to get a move on."

He headed off to take his shower, and I shook my head, glancing over at the thong lying across the floor. I supposed Jason had found his something blue for the day.

♡

When fifty minutes had passed and I'd gotten showered and dressed in my suit, I headed back to the guest room to retrieve Jason. The whole time I was getting ready, I couldn't stop thinking about Aaliyah and the shit situation she was about to be in by marrying an ass like Jason. She deserved better than him, and I very much doubted he would tell, which made me feel shitty. Because if he didn't, I had every intention of doing so.

Did that mean I was breaking some kind of bro code? Maybe, but I couldn't explain it. For some reason, deep down in my soul, I felt as if my loyalty was in Aaliyah's corner and not Jason's.

"Jason, hurry up, will you? We've got to get a move on," I called out as I walked into his room, thinking he was still in the shower.

When I didn't hear a reply, I called out his name once more.

Again and again.

I darted over to the bathroom to find it empty, and I swore my stomach dropped. I pulled out my cell phone and dialed his number—no luck. I called his number once more.

Again and again.

As I searched the space, I noticed a note sitting on the nightstand.

I can't do it.
I hardly even know this girl. What the fuck am I doing marrying her?
Let everyone know.
Tell Aaliyah I'm sorry.
-Jason

The letter crumpled in my tight grip, and I sighed, knowing today would be the worst day of Aaliyah's life.

TWELVE

Aaliyah

"I DON'T BELIEVE THIS," I WHISPERED, SHOCK TAKING OVER MY core. "I can't believe this…"

Oh God, this was the worst possible thing that could've happened. I couldn't believe everything around me was crashing and burning on today of all days. I looked at my phone as tears formed in my eyes. I felt an overwhelming amount of sadness. I couldn't even explain why.

Feeling alone on your wedding day was never a great thing.

I can't breathe…

I can't breathe…

"Why is this happening?" I asked Hannah as I stood in my dressing room, waiting for Marie to arrive. I wished I could say Hannah was a close friend, but I didn't really know her all that well. She was the wedding planner Marie had hired, and she was in charge of making sure I wouldn't have the exact breakdown I was currently partaking in.

I stood in front of the floor-length mirror wearing my wedding

Don't cry. Don't cry. Don't cry…

"Oh, my gosh!" I sobbed, covering my face with my hands.

"Oh, honey, don't do that! It's all right," Hannah told me.

"How can I not cry? Look at me! I'm fat!" I sobbed, staring at my stomach. Who thought eating a whole basket of bread was a good idea the night before their wedding? Even more so, who thought getting a mermaid dress was a wise idea when one had hips like mine? Why had I done that to myself? Why did I love to self-sabotage?

Jason was right. My ass was fat.

"You're not fat. You look marvelous," Hannah promised in such a monotone way. It was clear she had given the "You're not fat" talk to many brides in her lifetime. She reached for a tissue and started patting at my eyes. "Now stop crying, or we'll have to keep touching up your makeup."

I sniffled a bit and stared at myself in the mirror as a few stubborn tears kept falling from my eyes. "Do you think this is the right dress, Hannah?"

She snickered, placing her hands on my shoulders. "I think it's a bit late to be asking that question."

I nodded. "I know, it's just—"

"Butterflies," she cut in. "It's wedding day butterflies. I've been doing this for over thirty years now, darling."

"Thirty years?" She must've been dying her hair that shade of red. There was no way she had not one gray hair given her line of work. Nothing made a person go gray faster than a bridezilla.

"Yes, thirty long years and while all the small details are fun, they don't really matter much."

"They don't?"

"No. It's not about the dress, or the reception, or the first dance. It's not about the perfect photographer or a gorgeous bouquet. None of that matters. All that matters is you standing at the end of that long aisle with the love of your life and saying 'I do.' The only thing that matters is you two there together, at that moment, as you both start writing the opening chapter of your story."

I released the breath I hadn't even known I was holding.

She took my hand in hers and squeezed it lightly. "Okay?" she asked.

I nodded. "Okay."

There was a knock on my door, and we both turned to see Connor standing there. He looked so handsome in his all-black tuxedo. I was glad he'd gone with all black. It was so charming and classy.

"Connor, hey, you look great." I sighed, relieved. "It's so good to see you're here because that means Jason's here, which means this is really happening, and I was crying for no reason and—" My words trailed off as I stared at Connor. His lips were doing something strange, something I'd never witnessed before.

He was...frowning?

"What is it?" I asked, alarmed. "Is everything okay? Is Jason all right?"

He cleared his throat and slid his hands into his pockets. He looked at Hannah and then back at me, that frown still resting uncomfortably against his lips. "Do you think we can speak privately?"

"Oh no..." Hannah muttered quietly, shaking her head.

I shot my stare toward her, even more alarmed than before. "What do you mean 'oh no'? What's going on?"

Hannah gave me a broken smile and squeezed my hands. "I'll give you two space to talk." She left the room as if she knew what was about to happen, as if she knew how my world was about to be turned upside down.

Once she was out of the room, Connor stepped closer to me. The closer he grew, the sicker I felt.

I can't breathe...

I can't breathe...

"No," I whispered, my body beginning to tremble. "I mean, this is ridiculous. He wouldn't...I mean, he couldn't..." I laughed, fully in denial, and the more I laughed, the more Connor grimaced. "Why are you here right now?"

He lowered his head before raising it slowly and staring at me with those blue eyes. "I'm so sorry, Aaliyah."

"No." I shook my head. "Don't be sorry because there's nothing to be sorry about. I mean, he loves me. We love each other. Today's happening...it's just nerves. I had nerves, so I'm sure he had nerves, which is fine. We are fine." I swallowed hard. "Right, Connor...?"

"He, um…" Each word that left Connor's mouth was tainted with pain. Each word dripped with guilt as he said all that needed to be said for me to fully understand the situation at hand. "He left a note on the nightstand…"

THIRTEEN

Connor

ALL THE GUESTS HAD DISSIPATED, TAKING WITH THEM THEIR GOSSIP and judgmental commentary. All that was left in the church were Aaliyah and me. I was only still there to make sure everyone got the fuck out and left the poor woman alone.

Her back was to me as she stood at the end of the aisle, staring at the arch filled with beautiful flowers. The train of her gown was spread out behind her, and her shoulders were rounded forward.

"Aaliyah." I spoke gently, stuffing my hands into the pockets of my suit. "Where is your wedding planner?"

"I sent her away. I just couldn't handle being around people. Marie tried to comfort me, but I told her to go make sure her son was okay."

"Oh." Her body stood a bit straighter, yet she didn't turn my way. "I can have my driver take you home. Or if there's somewhere else you want to go…anywhere…anywhere you want to go, I'll take you." I took a breath, unsure what I should say next. There wasn't anything I could say to make the current situation any better for her.

Her head shook a bit, and she fiddled with her fingers. "Do you think he's all right?" She turned my way. "It just doesn't seem like him to run."

I took another step toward her but didn't speak. She must've known a different Jason than I had. The Jason I knew was a runner, through and through. When things got hard, he dashed. When he had to put in a bit of actual work, he'd throw a fit and end up in Bora Bora for a mental break. He was the definition of unstable, yet Aaliyah didn't see it that way for some reason. She seemed truly shocked by the events that had taken place. Me, on the other hand? The idea of me being shocked that he'd bolted seemed absurd.

How had he tricked her into believing he was someone worthy of her time?

"We were right for each other. I know we were. I felt it..." She shut her eyes for a moment and took a deep breath. "At least, I thought I felt it. I mean, I know he's been stressed with work lately, and..."

She was seconds from falling apart, and I didn't blame her. She had every right to fall into a million pieces right then and there. I had to get her out of that place. Out of that dress. Out of her tragedy.

"Aaliyah, we should go."

"He won't answer my calls." Her eyes were filled with water, but no tears fell. "Maybe there was an accident, and that's why he hasn't answered my calls. Maybe there was some kind of panic at the office, or maybe someone told him a lie about me. I heard people talking yesterday, but they were just making things up, Connor. I swear. But maybe he believed them. Maybe someone got in his head. Or maybe..." She took a breath. "Or maybe everyone was right. Maybe I was just another blip on his roadmap of women. Maybe I wasn't anything special." She choked on her next words. "Or maybe...maybe...maybe..."

She covered her mouth with her hand as her body curved forward, and the tears began to flood her face. She sobbed into her hands, shaking uncontrollably as realization set in, the knowledge that on that day—the day of her happily ever after—she was left standing at the altar alone, with no love story to hold her upright.

Well, fuck.

This was awkward.

I walked down the aisle to meet her.

Step by step, I headed in her direction, moving toward her as quickly as I could, and when her knees began to buckle, I was right there to catch her. She wrapped her arms around me, holding me tight in her beautiful white dress that looked as if it had been made solely for her. She looked like a goddess who'd been struck down by lightning. Shit wasn't fair. From what I could tell, Aaliyah seemed like a good person. This kind of crap shouldn't happen to good people. Jason was an asshole for what he'd done.

"Why wasn't I enough?" she cried, repeating those words over and over again as the pain in her heart poured out of every part of her being.

I didn't know what to say or how to make her feel better, so I pulled her closer to me, holding her weary body against mine. I remained quiet and still as she lost herself within my arms. I wouldn't try to fix her because one could never fix what was broken. Sometimes, you just had to stand in the wreckage and hope you could learn to live within the new shattered pieces.

"You don't have to stay with me," she said as we sat on the ground in front of the altar. We'd been there for quite some time, at least an hour, yet I wasn't going to leave her side until she was ready to walk away. The woman had just been stood up on her wedding day; the least I could do was sit with her.

"It's fine."

"No, it's not. I'm sure you have better, more important things you could be doing."

I didn't say a word. It was clear she was feeling lost, abandoned, and alone, and I knew if it were me, I'd hate to be by myself. So I refused to leave her there on her own. I saw it in her eyes each time she told me I could go, a small hope that I'd choose to stay. She just needed one person who wouldn't walk out on her that afternoon. Therefore, I stayed.

Her knees were bent and pulled into her chest as she hugged them, staring forward into the distance. "The reception would be starting right now," she whispered. "There would be music, and dancing, and happiness..." Her eyes were bloodshot and puffy with streaks of her mascara down her cheeks.

I didn't reply.

She hopped up. "I think I'll go."

"Go? Go where?"

"To the reception."

"What?"

She nodded her head, obviously in a state of shock because she was talking insane. "Yeah, you know…just to check it out."

"What? No. That's crazy."

"Yeah, it is. Can you drive me?"

"Huh? No," I flatly stated. "Of course I won't drive you there."

"But earlier, you said you'd drive me anywhere I wanted to go. You swore you would."

Women and their impeccable memories.

"I don't think that's a healthy choice…"

"But it's a choice, and I'm sure you're sick of sitting here, so we should go there."

"No."

"Yes."

"Not gonna happen."

"Connor."

"What?"

I looked at her eyes and the roundness of her shoulders, and she gave me the most pathetic puppy-dog-Sarah-McLachlan-commercial-eyes. "Please?"

For Christ's sake.

"Fine. Just go change out of your dress."

She gathered up her ridiculously long train in her arms and started full speed ahead. "Nope, no time. Let's go."

FOURTEEN

Aaliyah

E VERYTHING WAS PERFECT, FROM THE GOLD VASE CENTERPIECES filled with roses to the floodlights used to make the dance floor shine. The place settings were beyond stunning, and the dessert table held all of my favorite things.

Brownies.

Cookies.

Lemon bars.

A cake that took my breath away. Gold ribbons dancing across the tiers of fondant, the letters J and A written in the most beautiful frosting. One layer was red velvet another deep chocolate. His favorite flavor and mine…

All of it was perfect, a reception built for a forever kind of love story, and all of the workers were tearing it down. How was I ever going to be okay after this?

I stood frozen in the doorway as Connor stayed near me, staring as they all took the pieces away. My chest tightened as two individuals were about to recklessly place the fifty-pound masterpiece onto a cart with wobbly wheels. They'd probably push the cake into the back room, grab

"Wait! No!" I shouted, rushing into the space with my long train following me. "Don't touch that!"

They turned to me with narrowed eyes. They looked like dang teenagers, obviously too young to be handling such a prize. "Uh, what?" one muttered.

"I said don't touch that cake!" I probably looked wild in the eyes because I felt completely wild in my heart. "Don't move it." I turned toward the other caterers and ordered them to stop breaking down the place settings. I shouted for the DJ to stop unplugging his equipment. I cried for the bartender to stop wiping everything down.

I just needed the perfect room to stay that way for a little bit longer.

"Aaliyah…" Connor's voice was low and sad.

I cringed at the sound. It was worrisome when the happiest man in the world looked sad.

"Connor, make them stop. Please. I just—make them stop. Make them stop," I pleaded, staring his way as if he was my only ally.

"They have to do their job…"

I took a deep breath and swallowed hard as tears began to fall down my face. "I just need more time."

He narrowed his eyes. He didn't understand me. He didn't know where my irrational emotions were coming from. If there was any-thing Connor didn't understand, it was others' emotions. He never stayed around long enough to witness them.

"You're being unreasonable," he told me. Not rudely, just matter-of-factly. It seemed Connor didn't have a rude bone in his body.

"I know, but please."

He rubbed the back of his neck, and defeat deflated his shoulders as he turned to the crew. "Leave everything as it is," he told them.

"But, sir, we were ordered—"

"Everything is paid for," Connor said quickly. "The room, the time, your services. So the least you can do is let the bride partake in the festivities."

"But…she's not a bride," another said. "The wedding was called off."

She's not a bride…

I hadn't known words could sting until I heard those ones fall against my eardrums.

Connor gave that individual a look and then narrowed his eyes. He reached into his back pocket and pulled out his wallet. "I'll pay you each three hundred dollars to continue the reception activities."

For the first time that afternoon, guilt found its way to me. "No. I'm sorry, Connor, we can go—"

He held a silencing hand up to me, pulling out the cash.

The workers all glanced toward one another, then shrugged their shoulders as they walked over to Connor and began collecting their payment for keeping a wannabe bride from having a mental breakdown.

Or, well, for helping a wannabe bride partake in her mental breakdown.

Because nothing about what I was doing was sane.

The DJ started playing music, and I moved to the middle of the dance floor. The lights flashed, and I swayed back and forth, staring at the almost life I'd missed. Then the wave of emotions came crashing into me as a slow song came on. My knees began to buckle, and my eyes began to flood with emotion. The second I began to fall, with the aim of hitting the floor, I was surprised when Connor stopped me.

He pulled me up, and he held me in his arms. He swayed back and forth with me. "I got you, Red. I got you."

When I began to fall, he was there to catch me.

"I broke my promise to you," I said. I rested my tired head against his shoulder as he moved back and forth.

"What promise?"

"You said to never fall for a man who wouldn't dance with me. He wouldn't have done this," I whispered, crying onto his shoulder. "He would've never danced with me."

"Then why did you choose him?"

I sniffled and didn't reply because my answer felt too pathetic to face.

Because I was alone and scared of being alone and scared for the small remainder of my life that would've been experienced alone.

"Why did you say that the last time we saw each other? Why did you tell me not to marry him? Did you think I wasn't good enough for him?"

He arched a bewildered brow and shook his head. "No. Of course not. I just knew he was nowhere near good enough for you."

I wanted to believe those words, but still, it was hard.

We kept dancing until the crew had finally had enough and kicked us out.

"Where would you like me to take you?" Connor asked.

"I don't know. I have nowhere to go. I can't go to Jason's penthouse. It's not mine. It's his, and I have no one, nobody to…I have nowhere to go and—"

"You'll stay with me tonight," he said, cutting into the panic rising in my chest. "You'll stay with me."

FIFTEEN

Connor

SHOWED AALIYAH TO ONE OF MY SPARE ROOMS AND GAVE HER A change of clothes. She thanked me quietly before she went into the room, closing the door behind her.

If there was anything she needed that night, it was rest.

I headed back to my office. I felt exhausted but knew I probably wouldn't be able to sleep any time soon. Therefore I'd do what I did best: pour myself into work.

Around one in the morning, my phone dinged.

Jason: Hey. Did everything work out?

Did everything work out?

The nerve of the asshole. I'd sent him a million text messages that day, called a billion times, and left a trillion voice messages begging for him to reply. To at least call Aaliyah. To man up and answer for the massive storm he had created. To face the broken heart he had destroyed. Yet I hadn't heard a peep from him for almost twenty hours, and when

He couldn't be serious.

He couldn't be that idiotic to think there was any kind of scenario where Aaliyah was anywhere close to being okay.

I wanted to cuss him out. I wanted to rip the fucker a new one for thinking any of his actions toward that poor girl were okay. Sure, Aaliyah was a hot mess, but it was because she really cared about the dick. She was the first girl I'd seen Jason with who looked at him as if he were someone worthy of being with. Plus, when she wasn't completely destroyed, she was kind, graceful, and beautiful inside and out. She had a pure heart, and Jason had felt the need to destroy it.

He'd disappeared without anything more than a few words scribbled on a piece of paper, leaving me to clean up his mess, his mistakes. He'd left as if leaving was the easiest thing for him to do.

So that night, I ignored him. I ignored his messages, I ignored his fake concern, and I secretly hoped karma would find its way to him, if only for that night.

When I got up to head to bed, I was surprised when I heard sniffling from the guest room. She was still up and clearly crying. Without thought, I headed over and knocked on the door. When she opened it, I felt as if I'd been sucker punched. She looked drained. Destroyed.

"Sorry, was I being too loud?" she asked.

"No, no. It's not that." I frowned and crossed my arms. "I just wanted to say you're important."

"What?"

"You're important. I want you to know that fact to counter any person who's ever made you feel as if your existence isn't of value. This world is better because you're here."

She let out a low chuckle. "How did you know I was feeling unimportant?"

"Because even though I've only spent short amounts of time with you, I know you care and feel things deeply."

She leaned against the doorframe. "Can I tell you a secret?"

"Yes."

"I'm afraid that before I die, I'll never find my person or my family. I'm afraid I'll always be alone until my final day."

"That's not true. You're a leading lady."

"What if I don't get the hero?"

"That's fine, too. Contrary to popular belief, you can still have a happily ever after without another person being involved. Sleep tonight," I ordered, nodding once.

"I'll try."

"Sleep tonight," I repeated, brushing away the few stray tears that danced down her cheeks with my thumb.

"I will."

"You're lying."

"I am."

"Do you want me to sit with you? So you don't feel alone?"

Her lips parted for a second before she shook her head. "No. I can't ask you to do that. I'm okay. Really, it's fine."

That was enough to convince me she needed me to stay. She was terrified of loneliness. I saw how it was eating at her that night. I refused to leave her alone in that state of mind.

Walking into the room, I sat down on the desk chair. She climbed into the bed and quietly thanked me for doing that small act. It was the least I could do. I couldn't take away her pain that night. I couldn't unplug the wild thoughts racing through her mind. I couldn't even begin to understand an ounce of what she was feeling.

I did the only thing I could do for a woman who had been abandoned and left stranded alone. I did the only thing that felt right. I stayed.

SIXTEEN

Aaliyah

DAYLIGHT POURED INTO THE BEDROOM THROUGH THE CURTAINS, and I groaned as it hit my cheeks. I had yet to open my eyes, the pounding of my brain making me feel nauseous. I wanted to rip my head off my body for the way it was spinning. I was certain meeting the sunlight would only intensify the awful feeling.

I reached to my right to locate my phone, which I always plugged in at night and left on my nightstand, but I gasped when my hand fell straight down instead of tapping the table.

My eyes opened, and instant panic hit me as I sat up in the bed, realizing it wasn't my bed at all. Every hair on my body stood straight up as a strong panic began to overtake my whole system. Where was I? And whose bed was I lying on?

Then it all came back to me. The wedding. The night before. Connor.

I sat in his oversized T-shirt and gray sweatpants, which made my level of panic skyrocket to new heights. I started to recall the previous night, the ending of my relationship, the meltdown that came after-

I glanced to the other side of the bed, where a nightstand was located. Sitting on it was a glass of water and a piece of paper.

I crawled over to it and picked up the piece of paper.

Red,
You're okay.
-Captain

I made the mistake of glancing in the mirror, which reflected my heartbreak in smeared makeup and tearstains. I looked like a raccoon with the eyeliner and mascara spread around.

The apartment smelled like bacon, which meant Connor was up and active. With slow movements, I walked out of the bedroom to find a huge, open space. His penthouse had an open layout that was modern and bright. The floor-to-ceiling windows were soaked in the sunlight that had awakened me.

"Hey," I muttered to Connor, whose back was to me as he stood in his kitchen area, stirring something on the stovetop.

He glanced over his shoulder, which had a dish towel resting on it, and gave me a half-grin. "Morning, sunshine."

What an ironic thing to say. There was nothing sunny about my shine.

He turned back to the stove, turned off the heat, and then walked over in my direction. I'd already found my way over to his kitchen countertop, where I took a seat on a stool and lowered my head to the island in complete defeat.

"Sorry I wasn't in there when you woke up. I saw you stirring for a while and figured you'd be waking soon, so I decided to get up and start breakfast."

"You really stayed in there all night long?"

"Yeah, of course."

Even the saddest parts of my soul felt warmth from that. "Thank you, Connor. I'm sorry, for everything. I'll get out of your hair right away. I know I've been a burden but I won't be for any longer."

"How do you like your grits?" he said, almost as if he hadn't heard what I said about leaving.

"What?"

"Grits—how do you like your grits? I made bacon, too, along with some scrambled eggs."

"I don't even know what grits are."

The look of shock and hurt that hit his face almost made me want to laugh. If I hadn't felt physically and emotionally crushed to my core, he would've received a laugh.

"Grits are only the best breakfast in the whole world. It might be a Southern thing, but it's a good Southern thing. I normally make cheesy grits, but I ran out of cheese. You can add a little sugar on top of them, though, and muah!" He gave a chef's kiss.

"I'm not really hungry," I explained, feeling my stomach still flipping.

"I know, which is exactly why you need to eat," he explained, grabbing a plate from his cupboard.

I shook my head. "No, really, Connor. I just need to go home. I feel…"

Awful.

Sad.

Broken.

Free?

Wait, no. Not that.

He looked at me, and his lips turned down into the saddest frown. He felt bad for me. I couldn't blame him. I felt bad for myself, too.

"Are you sure you don't want any food? I left out some more sweats so you can shower and change into them, if you need. Plus, maybe after you shower, you'll want something to eat."

I gave him a half-smile. "Yeah, thanks. Then I'll get out of your hair."

"No rush, Red. Truly." Connor seemed unbothered by my broken-down appearance. He stood tall and calm as ever. "Your cell phone is on the dresser in the bedroom, fully charged. Take all the time you need, and when you're ready, I can have my driver take you wherever you need to go."

"Thank you."

"Any time."

I stood from the chair and began moving in the direction of the bedroom. Then I paused and looked back at Connor.

"Connor, wait." He looked over his shoulder toward me, and I swallowed hard. "I know I don't have a right to ask you this, but the thought just keeps running through my head, and I'm not sure I can make it go away unless I ask you…"

He stood silent, waiting.

I bit my bottom lip. "Was there another woman that you knew of? Was Jason seeing anyone else?"

The corners of his mouth twitched, and he slid his hands into the pockets of his sweatpants.

His silence was my answer.

"Did you know her?" I asked.

"Don't do this, Aaliyah," he whispered.

"Do what?"

"Make it hurt more than it has to."

His words stung me, yet it was my own fault, really. I'd known who Jason was from the beginning, and I still allowed myself to fall for him. I'd walked into his spiderweb, knowing I was an ant.

"Everyone always told me, in a way. At all those social events, they always hinted at the man Jason used to be."

They were all right. I was just another mark on the timeline of women Jason crossed paths with. I had wanted so desperately for them to be wrong. I'd wanted to prove them wrong, and I'd wanted to prove to myself that I was enough. Now everyone was laughing at me from their mansions, thinking, *I told you so.*

I rose my head up to look at Connor.

Except for him.

His eyes were on me, and he wasn't so quiet. I didn't mean in his tones but rather his stance. The way his shoulders were low and his lips slightly moved. The way his arms crossed and his head tilted to the left a little. The way his blue eyes seemed as calm as the ocean at nightfall.

Nothing about his body language read "I told you so." Nothing about Connor was laughing in my face at my stupidity for loving Jason. Nothing about him was calling me a fool.

All that sat in his eyes was sorrow.

He felt bad for me.

I had to tear my stare away from him because his sadness for me only made my heart ache more. I went to take a long, hot shower as my tears intermixed with the water droplets slamming against my body, and I welcomed the sadness. I didn't try to fight it. I didn't try to avoid it. I didn't try to talk myself out of the hurting. No, I allowed the pain into my heart. I let it burn.

SEVENTEEN

Aaliyah

OFTEN WONDERED WHO THE FIRST PERSON WAS TO EVER FALL IN love.

Did they know what it was right away, or did it feel like extreme heartburn? Were they happy? Sad? Was the love a two-way street, or was it a solo affair? How long did it take to get there? How many days, months, and years did they travel before the love arrived?

Were they scared?

Did they speak the words first or wait for the other to do the talking?

In all of my favorite storybooks, there had been an insta-love moment. I loved when a character said they fell completely in love the moment their eyes met. While I'd always been a hopeful romantic, it was hard to believe that would ever happen in real life, yet still, I loved the idea of it all. I loved that it could happen, maybe, even if only in make-believe worlds. I loved the idea that love worked in whatever way it wished. I liked the thought that love swept in at its own speed, not believing in time, space, or constraints.

It showed up sometimes welcomed, other times not, and it filled

Then in many cases, that love shifted. It cracked, it bled, it left scars that would never fully heal. It opened a door for distrust, self-doubt, and pain. I sometimes thought life would be better if love never existed because if love wasn't real, heartbreak couldn't occur either.

I lately wondered who the first person was to ever fall out of love. Did they see it coming? Was it a slow build? Did it start with small annoyances, or did they wake one morning and realize the love was gone? Did they mourn it? Did they walk away easily? How many days, months, and years did they travel before the love evaporated?

I wondered if losing love hurt them to the same extent it'd wrecked me over the past few hours.

Connor offered to ride back to my place with me, but I declined the offer. All I wanted to do was be alone for a while. As the car pulled up to the penthouse in SoHo, I grew nauseous. A part of me wanted to rush upstairs, pack my things, and hurry away without being seen. A bigger part of me hoped Jason was sitting up there, ready to tell me everything from the past twenty-four hours was a big mistake.

Ready to tell me he had just caught a case of cold feet, and he'd run off to the courthouse with me that instant and say, "I do."

How pathetic was that?

If Jason asked me to still marry him, I'd probably say yes.

I didn't know what that meant for my strength.

"Thank you, Luis," I told Connor's driver, who had been nice enough to take me home.

Jason's home.

It definitely wasn't mine to claim.

"Of course. If there is anything you need, I'm sure Mr. Roe would be all right with me transporting you to a different location today." He was so kind to me, and I was thankful for that. I needed all the kindness I could get.

"I think I'll be okay, thank you."

We said our goodbyes, and I took a deep breath before walking inside the building. The moment I went through the front doors, my stomach tightened. Katherine sat working at the front desk, and her eyes widened when she saw me. Katherine was an older lady who'd been working in that same spot for over twenty years. She was the face that'd greeted me for the past six or so weeks since I'd moved in with Jason, one I was happy to know and love.

"Aaliyah, hi, sweetheart." She stood quickly, and the heaviness that sat in her eyes held guilt. "How are you?"

I gave her a tight grin. "Seen better days."

"I can imagine. I'm sorry about everything that happened, but Mr. Rollsfield said to let you know you're more than welcome to stay here as long as you need."

I stood a bit. "You've talked to Jason?"

"Yes, ma'am."

"Is he here now?"

"No, ma'am. He stopped by yesterday to pick up some things before he headed out. Said he was going on a trip."

"Did he say where to?" I asked.

Katherine grimaced. "I think he mentioned France?"

"Our honeymoon." Or what was supposed to be our honeymoon.

"Look, sweetie"—Katherine rubbed the back of her neck and lowered her brows—"I was really betting on you being the one this time. I've seen Jason with many different women. Many, many, *many*—"

"I get it. Jason used to get around," I cut in. "What are you trying to say?"

"I'm just saying, it was different with you. He was different with you."

I huffed at her words. They annoyed me for many reasons, but mainly because even though he had been different, he'd still left me. I wasn't enough to make him stay.

I was never enough to make them stay.

"I wanted to be the girl who changed his life," I confessed. My mind was having a hard time coming to terms with the fact that he had truly stood me up. Before in my relationships, I could see all the red flags—but Jason had seemed like he truly cared. This one had blindsided me.

"You did change his life."

I rubbed the palms of my hands over my tired eyes. "I didn't. If I had, I wouldn't be here all snotty-nosed and teary-eyed. If I were the woman who'd changed his life, he would've been able to say 'I do.' But instead, he walked away."

"Even if that is true, you still changed his life."

"How do you know?"

"Because people can't meet you and not be changed, Aaliyah."

I smiled and thanked Katherine as I reached around to grab my key from my purse.

"Aaliyah," a voice said from behind me, making me turn around in haste. I knew the voice the moment I heard it, and the sound alone made my heart sink.

"Marie, hi." I breathed out as I looked into a set of eyes that had grown to mean so much to me. "What are you doing here?"

"Well, I was on a quest to try to find my son, but I just got word that he's taking a mini-vacation to France for a while." She frowned as she looked down at her hands and fiddled with her fingers. When she looked up, tears were flooding her eyes. "Oh, Aaliyah. It wasn't supposed to go like this." She covered her mouth and broke down into uncontrollable sobs.

It was an instant reaction of mine as I wrapped my arms around her. There I was, standing in the lobby, comforting the mother of the man who'd left me on my wedding day. I couldn't help it; seeing anyone falling apart made me want to comfort them.

"He loves you, Aaliyah. I know he does," she said, pulling away a bit. "Do you think you and I can have a word upstairs?"

I hesitated for a moment. I wasn't sure I was ready to face a conversation with Jason's mother. I wasn't even ready to face myself and my heartache.

Before I could reply, Marie seemed to read the words I wasn't able to express. "It's fine, really. I'm sorry. I'll give you your space. I want you to know you deserved more than what my son did to you. From the moment I met you, I knew you were something special," she said.

"Thank you, Marie."

"I know this sounds crazy, but do you think…" Sniffling, she pulled out a tissue from her purse and wiped her eyes. "Do you think you and I can stay in touch? Maybe still get coffee with one another? I know it sounds selfish, but in a way, I feel as if you are a part of my world."

I felt the same way, yet the idea of seeing her any time soon seemed a bit too daunting a task. "I think I just need time, Marie.

Honestly, this is all a lot to come to terms with. My mind is still spinning."

"I understand, sweetheart. I won't take any more of your time but know you're welcome to stay at this apartment as long as you need. I'll make sure to keep Jason away to give you the time you need to move into a new place. But I hope you know what my son did to you was cruel, and I do apologize for all the hurt he has caused you."

I let out a nervous laugh. "You don't have to apologize to me, Marie. You aren't your son's mistakes."

Now it was her turn to release an anxious chuckle. "You could tell a parent that a million times, and we'd still never believe you." She pulled me into a hug and held me so tight. I melted into her hug. I hadn't known how much I needed that—for someone to hold me. "You are the daughter I always wanted," she whispered, stirring up my own emotions.

She turned to walk away and paused as she held the door open for a moment before she looked back my way. "Just so it's clear, Aaliyah, you were always the catch in your relationship, not the other way around. My son was never good enough for you. You were the prize." She smiled and walked away, leaving me there with a set of nerves I wasn't sure how to work through.

I took the elevator to the penthouse and felt a sense of emptiness once I stepped foot inside. I hadn't lived within those walls for long, but somewhere along the way, I'd convinced myself I'd achieve my happily ever after there. Sometimes fairy-tale endings are only for the storybooks.

Everything was exactly as it had always been in the penthouse, except a little different. All the components of the house felt a little less like mine. I walked into the bedroom and noticed some of Jason's clothing was missing from the closets. He really had left me, and he wasn't going to come back.

I wasn't sure what to do with myself. I wasn't sure how to move forward with life. I had nothing to my name—no husband, no job, no home. I'd given all of that up to be with a man who'd left me on our wedding day.

I lay down on the bed that morning, feeling everything but love.

I hated the discomfort I felt in that home. I hated the way the walls echoed to me that I didn't belong there. I hated how my skin crawled with the idea that any moment now, Jason could show up and remind me of how much I didn't belong.

So I stood up from the bed and went to the only place where I felt less alone.

Every Sunday morning, I spoke to dead people. Well, not dead people—just one. It had become a tradition to visit Grant's grave and talk to him about life, about the ups and downs of my world. I'd read him comic books, and we'd watch the sun rise with one another. That morning, I'd missed the sunrise with him, but still, I felt his comfort.

I sat in front of Grant's tombstone with my legs bent and my arms crossed on top of my knees. My head rested against my arms as I stared forward at the one person who still made me feel loved. I didn't say anything that morning because I knew he wouldn't be speaking back to me at all, but in my head, I'd imagine he'd say I was okay.

Scattered around his tombstone were quarters. I'd leave a quarter every time I'd visit because it always reminded me of him. When I first met Grant, he was always flipping a quarter between his fingers. He had all his odd beliefs and sayings that stuck with me over the years. *"Find a penny, pick it up, all day long you'll have good luck, find a quarter, make it mine, and I'll be lucky for the rest of time,"* he'd say. There was never a day he didn't carry a lucky quarter around with him. So, whenever I visited, I left him a quarter, so he'd have a bit of luck on the other side.

As I sat there, feeling hopeless, another one of his lines popped up in my head.

"Rain makes rainbows, Aaliyah. Let the water fall," he'd probably tell me. *"Break first, fix later."*

I broke.

I shattered.

I let the water fall from my eyes as the comfort of Grant's almost words filled my mind. I was thankful for Grant's silence that still somehow managed to wrap me up in some kind of mystical safe love.

EIGHTEEN

Aaliyah

AND NOW COMES THE PART WHERE **I** PLEAD.

My stomach sat in knots as I rode the elevator up to the *Passion Magazine* office, where I would respectfully—okay, probably not—beg for my junior editor position back. Now that I had no need to move to Los Angeles, I was trying to put my feet back on somewhat solid ground. I was a New Yorker through and through, and what do New Yorkers do when life knocks them down? We get back up and start swinging, too—knotted stomachs and all.

I was a bit shocked when my boss Maiv agreed to meet with me after I drunkenly emailed her at four in the morning due to a sleepless night.

Jason still hadn't called me.

I knew that didn't matter much, but for some reason, it hurt me. You would think the man who stood you up on your wedding day would at least send an *LOL my bad, I overslept and missed our wedding* text message of sorts.

Still, somehow his lack of communication was what kept my mind occupied the night before. I thought about where he could be, what he could be doing…who he could be doing.

Of course he was cheating on you, Aaliyah. Hasn't history taught you anything? That's what men do. Now, look at you—wasted a year of your life on a man who left. Your time is ticking. Tick, tick, tick...

"Shut up," I muttered out loud to my own insensitive brain. My thoughts had been in overdrive, trying to convince me that what had happened was all because of me—that I wasn't good enough, that I wasn't worthy of the happy ending, that I was bad at finding love that lasted...that I didn't have time to find a real love.

My thoughts were currently controlling me, and all I wanted was to be able to be in control of them instead, even if that meant sometimes muttering at myself to shut up.

I walked into the front lobby of *Passion* and saw Greta's smiling face. She was the front desk receptionist, so I saw her face first each day I came into work for the past years.

"Hey there, sunshine," she frowned, looking my way. She was invited to the wedding, so I was certain she knew of the outcome. "How are you doing?"

I smiled even though I didn't mean it. "One step at a time."

"I hate him," she told me. "And I hope he has a miserable life."

I wished I could've wished the same for him...even though my heart wasn't there yet. All I wished was that he'd reach out and call me. "How's Maiv's mood today?" I asked, shifting the subject away from my failed attempt at getting wed.

"Mood is the same as it is every other day: *The Devil Wears Prada* Miranda Priestly." Greta frowned. "Did you really use fifty-four exclamation points in the email you sent to beg for your job back?"

"What? No. It was fifty-two at most."

She snickered. "You're a brave woman for having enough nerve to even ask Maiv for your position back."

"More like desperate, but here we go."

"Godspeed," Greta said before holding up her fingers like Katniss from *The Hunger Games* as a sign of her support and love. "May the odds be ever in your favor."

I swallowed hard as I headed down the long walkway to Maiv's office. Everyone in the space looked at me and gave me a mix of empathic expressions and shocked *Girl, what are you doing? Run!* looks. I didn't know which one to listen to, so I kept walking.

Maiv's office door was open, which wasn't a normal occurrence. Still, I knocked on the doorframe to get her attention.

"Hi, Maiv. Is now still a good time to—" My words evaporated as she lifted her head in slow motion to look my way. Her green eyes hid behind a set of green frames, and her lips pressed together as she met my stare.

Then the oddest thing in the history of Maiv Sun happened—she smiled.

"Aaliyah, hi, yes. Do come in and close the door behind you."

I swallowed hard and did as she said, unsure how to take her smile. I'd worked for the woman for years, and I'd never received a smile from her.

I took a seat across from her desk, and my heart sat uncomfortably in my throat.

Maiv smoothed her hands over her gray hair tucked in a perfect high bun, and she sat back in her chair, still staring my way. She picked up the pen from her desk and began twirling it between her fingers.

"So," she started, "that was quite the wedding—or lack thereof."

"You came," I muttered.

"Of course, I came. I told you I was going to come. The ceremony space was very modern. You did a decent job, minus the whole no wedding thing."

"Oh. Well…thanks?"

She nodded once. "I'm guessing you're here because you want your job back."

I tried to push my heart back down to its rightful place in my chest. *Time to grovel.* "Yes, ma'am. Even if I can't go back to being a junior editor, I'll take any position and work my way up to—"

"You have connections with Connor Roe."

I sat up a bit straighter, thrown off by her question. "What?"

"I noticed at your almost wedding that Connor Roe was in attendance. He's the one who dismissed us all from the venue."

"Uh…yes. I'm sorry, what does that have to do with—"

"Why haven't you ever told me you knew Connor Roe?"

What exactly was happening? "Um, I didn't think it was of importance. Plus, I don't really know him, know him, and—"

"But he came to your wedding? How would you not know someone who was invited to your wedding?"

"I'm sorry, Maiv. I don't understand what any of this has to do with my job and me getting it back…"

"Oh, yes. Well, I can offer you your position back—"

"Oh, my gosh!" I exclaimed.

She held a silencing finger up. "If you do one thing for me."

"Anything, Maiv. I'll do anything."

"Good. I was hoping you'd say that." She leaned forward on her desk, dropped the pen, and clasped her hands. "I need you to get an exclusive with Connor Roe."

I choked on my next breath. "I'm sorry, what?"

"Connor Roe is the biggest bachelor in New York City. He is on his way to being one of the richest men in all of New York, if not the world, and he has never once done an interview. Everyone in the industry is clawing at the opportunity to get him on their cover, but he's refused all offers."

Wow. Was Connor truly that successful? Jason had hardly ever talked about work people when we spent time together. Still, I didn't see how I could help Maiv.

"Well, if he doesn't want to be interviewed—"

"Senior editor," she cut in.

"What?"

"If you get Connor Roe to agree to an interview and to pose for the cover of our September issue, I will make you senior editor."

No way. Senior editors always received the best projects. They were able to travel and see the world. Just a few months ago, Abby had been in Iceland following a story about an explorer for two months. That was what I'd dreamed about, doing the big stories that allowed me to see the world at the same time, to experience different cultures, different lifestyles, to see lives bigger than my own.

"You mean it?" I pushed out, feeling as if I were dreaming. "I'd be able to travel for work and write the meaningful articles?"

"If you get Connor to do an exclusive with us, you can write whatever you want." She held up a hand quickly. "Within reason, obviously."

"Yes, of course."

"So"—she narrowed her eyes—"you can do it?"

What was it about Connor that made people crave to be inside his brain so much? It was almost as if Maiv was begging me to get him to agree to the article. Well, as close to begging as she'd ever get, at least.

I nodded. "Yes, of course. Not a problem. I'll have him on board ASAP."

"By Friday."

"Friday? Like…" I gulped hard. "This Friday? Like, in a few days?"

"Yes."

"As in one, two, three—"

"If you can't make it happen, that's all you have to—"

"No! No! I can make it happen. It's pretty much already happening. There is no doubt in my mind that Connor Roe will be on the front cover of this magazine come this September. Yup, that's right because he and I are buddies. Pals. Amigos. Friends. We're pretty much Phoebe and Joey. Yup, that's us. Ketchup and mustard. Tom and—"

"Aaliyah."

"Yes?"

"You can leave my office now."

"Right. Okay. Thank you, Maiv, for giving me this opportunity. This is my dream position, my dream job. I know I probably don't deserve this at all after quitting, so thank you so much for doing this."

"You said this is your dream job?"

"Yes, it really is."

"Then I will say this. Something I've learned after five failed marriages: never give up your dreams for a man again. Men die—dreams don't."

"Uh, thank you?" I said, uncertain how to take Maiv's pep talk. "Wait, I'm sorry, did all of your husbands die…?"

She shrugged. "Some are just dead to me. Some of the others I'm sure were accidental."

"Some?"

She smiled again, and well, that felt like an inappropriate time to deliver a wicked villain smile. "Why are you still in my office?" she asked.

"Right, okay, goodbye."

I walked out, feeling as if I was floating on air. After the week from hell, it appeared the sun was slowly trying to peek out from behind my clouded mind. I pretty much skipped all the way to the subway, humming to myself the entire time, until I took a moment to pause and reality set in.

I'd promised Maiv I would get Connor to do an exclusive interview with *Passion*. I'd promised an interview with a man who seemed to be anti-interviews as a rule, a man who'd already given me more of his time and kindness than I deserved.

I was hoping to never have to exchange another word with anyone connected to Jason ever again, yet without Connor's help, I'd be jobless and probably homeless soon enough. With his help, I'd have my dream position.

It was time for me to do what it seemed I did pretty well as of late: grovel some more.

NINETEEN

Connor

"**P**LEASE STOP CRYING," I BEGGED OF ROSE AS SHE SAT across from me in my office. I'd been dreading having the conversation we had to have, yet I knew once Monday came, she'd be sitting in my office as this uncomfortable situation unfolded.

"Okay," she replied, yet she kept at it.

God, her tears.

It was an uncomfortable sight, and I wished she'd stop crying in front of me. I knew I shouldn't feel bad for her, but whenever a woman cried, all I wanted to do was comfort her. Even though Rose was in the wrong, she was still human, and her sobs—even if they were only crafted out of regret and being caught in my home—were still her emotions.

I handed her a tissue.

With a loud blow, she cleared out her nostrils, then sniffled some more.

"I just, I know you're about to fire me, and, and, well…" More tears. She kept falling apart in front of me, and I pitied her. She was pretty pathetic, after all, the way she sat there with heavy eyes, whimpering lips, and unrecognizable words.

I sat up straight in my office chair as she sat across from me, her shoulders rounded forward with a handkerchief in her right hand.

I felt bad, but then I thought of Aaliyah and what Rose had done to her, and that guilt evaporated quickly.

"Yes. I'm letting you go."

"You can't be serious." She sounded stunned. "I am one of the best workers here! This is bullshit!"

What in the Dr. Jekyll and Mr. Hyde was that? I blinked, and she became a completely different person. Her whole demeanor shifted. She went from the shy, nervous girl to this moody, uppity persona.

Dammit.

Damian was right.

"It has nothing to do with your work—"

"You can't do this!" she scolded. "I am too good for this place, so I quit. I don't want your stupid job anyway. I'm hot. I can get a job anywhere. That's what Jason said, at least."

That's because he was trying to get in your pants.

"That's besides the point. What took place over the weekend was inexcusable, especially you entering my home."

"To be fair, I didn't know it was your home!" she offered, as if that made it any better.

"Did you know Jason was getting married? Or was that a detail you overlooked while at his celebration the night before?"

Her gaze fell to the floor as embarrassment overtook her. "He said he didn't really love her."

"I don't care what he said to you, Rose. You are grown enough to know better than that."

"Whatever. I'm over this." She stood and started off toward the door.

"Rose?"

"Yes?" she asked, turning to look my way.

"What did Jason say to you that made you think it was a good idea to do what you did with him?"

"He said he thought I was gifted, and he believed I'd be successful someday. He told me he believed in me, and I've never had someone like him say that to someone like me."

"He might not have been wrong, but he may have said it to get exactly what it was you gave him. Men are snakes, Rose. Don't let them taint your future by falling into their lies."

"Women can be snakes, too, Mr. Roe. I'm grown enough to know what I'm doing."

As she walked out, Damian was yet again walking in. For the first time since Rose began working there, he spoke to her.

"Bye, Rose," he stated flatly.

"Fuck you, Damian," she barked in reply. Once she left, he closed the door behind her.

"I love it when the trash takes itself out," he commented dryly, taking a seat across from my desk. "So!" He clasped his hands and leaned forward. "Is this the point when I get to say I told you so?"

"Touché."

"One day, you'll start listening to me." He opened the portfolio in his hold and slid some paperwork across to me. "I knew you were pissed after losing that last property, so I spent the weekend exploring some spots and found this abandoned property. It's in Queens. I figured you might be interested in flipping it. Not many people are looking at it right now. I searched and called around a bit to get more intel on it. Might work for your dream or whatever."

He talked so calmly about going out of his way to find me a property to look at as if it wasn't a big deal, but I knew it was. Damian didn't straight-up say when he cared about people, but his spending the weekend to help me out demonstrated that he cared about me.

I smirked. "You love me, don't you."

He rolled his eyes. "Don't make it weird."

"Okay, I won't, but…" I kept smiling ear to ear. "You do, don't you?"

He stood from his chair. "I'm done talking to you."

"I love you, too, Damian," I called out. Even though his back was to me, I could feel him rolling his eyes.

"Oh, by the way—that woman who got stood up called the office. Said she wanted to meet with you briefly tomorrow. I told her you probably didn't have time to—"

"Red?" I asked.

"What?"

I shook my head. "I mean, Aaliyah? She called?"

"Yeah. Said she needed to have a conversation with you if possible, but your schedule is packed and—"

"Cancel my morning meeting at nine. Call her back and let her know she's more than welcome to stop by."

He cocked a brow. "You never cancel meetings."

"Well, I will tomorrow."

I didn't know why, but the idea of seeing Aaliyah again seemed much more important to me than some morning call. Ever since she'd come back into my world, I hadn't stopped thinking about her. I couldn't help but wonder if she was doing okay.

TWENTY

Aaliyah

I SPENT THE NIGHT RESEARCHING CONNOR, AND I WAS FLOORED BY what I found. I'd had no clue he was so powerful. Not only had he built himself an empire from the ground up but he also made sure to give back tenfold to the different communities as he succeeded. It was hard to find much personal information due to him never doing interviews.

From what I read, it seemed he was a stand-up guy with morals that he stood by—which held true to how he'd appeared a few years ago. Giving back to the community seemed to be high on his priorities, and that intrigued me. Jason wasn't as big on giving back in the same way as his business partner had been, though it might've been because Jason grew up privileged. He hadn't struggled a day in his life when it came to his finances. From what I'd read, it seemed as if Connor had to fight tooth and nail for every cent that fell into his bank account.

The next morning, I found myself standing in front of Roe Headquarters with nerves in the pit of my stomach and a bouquet in my hands—because what do you bring to a person who you are about to beg to give you an exclusive interview? Red and white roses, of course. The pack of chocolates under my arm was a backup plan, too, if he didn't like the flowers.

After I called Connor's office, asking if I could meet with him, I was surprised he was so quick to give me some of his time. From what I'd read, he was a pretty busy man, and I had no doubt I'd taken more than enough of his time over the past few days.

My mind was running in extreme overthinking mode as I rode the elevator up to Connor's office. The moment I walked through the doors, the receptionist looked at me holding the flowers and box of chocolates as if I were insane.

"Hello, how can I help you?" she asked.

"I'm here to see Connor."

"You're Aaliyah?"

"Yes. Should I wait out here to—" Before I could finish my thought, the door that led to Connor's employees' offices and his own opened up. A tall, somber-looking man stared at me. His all-black suit matched his charcoal black eyes. He was built, his arms pressing against the fabric of his business shirt, and the dark earrings that pierced his ears tied together his whole vibe. To put it frankly, the man looked terrifying, the kind of person you did not want to piss off because he could end your life with one stern look—the complete opposite of Connor's bright, welcoming feel.

When he turned to look my way, chills raced down my spine to the point that the box of chocolates almost dropped to the ground.

"Aaliyah?" he asked, his dark eyes staring into mine.

"Uh, yes?" I asked, sounding unsure.

"You're here to meet with Connor?"

"Yes?" I said again—as if it were a question.

He nodded once. "Follow me."

I looked at the receptionist to make sure this man wasn't going to murder me, but she'd already moved on to a different task. We walked down the hallway, and the knots that sat in the pit of my stomach hadn't dissipated. I felt like an asshat walking down the halls with a bouquet. What sane woman brings a grown man a bouquet?

A desperate one, I supposed.

We paused in front of an office door, and the man knocked two times before being told to come in.

"Aaliyah is here for your meeting," the somber man stated, nodding in my direction after opening the door. Across the way sat Connor, who stood from his seat quickly. He wore a light blue button-down with navy blue slacks, along with a belt that had probably cost more than my whole wardrobe if he shopped anything like Jason.

"Thanks, Damian. You can close the door behind her," Connor said, nodding toward the man who escorted me. "Aaliyah, come in, have a seat." As I began to walk toward the chair, Connor slapped his hand against his upper thigh. "Wait, Damian—I almost forgot."

"Please don't do this right now," Damian said dryly.

"Come on, we can't avoid our daily banter," Connor insisted.

"It's not daily banter. It's you being idiotic."

They must've had a different kind of boss-employee relationship. If I'd said those words to Maiv, I would've been attending my funeral the following week. Cause of death would be a heel to my ass.

Connor rounded his desk and took a seat on the edge of the wooden structure. He crossed his arms, and a wicked smirk found his lips. "Why did the ketchup blush?"

Damian let out a dramatic sigh. "I don't know. Why, Connor?"

A childish chuckle escaped Connor before he proudly said, "Because it saw the salad dressing."

I couldn't hold in my laughter. It was clever and corny, two of my favorite things.

"Oh, please don't encourage him with your laughter. It only pushes him to find worse jokes," Damian said in a monotone voice.

Connor gestured toward me. "No, she just knows good humor. You have to admit, Damian, that's a good one."

"It was a good one, but it kind of makes me sad seeing that you are using the same jokes as before," I said. "I didn't take you as a guy who recycled jokes."

Connor cocked an eyebrow. "I used that joke on you before?"

"About two years ago, yup."

"No way…" He blew out a cloud of smoke. "I need to do better. Though, it is remarkable that you remembered the exact joke that I told you two years back."

"What can I say? You left an impression on me," I said with a shrug.

"You two know each other?" Damian asked, confused.

"We met once on a random Halloween night two years ago," I explained.

Damian seemed a bit intrigued, which surprised me. I didn't know he could look anything more than monotone. "That's Red?"

Connor grew a bit flustered as I smirked. "So, you talked about me to people, huh?"

"Just here and there," he calmly stated.

"Are you joking? You met me a few months after that situation. You went on and on about how that woman changed your life. You couldn't shut up about how perfect and wonderful and life-changing—"

"Okayyy, Damian, now is not the time for you to adopt a chatty personality. You can go get back to work," Connor said, hurriedly ushering Damian out of the room. He was quick to close the door behind him, and when he returned to the front of his desk, he looked like a boy who'd got caught in the act.

"I swear, the guy never talks, and this is when he decides to blurt out all his thoughts," he said, shaking his head.

"Sounds like I left an impression on you, too."

He smiled. "Without a doubt." The mirth that radiated from Connor's face stayed as he shook his head, but then a somberness fell over him. "I was kind of surprised to hear you wanted to meet." He narrowed his eyes, and the jollity he'd possessed seconds ago transformed into concern. "How are you doing?"

Why was that question almost enough to send me into a tailspin of emotions?

I shook my head and shrugged. "As well as one could imagine, but that's not why I'm here." I looked down at the gifts in my hand and shoved them out in front of me. "These are for you."

He raised an intrigued brow. "Uh, thank you?"

"Yeah. I mean, I don't know if guys like getting flowers, but if it were me, I'd love getting flowers. I went with roses because, basic safe route, even though I'm more of a sunflower girl myself. Anyway, here you go."

I shoved them toward him a bit too aggressively until he took them from my hold.

He leaned in and smelled the roses. "I gotta say, I've never had someone give me flowers. I'm not sure I have a vase for them."

"I didn't think of that. I should've gotten a vase. If you want, I can run down to—" I started to get up, but he held up a hand.

"No, it's fine. I'll have one of my assistants pick it up. Thank you for the gesture, though I'm not sure I know why you're bringing this stuff."

"Well, you did put up with me on Saturday. The least I can do is bring you a gift after wasting your time. I know how important time is, and I make it a habit to try not to waste it, and well, once time is gone, you can't get it back, so I was thinking, well—"

"Aaliyah."

"Yes?"

"You're rambling."

"I know, sorry." I began wiping my hands on my thighs because when I was anxious, sweaty palms were a given. I'd have bet my armpits were currently creating impressive pit stains, too. "I'm dealing with a new set of nerves."

"No need for the nerves. We haven't been nervous around each other since the first time we met. We shouldn't start now."

Easy for you to say—you aren't about to make a crazy request.

He continued. "Honestly, you didn't have to bring me anything. You've never been a waste of time in my life."

He was being too kind because I knew the level of destruction I'd been. Though, Connor wasn't the type to throw that fact in my face, which I was thankful for. We stood there smiling at one another for a minute, and I was probably cheesing like a fool trying to push out the words that had to come out of my mouth next.

"Okay, that's not the only reason I came here with gifts," I confessed. "Oh gosh, is it hot in here?" I began tugging on the top of my blouse, trying to air out my nerves.

Connor raised an eyebrow. "The air is on." He reached toward his phone and paused. "I can call for my assistant to bring you water, though."

"No, no. It's fine. I'm just on the brink of a breakdown, no big deal. But that does lead me to what I need to talk to you about. Or more so, ask you about."

"Oh?"

I clasped my hands and set them in my lap. "I was hoping I could interview you."

Inquisitiveness filled his stare. "Interview me?"

"Yes. I know this sounds crazy, but I work for *Passion Magazine*. Well, I did work for *Passion Magazine*. I put in my two weeks' notice before the wedding since I was planning on moving out to California with Jason, and well, now…" My words faded as my brain began to recall why I was in this situation and why I was seconds away from begging Connor to help me.

I cleared my throat and blinked a few times, forcing out a smile as I continued to talk. "I went to try to get my job back yesterday, and I guess my boss saw you at the ceremony hall. I don't know if you know it, but you are a hot commodity in the media sphere, and so many people are interested in getting an exclusive interview with you." The more I talked, the more the light evaporated from Connor's eyes. "Straight to the point, my former boss said I can get my job back if I'm able to convince you to do an exclusive interview with *Passion* by this Friday."

At this point, he was completely grimacing as he sat on the edge of the desk. His legs were stretched in front of him with his ankles crossed. His hands slid into his pockets, and the frown only deepened as he realized what I was proposing.

"I'm sorry, Aaliyah, I don't really take on interviews."

"I completely understand, but at *Passion*, we aren't the everyday interviewers. We take pride in showcasing our clients in the best light and using our words to inspire others who have enough nerve to dream big. I spent the night researching you and your story—at least the parts that are public knowledge—and I do believe what you've done is quite remarkable. I think many could benefit from knowing your full story, or at least as much as you are willing to share."

He scratched at the well-kempt scruff on his face. "I hear you, but I'm sorry. I think it's important to hold on to some privacy in one's life, and once you invite the media in, things can get twisted and messy. I'm not looking to add any more mess to my life. I just want to do good, even if it's in private."

Just like that, my already shattered heart began to crumble even more. I hadn't known the pieces to break into smaller shards, yet here I was, heartbroken and pained.

I couldn't even argue with Connor about his reasoning because I knew it was true. Once you opened the door to the world of media, they thought they deserved the right to flood into your privacy whenever they wished.

You couldn't ask for privacy once you invited everyone into your world.

I parted my lips to try to say something that could maybe convince him, but nothing came to mind, so I shut my mouth.

He frowned and shrugged apologetically. "I'm sorry, I really am."

"No, it's fine. I completely understand. Thank you for even taking time out of your day to meet with me. And thank you for everything you did for me on Saturday. You truly went above and beyond." I took in a deep inhalation and stood from the chair. My mind was already beginning to turn into panic mode as I turned away from Connor to leave his office.

"Aaliyah," Connor called. As I looked back, I noticed he'd stood up from the desk, with his hands still in his pockets.

"Yes?"

"I'm sorry for what Jason did to you. You're a good woman, and you didn't deserve that treatment. But"—he took a few steps in my direction and lowered his voice—"between you and me, I believe you dodged a bullet."

I let out a dry laugh and blinked a few times. "If only my heart could believe your words."

"Just feel what you need to feel, then one day you'll be okay again."

"Is that how it works?"

"Yes."

"Promise?"

"Promise, Red."

Each time he called me Red, I felt a little less alone.

I wanted to believe I'd be okay, but the tears began falling from my eyes, and I brushed them away quickly. I shook my head and tried to apologize for falling apart in front of Connor again. He wouldn't allow it and was quick to grab me a tissue to wipe away my tears.

"Gosh, this is so embarrassing. I'm really not a mess like this. I hardly ever cry. Unless it's like one of those videos where a soldier comes home to surprise their family. Those always bring on the water-works. Or a cute animal that's been through trauma but found a happy family. That chokes me up, but the amount of tears I've shed in the past few days with you is too much. You've probably seen me cry more than most people." I chuckled, embarrassed.

"VIP access to your emotions," he joked. "No worries here. It's a safe place."

"We should really stop meeting like this, though—with me having a broken heart."

"Hopefully, next time we cross paths, you get the happily ever after."

I pushed out a smile, but he knew it wasn't real. He frowned and studied me as if he wanted to say something but didn't know exactly what words to give. Therefore, I took that as my sign to leave his office and allow him to get back to his life. I'd already taken up enough of his time.

He looked down for a second, then reconnected his stare with mine. "Aaliyah?"

"Yes?"

"Can I hug you?"

I nodded slowly. "Yes."

He moved in and wrapped himself around me as if he were a weighted blanket and held on tight. I melted against him, not even knowing how much I needed his comfort until he unleashed it on me.

I breathed him in, smelling his cologne that rubbed against the fabric of my clothing. I lay my cheek against his chest as he rested his chin on top of my head. I remained in that same spot until I felt as if I were overstaying my welcome against his soul.

Then I let go.

"All right, well, I'm going to get out of your hair, but thank you for meeting with me this morning. And thank you, Connor, for being... you."

"Of course. I truly wish you the best, Aaliyah, and you're going to be okay."

I didn't know why, but the way he said it almost made it seem true, almost as if me being okay was the result of all the madness taking place.

"I lost my relationship, my home, and my dream job all within a few days. It's kind of hard to believe everything's going to be okay, but thank you for your kind words. Oh, before I go." I reached into my purse and pulled out two dollar bills. I placed them on his desk.

He snickered. "Making good on our bet?"

"I'm a woman of my word."

He gave me a sad smile, and I gave him one back before turning to leave, but I couldn't help but pause because I knew there was something else I wanted to say to him.

"I searched your name online last night," I confessed, meeting his ocean stare. "And I doubt it matters coming from me, but I'm really proud of you for everything you've done in life. It seems all your dreams are coming true. Not only that, it seems you're big on giving back to the world what it gives to you."

"It does," he said, crossing his arms. "It does matter coming from you."

Later that night as I sat in bed searching the internet for jobs, I was surprised when my phone dinged with a new email. A new email from Connor.

To: aaliyahwinters@passion.com
From: ConnorXRoe@roeenterprises.com
Subject: Saturday

Red,

You talked me into it. I'm hosting an open house tomorrow (Saturday) for one of my bigger properties if you'd like to come. No better time than the present to get started with the interview process, plus you can see me in action at work. Meet me at the corner of Smith & Hadley at

Trevon Tower around ten in the morning. If you have questions or get lost, here's my number. Call or text any time.

-Captain

P.S. You're going to be okay.

TWENTY-ONE

Connor

MY MOTHER BELIEVED IN MAGIC. NOT LIKE VOODOO SPELLS OR chanting kind of magic, but the magic of one's mind. She believed everything works together for the greater good and that life leaves clues for every person about the road they are supposed to walk down. My mother would've called the events of the past few weeks a sign from the universe.

I'd have been lying if I said I didn't somewhat think the same thing.

Aaliyah coming back into my life had to mean something, right? Or maybe I just wished and hoped it meant something. Either way, I wasn't ready to let her go again. On the one hand, I loathed the idea of doing an exclusive interview and bringing people into parts of my world. But on the other hand, I loved the idea of having more of her in my life. Sure, I didn't have time for a life outside of work, but in a way, this was work-related now so—business. That was what I was doing. I was taking part in my regular business tasks.

Whatever it takes to convince yourself that you don't just want to be around Aaliyah, buddy.

"Why do I feel as if I'm going to be stunned by the property you're about to show me?" Aaliyah asked as she approached me on the sidewalk. She looked as breathtaking as she always did. I wondered if she knew how effortlessly striking she was without even trying.

She wore a white dress that hugged her waistline. The way it highlighted her hourglass figure didn't go unnoticed. Aaliyah's curves should've come with a hazard warning. Her hair was pulled up into a large bun, and her lips were painted crimson.

Caution: Will Make Grown Men Weep.

"I think most people would be stunned by it. It's massive."

"I'm excited!"

"Me too. How are you?"

She pushed out a smile. "Good."

"Okay." I nodded. "But how are you really?"

Her smile faded, and she shrugged her shoulders. *Good. Be real with me, Red.*

"One day at a time. At this moment, I'm okay," she told me.

"Good. I'm glad to hear it."

"Thank you for doing this—for agreeing to the interview, even when I know you aren't fully comfortable with the idea. I want to give you my word that I will put my all into this project, Connor. I swear, I'll make this experience worth it for you." She shifted nervously in her heels as her lips turned upside down. She might've been the first person in the world who still looked beautiful while frowning. "I just don't want you to think I'm using you. I am really interested in knowing your story."

"You can use me," I confessed, shrugging. "If I'm going to be used by anyone, I'd like it to be by you."

She blushed a little. "How is it that you're still as nice as you were a few years ago? How has the city not made you jaded yet?"

"I visit home enough to still hold on to my Southern roots."

Her shoulders relaxed a little, and she locked her stare with mine. Her eyes were so soft and filled with confusion. "Why did you decide to do the article? You seemed certain that you weren't interested when I met with you."

I didn't really have a straight answer for that because I couldn't keep my eyes off her. Because I couldn't stop thinking about her. Because for the longest time, I'd imagined being around her once again. Because when she was sad, I wanted to make her happy.

Because she deserved some kind of win after so many losses.

"Two years ago in Wish Alley, I wished for more of you. I'd be an idiot to walk away when a wish came true."

"You're good at that, you know."

"At what?"

"Giving out flashes of love that help people forget they're sad for a moment."

"This can't be real life," Aaliyah muttered, walking around the penthouse. Her jaw had gone slack the moment she stepped inside, and she hadn't closed said mouth since. I'd invited her to come early to see the small details that went into setting everything up before potential clients began arriving to see the property.

That early morning, we stood inside a thirty-million-dollar property, and that wasn't even the most expensive unit I'd be showing in the coming weeks. It was a double-height duplex penthouse, and to put it mildly, it was fucking insane. The penthouse was almost nine hundred feet in the sky, giving the owners views of New York City that felt surreal. There was a 270-degree panorama of the city that featured the Hudson River, the Statue of Liberty, and the Manhattan skyline. Five thousand two hundred square feet of wealth. Four bedrooms, six bathrooms, a theater room, and a custom Bulthaup kitchen. All the appliances were smart devices, and the hidden pantry that led to a reading nook with a setup for coffee and tea was the icing on the cake.

Not to mention the private elevator, fitness room, private yoga room, and private spa suites, along with the swimming pool.

Needless to say, the modern space was unmatched, and I was ready for the offers to start rolling in.

"It's unreal, right?" I agreed. "We have our staging crew come in and make it shine with all the furniture and accent pieces. We also have caterers and bartenders come in to serve the guests."

"Connor." She breathed out. "What the heck?"

I smiled. She was in a state of shock, and I couldn't blame her. I remembered the first time I walked into a property like the one we stood in. I had dreams about the damn place for weeks.

"People really live like this?" she asked.

"A very small, small percentage of people."

"With very big, big amounts of money," she muttered under her breath as she swept her fingers against the sofa cushions. She quickly pulled her hand away and turned toward me and whispered as if caught doing a bad deed. "Am I allowed to touch this stuff?"

"Touch away." I laughed. "You can even sit on it if you want to be wild."

"Oh, no. I don't have a wild bone in my body."

"Why do I find that hard to believe? You did, after all, once run around New York City with a superhero."

She looked my way and gave me a smile. Why did my chest always tighten when she gave that smile to me?

"Connor, everything's a go. We'll have about fifty potentials filtering in and out. A lot of talk about offers being made today. We'll see what happens," Damian said, walking up to me and breaking my stare away from Aaliyah.

"Good, good. Only a bit more time before things get busy. Damian, let me reintroduce you to Aaliyah. She'll be around over the coming weeks because she's doing a piece on me."

He cocked a brow. "A piece of what?"

"You know…a piece. Like an article. For *Passion Magazine*."

He blinked repeatedly. "You're doing an interview?"

"Yes."

"You? The man who thinks interviews are the devil?"

"Yes. Me."

"The one who's turned down hundreds of thousands of dollars to avoid doing interviews?"

"Uh-huh."

"You do know your last offer was for half a million, right? Is this the half-a-million interview?"

I shook my head. "No. It's not."

"How much are you paying him?" Damian flatly asked Aaliyah, who was still rubbing down the sofa.

She looked at Damian and smiled. "Oh, only ten thousand but he asked for it to be donated to charity."

Damian shot me a 'What the hell is going on?' expression, and I shot him a 'Shut up and drop it' glare—to which he gave me a 'You're a fucking idiot' stare. I followed *that* up with an 'I know I'm a fucking idiot' look. Aaliyah didn't even notice that we held a whole conversation with just intense eye contact.

Sometimes, I felt Damian and I communicated better without words than we ever did with them.

"My boss is convinced Connor is one of the hot topics of this time," Aaliyah explained.

"The topics must be very underwhelming this year," Damian replied.

Aaliyah laughed, tossing her head back. "Yeah. We were really scraping the bottom of the barrel with this guy."

Hell, her laughter was beautiful, too. She had that intense kind of laugh that vibrated off the walls and into people's spirits. It was an infectious sound, the kind of laughter that made other people chuckle, too.

"Makes sense. I'm sure you asked others too and they declined the offer of being interviewed," Damian said. "Honestly, that's the only thing that would make sense."

"He was actually the third billionth person we reached out to this time around," Aaliyah chimed in, playing along with Damian. Most people didn't pick up on Damian's dry humor since it read as rude and dismissive a lot of the time, but Aaliyah fell right into place with it.

"You should've kept searching," Damian said.

Aaliyah shook her head and crossed her arms. "I know. I told my boss that over and over again, but alas, we had to settle with this one."

Damian almost smirked, and—*holy shit how did she get him to almost smirk?* What kind of witchcraft was Aaliyah into?

"Better get back to work. If you want to give her the bad joke today and save me from that misery, by all means," Damian said.

"Sounds good. And Damian?" I nodded his way. "Take the lead today."

He arched a surprised brow. "Seriously?"

"Yeah. I think you're ready."

"I've never shopped a property this big," he warned.

"Which is exactly why you should do it today. You got this. I'll be lurking in the shadows if you need me."

His brows knitted together, and he shrugged his shoulders. "Thanks, I guess."

"I love you, too," I joked, patting him on the back. He walked off to make sure everything was perfect around the property, and I knew he was excited. Even though he'd never pushed a property that size, I knew if anyone could sell it that afternoon, it would be Damian. Sure, he was cold in his demeanor when he wasn't working with clients, but he turned on the fake charm once he stepped into the business role.

It was amazing to witness. He could make himself give fake smiles to clients and speak elegantly and charm their pants off without a problem. Yet the moment the clients left, Damian's face would drop and he'd return back to his old Eeyore ways. The good ole bait and switch.

I bet he had to unplug completely from the world after engaging with other humans. It seemed exhausting to him.

Aaliyah kept smiling. "What a nice guy."

"Nice?" I laughed. "Most people call him unapproachable."

"I think he's funny. A very dry sense of humor. He doesn't smile much, now does he?"

"I'm still waiting to see it. I'm kind of scared for when I see a real, genuine smile from him. I don't know how I'll react."

Aaliyah let out a small chuckle, and it transported me back to Halloween night when she laughed and left that sound imprinted on me.

"Come on," I said, holding a hand out toward her. "Let me show you the rest of the place before people begin arriving."

TWENTY-TWO

Aaliyah

KNEW WEALTHY PEOPLE EXISTED. I WASN'T NAÏVE ABOUT THAT FACT. I'd seen enough episodes of *Keeping Up with the Kardashians* to know some people live a very different type of lifestyle than I had. Plus, for the past few weeks, I'd lived in Jason's penthouse. Still, I'd never seen anything like the property I was standing in.

I'd never seen so much luxury in one place, so much…money. When the people began arriving for the showing, I could tell they were the types who could afford a home like that. They moved like wealth, as if they belonged in said home. The level of confidence they oozed inspired me.

Marie always said I had to act more confident in situations, but it was hard for me.

"Fake it till you make it, darling," she'd say.

I was going to miss her knowledge. I was going to miss her.

Connor handed the reins of the showing off to Damian, who turned into the most well-spoken individual when interacting with potential buyers. That was the first time I'd seen him smile, which was a very nice look on him. He should've done it more often.

Yet the moment the buyers turned away from Damian, his smirk would drop and he'd return to his normal somber personality. It was funny how different he and Connor were. Damian was shadows while Connor was light. They balanced one another out nicely, it seemed.

"He's nervous, but you can't tell, can you?" Connor whispered as we stood off to the side, taking everything in.

"No. He's so well-spoken."

"He can turn it on and charm the life out of anyone. This is the biggest property he's had to pitch. I have no doubt he'll have an offer by the end of the day."

"I think it's sweet how much you believe in him."

"He's a good kid who was given a shitty hand. He deserves a shot at life, and he shows up daily, demonstrating exactly why he is going to take over the world one day." He brushed his thumb against his nose. "So, shifting gears—how is this whole interview process going to go?"

"Right. I was thinking about the interview and the next steps. I came up with three different topics I'd love to explore for the article. I think it would be great if you took me to three places that reminded me of your past, your present, and your future. For example, today is great for seeing your present. That way, I can see your complete story and where it is leading you."

"My beginning, middle, and end."

"The perfect novel."

"What if the ending sucks?"

I smiled. "There's no way Captain's ending would ever suck."

"I like that," he commented, nodding toward me. "That you still call me Captain."

"I like when you call me Red."

He grinned and looked away for a second as if he had something to say, but he shook it off before saying, "Anything else I need to be aware of?"

"Yes. I have some dates to shoot over to you for the photo shoot. We can always shift the date because I know you're a very busy guy, but I pulled at least five dates. Once we choose, we can set up a photographer and a shoot location."

"I'm not much of a model," he warned.

"Trust me, you don't have to do much of anything to look good."

He arched an eyebrow. "Did you just call me handsome?"

My cheeks flushed a bit, and I moved my stare from his blue eyes to a couple roaming the kitchen, opening cabinets. "Don't act surprised. You know you're good-looking. That's why people are calling you the hottest bachelor in NYC."

"Is that what they are calling me?"

"That is definitely what they are calling you. Don't be surprised if ABC calls you to audition for their show."

"Hard pass for me. Back in my hometown, my closest friend, Jax, used to watch that show with an older neighbor. I stopped by once and couldn't stand it. I could never survive being on that show."

"Why's that?"

"I don't want to go lady to lady, test-driving the car without any true desire to purchase while the whole world watched."

"Well, sometimes you have to taste a few different fruits before you know what you like."

"Yeah, but you don't shove a banana in your mouth while still chewing on a peach."

I chuckled. "Did you just so happen to pick the two most sexual fruits you could think of?"

"What? I get the banana, but what is sexual about a peach?"

Now it was time for me to raise a brow. "Are you serious right now?"

"Serious as two kangaroos fighting."

"You have the weirdest comparisons."

"And you have a beautiful smile."

I felt my cheeks heat, but I rolled my eyes to take away from that fact. "Oh my gosh, bachelor. Do these lines really work on other women?"

"Truth or truth?"

"Truth."

"They really work on other women."

I nudged him in the arm. "Let me guess—this is the part where you tell me I'm not like other women, right?"

"No, I never understood that." He shoved his hands into his

pockets and shrugged. "I mean, what's so terrible about being like other women? Women are amazing. All kinds. I feel like guys use that line to flatter a woman while at the same time putting down all other females. And who wants a cocky asshole who has to put others down to lift someone else up? It's like a backhanded compliment."

I pursed my lips. "I'm trying to determine if that's reverse psychology or not."

"Good. I'm hoping to keep you on your toes. So, back to the peach."

"What about it?"

"How is that sexual?"

The bashfulness came back to me, and I knew he noticed, but I tried to play it off. "It's what the youngsters use as an emoji to speak about someone's butt. You know because butts are...juicy and plump." I made a hand gesture to indicate a round bottom, and I regretted it instantly when Connor began cracking up in laughter.

He made the same motion as me. "So a peach."

"Yup."

"Aren't peaches fuzzy? Wouldn't a plum make more sense?"

I tossed my hands up in surrender. "Hey, I don't make the rules."

He looked so perplexed by the whole idea as he shook his head in disapproval. "I think we should start a petition to change peach to a plum."

"I'm sure that would take off if you get gen Z in on the switch. They can make some TikToks with plums. It would go viral in a week."

"Are you a TikToker?" he asked.

"I'm a professional lurker but refuse to post anything. I have a strong fear of people judging me."

"You know the best way to get over people judging you? Putting yourself out there and realizing their opinions don't matter."

I laughed. "Aw, but the fear is strong."

He shrugged. "We might as well do whatever it is that makes us happy. Life is short."

If only he knew how short life can be.

"So you're telling me you put yourself out there?" I asked.

"Oh, on the regular." He scrunched up his face and cringed a bit. "I have a confession to make. I'm a TikTok celebrity."

I burst out laughing. "What? No, you're not."

His hands flew to his chest, and he narrowed his eyes. "Wait, why is that so hard to believe? I'm definitely qualified to be TikTok famous. I have over three million followers."

"No way. That's insane. What do you do on TikTok that would make you famous?"

"I give real estate tips."

The way I laughed at him included a hardcore snicker and my head tossing back. "That's how you're getting our generation to engage on TikTok? With real estate tips?"

"Hey! You're never too young to learn about the real estate world. Plus, people get really screwed over when they purchase their first homes. They need to know more details. Plus, this way, I can help more people around the world find their dream homes instead of just in New York, and they don't end up broke doing it."

"Don't get me wrong—I think that's brilliant and just more proof that you are a genuinely good person. But...it seems bizarre that you'd have so many followers for giving useful tips."

He bit his bottom lip, and I watched as he nibbled on it.

I poked him in the arm. "What are you leaving out?"

"Hmm? What makes you think I'm leaving something out?"

"Uh, the fact that you have no poker face and you look as if you're avoiding giving me all the details of your TikTok. You know what?" I reached into my back pocket and grabbed my cell phone. "Let me just pull out my phone and look you up and—"

"Okay, wait!" he said, tossing his hand in front of my phone. "Okay. So there is a little bit more to my TikTok."

"Do tell."

"I give the tips while dancing..."

"You do TikTok dances?"

"As if it's my day job." He narrowed his blues and shook his head. "You're judging me."

"I'm not. I just...the image of you doing those dances brings me more joy than I thought possible. I bet you do them shirtless," I joked.

The way his face read guilty made me jump up and down.

"Oh my gosh! You do, don't you? Connor…" I glanced around the penthouse to make sure no one was listening, and I moved in closer to him. "Do you set up thirst traps?"

"I do not set up thirst traps!" he whisper-shouted. He went back to biting his bottom lip and sighed. "Okay, I set up thirst traps, but you have to understand…supply and demand is the way the world works."

"So you supply your knowledge, and they demand your abs?"

He gave me a wicked grin. "You think I got abs, Red?"

I rolled my eyes. "Look at your arms, Cap—your biceps are growing their own biceps. I'm sure your stomach exhibits that same level of fitness."

"What, these ole things?" He smirked as he not-so-casually flexed his arms, posing as if he was the freaking Rock.

"Oh my gosh, stop," I whispered, feeling my cheeks heat as people looked our way. "People are staring."

"Should I take off my shirt and give them a real show?"

"Only if you do a TikTok dance." I laughed. Even though he was so embarrassing, he made me laugh more than I had in a long time by simply being a dork.

"I like that, too, you know," he said as he stopped his dramatics. "When you laugh."

And just like that, he went from making me laugh to making me swoon.

I tried to shake off the butterflies that had no business existing within me, but still, they lingered.

"It weirds me out a little," he confessed, sliding his hands into the pockets of his jeans. "How easy it is to joke around with you. I mean, I have a pretty easy time being around most people—it's in my character as a people person—but being around you is effortless. You make it easy." He looked up toward Damian, who was staring our way. He gave Connor a single nod, and then Connor nodded back. "Those people Damian just spoke to will probably put an offer in tonight."

"How can you tell?"

"Because Damian almost smiled. It's a done deal. Come on, let's wander a little bit more."

I began walking with him and suddenly felt extremely light-headed. I blinked a few times as my vision blurred. The room began spinning faster than I could handle, and my heart began racing faster as I reached out for the closest wall to steady myself.

Connor instantly grew alert and moved in toward me. "Aaliyah, are you o—?"

Blackness.

Syncope.

Noun.

Definition: The temporary loss of consciousness caused by a fall in blood pressure.

Also known as the medical term for passing out.

Two years ago, I didn't know what syncope was. Two years ago, I didn't know a lot of medical terms. I didn't know the ins and outs of a hospital room. I didn't know that sometimes it took hours to be seen in an emergency room. I missed those days when I didn't know.

I sat on the uncomfortable hospital bed after being given a script for medications due to my fall. I didn't remember exactly what happened, but when I came to Connor was standing over me with concerned eyes.

I remembered a warm sensation tickling down my face as I placed my hands against my skin, then pulled my fingers back to see red painted against my thumb.

"I'm bleeding?"

"You hit your head on the side table on your fall. We should get you checked out at the hospital," Connor said.

I disagreed.

I didn't want to go to the hospital.

He disagreed with my disagreement.

He worried about a concussion.

I worried about my heart, and what the hospital might've told me.

I knew that wasn't a good reason to not go get checked out, but it seemed every time I went into a hospital, I came out with worse news than before. All I wanted to do was be normal for a moment. All I wanted to do was interview Connor, get a look inside of his world, and become a senior editor.

Regardless, Connor won the hospital visit argument. I was too tired, and my head pounded too intensely for me to put up much of a fight.

So, now I sat in the chilled hospital room, with a nurse bringing me my discharge paperwork and prescriptions. They'd given me five stitches to my forehead, and some pain medicine to help with the recovery.

I knew Connor was still in the waiting room, and the biggest wave of embarrassment flooded my mind thinking about facing him. Not only did I faint in front of him, but I did it in the middle of his work event. I passed out and bled inside of a multi-million-dollar home in front of dozens of people.

There were so many days I wished I wasn't me.

That day was high on the list.

"I'm going to need you to be more careful with yourself, okay sweetheart? If you ever start to feel lightheaded, find a close seat. Or, lean against a wall and lower yourself to the ground. Eating enough can help with the dizzy spells, too. And try not to take your heart medicine on an empty stomach, okay? And don't forget to follow up with your primary doctor." The nurse spoke to me as if I were her own child, filled with nothing but care and concern.

"I will, thank you."

She smiled and squeezed my hand. "Of course, honey. You take care of yourself."

Over the past two years, I was quick to learn that nurses were never appreciated enough for what they did. To them, I was nothing but a stranger each and every time, but they treated me as if I were their own family. They tamed my fear when it ran rapid.

"Come on," she said smiling. "Let me walk you out to the front lobby."

TWENTY-THREE

Connor

I HATED HOSPITALS. ESPECIALLY EMERGENCY ROOMS. THEY ALWAYS reminded me of the time I'd spent in them as a youth, waiting for my mom to come out okay. No matter what, she'd never allow me in the back room with her until the doctors made it clear she was okay. Mom worried about scaring me too early on with her first go at cancer.

The second time around, I was a teenager and old enough to know what was going on—but Mom still didn't allow me in the back. Instead, she always made sure I had cash in my pocket for the hospital vending machines. It was due to that time in my life that I vowed to always have cash handy. That afternoon, I was thankful for that as I waited for Aaliyah to come out from behind those two automatic doors that led people to the back for examinations.

I'd hit up the vending machine and emptied it of all the bags of Cheetos. The items looked as if they hadn't been changed out since the eighties, but lucky enough for me, the chips tasted fine as day.

When Aaliyah came out from the back, she thanked the nurse practitioner profusely, then thanked the receptionist repeatedly, and she thanked the other receptionist nonstop because that was who Aaliyah was as a person—she was thankful, even on the days when she had a million reasons not to be.

I stood from my chair the second she turned my way, and a small smile curved her lips as she nodded me over. It was so good to see her doing okay. When she'd blacked out, I had been terrified that she wouldn't be all right. She'd managed to hit her head when she fell straight onto the corner of the nearby coffee table.

"Now, that medicine they gave you will make you a little loopy," the nurse said to Aaliyah before glancing my way. "Are you the one in charge of getting her home safe tonight?"

"I am."

"Good." The nurse placed her hand on Aaliyah's forearm and squeezed it lightly. "And thank you again, Aaliyah, for the prayer for my son. It means a lot to me that you took the time to do that."

"Of course, Janet. I hope he aces his audition." Aaliyah beamed. "Nice meeting you, too, Randy!" Aaliyah waved to the other nurse. "Cheetos?" she asked as I poured the remaining chips into my mouth from the third bag.

I crumpled up the bag then pulled out the fourth—and last—bag that was tucked under my arm. I held it out to her.

Her button nose crinkled up, and she shook her head. "No, thank you. I hate Cheetos."

And just like that, the perfect woman revealed her first flaw.

"I think it's very rude of you to make such a harsh comment," I said, shaking my head in disbelief. "Cheetos are the chips of all chips."

"That's not true. They don't even make the top three list of chips."

"Okay, so what are the top three?"

Aaliyah's brows lowered, and she bit her bottom lip as she thought. "Okay, first is Doritos, obviously, then Ruffles Sour Cream and Cheddar, followed closely by Fritos."

"Are you kidding me? Those are such lame choices!"

She shrugged. "I'm not going to be judged by a man who orders boneless chicken wings."

"They are delicious."

"They are chicken nuggets. Besides, anyone who doesn't think those are the best chips on the market, are wrong."

"With each second that passes, you become much more terrifying."

She laughed. "Okay, chip snob, what are your favorites?"

"That's easy: Cheetos, Cheetos Puffs, and Cheetos Paws—though, I haven't been able to find those gems in ages, unfortunately, and they were my favorite."

"You can't just name Cheetos for your top three favorites! Those are all the same."

I cocked an eyebrow. "Clearly, you've never tried the variety of Cheetos. They are far from the same. One day, I'll teach you the ways of the most perfect chip brand in the world. For now, let's just get you home."

Just then, her cell phone dinged, and she pulled it out. The mirth in her stare slowly evaporated as her smile faded, too.

"Everything okay?" I asked.

"No...it's Jason. He said he's stopping by my place tonight." She paused and shook her head. "His place, I mean." Her eyes stayed glued to the cell phone, and I watched as her hand trembled with nerves. "That's the first message he's sent me since he left me. Do you know how many messages I've sent him since the wedding day?"

She turned the phone screen toward me. She began scrolling up, through dozens and dozens of text messages she'd sent him, begging him to contact her, begging him to reach out.

His responses were nonexistent up until that evening, and all he said was, "Hey. Back in town. Stopping by my place."

That was it.

What a piece of shit.

Her eyes glossed over when she looked up at me, and dammit, all I wanted to do was wrap my arms around her and tell her she was going to be okay.

"I'm not ready to see him. I can't go back there. Oh my goodness, I can't face him, not after what happened. I wasn't mentally prepared for this, and now I have to—"

"You'll stay with me tonight." I placed my hands on her shoulders, stilling her movements.

Her deep brown eyes looked at me with major concern. "What?

No. I already took up enough of your day today, Connor. I cannot expect you to take me in as a stray for the night."

"I'm not taking you in as a stray. I'm taking you in as a friend who's had a bad day. Besides, you shouldn't be alone with your injury."

She laughed a little, though it wasn't filled with amusement. More like disappointment. "Five stitches to the head."

"You need someone to be there for you tonight if the pain gets too bad."

"I don't think that's how it works. All I have to do is pop the prescription and call it a day."

"Listen, Doritos lady, you're going to let me take care of you tonight."

"Is that an order?"

I laughed as I finished off the Cheetos and tossed the bag into a nearby trash can. "It's an official order. Now, come on." I held my arms out toward her. "Hop in."

"Hop in?"

"Hop into my arms. I can't walk you out when you're injured."

The spark in her eyes slowly came back. "Don't be silly, Connor. I'm not getting into your arms for a head injury."

"You are. I'm going to carry you out of this emergency room come hell or high water."

"I promise you that you're not."

She shouldn't have made promises she couldn't keep because within a second, I scooped Aaliyah up into my arms, and I carried her away with me as she laughed nonstop and begged me to put her down.

The fact she was laughing made me feel like it was a job well done.

Plus, I liked how she felt pressed against my body. Almost as if she was meant to be there.

When we reached my apartment, I walked Aaliyah to the spare room. "You rest for a while, and I'll go pick up your prescriptions."

"You don't have to do that, Connor, really. I can handle it."

"I know you can, but you don't have to. Don't argue and let me do this." She nodded in agreement and handed me the paperwork needed for the prescriptions.

I headed off to the drugstore, and as I stood in line waiting to pick up Aaliyah's pain meds, my mind began to swirl back to memories I wanted to keep buried...memories of standing in lines and waiting to pick up medicine for my mother. Each step I took toward the pharmacist, my chest grew tighter. My breaths were becoming labored as I tried to inhale and exhale in a normal pattern.

When I reached the front of the line, the woman behind the counter smiled and said, "Hi, there. Picking up a prescription?"

"Yes. For Aaliyah Winters."

She walked over to the bins of pills and began thumbing through them.

My hands were sweaty, and I tried my best to ignore the thoughts that began flying through my mind. The recollections I'd worked to keep locked away within me were trying to resurface. I was fighting them. I was trying my best not to fall into the pain my mind was trying to unleash. Yet when she walked back and asked me if I had insurance, the wave of memories came rushing back to me.

TWENTY-FOUR

Connor

Sixteen years old

"**H**ERE ARE THE PRESCRIPTIONS. MAKE SURE TO TAKE ONE of the nausea pills before you go to bed tonight. It will help," the nurse instructed Mom as she walked through the hospital doors she'd entered over two hours earlier. I'd been sitting in the waiting room, waiting for her to come out. Waiting for answers. Waiting to know if she was okay.

I rose to my feet the moment I saw her and rushed over.

"Are you good?" I asked, my voice cracking. I'd eaten almost everything out of the vending machine and felt as if any bad news would send me into a vomiting rage.

Mom gave me a small smile. She looked a bit pale in the face, and even her smile felt as if it were a bit of a struggle for her.

"I'm okay." She grinned.

It felt like a lie.

It had to be a lie.

Mom always lied about feeling okay to make me feel okay.

"What do you need?"

"Just to go home and rest, sweetie. I'm tired."

I scratched at the back of my neck, my nerves not easing up any. "Do you need prescriptions filled? I can drive us to the drugstore."

"It's fine. I can pick them up later and—"

"Mom," I cut in, scolding her for the ridiculous idea.

She lightly chuckled. "When did you become the parent of the household?"

"I'm not," I said, shrugging and allowing her to loop her arm with mine. "I'm just your favorite sidekick."

She leaned against me and didn't feel heavy at all. "My favorite sidekick," she muttered as I walked her to our car. I helped her get into the passenger seat, and she sat back and allowed herself to melt into the cloth. Her eyes shut, and her arms rested in her lap as I buckled her in.

"I'm sorry about this, Connor," she whispered. "You're too young to have to deal with any of this."

"I'm the man of the house—it's what I'm supposed to do."

She tilted her head in my direction. Her eyes were filled with guilt and sadness. "It's not what you're supposed to do."

I ignored her because I knew the conversation wasn't going to go how either of us wanted it to go. I was never going to let up about being the one to care for her, and she was never going to let up about me needing to act more my age.

"Did they call in the prescriptions?" I asked, shifting the topic back to the things that mattered in that moment.

"They did. They should be ready soon."

I nodded as I buckled my seat belt and put the key in the ignition. We drove to the pharmacy, and I tried to convince Mom to stay in the car, but she knew she'd have to deal with the insurance issues. Therefore, she came inside with me.

I stood back a little as she spoke to the person checking her out. My stomach was in knots as I listened to their exchange.

"I'm sorry, ma'am. Your insurance doesn't cover the costs. It seems you've reached your maximum, so it will be one hundred and fifty today," the cashier said with a lowered voice. It wasn't lowered enough for me to miss the words, though, maybe because I was listening a little too closely.

Mom sighed and pinched the bridge of her nose. "I can't afford that until next week when I get paid, but I need them now." She studied the prescriptions in front of her. "Which ones can I get by without having at this time?" she asked.

Before they could reply to her, I stepped forward and pulled out the old tattered wallet I'd gotten at a thrift shop. I pulled out the money I'd made from my part-time job and laid it on the counter.

Mom turned to me with widened eyes. "Connor, no."

"It's fine, Mom. I got you."

"No, no. I can move things around in my account and—"

"Mom." I gave her a comforting smile, and the anxiety that sat on her shoulders deflated.

"I'll pay you back next week," she promised, moving the money over to the cashier.

She meant it, too.

I'd take the money so she didn't feel lesser than, but any money she gave me would somehow be routed back to her, even if it meant me picking up groceries or taking her on a movie date or whatever.

The money she paid me back with always ended up back with her.

We went home that night, and I stayed on the sofa with her, watching movies. My mind was running in circles the whole time, trying to figure out how I could fit another part-time job into my schedule to help some more.

TWENTY-FIVE

Connor

Present day

AFTER I RETURNED HOME, I MADE SURE AALIYAH WAS OKAY, then I buried myself in my work. Even as I worked on emailing people back and collecting more details from Damian on the property he'd found in Queens, I couldn't stop replaying the situation that'd taken place with Aaliyah. Seeing the way she had panicked once she saw Jason's text message, I knew it must've stirred up some intense emotions. She'd been pretty quiet since she arrived at my place, keeping to herself in the guest room.

After a few hours of working, there was a knock on my office door, which was already wide open. I looked up to see Aaliyah with a glass of water in her hand. Her lips were smiling, but her eyes refused to do the same.

"You're still up," she stated, leaning against the door, probably to keep from tumbling over from exhaustion.

"You're still up, too," I said, turning away from my computer.

She smiled, and I felt the broken cracks that were trying to break through that grin. "Are you a workaholic, Mr. Roe?"

"It depends on how fast my mind is spinning each day." That evening, after spending time in the hospital, my mind had been spinning extra fast.

She walked into my space and sat down on the floor. Then she patted the floor beside her.

An invitation I didn't think I could pass up.

I lifted my glass of whiskey and walked over to her, taking a seat on the floor. She sipped at her water and gave me that smile that looked so good on her.

"You really shouldn't work past a certain hour," she told me. "Your mind needs breaks."

"Sometimes, the only way my mind gets a break is if I'm working."

"Fair enough." She glanced around my office with awe in her eyes. "I think my boss would fire me if she found out I was sleeping over at my client's house again."

"To be fair, I wasn't your client when you first stayed over. Plus, I'm really good with secrets."

"Is that so?"

"The best, actually. I have a special location in my brain where I keep people's deepest, darkest secrets caged away."

"Well, it's very nice of you to be such a trustworthy source of secrecy."

"I take it to heart when someone tells me a secret. So, don't you worry. Your boss will never know about your night spent with me."

"Thank you. So, why does your mind do that?"

"What?"

"You said your workload depends on how fast your mind is spinning. What makes your mind spin so fast?"

I smirked. "Is this off the record?"

"Scout's honor." She saluted.

"Were you a scout as a kid?"

She cocked an eyebrow. "What? No, I'm a journalist."

"Then you can't say Scout's honor. It doesn't mean anything if you aren't a scout."

"Potato, po-tah-to." She waved me off in a dismissive fashion. "No matter what, I'm not going to tell anyone what we talk about tonight. Your secrets are safely locked in the secret chamber of my brain, too."

I thumbed the rim of my glass. "I overthink everything. I sometimes think I live in the future more than I live in the now. In order for me to slow the speed of my mind, I focus on what's in front of me. That normally includes working."

"Why are you so afraid of the future?"

I chuckled. "Who said I was afraid?"

"Your eyes when you talk."

"I'm having some déjà vu of when we first met, and you read me," I joked.

"I thought about you a lot after that night together," she confessed. "Even after we went our own ways, you stayed on my mind for weeks...months."

"That went both ways."

"Truth or truth?" she asked me.

"Truth."

"Did you ever go back to any of the places we promised not to go?"

I smirked. "Once or twice. I mean, you can only leave so much up to destiny. I just wanted to see you again. I apologize for breaking our agreement."

"It's all right. I broke it, too—mainly because the comic bookstore was epic in insane proportions. The nerd in me was called back to that place."

"Fair enough."

"I did, however, glance around the corners a few times, hoping to find you."

"Seems destiny handled the whole bringing us back together angle all on its own."

"Why are you sad tonight?" she asked, throwing me for a complete loop.

Her stare stayed intensely focused on me as if she was trying to peel back more layers of my story. After all, her job as a journalist was to get to the root of the story. Not only to explore what was on the surface but to truly dive deep into the meat of a person's soul.

She was the first person in my life who looked my way and saw past my smile.

Most people looked at me and believed the smiles. Aaliyah was different. I wasn't sure how I felt about that realization. The last thing I wanted was for her to see my scars from the past that still had enough power to haunt me.

"You don't have to answer that," she offered. She must've witnessed my discomfort, too.

I took her up on the offer because I wasn't ready to open up about how the hospital trip had taken me back in time to a period I tried to forget.

Luckily, she understood and smiled, then averted her eyes to go back to sipping at her water. "For a large chunk of my life, I lived in both the future and the past. Growing up without a family, you think about the past a lot. Like what made my parents give me up to foster care? Where did I come from? What are my roots? Then about the future—it's a whole new set of fears. Will I ever get to create my own family?" She lowered her head, and a somber look found her. "I guess that answer is becoming clear now with Jason."

"He's a dick and didn't deserve you. That doesn't cancel out your chance at a future."

"Sometimes, it just feels as if time is running out."

I nudged her in the leg. "You're young. You have your whole life ahead of you."

She paused and locked those brown eyes with mine. For a split second, she parted her lips to speak, but she shut her mouth quickly. Then she smiled. "Needless to say, living in the moment is important. This is all we truly have." She held her glass up and cheered. "To this moment."

"Cheers to this moment," I said, clinking my glass with hers.

"Hear, hear!" She took a sip. "Although, honestly, I'm a bit worried about my soon-to-be future. I need to find a new place to live, and the search has been hard. I can't keep living at his place. But, I also know my price point isn't great to get a decent place, at least not until I get my raise at *Passion*."

"Move in with me."

The words left my mouth without any thought or hesitation. The funny thing was, after they came out, I didn't have an ounce of regret. I meant it. She shouldn't have to live in that place. Plus, I didn't hate the idea of seeing her every single day. The more time I spent with Aaliyah, the more time I craved.

She laughed. "Yeah, okay, Connor."

"No, I mean it. Move in with me. It's a three-bedroom, three-bathroom pad. It's huge! Almost four thousand square feet, so there's plenty of space. You won't even have to worry about finding a place until you save up for a while and then don't have to move into a shithole."

Her laughter died down after she witnessed the look on my face. "You're joking, right?"

"You said it yourself, you love my place."

"This is ridiculous. There's no way you can be serious about me living with you."

"Why wouldn't I be serious? I think it actually works out great. My place is big enough that we have more than enough space for you and your things. I think it's a brilliant idea. Plus, it gives you more time to find your forever pad. Then you're not rushing into the market looking for a trash place to live. It could be an in-between, a place you stay before getting to the next one, especially since you're getting a raise when you become a senior editor soon—"

"If I do a good job with your article."

"You'll do a great job."

She released a low sigh. "That's too much, Connor. Plus, I can't invade your personal life like that. So thank you for the kind offer, but—"

"I haven't even shown you the best part yet," I urged, cutting her off. I stood and held my hand out to pull her to her feet. I led her to my bedroom. "I'm a bit of a nerd when it comes to hidden passageways, so when I saw this place, I knew I needed it." I walked over to my walk-in closet, and she appeared confused when she followed. It was gigantic, and everything was organized to a T. Still, she wasn't connecting the dots of what I was trying to show her.

I smiled, then pushed a button, which made the rack of clothes automatically shift to the right and reveal a hidden door.

"What does that lead to?" she asked, intrigued.

"Go ahead and find out for yourself."

I stepped to the side and allowed her to go open the door for herself. When she did, a staircase was revealed, leading to the rooftop of the penthouse. She followed the stairs, and when she reached the top, she gasped.

The space was filled with beautiful plants and flowers, along with stunning patio furniture. A two-person wooden swing sat facing the most perfect view of the city, leaving her in awe. You could see every single light that twinkled in the distance.

"The city lights," she whispered, placing her hands over her chest as she stood close to the edge of the railing.

"I know how you love the views," I said as I walked over toward her with my hands in my pockets. "There are no lights in the world like the eastern lights."

"That's the truth." She smiled as she stared into the night. The sky was fast asleep, yet the city was vibrant with life. "When I was a kid, I used to run away from my foster home whenever I felt overwhelmed and alone. I used to climb up the fire ladders of this one building in Queens, where I could see all the city lights. I'd stand there and breathe in and out as I stared into the night. I don't know why but seeing the city lights brought me an odd sense of comfort."

"Why's that?"

"It's silly and probably doesn't make much sense, but I always felt alone as a kid. I didn't grow up with friends, and I had no family. Lonely was something I thought I'd always be. But it was different when I saw the city lights. It reminded me that even though I felt alone in the world, I wasn't alone in a sense. Every light stood for a person to me, someone out there who felt love, felt pain, felt life. It was a reminder that even when my life felt dark, the light was around the corner."

Staring out into the night, I remained quiet, seeing what she saw and loving the way her mind worked.

"As I said, it's silly," she whispered, seeming nervous about her confession.

"No, it's not that." I shook my head. "I'm just trying to figure out how Jason was stupid enough to let you go."

Her cheeks reddened as she bashfully fiddled with her fingers. "It wasn't just Jason—every guy before him. Maybe some girls are simply meant to be temporary things."

"Maybe," I agreed. "But I don't think that's what you are."

She smiled. "Everything's temporary. We just wish it wasn't." She shifted around and released a soft sigh. "This is quite the view."

"If you think this is something, you should see it in the fall," I offered. "And in the winter, and the spring, and as long as you need to see it, you should see it."

"You really mean this, don't you? You're actually offering for me to move in with you?"

"Yes. Of course, you don't have to say yes, but I want to help. I have the ability to offer this to you, so that's exactly what I'm doing."

"That Southern boy heart." She lightly laughed.

"You can take the boy out of the country," I said as I shrugged, "but you can't take the country out of the boy. Take some time to think about it. No rush and no pressure—I just wanted you to have the choice."

She nibbled her bottom lip. "If we do this, we have to have rules."

I perked up. "I'm fine with rules. Rules and I go hand in hand. Shoot them my way."

"Okay. For starters, if it ever gets to be too much for you, you have to tell me."

"Easy."

"And if you have a girl over, I am more than willing to go stay at my best friend's house, so I don't cock-block."

Mirth filled my smirk. "Did you just say cock-block?"

"I did, and I mean it. I'm sure you have a rotating list of women you keep in contact with."

I gasped, and my hands flew dramatically to my chest. "Okay, did you just call me a manwhore? Red, I'm hurt."

"Hey, you said it, not me. I'm just saying I don't want to get in the way or change your life too much. I don't want to be a burden."

"Nothing about you is a burden."

"Please stop doing that, Connor."

"Doing what?"

"Being so ridiculously kind to me."

"Well, okay, now it's time for me to be a hard-ass and not so kind because I have a few ground rules, too."

"Okay, shoot."

"For starters, ESPN is the background noise during dinnertime."

She laughed, and I wanted to dive into the sound and allow it to swallow me whole. God, her laughter was addictive. "I think I can do that."

"And you can't get mad when I leave my socks around the apartment."

"I think that rule should go both ways," she agreed. "Also, you can't laugh when my socks are mismatched—which they always will be."

"Okay, and the last rule: you have to let me know when I'm talking to work Aaliyah or roommate Aaliyah. I don't want you to quote me on something in an article that I meant to say to my roommate and work Aaliyah got ahold of it."

"I think I can agree on all of those rules."

"Well, good. Then do we have a deal?" I held my hand out toward her.

"Deal," she said, shaking my hand. "But I will pay rent, you will accept it, and I am officially offering you an IOU for anything and everything you might need from me in the coming days, weeks, or months."

"Sounds good. I'll keep that IOU tucked in close to me for when I need it. Welcome home, roomie," I stated before she dropped my hand.

I looked out to the city lights, took in a deep breath, and released it slowly through my mouth. I didn't know why, but the idea of Aaliyah staying with me brought a level of peace over me, as if she was always supposed to be there. I was certain she thought I was helping her out, but I felt as if I was the one who'd won. Being around her felt like being around the better part of me.

TWENTY-SIX

Aaliyah

I WAS MOVING IN WITH **CONNOR ROE**, MY FAVORITE SUPERHERO. I couldn't even wrap my head around the fact, but I felt a strange sense of comfort about the idea. Whenever I was around him, I felt safe, which didn't make much sense. In the grand scheme of things, we hadn't known one another that long, but at the same time, I felt as if we'd been connected for years.

Even so, I couldn't really focus on the move until I handled a certain issue that kept popping up in my life. Ever since the wedding that never happened, I'd received an influx of messages from Jason's mother. Voicemails, text messages, emails—she'd tried to reach out to me on every platform multiple times.

Marie: Hey, Aaliyah. Are you coming to the book club meeting this week? The ladies are asking about you.

Marie: We should grab a coffee. I miss you, sweetheart.

Marie: Have you heard from my son?

Marie: I know you need space, so no need to respond to any of my messages. Just know that I'm here, and I'm sending them so you know you are loved, and Walter and I miss you. Maybe we can grab a drink, you and me? I'm worried about you.

Marie: You have your scheduled doctor's appointment this week, right? I had it marked on my calendar. I hope everything is going well. Please let me know, Aaliyah. I'm worried.

I was trying my best to set a boundary with Marie, letting her know I needed time and space to regroup, but I felt awful about the idea of her sitting and worrying about me and my health conditions. Therefore, every now and again, I'd shoot her a text message to let her know I was okay.

Greta from work told me I owed Marie nothing, not even a second of my time or energy. She said Marie was being passive-aggressive with all the messages she sent me, and perhaps that was true. But the guilt of ignoring her messages was getting to me, especially with all she and Walter had done for me in the past. Even though Jason hadn't treated me right, that didn't mean his parents hadn't. Jason and I ending our relationship was one thing, but ending the relationship I had with his parents—Marie more so—was turning out to be harder. I felt my bond with her more than Jason's and my connection. I considered her a friend.

But after the breakup, I knew Marie would become a casualty of our relationship falling apart. Over time, she'd create reasons in her mind that I was at fault for Jason and me not working out somehow. She wouldn't even know she was doing it, either. She'd just get information from her son, the child she raised, and he'd manipulate her thoughts into believing he'd been wronged by me.

In the end, she'd always side with her family member. That was how life worked.

I'd officially reached the point when I knew I had to cut the cord between Marie and me. Even if I'd miss her friendship, I knew I had to put a stop to it before it took a toxic turn.

"Thank you for meeting with me, Aaliyah," Marie said as we sat down in the coffee shop we used to frequent regularly. The comfort and ease I always had with her wasn't there that morning, though. If anything, I felt entirely out of place sitting across from her, as if I no longer belonged there.

"Of course. I figured after all the messages you've sent, we should just get it over with."

"Get it over with? What do you mean?" she asked, hurt in her voice.

"Aren't you looking for closure? I'm not sure what else could happen for us after everything that took place with your son."

"No, not at all. I refuse to believe you and I cannot stay in one another's lives. You don't know what it means to me that you've come into my world, that we'd crossed paths all those years ago right here in this café. I love you, Aaliyah, and I don't want what my son did to change our relationship. Plus…" She hesitated as if she wasn't certain she wanted to speak her next words. "He still loves you, honey."

I huffed, completely thrown off and disgusted by her words. "Excuse me?"

She reached across the table, took my hands in hers, and squeezed. "He loves you, Aaliyah. I know he does. He just got cold feet."

"His toes must be ice crystals by now, seeing as how he hasn't once tried to reach out to me."

"I think he's scared of how much he cares for you. He's never been that vulnerable with a woman before."

I pulled my hands away from her hold. "He cheated on me, Marie."

Her eyes widened, surprised by my words. "What? No. Where did you hear that?"

"I have my sources. Listen, I understand you're hurting and confused by all this, and I get it. I still am, too, but this is too much for me. You know I care for you, but Jason and I are over."

"Don't say that. You haven't even given a second thought to giving him another chance."

"I'm sorry…did you not hear me? He cheated on me."

"Young men cheat sometimes—that's what they do."

Her words baffled me to the point that I was left speechless.

That's what they do? That was her response to finding out Jason cheated on me?

"I'm sure it was an accident," she told me.

"Did his penis accidentally fall into some woman's vagina?" I mocked.

I saw the flush of color hit her cheeks, and I couldn't blame her. That was the most straightforward I'd ever been with her, but there wasn't really another way around it. He had screwed another woman. There was no accident involved. It was a choice he made.

"I know my son isn't easy, and he has a history of mistakes, but I see his potential. With the right woman, he could be as stable and grounded as his father. Walter used to be young and wild, too. I tamed him."

"Potential isn't something worth staying for because it may never come. Plus, it's not my responsibility to tame a man."

She released a heavy sigh. "Maybe if you meet with him. Maybe if you talk in person…" She was spiraling, and it was all becoming a little too much for me. When would she start connecting the dots that whatever it was Jason and I had shared was nothing more than a made-up story? There had been a point when I'd thought what we had was real, but it was wishful thinking.

He wasn't the only one in the wrong for what had happened. I had make-believed for too long in the situation. I was in a rush, trying to settle down before my time ran out. I wanted a family so much I fell into the arms of a man who was never strong enough to hold me.

I took the blame for the mistakes I'd made, trying to create love in a place where it was never meant to grow. I owned up to my flaws, and I'd have to deal with them in my own time. But I knew for certain that going back to Jason would never, ever be a situation I'd fall back into.

"If he wanted to meet with me, Marie, he could've, but he doesn't, and I don't want to meet with him either. I'm moving on with my life. I'm moving out of his place this Sunday, and I will be leaving the key at the front desk for him whenever he's ready to return. It's over."

"You can't truly believe that, Aaliyah. After everything we've been through…" The tears fell from her eyes, and she wiped them away, only to have more begin to fall. "You're our family."

I hated that she was crying. I hated that I was the reason behind her hurting. She'd come into my life at one of my lowest points, when I was scared and alone, and given me comfort, not to mention all the medical expenses she and Walter had covered for me without a second thought. They truly had been my family for a short period. But if I stayed in her life, I knew it would become toxic. I didn't want that for either of us.

"Plus, there's the issues with your health," she said, trying to compose herself. "You need me."

"What do you mean?"

"When we met with the transplant team, you selected me as your designated support person. If you do end up receiving a heart transplant, you'll need me. Remember how they told us that you'd need that person to look after you before and after a transplant? I have to stay in your life. You have no one else, Aaliyah."

I knew she didn't mean for her words to sting me, but they did. It felt like a punch to my soul.

I have no one else.

I cleared my throat and blinked away the emotions building up inside me. "If that becomes an issue down the line, we'll deal with it. I'll switch it over once I find someone new."

"But—"

"I'm sorry, Marie. I can't keep holding on to this. You've gone above and beyond for me over the years, truly. But now that Jason and I are over, I think it's time to let go." I shrugged my shoulders and grabbed my to-go cup of coffee. "Maybe some things just aren't meant to be forever. I'm sorry, Marie. I have to go pack."

"Where are you moving to?" she asked.

"I don't really feel comfortable telling you that information."

She combed her long straightened black hair behind her ears and shook her head. "You're making a huge mistake, Aaliyah, by walking away from my family."

It was already happening. She was beginning to shift blame to me, as if I were the one who'd caused the current issues. She made it seem as if I was the one who had called off the wedding and was severing our connection. That blame would only build over time, making me the villain in the story. Leaving now was the best option for everyone involved.

I cleared my throat and stood from the chair. "I wish you the best, Marie, but please, to make this easier for everyone…stop calling."

I hadn't received a message from Marie since I told her we needed to cut all ties. Therefore, my attention was completely on packing up my things and moving on from Jason's world.

Connor went above and beyond to help me with the move. When

I tried to talk him out of hiring movers for me, he told me he wouldn't take no as an answer. "It's a good reason to get together for an interview session," he'd said, giving me an excuse to have him help me pack up my boxes.

I took him up on the offer. The sooner the boxes were packed, the sooner I could be out of Jason's place.

"You're a collector," Connor commented, taking my snow globe collection off the bookshelves in the living room.

I looked up from the box of dishes I had sitting on the kitchen counter-top. "I like things to look back on. Each snow globe has a story behind it."

He arched an intrigued brow as he lifted one. "Where's this one from?"

After setting the plate inside the box, I walked over to Connor and took the snow globe from his hand. It was a woman sitting at a desk writing. My lips turned up at the memory that came rushing back to me.

"I got this one the day I graduated from college with my journalism degree." I placed the snow globe into the box.

"What about this one?" he asked, lifting up another globe.

The moment I saw it, my smile evaporated. I took it from Connor and stared at it. There were two ice skaters at Rockefeller Center right in front of the Christmas tree. I shook the snow globe and watched the snowflakes fall over the couple.

"Jason got it for me after his family took me ice skating for the first time," I explained. I walked over to the trash bin in the kitchen and tossed it inside. "I'd rather not hold on to that. Plus, looking back, it was actually his mom who pressured him to get it for me. He didn't even spend his money on it."

Connor crossed his arms. "For some reason, that doesn't surprise me. His parents are gems."

"Yeah. I figured over time, he could become more like them. Are you two close? You and Jason?" I asked. I'd been wondering about their relationship and about Connor's thoughts on the subject since it took place.

He laughed. "Close? No, not at all. Jason and I haven't always seen eye to eye. Not only on the business side of things but on the lifestyle side, too."

"Everyone said he was a party animal before me."

"That's true."

"I don't know why I thought he'd change for me...I don't know why I thought I'd be the one to tame him, but when we were together at first, it seemed real. He seemed really into me. He gave me all of his time and attention at the beginning."

"Love bombing—it's one of his specialties with his new girls. He floods them with time and attention, making them feel like they are the most important thing in his world. Then, he slowly starts to shit on them, making them feel unworthy of him."

I huffed. "So I was just another one of his targets. His whole persona changed when we moved in together."

"A fraud can only hide its true colors for so long. The mask always falls off."

Before I could reply, my cell phone began ringing, and Katherine's name popped up on the screen. "Hello?"

"Hi, Aaliyah, it's me, Katherine. From downstairs," she whispered, making me snicker a little.

"Yes, I know. Your name popped up on my screen. What's going on? Why are you whispering?"

"Oh, because I don't want anyone to hear me, but I needed you to know Jason is on his way up to you. Like he's on the elevator. Like, right now."

I stood straighter, alert. "What?"

"I just wanted to give you a heads-up since I know you're packing and all and—oh! Got to go." She hung up the phone, leaving me there as if I were a deer in headlights.

"What is it?" Connor asked.

"Jason...he's here. He's on his way up now." I locked eyes with him, alarm shooting out of every inch of me. "You need to go."

"What? Where?"

"I don't know, but you being here will just make it awkward. And I'm freaking out and sweating, and I, uh, I don't know. Can you go into, like, the spare bedroom for a bit? Because I can't face him and then also have him asking why you're here. It's all too much."

Without any more commentary, he headed to the spare room and closed the door behind him.

Within seconds, the front door opened, and I was face-to-face with the man who'd stood me up on the most important day of my life. As he stood there, staring at me, he looked weak. Pathetic. Like someone I never truly knew.

"Hi," he said as he crossed his arms. "What's up?"

What's up?

That was what he decided his first words to me in person should be? My blood began to boil as anger built up inside me. I had thought I would crumple the moment I saw him. I'd thought I'd fall apart and cry. Instead, I felt an intense amount of irritation.

"You didn't tell me you were coming here," I said.

"I know. I figured it might be best if I just surprised you by stopping by. My mom told me you were moving out today, and well…" He raked his hand through his hair. "Do you really think that's a good idea?"

"Are you kidding me? Why in the world would I stay?"

"I don't know, Aaliyah. This just seems pretty sudden, that's all."

He was talking as if I'd upped and decided to walk out on our relationship, as if I'd made a rushed decision to move on with my life.

"Jason, what in the hell are you talking about? You called off our wedding. There's nothing sudden about me moving out. Honestly, I should've been gone a long time ago."

"You don't have to raise your voice."

"I'm not raising my voice!" I snapped, clearly heightening my vocals at that very moment.

"See why I didn't reach out to you after calling things off? I knew you would react like this," he muttered.

"React like what? You know what, I don't even know why we are having this conversation. It doesn't matter. I'm moving on, and I'm assuming you're doing the same. So, if you'd excuse me, I'd like to finish packing so I can get out of your place."

"What if we didn't, though?"

"Didn't what?"

"Move on?"

My chest tightened. What in the world was he talking about?

He took a step toward me. "Aaliyah—"

"Stop," I scolded, holding my hand up in front of me. "Don't come closer."

"Why do you have to be so dramatic all the time?"

"Excuse me?"

"You're acting super emotional for no reason. Yeah, I messed up, and I get that, but that doesn't give you a reason not to give me another chance."

Was he drunk? High? Did he really believe there was any part of me that would want to give him another chance at hurting me again after he left me? I wanted to curse him out. I wanted to yell, and I wanted to scream, but I didn't. I didn't want to give him any more of me. I wanted it to be over.

"Jason, I'm going to finish packing, you're going to move on with your life, and I'm going to do the same."

"We took care of you," he said. "When you couldn't do things, my family had your back, not to mention the bills for your—"

"I get it, okay? Your family has gone above and beyond for me, and I'm grateful—but you can't toss that in my face. I never asked for any of what you've done for me. If needed, I'll pay all the money back."

"As if you have the time to pay it back. It would take you years."

Those words were meant to cut me deep, and they did. Just another reminder of time and how mine was limited, another strike to my soul that I'd spent my precious time on the planet getting into bed with someone like him.

"You and I are done," I said, not showing the emotion he'd come so close to pulling out of me.

He stared for a second, studying every inch of me. He was waiting for it to happen, waiting for me to crack, but I wouldn't. I couldn't give him what he'd come for. It was as if he derived pleasure from watching me ache, so I stood strong.

"Your loss," he said coldly. How had I ever thought that man was who I wanted to spend forever with? He was a monster. I'd climbed into bed with a monster simply because I was afraid of lying alone. "I should've never even listened to my mom about coming over here today. I knew it was a lost cause."

"Your mother told you to come here?" Why would she do that? Especially after I told her it was best to cut ties? A last-ditch effort to try to get me to change my mind?

"Yeah. She tried to pressure me to get back together with you and—"

"Do you love me, Jason?"

He paused and arched an eyebrow. "Why would you ask that?"

"Because it appears you were trying to please your mother by being with me."

He shrugged his shoulders. "She wanted you and me to be a thing more than I ever wanted us to happen. She thought you'd be good for me. That's why she pushed it so much and offered me..." His words faded, leaving me wondering where his thought was going.

"Offered you what?"

"It doesn't matter. It wasn't even worth it. Clearly, this is over. Good luck with whatever kind of life you have left. Leave my key in the foyer." He turned and left, slamming the door behind him. Even though he left, his words still struck me hard.

Whatever kind of life you have left.

At that moment, I felt nothing but regret for wasting more than a year of my life with that man. I couldn't believe I'd ever fallen into his arms. The truth was, I had only stayed because I loved his parents. I loved the idea of family. I loved feeling as if I were a part of something concrete.

I'd fallen in love with a lie in order to hold on to the idea of fake dreams coming true.

"You okay?" Connor said, coming into the living room.

I turned to face him and nodded. "I hate him."

"Good because I do, too."

TWENTY-SEVEN

Connor

"WHAT IN THE WORLD...?" AALIYAH'S WORDS FUMBLED out of her mouth as we stood in my apartment. It was the first time she'd been over since she decided to become my roommate, and the movers were just now starting to bring things inside. She turned around and faced me, stunned. "Connor. What the heck?"

"I figured we should've switched bedrooms. This one is bigger." I'd moved all of my crap out of the bigger room because I knew it was better suited for Aaliyah. She could easily spread out in the king-sized bed and relax to the fullest extent, which she deserved. Plus, the whirlpool tub was better in the master bedroom, and I figured she could use some peaceful nighttime soaks to unwind from the craziness of her current life.

"There's no way I'm taking the master bedroom. It's yours."

"Well, I already switched all of my clothes over to the other two spare bedrooms, so unless you want me to do that again...which, please don't make me do that again."

"Why?" she whispered, shaking her head in disbelief. "Why would

"I wanted you to watch the sunrises and sunsets."

She smiled, and I loved that she was doing that. She walked over to the bed, where a large basket sat. Inside of the basket was a bunch of bath bombs, candles, and bags of Doritos along with a variety of snacks. I tossed in some of my favorites, too, to enhance the snacking experience. Plus, I tossed in a few blank notebooks and fancy pens because what was a writer without a notebook and pens? Then the television remote because I figured that was the utmost important part of a bedroom experience.

On top of the basket was a note that read, "Welcome home, Roomie."

Aaliyah's fingers grazed over all of the items, and she shook her head in disbelief. She then moved her stare to the nightstands on each side of the bed where vases filled with sunflowers sat.

"Those are my favorite flowers," she said, stunned.

"Yeah. You casually mentioned it when you came to my office to give me roses."

"And you remembered."

I hadn't enough nerve to tell her that I remembered everything she told me. From her favorite flowers to the wishes she'd written in Wish Alley two years prior. Aaliyah Winters was someone I wanted to remember for the rest of time. To that day, Halloween night was still one of my favorite memories.

"I'm having a hard time believing that I haven't had a mental breakdown somewhere along the line, and you're just a figment of my imagination," she said.

I chuckled and crossed my arms. "Well, don't become sane anytime too soon. I kind of like existing in your imagination."

"I like that you're here, too."

She walked around the bedroom and entered the bathroom. "Holy shit!" She came dashing out quickly. "Connor! Did you see that tub?!"

"Yeah, I saw it."

"It's a freaking swimming pool!"

"Don't be dramatic. It's more of a hot tub if anything."

"There's a TV hanging on the wall! Who has a TV in their bathroom?!"

"People who exist in imaginary minds of a woman who is having a mental breakdown."

"Don't wake me up from this trip," she joked, shaking her head back and forth. "This is too much. You're too much."

"My mother's been telling me that since the day I was born. Now, let's get all these boxes moved in, and then we can order in some dinner or something. We can even eat out on the rooftop if you want to watch the sunset."

I turned to walk away, and Aaliyah called out to me. When I looked back at her, she stood still, and her brown eyes flashed with emotions as her perfect, full lips parted. "Thank you, friend."

"For what?"

"Existing."

After the movers came and went, Aaliyah and I ordered food and headed out to the rooftop to enjoy dinner with one another. It didn't take long for me to realize that Aaliyah was one of the healthiest people I'd ever come across, which surprised me a bit. Two years ago, she was downing chicken wings drenched in ranch as if she was a competitive eater, and now she didn't drink or touch fried food. As I ate my burger and fries, she chowed down on a kale salad with some kind of lemony vinaigrette.

"For a long time, I thought you were an all-around perfect girl, but tonight you kind of killed that idea as you began eating kale," I said, shaking my head in disappointment.

She laughed. "It's not that bad. It's actually good if you massage the dressing into the leaves and let it sit for a while. Plus, the grilled chicken is full of flavor. And my green drink—"

"Just admit you don't like things that taste good, Red, and leave it at that. You're eating grass and drinking grass."

"Listen, do you know how much fat and unhealthy chemicals are in your burger and fries?" she asked.

I held up a stern hand. "No, and you better not tell me. Otherwise, we will be roommates at war."

"I'm just saying. What you put in your body has a big effect on your overall wellness. A bit of kale wouldn't hurt you, Cap. Greens are your friends."

"And a few fries wouldn't hurt you either," I said, waving one in her face. "Life is about balance. And for your information, my burger has a slice of tomato and some lettuce. And what is that I see?" I took the top bun off of my burger and dangled a piece in the air. "Is that an onion and pickles? I'm pretty much the healthiest man alive."

She tossed her hands up in surrender. "Okay, health nut, my mistake. I need to be more like you."

I held a fry in front of her face, and she took a small bite of it. Her eyes almost rolled into the back of her head because Charley's Diner seasoned fries were the best fries in the history of potatoes.

I smirked. "See? What's life without a bit of deliciousness?"

She stabbed a piece of kale and held it in my direction. "Open up."

I pressed my lips together and shook my head. "Nuh-uh," I said through my closed mouth.

"Connor! Fair is fair."

I kept my mouth locked closed. "Life'snotfair," I mumbled.

"You're so dramatic."

"Iknowbutthat'swhoIam." I shrugged, she laughed, and my God, I was so happy she didn't marry that asshole.

She gave up and pushed the fork into her own mouth, allowing me to part my lips in victory.

"One day, I'm going to get you to eat a kale salad," she warned.

"Don't hold your breath. If my mother couldn't get me to do it, a beautiful lady won't be able to do it either."

"Don't flatter me."

"Don't be so beautiful then." Her cheekbones shined through as she grew bashful. I threw a french fry her way. "Don't blush like you don't know you're beautiful."

"I don't take compliments well," she said, tossing the fry back my way, and like the professional fry eater I was, I caught it with my mouth.

"That's because you're too humble. You should stop being so damn humble. You're the shit, Aaliyah. You work at one of the top magazines in the world as an editor, you are educated, you are a great person, and you are hot as fuck—"

"Don't say hot as fuck," she said, blushing even more.

I placed my hands on her shoulders and shook her back and forth as I hollered, "Aaliyah Winters, you are hot as fuck, and the whole world deserves to know it!"

"Oh my gosh, Connor, shut up!" she whispered, covering my mouth with the palm of her hand. "You're so extreme."

She wasn't wrong.

"I'm just saying. You are the shit, and you need to start acting like you're the shit."

"But I don't feel like I'm the shit. I honestly feel...weak."

"Who cares, though? Fake it till you make it."

She raised an eyebrow. "What?"

"Life is created by habits. We teach the world how to treat us, and that all comes down to how we treat ourselves. I learned this at a young age. When I moved out to New York, I had one thousand dollars to my name, and no idea what the hell I was going to do. All I knew is I needed to act like I was a rich man in order to get through the doors of real rich men. I faked it until I made it. I walked into every room as if I belonged there. I drank whiskey with people who are billionaires. I attended galas and parties for the elite when I still only had pennies in my bank account. You know why I was invited?"

"Do tell."

"Because I showed up as if it would be their loss if they didn't invite me. Confidence is a repeated habit. Act confident in your own skin until it becomes your outer layer."

She narrowed her eyes in thought. "Fake it until I make it?"

"Yeah, and don't take life too seriously. Life is short, might as well learn how to laugh at yourself sometimes, too."

"Sounds like you need to be my life coach." She laughed. "I mean, let's be honest, you kind of were my life coach on that Halloween night all those years ago."

"Yeah, which by the way, makes me extremely confused. Because afterward, you were falling back into self-love. I thought we really had some breakthroughs that night. Color me shocked when two years later I find out that you were engaged to the bane of my existence. Like, how, Red?! How did you end up going from where we left off to ending up with Jason Rollsfield? As your temporary life coach, I was hurt by that discovery."

She laughed lightly and shook her head. "What can I say? I didn't have enough time to observe your knowledge. You were a flash of love for me, and then reality came back, and I fell back into my old patterns. Maybe if I had more time to learn from you, it would've stuck better, but it was hard to hold onto something that came and went in a flash of an eye."

"All right," I said, rubbing my hands together. "We can start again."

"What?"

"We are going to get back to our training. It will be easier now, too, seeing how you are my new roommate, and I can help you discover the parts of you that I already know exist. So, this time, it's not about trying to get you to fall in love with me; it's getting you to finally, truly fall in love with yourself."

"Are you serious right now?"

"As serious as a heart attack."

Her eyes flashed with momentary emotion, and for a second, it almost looked as if she were going to cry? Did I say something wrong? It didn't take long for that look to evaporate from her eyes, and she gave me a lopsided smile.

"Why do I feel as if this is the best and worst idea in the whole wide world?"

"Uh, because it is the best and worst idea in the whole wide world." I leaned in toward her. "Say yes?"

She nibbled on her bottom lip, hesitating as she fell into deep thought. She released a weighted breath and shrugged. "All right...yes. I'm in."

"Hell yeah! This is going to be fun. I do have a few questions for you, though. To help me figure out the best direction to take this challenge."

"Like?"

"Do you care what others think of you?"

"Absolutely."

"Are you a people pleaser?"

"I aim to please."

"Do you ever say no when asked to do something?"

"Oh, gosh no. I like people to like me."

I shook my head. "What if I told you that people don't actually like you, but they like what you do for them?"

Her eyes flashed with an intense vulnerability. "Well, that would make me very sad."

"Why's that?"

"Because I think people only do like me because of what I do for them. And if I don't do things for them, then they probably wouldn't like me very much. Which means...I'd be lonely."

"Red...that's ridiculous. You are the most likable person on this whole planet. But people take advantage of that because you are too good. So I'm going to teach you to set boundaries."

She wiggled her body around. "That makes me uncomfortable."

"Good. It should. We aren't here to be comfortable; we are here to grow. And believe me when I say, once you fall in love with yourself, the right people will come who expect nothing from you at all."

"Promise?"

"Promise." I tossed a few fries into my mouth. "I think for research, perhaps we need to look into why you ended up with someone like Jason to begin with."

"That's easy...I loved his parents so much and the feeling of family that I lied to myself about who he really was."

"Why did you lie to yourself, though? I don't get it."

She tilted her head, seemingly baffled by my confusion. "Because the lie felt more comforting than the truth, and if I didn't have that lie, then I'd be alone."

"What's so scary about being alone?"

"Everything," she confessed. "Everything's scary about being alone."

That made me sad for her because I knew what loneliness felt like. Maybe not as deeply as her because I was pretty content with my loneliness. Sometimes, women came into my life for random flings, but I'd learned to enjoy my own company.

"I'd rather be alone by myself than lonely with someone else," I told her. She smiled, but it felt so sad. I reached across to her and took her hands into mine. "Red, by the end of this, you're going to be stronger than you ever thought. You're going to wake up and feel full without the need of another soul, but it will take some time. I'll be right here beside you, too. You're going to be confident, and strong, and not take anyone's bullshit even if their lies feel a bit comforting. You're going to learn quickly that it's so much better to sit in moments of ugly truths than swim in beautiful lies."

TWENTY-EIGHT

Aaliyah

"**T**HERE IS NO WAY IN HELL I'M PUTTING THAT ON," I said, standing in the living room with my hands on my hips. It had only been twenty-four hours since Connor had become my life coach, and he had already lost his freaking mind.

"Oh, yes the hell you are."

There he was, standing in the middle of his home, wearing a banana outfit. He was grinning ear to ear like a dork as he held my costume in his hand—a plum.

"You're insane."

"Yes," he agreed, then held the costume out toward me. "Now get dressed."

"No way. I refuse to become a plum."

"If you're interested, I have a peach costume in my bedroom," he offered with his devilish smirk.

"Where did you even get these?"

"Amazon Prime, same-day shipping."

Thanks a lot, Jeff Bezos.

He began shaking his banana around as he came toward me.

"Come on, Red. You had no problem exploring New York with me two years ago in costumes."

"That's because it was Halloween night! Everyone was in costumes."

"Since when do we care what everyone's doing?"

"Uh, since forever?"

He walked toward me, with his banana end poking me in the side. "Which is exactly why we are going to do this. We are going to step outside of the mold and do what no one else is doing. We are going to make fools of ourselves because the more comfortable we become with being uncomfortable, the more comfortable we will end up."

I blinked a few times. "Nothing about what you just said made any sense."

"All I'm saying is, we are going to have a fun day being weird and exploring the town dressed as sexually charged fruits because we don't care what other people think of us. Life is too short not to have fun and dress up like fruit on random Saturday nights."

"You're so weird."

"Yes." He held the costume out toward me. "Now, go get dressed." I parted my lips to argue some more, but he placed his finger against my lips, shushing me. "You promised you would let me coach you. Now, come on. Let's get this going."

Reluctantly, I put on the plum outfit and came out feeling like a complete fool. I was round, plump, and a nice vibrant purple.

Connor's face exploded with laughter as he stared my way. "Oh my gosh, this is so much better than I'd imagined it to be."

"There's no way I'm leaving the house like this," I told him.

"You are definitely leaving the house like this. Come on, we gotta go." He walked over to his dining room table and picked up a huge boom box. Why in the world did he have a boombox? This guy was so weird in the best of ways.

"Where exactly are we going?" I asked. "And why do we need a boombox?"

"We're going to Times Square to put on a show," he told me, grabbing his keys off the coffee table. "Let's go."

A show? What? No. Nope. I didn't sign up for any public acts of humiliation.

"I'm sorry, Connor. I'm already drawing the line at any kind of show performances. I don't have that level of confidence."

"I know. Which is exactly why we're doing it."

"We're not doing it."

"Oh yes, Red." He nodded with the biggest smile in the world. "We are."

"No." I stomped my feet. "We aren't."

Next thing you knew, I was standing in the middle of Times Square, dressed as a plum next to a male banana, as he put a cassette tape into the boom box. Where did he get a cassette tape?!

People were staring at us, but most of the people who looked on were tourists, which made me pleased to know that I'd probably never see them again. What made me less than excited? The cell phones in their hands as they began recording Connor and me.

"Connor, this is too much for me," I said, feeling silly.

"No, not yet. This is going make it too much for you," he explained, hitting play on his boom box. Within seconds, "What a Feeling" by Irene Cara came blasting through the speakers. Was he truly playing the song from *Flashdance*?

Then he began dancing around like a madman. He was humping his hips around with his banana, thrusting the air and spinning around and around. "Dance, Red," he said, waving my way.

I felt so extremely embarrassed as people laughed at him leaping around like wild.

"I can't dance like people aren't watching, Connor," I warned.

"Good. Dance as if they are. And then don't care what they think." He came over to me and took my hands into his. He squeezed them. "Aaliyah."

"Yes?"

"Do you trust me?"

His eyes were so sincere as he asked me. He was filled with hope and excitement, and trust...

Crap.

I trusted him.

So I allowed him to pull me into his arms, and the plum danced with the banana. We spun around faster and faster, taking the world on, and the more I danced with him, the more I laughed. The more I laughed, the more I forgot about the bystanders. The more he twirled me, the more freedom I found.

We danced to a lot of songs, each one filled with positivity, and when the last song came to a halt, when we hit the final note, I asked Connor to play the cassette over again.

Having Connor come back into my life felt like a blessing I didn't deserve. At times, I wondered if he were even real, or if I'd somehow slipped into an unbelievable make-believe world where superheroes really existed and swooped in to save the day.

Talking with Connor was like talking to an old friend you hadn't seen in years but truly cared for—effortless. All of the charm he'd had two years earlier was still there tenfold. He didn't know it, but I was in desperate need of his friendship.

Though, his life coach tasks were a bit overwhelming at times. He'd even given me a list of homework to tackle each morning.

1. Dance around my bedroom to a positive song.
2. Say no to someone you love.
3. Have a cheat meal.

I was still building up the courage to tackle number two and three on the list, but number one came pretty easy for me, seeing how Connor had left of list of positive songs for me to pick and choose from.

"Firework" by Katy Perry

"Best Life" by Cardi B (feat. Chance the Rapper)

"All I Do is Win" by DJ Khaled

"Can't Stop the Feeling" by Justin Timberlake

"You Got It" by VEDO

His list was a great start. At first, I felt silly doing the act. I didn't know how it helped me learn to love myself, but if I could dance in the middle of Times Square as a plum, then I could easily dance around my bedroom. I did it first thing in the morning after taking a shower. I'd wrap a towel around me and move my body as if I hadn't a care in the world.

I added more songs to the playlist, too.

"This is Me" by Keala Settle & The Greatest Showman Ensemble

"I Am" by Yung Baby Tate (feat. Flo Milli)

"Brown Skin Girl" by Beyoncé

Even on the mornings when my self-doubt was louder than the music, I danced. On those days, I danced more. I'd begun to dance in front of the mirror completely naked, looking at my body and all the flaws my ex-boyfriends pointed out. My stretch marks. My too small chest. My fat ass. All of it stared back at me as I moved my hips.

I began singing along with the songs, allowing them to vibrate all across my skin.

"Oh, hell yeah! It sounds like a dance party in here!" Connor said one early Monday morning, walking into my bedroom waving his hands in the air.

"Oh, my gosh!" I screamed, turning around to face him, completely naked. The only piece of fabric on my body was the towel wrapped around my hair.

"Boobs!" he shouted, hurriedly turning around and covering his eyes with his hands. "Oh, shit! I'm sorry, Aaliyah! I just heard the soundtrack from *The Greatest Showman,* and I always get excited about *The Greatest Showman*, and I'll be honest, I didn't expect to walk in on the greatest show, man," he rambled, making the redness deepen in my cheeks but also making me snicker a bit from how embarrassed he'd been for walking in on me. I think his face reddened more than mine.

"Also, sorry for yelling boobs. What am I? A teenage kid who just saw his first set of tits? I mean, it wasn't. I've seen boobs before. Many. Well, not many. But not few. Definitely not few. I'd seen a completely normal, average number of breasts throughout my adulthood. Not a weird low and not an absurdly high number either. But you know what I mean, your boobs aren't the first pair I've seen, which means I probably shouldn't be shouting out boobs toward you like a freaking psychopath even though, I mean, what I'm trying to say is your boobs are worth shouting for. I mean, fuck, I'm going to go now," he said, his nervous energy shooting throughout his system. He began hurrying away with his eyes covered.

"Connor, watch out for—"

Bam. He walked straight into the doorframe.

He held a hand up and waved. "I'm fine. I'm fine. Okay. Leaving. Bye."

With that, he was gone, leaving me with no discomfort. Only laughs.

TWENTY-NINE

Connor

BOOBS, BOOBS, BOOBS.

Fuck. Not just boobs. They were more than just boobs. They were breasts. Full-grown, homemade, deliciously plump and perky breasts. Aaliyah Winters was a masterpiece. I didn't need to see her naked to remind me of that fact, but holy shit, seeing her naked? Not a regret of mine.

Sure, I should've knocked on her door. That was roommate 101, but I wasn't thinking at all. When I heard good ole Hugh Jackman and his gang singing, my body just responded to the sounds.

Breasts, breasts, breasts.

Dammit, Red, why did you have to look like that? So perfect? So curvy, so smooth, so damn desirable.

All I wanted to do was walk over to her and let my hands wander— which were probably thoughts I shouldn't have been having for a new roommate. Especially seeing how I was her new unofficially-official life coach. My thoughts weren't really morally correct to have about my new client, but at the end of the day, I was just a man. A man with an extremely hardened dick sitting in my office the morning after finding

I listened to her music playing in her bedroom that morning, and I wondered if she were dancing again. Naked. With those breasts exposed.

I leaned back a bit in my office chair and closed my eyes, clearing my throat. My mind began thinking about her moving to the music, her hips swaying back and forth, her body moving in the most mystical way.

Her lips. Her collarbone. Her nipples. Her lips—different set of lips that time.

All I wanted to do was move with her, dance close with my body pressed up against her skin. Unfortunately, all I had was my hand and my cock to create some kind of pleasure. I slid my sweatpants down and gripped my cock. I began stroking it up and down, thinking of Red, of her body, her curves, her.

Fuck, I wanted to taste her. I bet she tasted like the greatest high.

I repositioned myself in my chair, leaning back more as the strokes became more intense. Gripping myself harder, I imagined it being Aaliyah's mouth moving up and down my cock, taking me all in as I pinched her nipples. I'd pull her on top of me next, having her sit on my face, letting me taste her, suck her, fuck her hard until she came all over my face. I'd lick up all of her delicious juices as she—

"Connor, I'm ordering in some—oh, my gosh!" Aaliyah screamed, forcing me to open my eyes as I was seconds away from an exploding orgasm hitting me and—oh fuck, nope. Couldn't stop that train from going because it had already left the damn tracks.

"Fuck!" I shot up from my chair and turned my back to Aaliyah. I hurried over to the corner of my office as I unloaded all of my dirty thoughts into my trash bin. "Fuck, fuck, fuck," I moaned. Yup. That was right, friends. I was moaning as I got off into a trash bin because even with my embarrassment, an orgasm was an orgasm, and shit, it felt good. Afterward, though, shame was all that was left.

I felt like a kid who got caught with a *Playboy* magazine. Aaliyah somehow was both the *Playboy* magazine and the individual who'd caught me with it.

I turned around to express my extreme humiliation and apologize for her walking in on what she walked in on, but when I looked behind me, the door was closed and she was on the other side of it. Thinking back on it, I should've probably shut the door before I started yanking my cock, but you know what they said, an idiot was always going to be an idiot.

"I'm sorry! I saw your door was open, and well, I was going to ask you if you wanted me to order you some breakfast," Aaliyah exclaimed from outside the door.

"Right, yeah, no big deal. Sorry about that."

There was a silence for a moment.

I felt like a complete moron.

A dirty, filthy moron.

Then Aaliyah's voice came back.

"So…" She paused for a moment. "Do you want scrambled eggs? I would offer you some sausage, but I think you're all set with that."

I snickered to myself, feeling my humiliation began to fade. She could've allowed the situation to be uncomfortable and odd, but she went with humor instead.

Damn.

I really liked that girl.

THIRTY

Aaliyah

THE FIRST FEW WEEKS OF LIVING WITH CONNOR WERE SO EASY—even with our embarrassing moments. If anything, those experiences made us more relaxed and comfortable around one another. After he saw me dancing naked, and I saw him, well…fully awake, we'd crossed off most of the awkward parts of having a roommate.

Check and check.

If I were honest with myself, which I was trying to be more and more each day, I'd say I wondered what he was envisioning as he sat back in his office chair, stroking his hands up and down.

Yup, both hands.

He needed both for his massive Captain America. His Incredible Hulk. His Iron Man. Thor's hammer. I bet he could knock a woman right out of Asgard with that thing.

Swing that hammer, Connor, swing.

After the unfortunate interactions—well, maybe unfortunate for him, but I didn't mind my view—we created rules where doors should be closed during a person's, um, intimate moments. And if a door was

Other rules were created, too.

We'd made up the rule that any interview topics would be left outside of the household, so he'd have a safe place to return to after his long days at work, which were frequently very long days. Even though I left the article aspect of his life outside of his home, he brought his workday into what was supposed to be his haven.

Some days, he'd get home around ten at night, and he'd go straight to his office and dive back into doing work until the wee hours of the morning.

On Sunday morning, I'd awakened early to go visit Grant's grave for my weekly trip, and I was surprised when I saw Connor still sitting in front of his computer. I knocked on the doorframe, and he looked up, appearing exhausted.

"Early morning or late night?" I asked.

He glanced at his watch and groaned as he rubbed his hands over his face. "Late night. What are you doing up so early?"

"On Sundays, I go out of the city to visit Grant's tombstone. I get up early so I can catch the sunrise with him and read some comic books."

He rubbed the sleep out of his eyes and gave me a lazy smile. "That sounds amazing."

"It's a tradition that I've adapted."

He stood up from his chair and walked in my direction. "Can I come with you?"

I was a bit taken aback by his request. I'd spent months with Jason trying to get him to join me, but he always said it was too early and just plain odd.

Connor asked without even being invited to come. Plus, he was running on no sleep.

"Aren't you tired?" I asked him.

"We can whip up some coffee to take with us," he said. "I remember you talking about Grant a few years back, about how important he was to you. I'd be honored to meet someone that special to you."

The way he said "to meet" made the butterflies swirl in my stomach. As if Grant was still alive and well.

"If you want to come, I'll be glad to have you."

"I do," he promised. "Let me get the coffee brewing, then we can head out."

Once the coffee was ready, we were on our way to see Grant with blankets and comics galore. When we arrived, Connor laid out the blankets for us to sit on and smiled as he stared at Grant's tombstone. I sat down, and he followed my steps, sitting right beside me.

"There're a lot of quarters," Connor noted.

"Yeah, I leave one every single time. Grant believed that if a penny was lucky, then a quarter had to be twenty-five times as lucky. Whenever I find a quarter, I figure it's a kiss from Grant. It's stupid, I know."

"There's nothing stupid about that."

"Jason thought it was," I told him.

"Jason also thought Italy was a continent. His opinion is mute and void."

I snickered. Touché.

"Can you tell me stories about him?" Connor asked, bending his legs and resting his crossed arms on top of his knees.

"You really want to hear stories about Grant?"

"Yeah. Stories about him and you together. I want to know everything you want to share with me."

That felt so odd to me. Jason never asked, and he never wondered. But Connor seemed so interested in knowing more about my past, more about what made me into the person I'd become. Talking about Grant felt like talking about a parent. He meant the world to me, and I loved how when I began to speak, Connor listened intently to every word that left my mouth.

Then he read the comics to Grant and me, which made my heart begin to beat for him. He didn't have a clue how much his showing up with me meant. It felt so special to have someone to watch the sunrise with as I sat at Grant's grave.

When it was time to leave, Connor pulled out his wallet, grabbed a quarter, and left it on the tombstone for Grant to have. I wondered if Connor had any clue how good of a person he was.

Each day, I loved waking up and not being alone in the household. Something was comforting about having someone else in the penthouse with me, even if Connor and I weren't always interacting. I liked knowing that if something ever went wrong, someone was right around the corner.

Still, I worried about Connor and his work habits.

One night, I woke up around three to go get a glass of water, and I found him sitting in his office typing away. His shoulders were rounded forward, and exhaustion sat heavily on his face. I didn't interrupt him, but the image stayed with me for a few days until I felt as if I needed to step in. I might've been crossing a line, but when he came home from work one night, loosened his tie, and sat grimacing, I knew he needed a break. I was even more certain that he wasn't going to give it to himself.

His office door was closed around ten p.m. that night, and I could hear his heavy sighs. I knocked twice, and he invited me to come in. I carried a package behind my back to help persuade him to take a break.

"Hey, Red. What's up?" He smiled genuinely, but I saw how tired his eyes were.

I leaned against the doorframe. "You need an RB."

He raised an eyebrow. "A what?"

"An RB—a roommate break. Come on. You've been killing yourself in the office, working way too hard, and you need a break."

"As nice as that sounds, I don't really have time for a break."

"Well, you need to make time. Otherwise, your body will start to break down, and you need your body to function correctly. Nothing good comes from working yourself to death."

"You sound like my mother," he muttered before growing wide-eyed. "Ah, shit, I forgot to call my mom back. She's going to leave me a million messages about it."

"It's okay. You can call her tomorrow after a night of good rest and some RB time. Come on."

He raised an eyebrow. "You aren't going to let up on this, are you?"

"No, I'm not. Plus, I have a surprise for you if you agree." I pulled the box from behind my back and held it out in front of me.

His eyes narrowed. "What's in the box, Red?"

"I guess you'll have to stand and walk away from your paperwork to find out, Captain."

With hesitation, he pushed his chair back and walked in my direction. He ripped the tape off the box and gasped when he saw what was inside.

"Are those...?" he whispered.

"Yes."

"And they're for me...?"

"Uh-huh."

He reached into the box of treasures, also known as Cheetos Paws, and I smacked his hand away before he could grab a bag. "Nope! None for you until RB is agreed upon."

"Where did you even find these?"

"A good player in life never shares her secrets. Now, what do you say? Do we have a deal?"

He swiped one of the bags from the box, opened it, and began shoving the Cheetos Paws into his mouth. "Deal," he said with his face stuffed, grinning like a kid on Christmas morning.

We took the chips along with some other snacks and drinks up to the rooftop to talk. My only goal for the night was to get Connor to relax a little. I could tell he put too much pressure on himself to take over the world and do good with the power. All I needed was for him to take over himself for a bit of time and learn to slow down.

We asked each other all kinds of questions. Like always with him, the conversation came easily, and I witnessed when the relaxation finally began to settle over him as he chose to live in the moment.

"If you could have any animal as a pet, what would it be?" he asked me as he finished off his third bag of chips.

"Oh, that's easy. A dog."

"I knew you'd be a dog person."

I nodded in agreement.

"I used to volunteer at a humane society for abused dogs. It blew my mind the kind of torture humans would put those poor babies through. We'd gotten some who had been hurt and harmed more than they ever deserved. They had a lot of trauma, anxiety, and depression when they arrived, but they let us near them over time. Did it take a while for them to build up their trust? Yes, but once it was there, they gave us love so freely. No creature on the planet loved unconditionally like a dog. Sadly, if their abusers came back, they'd still give them love. This world doesn't deserve dogs."

"I couldn't agree more. If I had time for a dog, I'd definitely get one."

"Sometimes, you have to make time in life."

He smiled. "I think I'll start with RB time and ease my way into getting a dog."

"Make sure to adopt, don't shop! There are a lot of babes out there who would change your world for the better."

"Yeah," he said, his blue eyes looking into mine. His dimples deepened. "I bet there are."

I had to look away from him because whenever he stared for too long, my stomach filled with butterflies. I began picking at my fingernails to distract myself. "You know what saying I've always hated?"

"Do tell."

"Men are dogs. Why would people disrespect dogs like that? Dogs are loyal, even on your shittiest day. You can yell and scream at them, and they are still going to crawl into your lap and love you. Sure, maybe they have accidents in the house or chew on your shoes, but you see the real guilt in their eyes from making the mistake. And they learn. Dogs are loyal, and they learn! Men are just...men. And that's the worst thing I could think to call them. Not pigs. Not rats. Not snakes. Men are men." I looked toward him and offered an unapologetic smile. "I mean, no offense."

"None taken. You can include me in that group."

"But you don't treat women badly. You actually avoid getting involved with them and wasting their time. That's different. Jason gaslit me. He said the right things in the beginning until he thought he had me locked in. After I moved in with him, he showed me his true colors. It was always a game with him. You don't play games. You don't even enter the ring because you don't want to waste a woman's time. That's noble."

He waved his hand back and forth. "Er, I'm not sure if it's nobility or just blatant fear."

"What in the world could you be afraid of?"

He smiled. "A lot, Red."

Gosh, those dimples should've come with a warning. Connor Roe was almost the perfect package. He had the looks, he had the personality, he had the charm. The only thing missing was his commitment to having actual relationships.

"I lie to myself on the regular."

"About relationships?"

"Yup. I mean, I do work a lot, and I am a workaholic, but if I wanted to, if I really wanted to, I could be in a relationship."

"Then why are you single? You could get any woman you wanted. You're far from a jerk. You're charming and giving, and I've recently learned you are TikTok famous. You'd probably go all out and record your partner's TikToks for her and make her famous, too. So what's the reason?"

"Do you want a bullshit excuse or the truth?"

"I think you and I do truths best."

"I haven't found love because I haven't been looking," he explained. "I think love is beautiful. Hell, that's why I live for flashes of love in my life. But the forever kind terrifies me because I know how much it can hurt when it goes wrong. My mother almost died twice in my lifetime. It wasn't a sudden thing, either. She had two battles with cancer, and each time, I watched her suffer. I had to come to terms with the idea that I wouldn't have a mother at a young age.

"That nearly killed me. I never wanted to go through losing someone I cared about that much again, so I don't let myself get close with others on that personal level. I'm afraid of the forever kind of love because with love comes loss, and nothing truly lasts forever."

We'd shared many pieces of ourselves throughout our interactions with one another, yet I felt like Connor's current information was actually the rawest he'd ever been with me. He was sharing things with me that I was almost certain he hardly shared with himself.

"It's funny," I replied, combing my fingers through my hair. "I think I'm the opposite of you. I chase after love because I've never had it. If I had a chance to have a mother, I would scoop it up, even with the idea of losing her. Having love once, to me, is better than never having had it at all. The problem with the way I chased love, though, is I ended up with people like Jason and my ex before him, Mario. I gave myself freely to people who probably didn't deserve me at all."

"Wow." He breathed out, shaking his head back and forth as he slow-clapped.

"What?"

"It's just nice to hear you finally realizing what I realized from the first moment I met you—that you're a prize."

I crinkled up my nose and shrugged. "Only took two men cheating on me, a failed marriage attempt, and a pretend life coach to get me here."

"Doesn't matter what it took as long as you arrived. Is it my turn for a deep question?"

"Shoot it my way."

"Did you ever try to find them? Your parents?"

I pushed out a short-lived chuckle. "Yes, and I always ended up with dead ends. I gave up a few years ago because what was the point? How long could I search for someone who wasn't searching for me?"

"How unlucky of them to have never known you."

My lips parted as our eyes locked, and I swore my damaged heart started beating for him. I gave him a shy grin before shaking my head. "Don't do that, Connor."

"Do what?"

"Make me feel important."

His dimples deepened.

Goodness, I shouldn't have liked that so much, but I did.

"Hey, Red?"

"Yes, Captain?"

"You want to go record a TikTok dance with me?"

THIRTY-ONE

Aaliyah

THE HARDEST PART OF LIVING WITH CONNOR WAS THAT HE WAS insanely attractive and kind. It truly should've been illegal. No one should've been that handsome and nice—it ruined all other men. One of his favorite hobbies was to walk around shirtless on the regular. Some days, he'd come into the living room area dripping in sweat, and my lady parts tingled as if they hadn't seen a shirtless man in ten years.

It wasn't only his fit, muscular body that oddly turned me on, though. It was the way he went business mode on phone calls and spoke as if he was the HBIC—head bachelor in charge. He was thorough with every conversation he held and spoke with authority. His strength was sexy.

On the flip side, his bad jokes turned me on, too. Just watching the way his mouth moved when he spoke, how sometimes he'd bite down on the corner of his lip when he was trying to recall a punchline. Sexy.

And when he cooked? Holy crap. He turned me on when he made eggs. I was hot and bothered when he burned toast.

His laughter, his frowns, his goofy smirks. Everything about him pulled me in, and I didn't know if once it was time for me to move on, I'd be able to let go. The more he existed in my world, the more I craved for him to stay. The more I hoped he'd notice me as more than his roommate, more than his friend.

"You sure this looks okay?" Connor asked as we stood inside an old warehouse for his photo shoot for *Passion*. He was dressed in a designer forest green velvet suit that fit him in all the right places. His hair was gelled back, and he had a makeup team touching up his face as I stood nearby watching.

The whole crew around us was setting up for his photo shoot with one of the top photographers in the industry, Jean Paxon. She'd shot for the royal family in the past, so having her at our shoot felt extraordinary.

"You look amazing," I told him as I held his coffee and my tea in my hands. "Besides, there will be outfit changes and whatnot. You're in the best hands, and remember, you're already a pro at this kind of stuff with your TikTok."

"Uh, this is kind of more advanced than some silly social media app. They have like fifty lights set up! Plus, this magazine is going to be in stores. The last thing I need is to end up taking crappy pictures because of my ugly face."

I rolled my eyes. "You don't have an ugly face, Connor."

"You think I'm pretty, Red?" he said in a whiny, annoying voice.

"No. You're hideous. Your nose is crooked, your lips aren't full, and your eyes are too far apart—but we can fix all of that in editing. I just need you to get a somewhat decent shot so I don't lose my job. Now here, take the coffee and stop whining."

He smirked and nudged me in the arm. "Aw, I think you're kinda pretty, too."

What a dork.

"Also, I like your lipstick. Red on red. That's a good color on you."

My cheeks flushed.

I hated that I loved when he complimented me. It only made me secretly want him more.

If he felt any kind of nerves about the photo shoot, I couldn't tell at all. The moment he was given direction from Jean, Connor fell right in line. His skill at looking professional yet sexy as hell was impressive. He also came off as soft and approachable in some of the laid-back photos he took. I loved the stills of him laughing the most because they captured his heart.

When it came time for the shirtless photographs, which Jean insisted on taking, my cheeks heated up instantly.

"Holy shit," a crew member muttered beside me as she stared at Connor's rock-hard body. "I can only imagine what's hidden in those pants."

Thor's hammer, ma'am.

Thor's hammer rested inside those pants, and it had powerful force behind it.

Did you know if you looked up the word Connor on Urban Dictionary, you'd find the second definition to say it stood for a huge penis? I couldn't make that up if I wanted to, and from my own personal observation, it seemed Connor's name was very fitting for his... assets.

Sometimes, my internet searches took me to odd places.

"Is he seeing someone?" she asked. "I might have to shoot my shot."

The hairs stood straight up on my body as she said those words. "Uh, yeah, he's seeing someone," I lied.

Yup, that's right, I lied.

I lied because the idea of any woman shooting her shot with my guy—err, my *roommate*—made a rage begin to rumble inside me. Who did this woman think she was talking about shooting her shot? Talking about his privates? Had she no shame in drooling over a grown man who was simply trying to do his job?

He's not a piece of meat, lady! He's a human being! Have some respect.

Also, did she not pick up on my context clues? I'd been throwing them out all day. I wore red lipstick because I'd hoped Connor would notice—which he did. My blouse wasn't buttoned all the way to the top. Actually, two buttons were undone, *thankyouverymuch*. Also, my calves were on full display and looked amazing in the four-inch heels I would regret later that night due to foot pain.

For goodness' sake! Did she not notice I was on the verge of physically humping his leg on set? I was seconds away from throwing my bra at his face. My *red* bra. Red!

How didn't she see that? Didn't she pick up the vibes I was spewing?

The level of disrespect was disgusting. Connor Roe was off-limits.

I tilted my head, not taking my eyes away from Connor's abs.

"Gosh, lucky girl. I'd give anything to have just a day with him."

"I know, right?"

"And his lips…shit. I bet he could do the craziest things with that mouth of his. I'm probably going to dream of that man tonight."

Don't you fucking dare!

I almost felt bad for lying to her, but was it really a lie? She asked if he was seeing someone, and Connor kind of was. Me. He was seeing me. He saw me in the living room, the kitchen, and on the rooftop. He saw me doing yoga some mornings, and he saw me at the dining room table at night. You could basically say we were getting pretty serious.

Oh, God. I was losing my marbles. Connor needed to put on a damn shirt ASAP.

For our last location of the day, we moved to Central Park, where Connor wore gray slacks and a button-down white shirt with the sleeves rolled up. He looked perfect in the most effortless way. I couldn't help but notice people—men and women—passing by and taking in how handsome he was.

It was impossible to not take note. If he hadn't been in real estate, he could've easily been a model.

"Red, get in here," he said, snapping me from my thoughts that had been all about him. "I need some shots with you."

I laughed. "Oh no, I'm good. I'm better behind the camera."

"No. I need shots with the one and only person who's ever interviewed me. This is a big milestone, so come on."

"It is a good idea," Jean agreed. "For the records. Even if not in the magazine, it will be a nice memory. Come on, will you?"

I looked down at my overtly exposed chest, and then I heard Connor groan. "Stop it. You look breathtaking as always," he said, waving me over.

The hesitation was strong, but I didn't want to keep the crew from packing up and finishing their day. Maiv would kill me if we went over our time slot and spent more of the budget.

I hurried over to Connor, and he quickly instructed me on the positions we were supposed to take. "Just pretend we are a power couple, like Harry and Meghan, or Beyoncé and Jay-Z," he whispered. "Stand back to back with me," he said.

I did as he told me.

We stood back to back, side to side, and then, without prompting, he scooped me into his arms and swung me around, making me crack up laughing.

"Oh, my goodness, stop, Connor!" I screeched, but he kept going, spinning me round and round, faster and faster until he brought me back to solid ground. I felt dizzy and lightheaded. As I began to stumble a bit, he caught me, holding me in his arms.

He rested his forehead against mine, freezing my movements, and it felt as if he'd frozen time. "Sorry, too fast?" he whispered.

"Too fast," I replied.

"I'll take it slower next time."

I laughed. "There won't be a next time."

"I think we'll have a lot of next times, Red," he said, his breaths falling against my lips.

His lips were close to mine. Were his lips always that close? Were they normal roommate distance apart, or was he going to…?

Oh, boy.

This boy.

For a moment, I forgot we were in the middle of Central Park. For a moment, I forgot a photo shoot was taking place. At that moment, all I felt was his heat and mine, and all I wanted to do was fall into him and taste his lips, allow him to taste mine, and then take him back home for more of the same.

"Okay, I think we got it," Jean said, breaking me away from the fairy-tale story I was making up in my mind.

I took a step away from Connor and looked up at the crew, who were all staring at us as if they'd just walked in on us having sex.

The embarrassment hit me fast, but I tried my best to shake it off.

I clapped my hands together and cleared my throat. "Okay, everyone, that's a wrap."

After the photo shoot, we headed home, and I decided to allow myself a cheat meal for the first time in months. My meal of choice: Chinese food.

"I was wondering if you'd like to come down to Kentucky with me," Connor asked as he unloaded enough food for an army. When I told him I was going to have a meal off my regular plan, he decided to order almost everything on the menu to celebrate the occasion.

"Kentucky? Home base?"

"Yeah. I was thinking of going down there for a weekend to visit. I thought it might be good for the article to see me in my true Southern element. To see the past of where I began. My roots."

I smiled. "I think that would be a great idea. Maiv is all about us writing articles with the complete heart of our subjects, and from what you've shared with me, your mom is a big part of your life."

"The biggest," he agreed.

"How long has she been cancer-free?"

"This will be year ten, which…" His smile spread wide. "It's just really good to hit the ten-year mark."

"I'm so happy for her."

"Yeah. She's been through a lot of hard battles. I still deal with a lot of worry and fear that it will come back someday, but so far, so good."

"Stay positive. Ten years is a long time."

"I know. Sometimes my thoughts just spiral, but I'm thrilled she's okay. I know the invite is a bit last minute, but I'm planning to go down two weekends from now."

I smiled. "Lucky for you, I have no life. I cannot wait to see what small-town life is all about. I've never been to a small town."

He laughed. "It's a bit different than the New York life, that's for sure. The people are everything you'd imagine them to be—gossipy, caring and closed-minded but fun. Everyone's involved in everyone's affairs pretty much."

I rubbed my hands together. "I can't wait."

"Just a heads-up, not to sound cocky, but I'm a bit of a superstar down there. I'm like the small-town celebrity, which is ridiculous but also flattering. Last year, they named a street after me. Had a full-blown festival to do it, too. It's insane, and a waste of money, but they love me."

"What's not to love?"

He looked my way and smiled before grabbing a plate to pile high with Chinese food. "I'll book the flights for us tomorrow if that works?"

"Perfect. I'll email Maiv later tonight to keep her in the loop of what's happening."

"Okay, so we have General Tso's, egg foo young, shrimp fried rice, and…" He opened a carton and arched a brow my way. "Crab rangoon. What would you like?"

"Everything."

"Thatta girl," he said as he began making a plate for me. I would've argued that I could've made my own plate, but something was so sweet about him wanting to serve me before he made himself a plate.

He handed it over to me, and then after he had his plate in front of him, he sat beside me on the couch, and we both dived into the food.

"I want to give you fair warning that when I bring you home, people are going to assume we are in a relationship because I've never brought a girl home before."

I laughed. "Then we'll just have to work hard to convince them that we aren't." Even though the thought of us being in a relationship made my stomach fill with butterflies. Connor was only my roommate and my friend—nothing more, nothing less. But sometimes, like at the photo shoot today, he'd touch my skin, and I'd feel a million different emotions all at once. It was as if his touch, his smile, his warmth, his whole persona shot flashes of love throughout my body every single day.

My favorite kinds of flashes of love came solely from the man sitting across from me.

Connor kept talking about anything under the sun, and then, he paused his words and looked at me. His blue eyes smiled brighter than his lips, and I shifted around on the couch cushion.

"What is it?" I asked.

"Nothing. It's nothing. I was just thinking…" He laughed lightly and shook his head. "My mom's going to love you."

And just like that, his flashes of love crashed straight into my heartbeats.

THIRTY-TWO

Connor

ALIYAH WINTERS LIVED RENT-FREE IN MY MIND.
There was so much to like about the girl. A day did not pass where she didn't put a smile on my face. I found myself picking up on her little quirks, and the more I saw them, the more I loved them. Like how when she typed on her laptop and she couldn't think of how to spell a word, she'd snap her fingers in the air repeatedly until it came to her. Or whenever she was about to eat food, she'd do a little excited jig.

When we'd be out in public and she saw a dog, she'd always react as if she just met an angel and she'd beg the owner to let her cuddle the fur ball.

I loved how she tried to tell me corny jokes, but always forgot the punchline. I loved how when she had a bite of food, she'd moan a little and then always offer me a bite, too, so I could moan along with her.

I loved her ass—I know, shallow—but damn, her ass. The way it moved in dresses, in skirts, in jeans. Fuck, in jeans. I could get a stiff one solely from watching Aaliyah Winters move in some blue jeans. Must've

Sometimes, when we'd leave a restaurant after tackling some interview questions, I'd let her lead so I could watch her walk away. The way her cheeks moved side to side. The way I wanted to move those cheeks side to side.

"What are you doing?" she asked the last time I trailed behind her. "Is everything okay?"

"Yeah, everything's fine." I slid my hands into my pockets and smirked. "I just had the craziest craving for some plums."

I knew she blushed after I said that, and I loved that, too.

I loved how she blushed when she was around me. It made me think that maybe this "catching feelings" thing was happening on both sides of the fence.

Catching feelings.

I didn't know my heart knew how to do that.

"You sound well-rested," Mom said as I sat in my office after giving her a call during my lunch break. I couldn't recall the last time she said those words to me, and I knew they were solely due to Aaliyah and her forcing me to slow down a bit. Roommate Breaks were becoming my new favorite thing.

"Yeah. Been getting a good amount of sleep each night."

"Oh, sweetheart! That makes me so happy. It's good to hear you're taking some time for yourself. Speaking of time for yourself, how's that promise you made me? About finding a hobby?"

"You'd be happy to know that it's going swimmingly."

"Are you serious?" she exclaimed. I could feel her joy through the phone. "What is it you've been up to? What's the hobby?"

I sat a bit straighter in my chair as pride beamed against my face. "I'm a life coach." Silence hit the line with a deep, painful hush that made me raise an eyebrow. "Uh, Mom? You there?"

"I'm sorry, I'm just trying to understand, sweetie. It sounded as if you said you were a life coach."

"Yeah. I did."

"Well, okay. Honey, my sweet, sweet child of mine. I mean this in the most loving, nurturing way possible, but, um… How can you be someone's life coach when you don't have your own life?"

"What?! I have a life."

"No, honey. And I mean that from a place of love. All you do is work, work, work. No play at all."

"I'll have you know that I've been getting a lot of play lately thanks to my roommate forcing me to take breaks."

"Roommate? What do you mean roommate? I haven't heard anything about this."

It'd been a while since I'd spoken to Mom, seeing how work had become so busy. I felt instant guilt for that fact. "Oh, a friend of mine was in a bit of a pickle. I didn't want her to struggle too much, so I offered to let her move in with—"

"*Her*?!" Mom exclaimed. "Oh, my lanta, you're living with a woman?! Tell me all about her? Is she pretty? Is she kind? Is she your girlfriend? How long have you been seeing her? Have you two been in a relationship for a long time? Oh, my goodness, my baby has a girlfriend. This is so amazing," she cried out, clearly spiraling down a tunnel of insanity.

"Mom. Chill. Aaliyah's just a friend. Nothing more."

"Well, you need to bring her down here for me to meet. It's been far too long since I've seen you, anyway. Oh! I have to bake her a pie. You know, everyone loves my apple pies."

"Yeah, actually, that's why I was calling. Aaliyah is a journalist and she was assigned to interview me and do an exclusive article for the magazine where she works. I wanted to show her my hometown, show her where I grew up. I figured it would—"

"Oh, my goodness, you're bringing home a girl! I have to tell Danny!"

Not this Danny guy again. Was he really still in the picture?

"Mom. Remember. She and I are solely friends. That's it."

"Yeah, okay, I hear you. I'll just make sure everything's perfect for when she arrives. Oh, my goodness, a girl!"

My mother was officially losing her mind. I was convinced that she was already planning a wedding for Aaliyah and me. I prayed to God that when I got down to Kentucky, the church doors weren't opened wide for me to say, "I do."

"Can we change the subject?" I asked.

"Do we have to? I just love the idea of this all, but I can hear it in your voice that you are getting irritated, so we can shift directions. Tell me more about this life coach thing. Who are you coaching?"

Somehow the conversation went right back to the girl I was trying to shift from.

"Aaliyah, actually. She's been through a lot of shit from crappy men. I wanted to help her find some self-love again. She's truly amazing and deserves to know it." Mom began sniffling on the phone, trying to muffle the sound, but I heard her. "Stop crying, Mom."

"I'm sorry, but that's so sweet of you. You're a good man, Connor Ethan, and I'm so proud of you."

I rolled my eyes but felt a slight tug at my heart. Something about your mama saying she was proud of you hit a certain chord of emotions. "Thanks, Mom."

"Although, I have to say, it sounds like she might be coaching you, too. Didn't you say she talked you into taking some breaks from work?"

"Yeah, she did."

"Maybe at the end of the day, you needed her as much as she needed you."

I smiled at the thought.

Maybe.

"Oh goodness, Connor. I really like this girl, just from the sound of everything. She sounds wonderful."

I knew she'd love Aaliyah. It was kind of hard not to think she was wonderful.

Before I could reply, there was a knock at my door. I looked up to see Marie standing there with a basket in her hands. She smiled brightly, and mouthed, "Is this a good time?"

Perplexed, I arched an eyebrow. "Hey, Mom. I'm going to need to call you back."

"All right, sweetie. I love you."

"Love you, too."

"Tell Aaliyah I said hi!" she added in before ending the call.

I placed the phone down and smiled over to Marie. I hadn't seen her since the wedding had been called off. All I knew is that Aaliyah had to tell her to back off a bit and give her space to breathe. I understood both sides of the situation. When a relationship ended, it wasn't only two people who had to deal with the heartbreak; it was everyone who loved the individuals. It was clear that Marie loved Aaliyah. She treated her like her own, so losing someone you'd grown to love, someone you thought would be in your life forever, had to be challenging.

"Well, good afternoon, Connor," Marie said, walking into my office after I waved her in. "I was in the neighborhood, visiting Walter at work, so I thought I'd stop by. Last night I went into a baking frenzy, and I needed to get some of this food out of my house." She set a container with treats in front of me and then took a few steps back.

"I would say you didn't have to do that, but I'm glad you did," I said, opening the container and finding my favorite cookies: oatmeal chocolate chip.

I could've shoved all of those into my mouth in a heartbeat, but I didn't want to appear like a slob in front of Marie.

"Yes, well, I know those are your favorites. Now, I don't want to keep you, but I wanted to see if you'd heard from Jason recently."

"We emailed back and forth a few times to finalize some paperwork and had a call last week, but that's about it."

"Oh, right. That makes sense. The two of you boys are just work, work, work. Just like Walter. I'm surrounded by workaholics," she seemingly joked. She shifted around in her high heels before saying, "I don't want to hold you up, but do you have a minute for us to talk?"

I tilted my head in confusion but then gestured toward the empty chair beside her.

She sat and crossed her legs. Her lips were painted a fuchsia color, and her fake eyelashes batted my way. I swore, Marie was always made up as if she were on her way to a runway show.

She pursed her lips together and began to tap her fingers against her thighs. "It was a shame, wasn't it? What happened at the wedding."

"Yeah. You could say that."

Or the biggest blessing in the world.

"I just feel awful for all sides. I know my poor Jason just got cold feet and panicked. Now, I'm not making excuses for him, but he's just not used to having someone as good as Aaliyah. All of the girls before her were exactly that—girls. They played games and always got Jason in trouble. But Aaliyah…" Her eyes flashed with emotions, and she shrugged her left shoulder. "Aaliyah is a saint. She is a grown woman with a good head on her shoulders."

I couldn't disagree with that, but for the life of me, I couldn't connect the reason Marie was telling me this information.

"I'm sorry, Marie. What happened was terrible, but I don't know what this has to do with—"

"I heard a rumor about you doing an interview for *Passion*. Is that true?"

I sat up a bit straighter. "Uh, yes. It's true."

"And Aaliyah is interviewing you?"

Why did I get the feeling this conversation wasn't going anywhere good? "Yes… After the wedding, she was in quite a situation because she'd already put in her notice at her job. Her boss said she could have her position back and get a raise if she could land an interview with me. I felt bad not helping."

"Oh, my goodness, of course. I'm so thankful you offered your services to her. Jason didn't leave her in the best situation, that's for sure. You're a good man, Connor. You've always been a good man."

I blinked a few times, not knowing what to say.

She blinked a few times, giving me the most uncomfortable smile.

I began to shift papers around on my desk. "Well, I actually have a lot of work to get—"

"Can you put in a good word?" she spat out.

"I'm sorry, what?"

"A good word, for Jason. Can you tell Aaliyah that he made a mistake and wants her back? Because he does, he does want her back."

That wasn't what he'd expressed on the day Aaliyah moved out of his penthouse.

"Uh, I don't think it's a good idea for me to get involved in other people's issues."

"Right, of course. I get that. But if you could just sell the idea of them getting back together, it would make the whole situation much easier. You're a trustworthy person, Connor. People value your opinion."

"I'm not really comfortable doing that. I'm sorry, Marie."

A flash of irritation hit her eyes before she forcefully delivered a smile. A fake, big grin that was only hiding the anger behind her stare. I knew she was upset about the breakup, but she seemed to be taking the over-involved mother role a bit too far.

She stood up from her desk, walked over to me, and patted her hand against mine. "Just think about it, will you? I'm sure once you give it time, you'll see vouching for Jason is the right choice."

How about absolutely fucking not?

I pushed out a smile. She probably knew it wasn't sincere, but at that point, I didn't care. "Well, you have a good day, Marie. Thanks again for the cookies."

"You're more than welcome, sweetheart. Now you take care." She pushed her purse up on her shoulder and as she began to walk away, she turned back to me. "Oh, and I heard about you finding a new place for your passion project with Walter. Good for you never giving up on your little dream." She flashed a big grin. "I hope it works out this time. It would be a shame if this one fell through like all the others."

She left the room, leaving a lingering unease behind. Did she…? Did she just threaten me somehow with a big smile on her face? No. Marie wouldn't do that. She was as sweet as pie. As sweet as those damn cookies she brought me. Although, the way she spoke about my low-income apartments made it feel…dirty.

I tried my best to shake off the feeling, thinking she was nothing more than a depressed mother who'd lost the future of having an amazing daughter-in-law. I'd be crazy, too, if I lost Aaliyah.

Before I could fully analyze the situation with Marie, Damian came walking into my office.

"Hey." He nodded once before taking a seat across from me. "Aaliyah's going to Kentucky with you?"

"How did you know?"

"Your mom just texted me in full-blown glee."

Damian and my mother were the best of friends. He hated almost everyone else in the world, except for my mom and me. They probably talked more than I did.

"Yeah. I figured it's a good opportunity for the article. For her to see where I came from."

He blinked a few times, then said, "Okay."

I arched an eyebrow. "What's that supposed to mean?"

"All I said was okay."

"Yeah, but you said it in a very non-okay way."

"I just think it's weird that you're pretending to take her down there for work when really, you just want to bring her to your hometown."

I snickered. "What?"

"Never mind. I think it's great you're taking her."

I arched an eyebrow. "You do?"

"Yeah."

"That's it? That's all you have to say?"

"What do you want me to say?"

"You're the grave digger. You find out crap about everyone, and you've met Aaliyah a few times now, so I kind of want to know your thoughts on her."

"Why do my thoughts matter? I'm not the one being interviewed by her."

"Yeah, but you're my person."

"Don't be weird, Connor."

"I mean it. Your opinion matters to me, Damian. Honestly, I should've listened to you about Rose and a few other employees in the past. So if there's something about Aaliyah that I should—"

"You like her."

"What?"

"You have feelings for her. You've made it pretty obvious from the jump, but you've been too damn scared to admit it because you are terrified of commitment. Even so, you set yourself up to have this woman in your life because you don't like the idea of her not being around. Exhibit A: You agree to do an interview. Exhibit B: You ask her to move in with you. Exhibit C: She's going to your hometown to meet your mother."

"She'll be meeting other people, too," I urged.

Damian rolled his eyes. "You're basically fucking her without fucking her."

"What? No. We're just buddies. Pals. Roommates. That's it."

Oh, the lies we told ourselves on the daily.

"Whatever makes this easier for you, champ. Although, you could admit your true feelings for her and see where they'd take you. But alas, you're too chickenshit. Here I was, thinking I was the messed-up one who needed therapy, but I guess even millionaires like you have some trauma, too."

I blankly stared at him for a few moments, blinking rapidly. "Uh, I'm sorry. I didn't ask you to tell me about myself. I was asking about Aaliyah."

"Oh. I already looked into her weeks ago." He shrugged. "I like her. She's a good one."

The only other person I'd ever heard him say that about was my mother, and she sent him care packages every month.

"Anyway, I gotta get back to work. Also, did you see the email from Walter?" Damian asked, standing up from the chair. "He replied about five minutes ago about the Queens property. It's all but a done deal. Just need to draw up contracts and sign on the dotted line. Congratulations, Con. It's yours."

Holy shit.

I got the property.

Ever since Damian told me the good news, my mind hadn't stopped spinning. No, the great fucking news. I'd been working for years to make this happen, and the fact that it hadn't fallen through like all the other locations made me want to cry like a damn child.

It was really happening, and I knew exactly who I wanted the first person I told to be.

"Do I really need to be blindfolded for this?" Aaliyah asked, laughing. "This seems a bit dramatic, and I've watched a lot of true crime, so if you are going to murder me, just tell me now so I can say a few prayers to try to get into heaven."

I snickered. "Don't be dramatic. If I wanted to kill you, I would've done it on Halloween night."

"Well, that's comforting."

"We're almost there. Luis is pulling up right now."

Luis parked the car, and I hopped out quickly, then guided Aaliyah out of the vehicle, with only a few fumbles and hiccups. The whole time she laughed, making me chuckle, too.

"You okay?" I asked.

"Yeah, I'm good," she said, standing straight as we stepped onto the sidewalk. "Now, do I get to take it off or...?"

"Wait. Let me set the scene. I thought this would be great for the article. You remember how you said you wanted to showcase the past, present, and future of who I am?"

"Yes."

"Well, we've only covered the present day. You've seen me in my work element, but I wanted to share the next chapter with you for myself. The future of Roe Real Estate is here." I moved behind her and began untying the blindfold. The second it fell, Aaliyah looked at the run-down building in front of her.

Her eyes widened as she stared at the building, then at me. "Is this it? Is this your location for your low-income luxury apartments?"

I nodded.

Her face filled with a level of excitement as she began jumping up and down, grabbing my arms and forcing me into her leaps, too. "Oh, my God, Connor! Oh, my God! You did it! It's happening! *Ohmygoodness!*" she screeched, her excitement level rocketing from the sidewalk and straight to Mars. The way she celebrated my dream made me almost choke up. The only other person who'd ever shown so much excitement for me was my mother.

"Shit, Red, you're gonna make me cry," I semi-joked.

When I looked at her, my heart, which already beat faster whenever she was near me, almost exploded. The tears I felt were falling from her eyes.

She blushed as she wiped them away. "Sorry, but Connor...you did it." She stopped her quick movements and placed her hands on her hips, looking up at the building's broken windows and graffitied walls. It looked like a disaster, but somehow, she was able to see past its current brokenness and focus on its potential.

She turned to me, and her smile felt so warm. "You did it, Connor. You did this, and I'm so proud of you."

Cue the fucking tears.

I pinched the bridge of my nose and cleared my throat. The tears were on the brink of falling. Something about her saying she was proud of me struck a chord I hadn't even known could be reached.

"Thanks, Red. That means a lot to me. Now, off the record, I got the seller to loan me the keys for three hours."

She held her hand out toward me and smiled. "Come on, then," she urged. "Show me."

The skies of the city were dark, a clear sign a storm would be moving in soon. Even still, I swore I could feel the sun when I looked at Aaliyah.

I took her through the seven-story building, stopping on each floor to explore. Each level had ten apartments, so we'd be able to house seventy families. We stopped in every unit of the building, too, because Aaliyah wouldn't allow us to do anything else. Even when she seemed short of breath, she kept a smile plastered on her face.

Her happiness made me happier.

"Do you see it, Captain?" she asked as we stood in the final apartment on the seventh floor. "Right over here, the family can put their entertainment center. That over there will be little Timmy's bedroom, and over there is Sara's. The parents' bedroom suite will have a soaking tub with all the luxury amenities, with locks on the door so Mama can get a few moments to herself. They'll make memories over here," she said, dancing on her tiptoes to the dining room area. She pretend-sat as if she were at a table. "They'll laugh here over dinners. They'll discuss life, do homework, and love one another right here." She stood and walked over to me. "All because of you."

"This world doesn't deserve you, Red," I confessed. I didn't deserve her, but each day, I wanted her a little more than the last. I hadn't really faced the fact that my feelings for her and my connection to her were growing more and more each day.

"Come on," she said. "Show me more."

I took her to the rooftop. The clouds were darker than when we'd first arrived. The thunder roared throughout the sky, signaling that the storm was moving in.

She moved around the space with her arms wide open. "Is this where the community garden will go?"

"Yes. It will be over here, and there will be gas grills and seating throughout the area. The families will be able to pick up the fresh vegetables as they please, and there will be a worker to help tend to it at all times."

I felt the first raindrop fall against my face, and Aaliyah must've felt one, too, as she looked up at the sky. Her brown eyes moved to me, and she shook her head. "Your dreams are coming true."

I bit my bottom lip and nodded. "They are." I moved in toward her and took her hands in mine. "Dance with me?"

There wasn't a moment's hesitation from her. She moved in close to me, and I took her into my arms. We swayed back and forth, pretending there was music as the raindrops began to fall a bit faster. I offered to run inside with her, but she declined.

"A little longer." She rested her head against my chest as we moved in slow motion in the rain. "I can hear your heartbeats," she whispered.

"They're beating for you," I confessed. At first, I didn't know if I'd spoken the words out loud, but when I saw how she looked up at me, I knew she'd heard them.

I was terrified of speaking about my true feelings for her because I couldn't take them back once they were out there. But Damian had been spot-on about everything he'd said to me about my feelings for Aaliyah. The idea of her not being in my life drove me wild. The idea of her not being across the hall from me made my chest ache. The idea of never knowing what her lips tasted like…

Those lips.

Those full, beautiful, juicy lips.

God, all I wanted to do was lean down and taste them. Suck them. Fuck them…

I parted my lips to answer her question, to skip past my fears and let her know my secrets, but before I could, a deluge fell over us and lightning flashed throughout the sky. The pouring rain broke us away from the moment, but then I stood there, thinking about one thing and one thing only—I wanted to kiss her.

I stood there still as the raindrops hammered over us. I didn't care that I was getting soaked; I didn't care that every inch of me was wet. All I cared about, all I wanted to know was if she wanted to kiss me, too.

THIRTY-THREE

Aaliyah

HE WAS GOING TO KISS ME.

Maybe. Or perhaps, I imagined him leaning down to kiss me in the rain. Maybe I was just hoping and wishing, dreaming of the possibility of his lips finding mine and his tongue parting my mouth to slip inside.

My skin began to tremble as we stood in the rain, staring at one another without saying a word. We should've moved inside once the downpour began. We should've run for shelter, but we stood there, still. Dripping water from head to toe. Eyes locked, souls exposed.

Gosh, I wanted him to kiss me. I wanted him to tell me his truths, tell me if what I felt were his feelings, too. I wanted to fall against his mouth and have him swallow every piece of me as I gave him my all.

I wanted to kiss him.

And I wanted him to kiss me, too.

He looked down at the ground for a moment, and when he brought his gaze back up to meet mine, he looked as if he were seconds away

"You terrify me because every single day, I wake up with you on my mind. Every single night, you stay there, too…I'm falling…" He cleared his throat, and I knew how hard it was for him to open up to me. I knew how relationships scared him, and I knew about his hesitations. But still, he kept speaking his truths. "I am overwhelmingly falling for you, Red."

My heart skipped a beat. Maybe five beats. Maybe it stopped altogether. Maybe his words healed it. All I knew was all the broken pieces of my tattered and tired heart belonged to him.

I looked at him, completely stunned by the words leaving his mouth. Had I been imagining them? Because everything he was saying was everything I'd wanted to hear. I didn't know what to say because a part of me worried that I'd realize it was nothing more than a dream by morning. by morning. I was scared that maybe by morning, he'd retreat back to his fears of love.

Then as if he knew of my worries, he kept talking. "I'm scared because I've never felt this way. I'm scared because you make me want to take breaks from my work. You make me want to experience things outside of my career. You make me want to live because everything about you is magic."

"Connor…"

"You don't have to say anything, really, Red. I know you just got out of that relationship. I know you are still healing, but I just…I want you. I want you more than I'd ever wanted anything else in this world. I don't care how long it takes for you to be ready because I'll be waiting…because this…I want this… I want—"

"You," I murmured, placing my hands into his. I looked down at our intertwined fingers and looked up at him. "I want you, too. I wanted you to say those words more than you know," I said. "I thought I was the only one feeling this way."

"No. I've felt this for a while now, but I didn't want to bring it up. I was scared to bring it up. Shit, I'm still scared, Aaliyah…but I'm more scared of not giving us a real shot."

"Connor?"

"Yes?"

"Kiss me."

He did so without any hesitation.

The raindrops kept falling as his mouth fell against mine. He tasted like my favorite fairy tales, full of wonder and love. He kissed me as if he were trying to show me the truth behind his feelings, that they were real. That we were real, something powerful. Something that neither one of us expected to happen.

Or perhaps we did expect it. Maybe we'd known all along, ever since that Halloween night when I decided to try to fall in love with a stranger.

And there I was, two years later, falling, falling, falling.

I kissed him back with the same intensity he gave me. His hands wrapped around me, and I moaned against his mouth as I felt one hand slowly moving across the fabric of the dress resting against my thighs. The clothes were soaked against our skin, showing our every curve and every muscle.

I liked how his hands wandered. I liked how his tongue danced with mine. I liked how he touched me. How he kissed me. How he sucked my lips between his.

I loved how he touched me in the rain.

"Tell me to stop, and I will, Red...but I want this...I want you... all of you. If you say stop, I'll stop. But if you say go...Fuck, Red." He pressed his forehead against mine and moaned against my lips as he closed his eyes. "Please. Tell me to go."

My hands fell against his chest. I felt every muscle he had as his gray T-shirt clung to his skin. My lips parted against his, and I whispered, "Go."

Within seconds, he was undressing me as I tore at his clothing. We went after one another as if we were seconds away from discovering our full destiny. He lay me down on the ground gently and spread my legs apart. Without a moment's hesitation, he placed my legs over his shoulders as he leaned down between them. His fingers moved across my lower thighs, and his mouth trailed his fingers, leaving kisses and gentle sucks the entire way. He licked at the raindrops that kept hitting us, sucking them from my bare skin, making the chills intensify every second he grew closer to my core.

He moved in closer, so close that his hot breaths fell against my upper thighs. His mouth stayed in one location as he sucked my sensitive skin between his full lips, shooting a rocket of desire and anticipation through my whole system.

"Please," I begged, knowing exactly where I wanted his mouth to land, knowing what I wanted him to kiss, lick, suck, fuck...

Fuck...

My breaths were uneven as he found his way to my clit, and he worked at it as if I were his queen and his only duty in life was to bring me to a state of ecstasy. He took my soul to a new level as his mouth made love to my core. His tongue slid against my clit as his fingers worked their way inside me. The motion and speed of his actions intensified as he drank the raindrops intermixed with my own wetness. He tongued me hard, drinking up every sip of nourishment I'd given him. He swallowed me as if I were his source of livelihood. I moaned as my hips pushed up, begging for him to go deeper...to have all of me...to give me all of him.

I wanted him inside me. I wanted him to push his hardness against my core. I wanted him on top of me, staring down at me as he fucked me like he meant it.

"Purse," I breathed out, gesturing to the side of me where my purse lay in the rain. "Condom," I muttered, unable to build up any other words. Luckily, that was enough for him to connect the dots. He rushed to my purse, dug inside, and grabbed the condom.

After he finished tasting me, he climbed on top of me, exposing his big, throbbing cock. My mouth began to water from the sight of his massive hard-on. He tilted his head as he hovered over me, almost as if he was asking permission to enter.

I nodded once, knowing words were too much to give at the moment.

He engulfed my lips against his, kissing me hard and long. I gasped as I felt him sliding into me, giving me all of him. As he thrust his hardness inside me, my fingers wrapped around his back, and my nails dug into his skin. I didn't know it could feel like that. I didn't know making love could feel like life and death, prayers and sins, heaven and hell. His normal playful demeanor was gone, and when I looked into his eyes, I saw his dilated stare filled with desire, with passion, with love.

"Oh, gosh, yes, Connor…please…keep…" I breathed out, exhausted yet completely in bliss and wanting more of him. Wanting all of him.

"God, you feel as good as you taste," he muttered against my mouth before kissing me harder and thrusting into me deeper. His words mixed with his movements and the rain made it impossible for me to hold back any longer.

"I'm going to… Connor…I…"

"Do it for me, come for me," he whispered, making me even more hot and bothered. My hips rolled up and down as he continued to fuck the life out of my body. Connor had many personalities, but I didn't know the dirty talker was one of them. That made me crave him even more than I had before.

I came hard against him, my whole body trembling as I released. He thrust hard into me once as his hands rested against my shoulders.

"Shit, you're going to make me come next," he said, still pumping into me.

"Please," I begged, opening my eyes to find his blues staring at mine. "Please come inside me. I want all of you. Connor…please… fuck me like you mean it."

Those words sent him into overload as he pressed his arms against the hard ground and began going more and more, in and out, in and out, fucking me as if he'd find forever between my thighs and our future against my lips.

A few moments later, he lost himself inside me, giving me everything he had, breathing heavy as he unloaded himself. When he finished, he fell to the left side of me onto his back, and we both lay there for a moment, completely out of breath as the rain hammered against our skin.

"Holy," he whispered.

"Shit," I finished.

"That was…"

"Amazing."

Silence fell over us as time passed for a few moments. We both worked on catching our breath before he rolled over onto his side to face me. He had a goofy grin on his face that I loved so much, and he trailed his lips down every inch of my body. "You're perfect. You're perfect," he whispered with every kiss landing against my lips. "You're perfect."

I sighed, feeling whole for the first time in a long time as his mouth rested against mine, and said, "We're perfect."

THIRTY-FOUR

Aaliyah

FOR THE NEXT FEW DAYS, CONNOR AND I WOKE UP MAKING LOVE, and we fell asleep doing the same. We switched back and forth with whose bedroom we'd fall into, and sometimes it just ended up happening on the kitchen countertop. Or the living room sofa. Or the rooftop.

That was my favorite, the wind blowing against our warm flesh as he drove deep inside me, the moon shining bright as he made me weak in my knees. My favorite thing about the way our bodies fell together was how he made it both gentle and hard. Soft and rough, kind and dangerous. I loved how he inhaled my entire existence. Even though there were times I thought I'd fade away from overexerting myself, I didn't even care because it felt so good with him inside me.

He made love to me as if it was both the first and last time. Therefore, that meant every single session quickly became the best sex I'd ever had. He never stopped until I got off multiple times, too. It must've been that Southern gentleman in him because he always made sure I came first. Ladies first.

I always returned the favor.

I didn't know it was possible—having two humans both end up fulfilled.

It felt as if I were living in a dream world, but sadly, every dream had to come to an end.

One morning, Connor had an early conference call, so I woke up in bed alone. I woke up in pain. It wasn't out of the blue. I knew over the past few weeks my symptoms were building up.

I was more tired than normal. Walking short distances winded me. My ankles were swelling again. Connor even noticed the swelling, but I blamed it on wearing a pair of heels all day at work. He gave me ankle massages, and when he'd fall asleep at night, I'd cry thinking about how seriously wrong I'd been feeling.

I just needed a little bit more time.

I had a doctor's appointment coming up after my trip to Kentucky, so I was doing my best to push through. To enjoy the current moments of happiness with Connor. To live. To pretend for a while that my life was normal.

Yet that morning, I couldn't continue lying to myself.

My body ached, and my head was clouded. The chills that found me were the worst part. I could hardly sit up in bed. Every little movement I made felt as if someone was slamming into me.

"No," I whispered to myself, unable to open my eyes because that brought about another wave of dizzy spells.

Time.

Just give me a little bit more time.

Connor and I were supposed to fly out to Kentucky soon, and I didn't want to cancel the trip. Not only was it important for the article I was writing but it was also important to me. I wanted to see him in his hometown, wanted to meet the people he grew up with, and I wanted to walk the streets that raised him. I couldn't miss it.

I placed my hands on the edge of my bed and pulled myself up to a sitting position. As my feet hit the wooden floor, I groaned. Everything hurt. I knew most people couldn't understand that level of pain, but just sitting up felt like the ultimate chore to me. I wanted to crawl back into a ball and sob. The pain's intensity made it hard to even breathe in a normal pattern.

"You're okay. You're okay. You're okay," I repeated to myself, borrowing the words Connor had given to me time and time again over the past few weeks. Even though I said the words, the aches made them feel unrealistic.

I tried to push myself up from the mattress, but I failed. I felt weak, tired. So very tired. Tears formed in the backs of my eyes as they remained shut, and they slowly began to fall down my cheeks.

"You're okay. You're okay. You're okay," I repeated, feeling as if I were going to vomit from the way my mind spun.

I began coughing into my hand, trying to clear my throat. Trying to make a passageway for more air to inflate within my lungs.

I hated this. I hated my heart and how it was quitting on me. I hated that I'd gone so long feeling good, only to have my life turn upside down in the span of two years. I hated that the good days always made the bad ones feel like complete hell.

I hated knowing that more bad days were on their way.

Time.

I need more time.

I was going to be nauseous. It was only a matter of time before I was hugging the toilet seat. The spinning in my head made that painfully clear. The last thing I wanted to do was throw up as Connor was in his office having a meeting.

Connor.

Time.

We needed more time.

To my surprise, he came into the bedroom with a big smile on his face. In one hand, he had a box, and in the other, he had a green drink. "Morning, sunshine. I finished my meeting early and ran down the street to get you some breakfast. I know you're healthier than me, so I got you a green drink and an omelet."

The thought of eating anything at that moment made my stomach turn in a way stomachs shouldn't be able to turn.

The second he caught sight of me, a heavy look of worry filled his face. "Aaliyah, what's wrong?"

I must've looked hideous.

"Hey there," I said, thinking I'd head over to thank him, but instead,

I began to experience a dizzy spell as I attempted to walk. Connor hurriedly set the box and drink on the dresser and rushed to help me stand.

"Sorry," I muttered.

"Don't be," he replied, lowering me back down to the bed. He then kneeled in front of me, looking as perfect as he always did. Christ, I felt so embarrassed. If I looked anywhere near as bad as I felt, he probably thought I was on the verge of death.

Maybe I was.

"What happened?" he asked. "What can I do?"

"Nothing, nothing, it's fine. I just woke up feeling a bit off. That's all." I didn't want to go into the full scope of what was really happening. It all seemed too much, and the last thing I wanted from Connor was for him to worry about me.

He rolled up his sleeves and walked toward the bathroom. Within seconds, he came out with a warm hand towel and placed it on my forehead.

The warmth it brought me soothed me more than I'd thought it would as I kept my eyes shut. "Thanks," I said, trying my hardest not to cry. "It's probably just a cold."

"We were in the rain a few days ago for a long period. Damn. I should've taken you inside. This is my fault."

"No. It's not. Trust me."

"Regardless, I think it might be best to stay in today, get better fully. When I get a cold, I get knocked on my ass like no other, so I completely fall into sick mode and disconnect from the world until I'm better."

If only it was that easy for me.

"I'll rest up today, and I'll be better by morning," I said as I began to push myself to a better sitting position. Instead of being successful with that, my vision blurred, and I found myself rushing to the bathroom, where I threw up. The pounding in my head was too intense. Not only was I falling apart, but I was falling apart in front of Connor, which made it that much worse. By this point, I felt as if he'd seen me at my worst a lot more than at my best.

Still, he stayed, joining me in the bathroom, holding my braids back.

"Maybe it was something you ate last night? Maybe something bad with that salad you ordered? If it's a bad cold, maybe we need to shift our flights—"

"No!" I quickly said, shaking my head. "Don't. I'll be fine, I swear, Connor. By tomorrow I'll be my normal self."

"I can stay home with you today."

I sat up a bit and forced a smile. "No, truly, it's okay. I know you have a lot of work. Really, Connor. I'm good."

He was hesitant, but he agreed. He helped me back to the bed, making sure to tuck me in. "If you need anything, just call me—even if it's just to talk. I'll answer."

"Thanks."

He leaned forward and kissed my forehead. "Feel better, Red."

"Will do."

The moment he left for work, I went ahead and called my doctor.

"I'm sure it's just a cold," I explained to Dr. Erickson as I sat in his office. "I made a mistake and got caught in the rain a few days ago, so I'm sure my body is just fighting off the virus." At least that was the lie I'd been telling myself over the past few days.

I could see the concern in Dr. Erickson's eyes after he ran some tests. The worry on his face made me realize the fear I'd been running from was catching up with me. The medicine wasn't enough to keep me going anymore. My body wasn't working the way it needed to in order to function.

"Sadly, Aaliyah, it's not just a cold."

He pulled up a chair beside me and gave me a broken smile as he took off his glasses for a moment and pinched his nose. "Unfortunately, it appears everything we've been doing has run its course. It's time we get more aggressive with treatment and switch gears."

"You mean surgery?"

"With your condition, a surgical procedure is too much of a risk. We need to move forward with a heart transplant. It is the only option available at this time. Without it…" His words faltered, and he gave me another fake smile. "You're getting higher on the transplant list. Your time could be coming any day."

"Any day, or any week? Or months? Or years…?" I said, knowing I'd already been waiting on that list for the longest time. It had been over three hundred days since I'd been placed on the transplant list, and nothing had come from it.

"You know it's impossible to say, Aaliyah, but you are coming up close. For the time being, we do need to keep your health up the best we can. I have a few new medications we need to get going in your system. The next step also might be hospitalization up until the point where we can get you a transplant because—"

"Wait, no." He raised a confused brow as I shook my head. "I have a trip to Kentucky coming up. I am flying down there in a few days."

Dr. Erickson looked at me as if I were insane. "Oh, that's not possible, Aaliyah. I'm sorry, but you cannot travel at this time. For one, with your condition, you are at a higher risk for blood clots, and sitting on a cramped airplane isn't wise. Also, you are at risk of infection, and being around other travelers isn't safe. Then there is the biggest reason—you are high on the donor list. You need to be in the area when the call comes through. I'm sorry, but a trip to Kentucky isn't going to happen."

My damaged heart began to break some more. "What?"

"I'm sorry. That's just not a possibility. Travel is completely out of the question."

He kept talking, but my mind was already slipping away from the conversation.

For the past few weeks, I'd been falling in love with myself and Connor. I'd been forgetting about my health situation and falling into him. He'd been the escape I craved, making me dream past each day. Kentucky was just another part of the fantasy that excited me, but all of those dreams, all the make-believe came to a crashing halt when Dr. Erickson expressed how dire the situation had become.

Time was running out, and there was a strong possibility that when my heart stopped beating, it wouldn't begin again.

That reality was too much to take in. I'd been trying my best not to allow it to settle into me, but now I had to face the facts. My time left was short, and unless a transplant came through for me, I was a hopeless case.

I was dying.

I went back home and lay on the sofa for the remainder of the day. Maiv said I was able to work from home, but I hadn't been able to do any work at all. The new medicines made me drowsier than I wanted to be. All I could do was rest and hope things began to shift.

When Connor came home, he walked in alarmed. The moment he saw me laid out on the sofa, he hurried over to me. "Hey."

"Hi," I replied, sitting up a bit.

"Still feeling awful?"

"Still feeling awful."

He nodded slowly and gave me a broken smile that read more like a frown. "God…I should've never had you standing in the rain on that rooftop. I'm sure that didn't help the situation."

"This isn't your fault."

"I know. It's just that…" He paused for a moment and looked down at the floor before bringing his blue eyes to meet my brown ones. Those eyes flashed with such hurt that my own chest ached. His lips parted again as he found his lost words. "It's just that if there was something wrong with you, my heart would break."

I loved him.

It wasn't the kind of love I'd ever experienced in the past. No, this love was authentic. It was both exciting and scary. Powerful yet calm. I knew if I had to die, I'd be lucky because for the first time in my life, I knew what true love felt like. Connor gave me himself day in and day out. I couldn't imagine a better person to love.

"Connor," I started, feeling the emotion sitting behind my eyes. I wanted to tell him how I felt about him, how he made me feel safe in an unsafe world. How he healed the cracks of my broken soul, which others had left battered and bruised. That if ever he wasn't okay, my heart would break, too.

Instead, I pushed out a smile and tried to ignore the feelings overpowering me. "Thank you for checking on me," I said, leaning toward him, feeling faint but not wanting him to know it. Because in our make-believe world, I wasn't sick. I didn't have any kind of illness, my body didn't ache, and my chest didn't burn.

"I'll always check on you." He shifted a bit on the cushion. "Do you need anything? Soup? Crackers and clear soda?"

I shook my head. Honestly, I hadn't been able to keep anything down. The idea of eating anything else made my stomach turn.

"I'm okay."

"Are you going to be resting on the sofa?"

"Yeah. I haven't moved much from this position."

"Do you need someone to rest on the sofa with you?"

Gosh, that man made my heart feel things I didn't know hearts could feel. If his care and attention to me had been enough to heal, my heart would've lived forever.

I nodded, and he was wrapped around me within seconds.

We lay on the couch, and he became my pillow as he wrapped his large arms around my body. Connor was the weighted blanket I'd always needed in my life. Just by holding me, he made me feel safe in an unsafe world.

"Doesn't *The Bachelor* come on tonight?" he asked, glancing down at his watch.

"Yeah, but I know you don't like that show. I'm recording it so I can watch it later."

Without question, he picked up the remote and turned on the television, putting on *The Bachelor*. I breathed through my mouth because my nose was too stuffed up.

"How was work?" I asked, trying to ignore my aching body. Everything hurt. Even holding my eyes open felt exhausting.

"I couldn't focus." He shook his head. "Too worried about you."

"Please don't do that. Please don't worry about me, Connor."

"Too late, Red. I already am."

I snuggled up against him and didn't make it through ten minutes of the show before I fell asleep in his arms. When I woke up in the middle of the night to go to the bathroom, to my surprise, he was still there. He stayed.

Connor wouldn't let me out of his sight after me being sick. He'd already canceled our trip to Kentucky, thinking it wasn't a good idea for me to travel while I wasn't feeling well. I was thankful for that because I didn't want to tell him how I couldn't make the trip, even if I wanted to go.

I was still trying to play it off as if it were nothing more than a cold, but the seriousness of the situation weighed heavy on my heart. I knew I had to make some big choices sooner than later and come back to the reality of what my future, or lack thereof, looked like. But instead, I fell more into Connor. More into his warmth, more into the haven he'd created for me. I wanted to pretend for a while that I wasn't as sick as I was. It just so happened that that was easiest when I was in his arms.

One night as we were tangled up in one another, Connor frowned as he looked down at his cell phone.

"What is it?" I asked, noticing the alarm in his eyes.

"It's work. There seem to be some issues happening at our West Coast location."

"The one Jason runs?"

He nodded. "Yeah. Some deals fell through, and there seems to be some missing paperwork that needs to be accounted for. I'm going to have to fly out there to deal with it." He turned my way and kept grimacing. "How much would you hate me if I flew out to California tomorrow? I just want to make sure he's not fucking up the company too much."

"That's completely fine. Why would it matter what I thought?"

"I feel bad leaving you here alone since you haven't been feeling well."

I laughed. "Connor, I'm a grown woman. I can handle not feeling well." I began coughing, and he frowned.

"That sounds painful in your chest."

"I'll be okay."

"You better be. Or else I'll kick your plum." He snuggled into my side and pulled me into him. I fell against him as if we were always meant to be together.

"I hope Jason didn't ruin too much out there," I told him, needing to shift the conversation.

"It's fine. Whatever he breaks, I'll fix. Not a big deal. Now, the last thing I want to do is talk about him. I just want to be here now with you."

Be here now.

I melted into him, still feeling awful yet embracing the moment. At that moment, I was wrapped up in a man I was falling in love with. That was the only moment that needed to count.

THIRTY-FIVE

Connor

INSTEAD OF BEING WITH AALIYAH, I HATED THE FACT THAT I WAS ON my way to deal with Jason and his fuckups. I wanted more than ever to tell Walter that his son was sucky at his job, but alas, I knew that wouldn't do any good. So, I'd do what I knew I'd end up doing: pull Jason out of the hole he'd dug for himself.

If that guy ever had to fix his own messes, he'd really be screwed. Or maybe he'd learn to actually grow up.

When the plane touched down in Los Angeles, I checked into the hotel, then headed straight to the office to meet with Jason. I didn't want to waste any time and be in California longer than I had to be. All I wanted to do was get back to Aaliyah, snuggle the shit out of her, and be happy.

When I walked into the building, I was stunned to see a familiar face sitting at the receptionist's desk. "Rose. What are you doing here?" I asked, baffled by her appearance. Last time I saw her, she was having her Dr. Jekyll and Mr. Hyde moment in my office after I fired her.

She gave me a smug smirk and shrugged, pushing her overly ex-

"You can't be serious."

She was smacking down on her chewing gum and twirling her hair with her finger as she kept grinning like a villain from a fairy tale. Ursula? Was that you? "It turns out having some good dirt on people could land you a solid job."

"Who did you have dirt on?"

"You." She said the word, but it didn't register instantly.

Because what kind of dirt could she have on me?

"You didn't really think Damian was the only one who could find out shit about people, did you?" she sneered.

My God. She was really unpleasant to be around. I couldn't believe I fell for her Goody Two-shoes performance.

Brava, Rose, brava.

"What do you mean you have dirt on me?" I asked.

"I saw it all over your TikTok. You had Jason's ex-fiancée doing dances with you. It was obvious that you two have been fucking. Nobody looks at each other the way you do if there's not sex happening. Then people got photographs of you two pretty much making out in Central Park during a photo shoot. And to think you judged me for screwing Jason when you ended up going and screwing his ex. The double standard."

"I don't think you know what a double standard actually is. Also, none of that is your business."

"Yeah, well, it became my business after you fired me."

"I don't have time for this," I said, tired of talking to a child. I marched past the front desk and straight into Jason's office.

"Connor. I didn't expect you before lunchtime," Jason commented as I walked in. His desk was stacked high with paperwork, and he had a smug look on his face. For someone who was failing at life, he sure had a lot of nerve to look smug. "Take a seat," he said, gesturing to the chair in front of his desk.

I did as he said and clasped my hands. "You said some paperwork was missing and that a few deals fell through?" I asked.

He waved a hand my way. "Nah, I only said that because I knew it would get you on a plane out here. Everything's fine business-wise."

"What the hell, Jason? Why am I here then?" The irritation hit me fast, but that wasn't shocking. Being around Jason had a way of pulling out my annoyance at a record speed.

He sat back in his chair and placed his hands behind his head. "Did you think it wouldn't get back to me? You and Aaliyah? Rose told—and showed—me everything."

"That's why you had me fly across the damn states? Because you're mad about some TikToks and photographs that people took of us?"

"You say 'us' as if there actually is a you and Aaliyah. But that would be ridiculous."

I stayed quiet because I didn't need to say or prove anything to Jason of all people.

He arched an eyebrow and leaned forward. "No way. You really are with her?"

"It's none of your business what I do in my private life."

"The hell it isn't when you're dating my Aaliyah."

"She's not yours, remember? You stood her up on your wedding day. That was the end of any kind of relationship you had with her."

"So, you figured you'd pick up my crumbs?"

I took in a deep inhalation and shook my head as I pushed myself up from the chair. "I don't have time for this. I can't believe you had me come all the way out here due to you being butt-hurt that Aaliyah moved on."

"She moved on to you, though? That's just disrespectful."

I rolled my eyes. "Let's not pretend you and I are close, Jason. We both know that isn't the case."

"Where's the bro code, though? Where's the respect?"

"We're adults. We are business colleagues, not friends. There's no bro code here."

"You're a fucking asshole."

"On that note, I'm going to head out." I turned to walk away but paused the moment he spoke.

"Have fun with all the hospital trips," he spat out.

I turned back and cocked an eyebrow. "What?"

"With her condition, the girl's always getting sick. It's a damn headache. I wasn't trying to spend every other weekend in the emergency room, but I had to do what I had to do to get this," he said, gesturing around his office.

What the fuck was he going on about?

"What are you talking about?" I asked.

He raised a brow. "You didn't know...? Oh shit, you don't know. She didn't tell you. Dude—Aaliyah's ya know..." He made a croaking face. What a fucking fucker.

"What?"

"She's literally dying."

"What? No, she's not."

"Uh, yeah, she is. Honestly, it seems impossible that you haven't noticed. I picked up on the signs early on, her fat ass ankles, her nonstop heavy breathing. I knew something was off, but my mom was the one who actually told me."

"Told you what?"

"She has heart failure. She was diagnosed like two years ago. They said she only has a few more years, which is why, when my parents said I could get this position if I married her, I jumped on board. I figured a few years with the sick chick was worth it if I ended up running the company out here, but I couldn't go through with it in the end. Plus, by that point, all the contracts were signed, and it was a done deal. So, I won without the sick girl."

He kept calling her sick, and it made me want to punch him in his throat. She wasn't sick. She just had a cold. It was only a cold. It was nothing more than a...

My mind began racing, connecting all the dots that had been right in front of my face the whole time, signs I'd decided to ignore because my feelings for Aaliyah were growing too much.

She was tired a lot.

She got winded easily.

No...she couldn't be...she would've told me...

"Anyway, whatever, man. Have my leftovers while you can. The clock is ticking on that one, so don't be surprised when you're at a funeral. One I'm not paying for because I didn't marry the bitch."

"Fuck you!" I said, barging toward him and grabbing him by his collar. He stared at me and began snickering as if he was enjoying the show of me finding out that the one girl I'd ever cared for wasn't going to be around for much longer.

"Yeah, fuck me. Let me go before I call security," he warned, ripping himself out of my grip. He smoothed his shirt with his palms and cleared his throat. "Now, go ahead—go back to New York to your fucked-up prize. I just wanted to tell you face-to-face that you screwed up getting together with her. In the end, you lost, dude."

I went back to the hotel and pulled out my laptop. My heart hadn't stopped racing since the conversation with Jason. I searched congestive heart failure. I read about every symptom, every cause, every treatment. I watched YouTube videos about patients who had it, watched videos about people who'd lost loved ones to it. My panic and worry were at an all-time high as I read more and more details about the severity of heart failure.

Then I searched the timeline of those diagnosed with it.

I searched their survival rate.

My own heart cracked into a million pieces.

Most don't live past five years.

She had been diagnosed two years ago.

Who knew how much time she had left?

How was this happening? Why hadn't she told me? Hell, why hadn't I realized it?! I fucking knew. Some part of me was aware, but I ignored all the signs because I didn't want it to be true. I didn't want the hurting of my past to come back to my present. Yet here I was, doing exactly what I had done as a child. I was searching for answers. Searching for some light. Searching for a cure to the uncurable.

I sat in my dark hotel room, falling apart as the laptop light shone against my face, realizing the woman I loved was going to die.

And nothing I could do would stop it.

THIRTY-SIX

Connor

Ten years old

MOM WAS TRYING NOT TO CRY WHEN SHE TOLD ME ABOUT THE cancer.

I didn't even know what that was, but I knew it was bad if she was trying not to tell me. I knew she'd been sick, but I didn't know how bad. I thought she just had a bad cold or something with how she was always coughing stuff up.

"Do you understand, Connor? Do you understand what I'm telling you?" she said as a few tears fell down her cheeks. She brushed them away fast, trying to pretend they never happened, but I'd already seen them.

"Are you dying?" I asked, feeling like my insides were twisted up in knots. My tummy had hurt ever since Mom said that word to me. Cancer. It was hurting her. It was making her want to cry, but she was acting like she didn't because she didn't want me to cry. Even though I wanted to fall apart.

I want to fall apart.

But I couldn't because Mom had already had to cry enough when Dad left us, and whenever I cried, she cried. I didn't want her to do that anymore, so I couldn't do it either. I had to be strong for her.

"No, sweetheart," she said, placing her hands against my cheeks. "No, I'm not dying. We are going to fight this, okay? We are going to fight this and win."

I sniffled a bit and nodded, wanting to be strong, but I was just a kid, and sometimes kids hurt. I gave her a hug and held her tight. Then I pulled back. "Can I go to bed?"

"Are you tired already? It's kind of early."

"Yeah. I just want to go to sleep."

She frowned but nodded.

I went to my bedroom and closed my door. I lay in my bed, put my pillow over my face so Mom couldn't hear me, and then I started crying. My whole body shook as I kept thinking about Mom being sick. She couldn't be sick. I needed her. She was my bestest friend. I couldn't handle something being wrong with her, and I hated that I couldn't fix it. I should've been able to help her, fix her, be the man of the house.

I couldn't stop crying like a stupid kid, and I knew I had to do better because Mom needed me to be strong, but I was scared, and I didn't know what I'd ever do if she wasn't okay. I needed her to be okay. I needed her to be okay. I needed—

"Connor Ethan," Mom said, walking into my room. I kept my pillow over my face because I knew if she saw me, she'd know I was sad, and I didn't want her to know. I had to be strong for her. For us. I had to because Dad was gone now, and there was no one else to be strong.

"Sweetheart, look at me," Mom said, walking over to my bed and sitting beside me. She tugged at the pillow, and I tugged back.

"No!"

"Connor, please. It's okay."

"No. It's not! It's not okay! It can't be okay if you're not okay!" I cried, my tears still falling, soaking my pillowcase. I sounded like a big baby, but I didn't know how to sound like anything else. Mom was sick. She wasn't okay, and that made me really scared.

She managed to remove my pillow, and she set it on the other side of the bed. I pushed myself up to sit, pulled my knees into my chest, and wrapped my arms around my legs.

"Look at me, Con."

I couldn't. I couldn't look at her because it would just remind me that she wasn't okay.

But she made me. She placed her hands on my cheeks and forced me to look her in the eyes. She then took my hands and placed them against her face.

"I'm okay. You see? You feel my face? You feel my skin? I'm still here, and I'm okay. Do you understand? I am okay. You are okay. We are going to be okay. Do you understand?"

I nodded as I kept sniffling.

"Do you want me to sleep with you tonight?" she asked.

I shook my head. "No. I'm a big kid." Even though I wanted her to stay with me that night. I didn't want to be alone. I wanted to wake up in the morning and see that she was still okay.

She smiled. "Do you want me to sleep with you tonight?"

I shrugged. "Will it make you feel better?"

"Absolutely. I think I need you tonight."

"Okay then, but we'll go in your room 'cause your bed is bigger."

"Sounds good to me." She wiped my tears away and kissed my forehead. We headed to her bedroom, and it wasn't long before she fell asleep. After she was sleeping, I snuck out of bed and went to grab her laptop. I went into her closet and closed the door so the light from the computer wouldn't wake her up.

I pulled up the search engine on the internet and began typing with one finger at a time as my heart pounded hard in my chest.

What is cancer?

What happens if my mom dies?

How long will my mom live with cancer?

Is my mom dying?

Each word I typed made my tummy hurt even more. If Mom died, who would take care of me? Where would I go? How could I live without her?

I couldn't.

I couldn't live without her.

After typing too many words and feeling even more sad than before, I climbed back into bed with Mom and wrapped my arms around her. I laid my head on her chest to make sure her heart was still beating and her chest was still rising and falling.

"Mom," I whispered, knowing she couldn't hear me. Tears started falling from my eyes as I lay against her. "Please don't do it, okay? Please...please don't die."

THIRTY-SEVEN

Aaliyah

Present day

I HADN'T HEARD FROM CONNOR SINCE HE'D TEXTED ME THAT HE'D landed in California. I'd sent him a lot of messages, and when I began to worry, he texted me back once. It was a vague and short reply.

Connor: I'm okay. Busy. See you once back in town.

I hated that when I read his message, worry and doubt hit me.

Don't overthink it, Aaliyah.

The day he was supposed to return to New York, I went ahead and prepared dinner for him. I made a spread of his favorite foods and laid out a tray with every type of Cheetos I could find.

He came in two hours later than he said he would be home, and when he did, he looked destroyed. His tie was loosened, and his eyes were heavy. He smelled like whiskey, and I couldn't for the life of me figure out what was happening. Had Jason burned the building down to the ground in California? What was weighing so heavily on Connor's shoulders?

"Hey," I said, moving closer to him.

He pushed out a forced smile. "Hey." He walked past me without greeting me with a kiss, no hug—nothing. The alarm started building in me, but I tried my best not to let it show.

"I figured you might be hungry after the trip, especially dealing with Jason and his crap, so I made you some of your favorite foods. And—"

"Are you dying?" he spat out, looking at me for the first time since he'd stepped into the house.

His words made my whole system go into shock.

My lips parted to speak, but no words came out at first. Then, I whispered. "What?"

He took a few steps toward me. He lowered his head before looking at me with pain-filled eyes. "Are you dying, Red?"

"How did you find—"

"Jason. I guess it got back to him that you and I were…a thing. That's why he called me out to California—to throw it in my face that I was picking up his leftovers, and then he told me you have heart failure. So, I came here to have you tell me it wasn't true. Please…tell me it isn't true," he begged, his voice cracking.

My lips parted, but I couldn't cohesively collect my thoughts to say anything that made sense. "I'm sorry, I…"

No words came to me.

He looked seconds away from completely falling apart.

I did that to him.

I made his soul ache.

I took a step in his direction, and he held his hand up. He put his head down and stared at the floor before sliding his hands into his pockets.

"I'm…I'm sorry," I said, uncertain what else I could tell him.

It was all I could think to say. When he looked up at me, his eyes were glassy, as if my apology was enough to tell him that I was, in fact, sick…that I was dying. It was at that moment that I saw the switch go off. I saw the moment he began to pull away from me.

"Listen, I think we kind of rushed into things," he started.

No…

No…don't do this…

"It's probably best if we keep our situation friendly instead of diving into more. Honestly, I've been falling behind on work, and I need to truly refocus on the projects I have on deck. I don't really have time for—"

"Me," I whispered, my voice shaking. "You don't have time for me."

He grimaced and brushed the palm of his hand against the back of his neck. "Cutting it off before feelings get involved is probably the best idea. We can go back to just being friends. This is all moving too fast, and I need time to regroup."

How could he say that? How could he act as if we hadn't already developed feelings for one another after all we'd shared?

"I, uh, I'm going to get to work," he said. That was it. There was no more conversation to be had. He walked into his office and shut the door behind him.

I didn't see him for the remainder of the night. I couldn't sleep at all. My mind was spinning too fast. All I wanted to do was go across the hall and knock on Connor's door, try to explain everything to him, try to express how sorry I was for lying about the severity of my illness. So, I did. I went to his office and knocked. When I didn't get a reply, I turned the knob and opened it. He wasn't in there. I checked his bedroom, and he wasn't there, either. I checked every other place in the house, including the rooftop, and I had no luck finding him.

He was gone.

A few days passed, and Connor never came home. After about four days of silence, I showed up at Connor's job to talk to him. I knew the conversation we had before he left hadn't gone well, but I wasn't ready to give up on us. I needed to be able to get through to him and make him understand I didn't mean to lie to him, let him know I wanted to be as open as possible. I just needed a chance to speak to him face-to-face again, now that we both were aware of the situation.

"Jason?" I gasped as I walked into the lobby of Roe Real Estate and saw my ex-fiancé standing there. He turned to face me. At first, he appeared shocked, but that quickly evaporated into a look of disdain.

"Wh-what are you doing here?" I choked out. I hadn't seen him since I was moving out of the penthouse, and I'd hoped I'd never have to cross paths with him again. If he was nothing more than a distant nightmare to me, I'd be perfectly fine with that fact.

He looked smug as he fiddled with the designer cuffs on his designer suit. "I actually am part owner of the business you're standing in, so I should be the one asking you that question. Flew in to finish a conversation with Connor." He slid his hands into the pockets of his slacks and arched an inquisitive brow. "What are you doing here?"

My mind shot back to the reason I'd shown up to Connor's office. To talk to him. To see where his head had been. To figure out how we could make what we had work. Yet I couldn't say that to Jason.

Even though I shouldn't have cared—he had, after all, stood me up on our wedding day—I did.

A wicked smirk curved his lips. "So those fucked-up rumors were true, huh?"

"What are you talking about?"

"You've been screwing my partner? News travels fast. I just didn't think you had it in you."

"It's not what you think, Jason."

"Oh, sweetheart, it's exactly what I think. I think you're a whore who got her feelings hurt and tried to latch onto whatever she could to keep her head above water."

"That's not it at all."

"Was this your way to get back at me for standing you up? You thought you could screw my partner to get me to care?"

"What? No...I—"

"Here are the facts, Aaliyah," he said, stepping closer, making me feel as if I was boxed in even though we stood firmly in the middle of the lobby. "I couldn't care less about who you're fucking because I couldn't care less about you. You've never been anything but arm candy to me, nothing of substance. You're a pretty girl and a decent fuck, but not someone any guy would want to really take home."

"You almost did," I choked out, feeling tears burning behind my eyes. "You were going to marry me."

"Yeah, and thank fuck I came to the realization that I was making a huge mistake. I mean, let's be honest—you'll probably drop dead any day now, judging by how ghostly you're looking, and I, for one, didn't want to foot the bill for that. You were just a business transaction for me. If I agreed to marry you, I got the West Coast division. That was it. I didn't want to deal with you. I doubt Connor would feel any different about it than I do."

"You're wrong. Connor's not like that."

He laughed mischievously. "You really think Roe gives a damn about you? I know that guy. I've worked around him for years. The truth is, if you aren't making him money, you aren't worth his time—especially someone like you. Connor is a businessman, and he doesn't make bad deals. Let's face the facts: you are a bad deal. If anything, you're a liability. He doesn't have the space for you in the empire he's trying to build." Jason moved in closer and ran his finger against my cheek, cruising it down my jawline. "Don't you get it, Aaliyah? You're no one's forever. You're just a temporary fix. Besides, after all the shit Connor has been through with his mother being sick, it's really fucked up that you'd put him through your drama. You're showing up, just to drop dead on the guy. Real classy, Aaliyah."

I swung his hand away from my face and took a giant step back. My mind was swirling faster than I wanted to admit. My vision was blurring as the emotions pushed to the front of my eyes. I turned away from Jason and rushed out the door, straight onto the streets of Manhattan.

I hated Jason. I hated him, and everything he stood for so much. I hated how he'd abandoned me on my wedding day. I hated how he lied. I hated how he betrayed me and made it hard for me to trust. I hated his anger, his personality, his heart. I hated how cruel he'd been.

But what I hated most about him was how he made sense, how I could see how someone wouldn't want a forever with a girl who had limited time.

I hated how his words aligned with Connor's fears.

I hated how Jason was right.

THIRTY-EIGHT

Connor

"**W**HAT IN THE HELL DO YOU THINK YOU'RE DOING?" Marie snapped as she burst into my office.

I'd been working on overdrive the past few days, avoiding facing reality with Aaliyah, and the fact that Marie came barging into my office left me stunned. She didn't even notice Damian, who was sitting in my office chair.

I raised an eyebrow. "I'm sorry, did I miss something…?"

"Is it true you are seeing Aaliyah?"

Jason must've brought his mother into the loop, and that was the last thing I wanted to deal with. I didn't want to face the fact that Aaliyah was sick, that she was dying. I didn't want to face the fact that there was truly going to be a day where she wasn't around. So, the last thing I needed was Jason Rollsfield's mother in my face, hollering at me about what was going on between Aaliyah and myself.

"Listen, Marie, this isn't a good time right now."

"It sure the hell is, and I need you to end it, okay? Whatever it is that is going on between you and Aaliyah needs to come to an

It already had, but I didn't need her to know that. All I needed from Marie was for her to leave my office.

"Whatever is going on between Aaliyah and myself is none of your business, Marie—"

"The hell it isn't," she spat out, pacing my office as if she'd lost her damn mind. "No. No. She has to be with Jason. They are meant to be together! I didn't go through all of this for her to end up with you!"

"What do you mean you didn't go through—"

"Leave her alone, Connor. She's not yours to have. I fought for this, fought for her, and I'll be damned if you come in and ruin this for my family!" she barked, tears sitting sternly at the back of her eyes. "End things, or else," she said sternly before pushing her purse strap higher on her shoulder, turning around on her heels, and marching out of my office.

Damian looked at her with a raised brow as she was leaving but didn't say a word. He then looked over toward me, confused.

"What the hell was that?" he asked.

"I have absolutely no fucking clue."

"Well, regardless of that, you look like shit," he stated. I knew I looked like shit. I hadn't slept in days. My mind was working in overdrive, and I couldn't focus on anything but the idea of Aaliyah dying. "What's going on?"

"Nothing. I'm fine."

"Bullshit. What's going on?"

"Just work stuff."

"Bullshit again. I know your looks when work stuff is bothering you. That isn't it."

"Can you just drop it, Damian? I don't want to talk about it," I snapped. Yeah. I snapped at him. I felt guilty about it instantly, too. "Sorry. I didn't get much sleep last night."

"Obviously. Like I said—you look like shit." He took a seat across from me. "Is it something with Aaliyah?"

"I'd rather not talk about it."

"Yeah. So, let's talk about it. What happened?"

I pinched the bridge of my nose and shrugged. "Nothing. I ended whatever it was that we were doing with one another. I figured it was best if I focus on work instead of putting my focus in other places."

He snickered. No shit, Damian actually laughed. "You got scared, didn't you?"

"You don't know what you're talking about."

"I do. I'm not an idiot." He paused and cleared his throat. "Is it because you found out she was sick?"

I looked at him, stunned by his words. "What? You knew?"

"Yup."

"How?"

"I told you, I researched her. I did digging when I realized you liked her to make sure she had no skeletons in her closet."

"And you found out she was sick?"

"Yup."

He said it so calmly, which pissed me right the hell off. "Why the fuck didn't you tell me?!"

"Because I knew you'd push her away, which clearly that's exactly what you did."

I raked my hands through my hair. My blood was boiling as Damian told me all of this as if it wasn't dire information that I could've used. If I knew Aaliyah was sick, I would've never let my feelings grow in the way they had. I would've never opened up. I would've never allowed myself to fall.

I knew better than this.

I knew better than to get close with someone.

"You should've told me," I said.

"I'm glad I didn't."

"What the hell do you mean by that? You wanted me to feel shitty like this?" I barked as the rage built more and more.

"No. I just wanted you to feel." He shifted in his chair and leaned forward. "I get it, man. I'm heartless. I don't feel deep for anyone. I wasn't built that way. But you're different. You were made to love, but you let your fear of losing people get in the way. I knew if you found out Aaliyah was sick, you'd push her to the side because of fear."

I knitted my brows together and grimaced. "That's not why I stopped things with her. I stopped because she lied about it."

"But she didn't."

"Omitting the truth is a lie."

"I don't tell you when I go to shit, but that doesn't mean I lied about it. It just wasn't something I told you."

"I'm being serious, Damian."

"So am I. Stop acting like she's some kind of devil because she didn't tell you how bad off she was. You're acting like a dick."

"Fuck off a bit, will you, Damian?"

"Nah. I'm good." He made himself comfortable in his chair. "Let's unpack this situation."

"There's nothing to unpack."

"There you go lying. Your baggage is heavy, shit, maybe heavier than mine."

"What do you want me to say?"

"That you pushed Aaliyah away because you're scared of her dying."

I started shifting paperwork around on my desk. "I really don't have time for this, Damian. So, if you don't have anything work-related to tell me…"

"I don't."

"Then you can leave. And you know what? Fuck you for not telling me about her. That was really shitty."

"What can I say? I'm a shitty person. Go ahead, be pissed at me, I don't give a fuck. Take as long as you need to throw your anger my way. Whatever makes you happy. But then, at some point, you're going to have to face the fact that you're throwing away something good because you're afraid."

"What do you want me to do, huh? She's dying, Damian, and—"

"We're all fucking dying!" he snapped, tossing his hands up in irritation. "The day we take our first damn breath, we begin to rot. The only real guarantee in life is that we will all meet our maker someday. Life's clock is ticking loud for all of us, man. We could walk outside and get hit by a semi and have our lives ended in a split second. That's it. That's the only thing this world promises us—death. But with Aaliyah, you have an actual shot at living. A lot of assholes are alive but aren't living. They aren't tapping into the deepest levels of happiness, and you could do that with Aaliyah no matter how short that time would be."

"You don't understand…"

"Sure, I do. Before you met me, I wasn't living. I was merely existing, but then you came into my life and gave me drive. You gave me family. So, don't tell me I don't understand. Whatever, man. Be pissed for as long as you need to, but don't miss out on that level of happiness due to your own stubborn fear. Most people don't get a shot at real love before they die. Don't be those people." He stood from his chair. "Knock, knock."

"Who's there?"

"Stop being a fucking dick and talk to Aaliyah."

I lowered my head and released a weighted sigh. He was right, but I wasn't sure how to go about any of it.

"Hey, Damian?"

"Yeah?"

"Can you do some digging on Marie Rollsfield?"

He seemed surprised by my request. When we first met, I made it clear that I didn't want him digging up anything on anyone I knew before meeting Damian. But something felt off with Marie. I knew something was wrong with the whole Jason situation, but I just couldn't put my finger on it.

Without question, Damian nodded. "On it."

I knew I needed to talk to Aaliyah because Damian was right. There weren't a lot of times when the guy was ever wrong about anything. I just needed to build up the courage to go home to see Aaliyah and actually hold a conversation with her. Yet all of my plans evaporated the moment I showed up late one night and found her in her bedroom, packing some boxes.

"Hey," I said, walking to her open door. She paused her movements and looked over at me. "What's going on?"

She blinked a few times, seemingly confused. She was probably thrown off that I was actually at the house after being MIA for days.

"I'm packing."

"For what?"

"I found a new apartment. I'm moving this weekend."

My insides twisted at her words. Shit. I knew I was dealing with my own demons, but I didn't want her to leave. I wanted her to stay. I wanted her to stay so bad, but I'd been a fucking idiot over the past few days. "You don't have to go."

She didn't look at me as she shrugged. "No, it's fine. My boss gave me an early raise, and I'd been able to save up enough for a decent place. This situation between you and me was always temporary anyway, right? So, I'm moving on to my next chapter."

I wanted to tell her to stay. I wanted to man the fuck up and stop being a dick and tell her that I was just scared. That I didn't know how to deal with the fact that she wasn't going to be around forever. I wanted to tell her that I didn't know what the fuck I was doing or how to process my emotions.

But instead, I said, "What about the interview?"

I wished I hadn't said that because I saw the flash of hurt that washed over her face from my words.

"What?"

"We never finished the interview. You were supposed to come down to Kentucky to see my past."

"Yeah, well, that's not going to work out. Besides, my doctors don't think it's safe for me to travel with my condition."

With her condition.

Those words were another reminder to me that she was sick. That she was dying. That she was facing a time limit against life, and she was losing. *Please don't die…*

Emotion sat at the back of my throat. I was on the brink of falling apart, but I couldn't do it. I couldn't express myself; I couldn't tell her how I felt, so like a damn idiot, I stayed quiet.

"Besides, I think I have enough to write the article. I have everything I need," she explained.

I knew what I wanted to say, but I couldn't be man enough to actually spit out the words. I should've told her to stay. I should've told her I'd be in her corner no matter what happened. I should've pulled her into my arms and comforted her because she had to be scared. She had to be terrified of everything that was happening.

I should've begged for her to stay, but, instead like an idiot, I let her walk away.

THIRTY-NINE

Connor

I LEFT NEW YORK AND FLEW DOWN TO KENTUCKY WITH MY TAIL between my legs. I knew I'd made a huge mistake ending things with Aaliyah, but I couldn't figure out how to make it right. Also, the idea of losing her was still so heavy on my chest. I couldn't stop researching heart failure ever since I'd found out. I'd been looking for treatments, calling specialists, falling apart and hating the universe for bringing Aaliyah back into my life only to take her away from me again.

This shit wasn't fair.

As my plane landed in Kentucky, I was greeted at the baggage claim when Mom rushed over to my side. Within seconds, her arms were wrapped around me, squeezing me so tight. I got choked up just from the comfort of her embrace. You'd never knew how much you needed your mother's hug until you were on the verge of a breakdown.

"Oh, sweetie! I'm so happy to see you!" She looked around the area with wide eyes filled with hope.

My chest just about caved in when I realized she was searching for Aaliyah. "She's not here, Mom."

"What? But I thought you were bringing her into town to show her—"

"She's dying," I spat out. I couldn't hold it in anymore as I choked on my words. Tears began falling down my cheeks as I whispered. "She's dying, Mom."

We got back home, and I fell into a deeper depression, just thinking about Aaliyah. I hated myself for being such a little shit. I hated myself for being afraid of losing her. I hated myself for abandoning her.

"Heart failure? But she's so young," Mom said as she made a pot of coffee. "That's so heartbreaking."

"Yeah," I said. It was all I could manage.

Before she could say anything else, the front door opened, and a man walked into my mom's house as if he owned the place.

"Honey, I'm homeeee!" he said in a singsong voice. He came marching into the house, and the moment he saw me, he clapped his hands together. "Oh, my goodness! Connor! Put it there!" he said, grabbing my hand and shaking it aggressively. It must've been that Danny guy Mom had been going on and on about. Great.

Clearly, he couldn't read the energy of the room because he was smiling and giddy as ever. He was dressed in a Hawaiian shirt with pink and yellow flowers all over it, neon green pants, and a tie-dye hat on his head. The dude was well into his sixties, dressing as if he were a toddler who got to dress themselves for the day.

Really, Mom? Him?

"Yeah, good to meet you, too, Dan."

"It's Danny," he said. "So, where's this special lady that I heard you were bringing home today?" he asked.

I knew he didn't mean for it, but that question was a sucker punch to my soul.

Mom walked over and wrapped her arms around Danny's waist. "I wish this was better news, but it turns out Aaliyah has some serious health issues. She wasn't able to make it."

"Is she going to be okay?" Danny asked.

"No. She's not. She's fucking dying and I can't save her. I broke up with her because I can't sit there and watch her die."

Mom's face dropped. "You broke up with her? You two were dating?"

"Yeah, we were, and yeah, I did. She's moving out of my place as we speak. It's over."

"No...Connor. You can't do that...I mean...I know this is a lot, but you can't abandon her...I know you're scared but—"

"I'm not scared, Mom. I'm fucking terrified. I'm terrified. But I can't do it again. I can't sit there and watch someone I care for lose the battle of their life. I can't go through that. I did it twice with you, watching you fight, and I can't do it again."

Mom's eyes watered over, and she covered her hand with her mouth, choking up. I didn't want to make her cry, but I was being honest. I couldn't suffer through that trauma again. I couldn't spend late nights sitting up wondering if Aaliyah was still breathing. I couldn't sit on the edge at all times, wondering if today was the day I was forced to say goodbye. I couldn't watch her die.

Danny stepped forward and gave Mom a half-smile. He was much more somber than before, his energetic personality taming. "Can I talk to him alone for a minute, sweetheart?"

Mom nodded, and left the room, leaving me uneasy with the idea of interacting with Danny. I didn't even know this guy.

He sat down at the table with me and released a weighted sigh. "Life is shitty sometimes, eh?"

"No offense, Dan, but I—"

"Danny."

"Right. Danny. No offense, but I don't want to talk about this. Especially with someone who is pretty much a stranger to me."

"I get it, but I understand where you're coming from."

"No, you don't."

"Yeah, I do, Connor. Probably more than you'd believe."

"No. You have no clue what it's like to go through what I've been through. You have no clue how hard it is to watch someone you love battle cancer two times. You have no clue what that can do to your head. Then when you get past that trauma, you have no clue what it's like to fall for someone who will bring up those same fears. You don't fucking know."

He brushed his thumb against the bridge of his nose and sat back in his chair. He stared forward as if he were looking past me, and he pushed out a forced grin that didn't have a drop of happiness in it. "You might not think I know what it's like, but I do, young man. I was married before I met your mother. Her name was Jules, and she was phenomenal. I was by her side through her first cancer scare and through her second that took her life."

Danny's brows knitted together as he lowered his hands to his lap and fiddled with his fingers.

My heart sat heavily in my throat as he revealed his truths to me, and I felt like a complete jackass because I didn't have a clue what he'd been through.

"No one suffers more than the victims of that ugly disease, of any disease, truly. No one knows what the pain those individuals went through was like. But I remembered I'd prayed to God that he'd shift it. Shift her pain to my body. Give me her hurts so I could feel them for her."

I remained quiet but invested.

I prayed that prayer one too many times, too.

"But the people who hurt the most after the ones with the diagnosis? Their loved ones. I never showed her my sorrow because I didn't want her to have any more of a burden to bear. I knew her sadness and fear was tenfold more than my own. She was already suffering more than words. What kind of asshole would I have been if I told her that I was hurting, too? Instead, I cried in my car. Before work. After work. During my lunch break. Whenever I had a chance to fall apart, I'd fall. I'd fall apart because the woman I loved, the woman I cherished with all of my heart was slipping away from me and I had no control over it."

He took a deep breath and clasped his hands together. "Please believe me when I say, I know the fears you have with Aaliyah. When I met your mother and found out about her past run-ins with cancer, I hesitated just like you. I thought what if it comes back? What if she leaves me sooner than I'd hope? What if I have to go back to that part in my life of falling apart in my car again? The what-ifs are the worst part of it all because there's no way to truly ever know."

"How did you get past it?"

"With her smile, with her heart," he said effortlessly as if loving my mother was the easiest thing to do. "You don't meet a woman like your mother and skip the chance of happiness because of the fear of loss. No, you dig your feet in deeper. You hold on to her tighter because you know her love will be worth it, time and time again. I realized that I couldn't live my life, waiting for the unknown, but I had to take the leap. Besides," he breathed out a cloud of hot air and smiled. "What kind of lucky bastard like me gets to fall in love with two extraordinary women in his lifetime? If life needed a reason for existence, love is the solution."

Damn.

I really wanted to hate that guy.

"I already messed things up with Aaliyah," I said, feeling gloom and doom about the whole situation. Fuck, I missed her. I missed her so much that I didn't even know how to cope. I didn't know my heart could do that—I didn't know it could keep shattering into a million pieces each day that passed. It was my own fault for pushing her away, too. Due to my struggles. My fears. My past.

"Do you love her?" Danny asked.

"Yes, I love her." That was the first time I'd admitted it. It was the first time I'd allowed those words to leave my mouth even though they'd been sitting heavily in my chest for weeks.

"Does that scare you?"

"Terrifies me."

"Good." He nodded. "Sometimes you have to be afraid of the things you love in order to make sure you don't ever lose them again."

"She's already gone. I can't even blame her because I'm the asshole who pushed her away when she was struggling the most."

"Do you think she loves you, too?"

I nodded slowly. "I believe so. I hope so."

"Then it's not over. When two people love each other, you work through the pitfalls. You fight for one another. You don't give up. Now, just figure out a way to prove to her that no matter what, no matter when times get hard, that you will not run anymore. From the sound of it, this poor girl has been abandoned in her life. Prove to her that you're here to stay."

The next morning, I woke up feeling even more exhausted than the night before. Perhaps drinking half a bottle of whiskey with my newfound friend Danny-boy wasn't the greatest idea, but at least I wasn't drinking alone.

"Connor! You have a visitor!" Mom hollered through the house, making me groan.

My head was pounding as I pulled myself out of bed and headed to the living room. A small, broken smile hit me as I looked up to see a familiar face.

"Hey, kid," Jax said, frowning. He slid his hands into his oil-stained jeans. "Heard you were in town."

"My mom called you?"

"Yeah." He cleared his throat. "She said you were going through some major shit."

"Yeah."

"As you know, I'm not really good with dealing with emotions and stuff...so how about instead, we go old school, and you join me on a plumbing job this morning?"

"Like the good ole days?"

"Yup. Come on. I made you a protein shake."

I grimaced. "Can we just grab some donuts?"

"Never. Go get dressed fast, will you? You're late."

I hurried off and went to get ready. About fifteen minutes later, I was hopping into Jax's passenger seat, and I instantly was transported back to when I was seventeen-years-old, having my daily drives with him. Sometimes I wished I could go back to that time just so I wouldn't have to feel the way I felt today.

"How's Kennedy and Elizabeth doing?" I asked about his wife and daughter.

"Good, good. Elizabeth's into gymnastics nowadays, and let me tell you, that's not a cheap fucking hobby. But I can't say no to the girl, even if she's a demon child as a preteen. Kennedy's pregnant again. We just found out last week. I'm not supposed to tell anyone yet, but you're not anyone, you're you."

"Me, your bestest friend in the whole world."

He rolled his eyes. I smirked.

Some things never changed.

We showed up at Old Man Mike's house, which was fucking disgusting. Mike was a hoarder with at least thirteen cats running around his house. Everyone in town knew that the idea of going into Mike's house was hell. Whenever he made pies for the town's festivals, people smiled in his face as they took a slice, then tossed it into the trash.

We were working on Mike's toilet, which looked as if it's been backed up for years. The color of the water, along with the smell, almost made me gag.

"I don't miss this job," I confessed, holding my shirt over my nose. Jax seemed unmoved by it.

"Mostly, I focus on the landscaping business, but every now and then, I pick up a plumbing job. Keeps me connected to my roots," he explained. "You see, the thing about these pipes that Mike has is they are old, and he allowed them to build up junk for too long. He didn't face the damage right away and just looked away from it. Never really acknowledging the shit that's been building for years up until one day, it began to overflow."

He grumbled as he worked the snake down the drain, fishing it around as he kept talking. "But it's never too late to start clearing out the shit that's been sitting there for so long. The shit he overlooked, the shit he tried to pretend didn't exist"—he hit a mark with the snake, and the toilet automatically flushed, signaling his breakthrough—"can all be fixed with time, forgiveness, and care."

I narrowed my eyes. "Are you trying to use a poop analogy on me, Jax?"

"I'm a small-town man. I don't know what an analogy even is," he joked.

"No. You're saying my soul is full of shit, and I need to deal with my emotional trauma from my mom, so I can flush this stuff out and be there for Aaliyah."

He grabbed a rag and began wiping his hands clean. "Is that what you heard from what I said?"

"Yeah. You said I was full of shit."

"That's because you are full of shit." He shrugged. "Kennedy's my best friend. If I found out we only had today left, I'd do everything in my power to spend every last second with her. So do it, Con. Clear out your shit."

"Do all middle-aged men in this town just have powerful words of wisdom up their sleeves?"

He stood up and patted me on the back. "Call me middle-aged again, and I'll knock your teeth out."

"Whatever you say, old man." I paused for a moment. "Are you currently touching me with your shit hand?"

"Yeah, I am."

"And this is exactly why I don't miss this job, but I do miss you."

"Don't be corny, kid."

"I love you, too, Jax."

Just then, my phone dinged with a message from Damian. I opened it and felt as if my chest was seconds away from collapsing.

"What is it?" Jax asked, noticing the look of panic on my face.

"It's Aaliyah. I have to get back to New York."

FORTY

Aaliyah

EXHAUSTION WASN'T A STRONG ENOUGH WORD FOR WHAT I'D been feeling as of late. Each morning, I felt worse than the previous day. All I wanted to do was stay in bed and fall into a deep slumber, but I still had a job to do. I was trying my best to hold on to any kind of normality even though it was seeming more and more impossible each day.

I'd turned my article on Connor in to Maiv for approval right when he showed up to my office. Greta texted me straight away when he'd entered the building. When he reached my office, I felt as if I would pass out simply from my nerves.

"Hi," he breathed out, days after he'd gone off to Kentucky. I figured that was the end of our story. It had to be the end of our story. I couldn't allow myself to give him any more of me. It wasn't healthy for us. It wasn't right.

"You shouldn't be here," I said, trying to hide any true emotions. I couldn't let him see how his proximity made me want to step in closer. I couldn't show him how much I missed him, how much I wanted him

"I hurt you." He sighed. "I'm sorry, Aaliyah. I panicked and pulled away."

"I'm over it."

His brows lowered as he stared at me. My coldness toward him probably threw him off, but I couldn't help it. I had to be cold so I could be strong.

"Give me another chance, Red. Please."

I wanted to cry, but I didn't. "You're too late."

"I love you," he breathed out, his voice cracking and pained.

I looked at him, and I was certain my eyes were flashed with emotions. Then I parted my mouth and whispered the words, "I loved you, too."

"Loved?"

"Yes. Loved."

Past tense. It was a lie, but one I had to tell him.

"Aaliyah—"

"Please leave," I stated sternly.

"But I...I hurt you," he whispered again, his voice pained with the realization of what had taken place.

I nodded. "Yes."

"Let me try again."

"No."

"Why not?"

"Because the first time it was you hurting me. If I let you come back, the second time would be me hurting myself."

"Aaliyah—"

"I don't have time for this, Connor. I don't have time to waste anymore. I can't do this back and forth thing with you."

He slightly gave a nod, before parting his mouth to speak. I couldn't let him do that, though. I couldn't allow him to give me another word because his sounds made my heart skip beats. His sounds made me want to fall into him and forgive him. His sounds made me weak.

I couldn't be weak anymore.

Still, his voice...

The way it spoke to me...

Just a little bit more of him...I just wanted a little more...time.

"I know you're upset with me, and I know I'm a fucking idiot, but I need to tell you something, Aaliyah, something really important," he urged.

"Can you leave?" I asked, not wanting him to go but needing him to leave.

"I will, but I need you to know that—"

"Connor, I mean it, can you—"

"She's your mother," he blurted out, making me still my body completely.

"I'm sorry what?" He took a step in my direction, and I took a step backward. I held up a hand. "Stop, what do you mean? Who's my mother?"

"Marie. She's your mother. I, uh…" He cleared his throat and rubbed the back of his neck. "I had Damian do some digging into her after she showed up to my office acting like a nutcase. She was going on and on about how she didn't go through all of this only to have you end up with someone other than Jason. Honestly, it was erratic, and crazed, and made no sense until Damian brought me proof."

"Proof," I huffed, shaking my head in disbelief. Why was he doing this? Why was he saying those words? There was no way that Marie was my mother. I would know if she was my mother. I would know if I was her daughter.

There's no possible way…

I felt lightheaded as my mind began spinning, trying to recall every situation I'd been in with Marie. I met her at my barista job, and she was always so kind to me. She introduced me to Jason and she told me she always wanted a daughter like me. She cried every time I called her a good mother.

No.

There was no way that could be true.

"I need you to leave," I pushed out, feeling as if I was on the edge of having a mental breakdown. This was all too much for me to deal with. I was already swimming in a pool of issues, and I didn't have the mental strength to add something this massive to the pile.

"Aaliyah—"

"Please," I begged, closing my eyes to try to still my dizzy spell.

When I reopened them, his blues were pinned on me. "Please leave, Connor."

He swallowed hard and nodded slowly. "I'm sorry, Aaliyah. For everything. I know this is a lot, but I figured you should know. I love you, Aaliyah. I always will, and I hope you truly know that." His eyes locked with mine for a brief second before he slid his hands into the pockets of his slacks and whispered, "I'm never giving up on you. On us. I'm going to keep showing up for you. I love you, Aaliyah, and I'm not going to give this, give us, up." He turned around and walked away.

If it weren't for my brain, my heart would've begged him to stay. I didn't let him walk away because I hated him. I let him go because I loved him. I knew he was sorry, and I knew if I allowed it, he'd stay. But I didn't want that for him. I didn't want him to suffer as my life came to an end.

I knew his past traumas and I couldn't put him through more. Therefore, I lied to him in order to allow him to let me go. As he walked away, he hadn't even known that he took a piece of me along with him.

I melted into my chair and tried to push down my emotions. My mind went right back to Marie. Breaths became harder and harder to breathe as she filled my head. Before I could process everything that had taken place, Maiv was standing in my doorway with a stern look on her face. Which wasn't surprising, a stern look was Maiv's default.

"Aaliyah. I read the article," she said with lowered brows.

"Oh? If there's anything you need me to change—"

"Congratulations on the promotion. You're going to make a great senior editor."

My heart didn't know what to do with itself. It was broken from losing Connor, but proud for myself. I knew I wrote the hell out of that article because I wrote it straight from my heart, broken pieces and all. I bled those words onto the page, highlighting Connor in the only way I knew how—the brightest of lights.

It was easy to write about someone as special as him.

"I'm thinking we'll title it 'The Modern Day Gent.' This is one of the best reads this magazine has ever had. You should be proud of your hard work. I expect nothing less than this moving forward."

"You have my word," I told her. She left my office as I sat and thought about the title. "The Modern Day Gent" was fitting. It described Connor Roe perfectly.

After my workday, I hopped right into a taxi and headed to Marie and Walter's home. I knew for a fact that I wouldn't be able to do anything else until I looked into her eyes and asked her the question that had been sitting heavily against my chest.

She wasn't home when I arrived, so I sat on her front porch, waiting.

Hours passed as day kissed nightfall, and I kept waiting. When her car pulled up, and she climbed out of the vehicle, she seemed stunned to see me sitting there. She hurried over to me with a look of alarm. "Aaliyah, sweetheart, are you okay?" she asked, probably noticing the paleness to my skin and the heaviness that sat in my eyes.

I stood up from the steps and looked her straight in the eyes as my whole body began to tremble. "Are you my mother?"

The moment's hesitation and guilt that flooded her stare told me more than any words she'd deliver ever could've.

Oh, my goodness, I was going to be sick.

"You can't be serious!" I cried out, my voice cracking as I placed my hands on top of my head. My heart pounded at an unbelievable speed against my chest as I sat on the verge of a panic attack.

Tears hit Marie's eyes as she took a few steps toward me. "Sweetheart—"

"Don't," I cut in, holding a hand toward her. "Do not call me sweetheart."

"I don't know how you found out, but..." She swallowed hard as her hands trembled. She placed her palms together in prayer formation and held them against her lips. She shook her head. "You weren't supposed to find out. I had it worked out so you'd never find out, but we were going to be a family. You were always going to be a part of my family when you married Jason. I know it sounds insane and odd, but I knew that there would never be a good way to bring you back into my life without all of the guilt and trauma attached to the fact that I—"

"Abandoned me. You abandoned me at birth."

Her tears fell down her cheeks, but I refused to allow mine to do the same. "It's not that simple."

"Don't make it simple. Just tell me the truth."

"I grew up like you…I was young and alone. When I met Walter, I felt as if I meant something to the world for the first time. Someone wanted little ole me. It was magical at first. Then Walter began to work later. He became obsessed with success, and he did anything—and any-one—to climb up the ladder. When I found out he was having an affair, my whole world crashed, and I felt betrayed. Disgusted with him, with me. So, I figured I should be a better wife. A better woman to him. I tried to get pregnant, and I couldn't. He kept cheating, so I went and gave myself to another man. I figured if he was a cheater, I should be, too."

I waited for her to continue. I needed all the pieces to the puzzle I'd been searching for my whole life. No matter how much it burned me.

"I, um, I met a man at a bar. His name was Cole Simms. He was smooth and funnier than any person I'd ever met. He was a jazz per-former and played at Ralph's in Queens every Saturday night. I went for weeks to listen to him play. I fell into his bed, and came out pregnant with you. I told Walter everything. He told me that he'd never take me back unless I'd give the baby up at birth. He told me he'd leave me with nothing and ruin my life. I know it sounds insane, but Aaliyah, I had nothing. I was just a poor girl with nothing to my name, and I didn't ex-pect to get pregnant. All I wanted to do was make Walter feel an ounce of what he made me feel."

"So, you gave me up to stay with a man who'd been unfaithful to you."

"It's so much harder to explain…" she told me, but I knew it was a lie.

"No. It's not. You gave me up, you left me alone and abandoned, then you adopted a little boy to call your son."

She lowered her head. "I know how it sounds…"

"It sounds like you're the devil," I agreed, feeling short of breath. *I can't breathe…*

"I think it was Walter's punishment for me. After I had you and gave you up, he began to speak about how much he actually wanted a child. A boy. He said if he could have that, he'd start therapy with me. So we adopted Jason…a five-year-old because Walter didn't want to deal with diapers and those early years."

"You chose Jason over me."

"You need to understand—"

"The-there's no-nothing to under-st-and," I breathed out, feeling an ache in my chest.

I took a step backward, and Marie moved in my direction.

"Aaliyah, you should sit. You're really pale," she ordered.

"What happ-ened to my fa-father?" I pushed out, feeling faint.

Syncope.

Noun.

Definition: The temporary loss of consciousness caused by a fall in blood pressure.

Also known as the medical term for passing out.

I felt it coming as my vision waved in and out.

"Aaliyah, please," she urged.

"Tell me."

She grimaced as more tears kept falling from her eyes. "I went back a few years ago when Walter and I hit a tough patch, to see if Cole still played jazz music. I found out he passed away."

"How?"

She swallowed hard. "He had a heart attack. He had a genetic family trait that was passed down the line, and…" She shook her head toward me and cupped her hand over her mouth. "I'm so sorry, Aaliyah. I'm so sorry. The moment I found out about his condition, I went on a mission to find you. I found out where you worked, and I knew after meeting you, I couldn't go on not having you in my life."

So many thoughts crashed into my head. So many feelings, so many emotions, so much pain.

Pain.

I was in pain.

I began to fall backward, catching myself as I hit the step of Marie's porch. I lowered myself down and placed my hand over my chest as I fought for every breath that came to me.

"Marie?"

"Yes?"

"Call 911."

FORTY-ONE

Aaliyah

MY BLOOD PRESSURE PLUMMETED QUICKLY AT MARIE'S HOME. I was rushed to the hospital and put on oxygen. Each breath felt exhausting to take. Once Dr. Erickson found out about my condition, he showed up to the hospital to check in on me. The paleness on his face showed me how dire my situation had become. Then again, I didn't need him to tell me what I already knew, what my exhausted heart had been telling me for so long.

I was dying.

Marie tried to visit me, but I refused to grant permission to see her. I wasn't ready to deal with her when I was trying to come to the realization that my life was ending.

I wasn't leaving the hospital, and I knew that for a fact. Not in my condition. A full day passed as I was being monitored. The room felt so cold as doctors and nurses filtered in and out of the space. They pricked me with needles and watched my numbers, making sure I was still stable.

I felt tired all the time.

All I wanted to do was sleep.

All I wanted to do was close my eyes and make the pain go away.

To my surprise, on day two of my stay in the hospital, I had a visitor. One I'd never expected to be standing in my doorway.

"Damian. What are you doing here?" I asked as he walked into my room. He looked down and somber as he always did. "How did you know I was here?"

"I'm pretty good at finding things out. Can I come in?"

"Sure, but...I'm confused as to why you're here." It was no secret that Damian and I weren't close. We'd only crossed paths a handful of times.

"I'm here on behalf of Connor," he said flatly.

"I don't understand."

"He loves you. You probably don't want him here because he hurt you. But I'm here because he loves you, and he wouldn't want you to be alone, so I'm going to sit here."

"Thi-is is crazy," I breathed out, fatigued. Exhausted.

"Yeah, well, I hear love can make situations a bit crazy." He scratched at the stubble on his chin. "You need to give him another shot."

"Damian—"

"Listen, I'm not here to stress you out or anything. Clearly, you're going through some serious shit. But I just needed to say that. I get it. I grew up in the foster system, too. I got a lot of jaded thoughts about people and trust issues. I have abandonment issues that I can't even begin to express, but Connor isn't the bad guy, Aaliyah. The rest of this fucked up world is."

"I don't know..."

"I get it. You're hurt. Be hurt. But then, give him another chance."

"It's not that easy, Damian."

"It has to be. Because this is personal to me."

"How so?"

He clasped his hands together and leaned forward. "You saved me."

I raised an eyebrow. "What?"

"You saved my life. Almost three years ago now, I was at my lowest point. I was thinking about ending my life. I felt lost and alone. I had nobody who gave a shit about me, and I sure as fuck didn't give a fuck about myself, so I figured what was the point. Then out of nowhere this goofy-ass guy with bad jokes came into my life and kept hammering at me to open up to him. He wouldn't let up, either. He kept pushing me with his sunshine and corny persona to get me to let him in. After all that work, I asked him why it was so important to him. He told me he met Little Red Riding Hood, and she changed his life for the better.

"He wanted to be able to do the same for someone else. If you never existed...if you never changed Connor's life, he would've never changed mine. I wouldn't be alive today if it weren't for you, Aaliyah. You brought someone into my life who believed that my life was worth living. Someone who gave me a shot to make something of myself when the rest of the world ignored me. So, understand me when I say this is personal to me."

His words soaked deep into my soul. I hardly could believe what he was sharing with me, but then again, I could because that was the type of person Connor was—he helped people. Still, I was scared of letting him back in.

"Have you ever been in love, Damian?"

"No," he quickly replied. "But I'd be damned if I ran from it when it came to me. People like us don't get the happy beginnings, but that doesn't mean we don't get the happy endings."

I knew Damian coming to speak to me was a big deal. Damian didn't often speak to anyone. Every time I crossed paths with him, he only offered up a few almost smiles here and there before he'd go back to minding his own business and living solely in his thoughts.

"Aaliyah," Damian said, stepping a bit closer to me. "Don't do this."

Even though he looked so tough all the time, so hard and cold, his eyes were currently washed over with empathy. With care. Every piece of him at that moment felt like a warmth I hadn't seen in a very long time.

"Don't do what?"

"Run away from something good because you're afraid that some-day that person will run away first. Connor's not a runner. Yeah, he fucked up and hesitated, but fuck, he's human. He spent his whole child-hood thinking his mother was going to die. Then when he found out you were sick, he fell into the old thought process that had haunted him for so many years. He's scared, Aaliyah. The guy is fucking terrified of losing you, but he wasn't going to run. He just stumbled a little."

"I know how hard it is for him, Damian. Truly. I get it. That's why I can't do this to him."

He looked at me confused. "What?"

"I'm dying, Damian. I know I don't have long, and I don't want to put him through that. I don't want him to have to watch me suffer be-cause it will break his heart."

"You're sitting here worrying about his heart breaking when yours is literally falling apart. If that's not love, then I don't know what is. He should be here."

"I can't do that to him...I'm sorry, Damian. I can't have him watch me die."

Damian's brows knitted as he pinched the bridge of his nose. Then he sat down in a chair.

"What are you doing?" I asked.

"Sitting."

"Why?"

"So you aren't alone."

"Dam—"

"I get it. You want to protect him from hurting. It's noble. Stupid as fuck if you ask me, but noble. But that doesn't mean you deserve to be alone. If you're dying, you're dying. It's shitty, and it's scary and fucked-up because I could name a million people who deserve to die more than you do. The world is a messed-up place, and it shits on good people. I'm sorry it's doing this to you, Aaliyah, but you're not going to do this shit alone. All right? I'm going to sit here and," He reached into his back pocket and pulled out a comic book. "I'm going to read you comics because that's what Connor would do."

"Damian. You don't have to stay here. Really. I'm fine."

"No, you're not, and that's okay. I don't need you to be fine. I just need you to let me read to you right now, so you're not alone."

"Loo—"

"Aaliyah," he said with a controlled, deep tone. "Just listen."

I sighed, and I did as he said.

Before he could start reading, a familiar face came darting into the room. Marie appeared dazed and full of worry.

"Oh, my goodness, Aaliyah. Are you okay?" she breathed out.

"What are you doing here?" I asked, sitting up a bit, feeling nauseous the moment she stepped inside my room.

"Well, after the ambulance brought you in, I had to gather my things and I had a heck of a time trying to get them to allow me in to see you. And since I am the designated support person for you—"

"You have a lot of fucking nerve, lady," Damian snapped, shooting her a look good enough to kill.

"What are you even doing here? This has nothing to do with you," Marie replied.

"No. It has nothing to do with you," I said.

Marie's brown eyes locked with mine. They were packed with sadness, and I hated her eyes in that moment because they reminded me so much of my own.

How didn't I see it before?

"Aaliyah. I understand you being angry with me, but these are the rules that the transplant coordinator shared with us. You must have a caregiver afterward. Without me, you don't get your transplant if one comes available. You need me."

"I do—don't," I said, taking deep inhalations. "Need you."

"Yes, sweetheart. You do," she disagreed.

"How about you not call her sweetheart. It's condescending," Damian ordered like a protective pit bull.

"How about you mind your own business?" Marie sneered.

"My brother is in love with this woman, which in turn makes it my business," he said without a tremble in his tone. "And clearly she doesn't want you here, or as her designated support person, so you might as well leave."

"She has no one else," Marie said.

"That's not true. She has me. If she'd like, that is." Damian looked over to me for approval of his words. I bit my bottom lip and nodded. He looked back to Marie. "See? Your services are no longer needed."

At this point, Marie was turning red with anger as she stared intensely at Damian. "I don't know who you think you are, young man, but I've been there for her for the past two years throughout her health scares. I've taken care of her these past two years night and day, whenever she needed me. I was there for her. I showed up to every hospital visit and every time she needed to cry, I was her shoulder. I did that for two years; you have no clue how much I've put into this responsibility."

"Twenty-four," he dryly replied.

Marie raised an eyebrow. "What?"

"You should've been there for her for twenty-four years, not two."

That statement hit Marie like a ton of bricks. She stumbled back a bit, shaken up. I felt the impact of Damian's words, too, but stayed quiet.

What was there for me to say?

"Listen, lady, I'm not here to listen to your sob story about how your life didn't go the way you wanted. I'm here for Aaliyah and Connor. So, how about you stop adding stress to her life. If you really give a damn about her, you'd go with me to shift the designated support person to me. Then, you'd leave her alone," Damian stated.

Marie looked at me, tears hitting her stare. "Is that what you want, Aaliyah?"

I nodded. "Y-yes."

With complete defeat, Marie pushed her purse up her shoulder and turned back to Damian. "There will be paperwork to fill out."

"I have a signature."

She frowned. He grimaced.

Then they left to handle the business that needed to be handled.

Twenty-five days.

Damian showed up for twenty-five days straight to read to me, making sure I wasn't alone. He'd studied up on what it meant to be a support person, and he'd made plans to be by my side throughout it all. Sometimes, I wanted to ask him how Connor had been doing, but I didn't have the guts to push out the words. I missed him too much to allow myself to ask.

FORTY-TWO

Connor

TWENTY-FIVE DAYS.

I'd been sitting in the lobby of the hospital since Damian informed me that Aaliyah had been admitted. She wanted nothing to do with me, so Damian showed up each day to sit with her. She had no clue that I was waiting right outside of her room, but I needed to be close, even if she didn't know. I couldn't imagine being anywhere else.

All I needed was for her to be okay. I needed her to recover, to come back to me whole again.

Each night, Damian would show up and give me an update on Aaliyah's condition, and I'd give him new comic books to read to her. He'd tell me about how she was a fighter, and even though it was clear she was struggling, she'd try to keep her spirits high.

He'd tell me that she missed me—not that she said that, but he could tell.

I figured he told me that because he knew I needed to hear it, not because it was true. But fuck, I'd hoped it was true.

As I waited one night for an update on Aaliyah, I received an email

To: ConnorXRoe@roeenterprises.com
From: maivkhang@passion.com
Subject: Article Approval

Hello Connor,

I hope you are well. Attached is the article written by Aaliyah Winters on your behalf. I am sending it to have you look over it to give your approval as we move forward with publishing the September issue. Thank you for taking the time to be interviewed. Passion appreciates your kindness and openness during this whole process.

Let me know your thoughts and if you have any concerns or issues, but after reading the article myself, I doubt there will be any complaints.

-Maiv

P.S. I attached some of the pictures from the photo shoot. The one with her looking at you is my favorite. Thank you for proving to me, and Aaliyah, that some men are worth it.

I opened the pictures attached to the email, and my heart almost burst when I saw Aaliyah and me together, wrapped in one another's arms, smiling and laughing. The world froze in those images, and all I wanted to do was create more moments like those ones. I need more time with her. I needed more time with us.

After I stared at the photographs for way too long, I went ahead and opened the article, allowing myself to fall deeply into the words Aaliyah created for me.

The Modern Day Gent:
My Weeks with Connor Roe, by Aaliyah Winters

Connor smiles as he takes a sip of his coffee.

It's our third day meeting after he agreed to do this interview, and everything about him expresses the fact that he doesn't realize how powerful he is—in the best of ways. He sits back in his chair with his right leg resting across his left knee. His broad shoulders are fully relaxed, showing his comfort.

His coffee has a splash of coconut milk and three sugar cubes—never two, never four.

He has nothing less than an approachable feel to him. It's refreshing to see how calm and easygoing he is in a city that's always moving at the speed of light to reach the next big thing. Connor Roe isn't in a hurry. He takes it slow. He never checks his watch to see the time, as if there is nothing more important than the present moment.

That's my biggest take away from my weeks spent with Connor—he's a man who lives in the moment. And every moment with him, one dreams to hold onto for eternity. When the waitress brings our breakfast items, she stumbles a bit, and the bowl of oatmeal almost goes crashing to the floor. Connor moves swiftly, alert and attentive, catching the bowl in his hands at a record speed. Not even spilling a drop or burning his hands. The waitress blushes, growing timid from embarrassment, but Connor gives her that award-winning smile and easies her anxiety.

"No worries," he states, soothing her shame. She blushes some more—a normal effect of being around this man.

No worries—a motto I've quickly picked up from the modern-day gentleman.

Connor believes in the magic of giving back to the world. He gives more than he takes, he fights for others more than he fights for himself. He pushes himself day in and day out to create a better life for those who weren't born into wealth and privilege. He dreams of a world where elders are treated fairly, where lower-income individuals never have to worry about how to pay their rent, and where foster children never for a second have to feel lonely.

He dreams of a world where no kid goes hungry. No single mother is left without electricity. No elderly is left abused and alone.

From his charity involvement with Adopt a Grandparent, Twisted Food Trucks (a program that offers free lunches to children in the summertime), and A.C.T.L. (act, care, teach, love), Connor Roe pushes for a better tomorrow by focusing on the issues of today.

He fights the good fight, day in and day out. He's the definition of a good man, which is why I must say, he's not only New York's modern-day gentleman with so much Southern charm—he's this generation's superhero. A doer of good. A giver of hope. A masterpiece of human existence.

I know what you're probably thinking, because I thought it at first, too. He's too good to be true. There must be a flaw that he holds somewhere within him, and I am here to tell you the facts about that: no flaws detected.

Not. A. Single. One.

Connor Roe is built by faith, powered by love. Every act he creates comes from a genuine place of care and gentleness. Even when he is afraid, his fear is due to his heart being overpowered with love. That isn't a flaw by any means—that is Roe's superpower—his power is to love.

If you ever get the chance to cross paths with Connor Roe, he'll give you love. Even if it's only for a moment's time. A flash of love, if you will. He'll hold the door open for you, and he'll offer to pay for the coffee cup of the customer behind him. He'll tell you really bad jokes that make you laugh so hard. He'll listen to every story you bring to him—even if it's incohesive. He'll hug you when you need it, and even when you don't. He'll look at you as if you are both the sunrise and sunset.

He'll be your friend when you have no one to talk to. He'll be your anchor when you feel as if you're floating away. He'll make you smile.

My gosh, will you smile.

That's the superpower he gives to this world. He creates millions of smiles in a society built on struggles and fears. He cherishes every single person, every single life, and he makes it impossible to not fall head-over-heels in love with him.

By the end of our time together, I am a victim of his powers. I fall, and I fall with ease and confidence, because I know at the end of the day, no matter what, he will catch me.

In his arms, I am safe.

In his arms, I am loved.

And in his arms, I love.

I am overwhelmingly in love with this superhero of mine.

Connor Roe is many things: a powerful businessman, a from rags-to-riches Cinderella story, and a force to be reckon with in the real estate world. Yet the best thing that he is?

Love.

Connor Roe is love.

Anyone who crosses paths with his love, will never be the same again. I know I won't.

Connor smiles as he takes another sip of his coffee.

And I cannot help but smile back as I take a sip of my own.

-AW, Senior Editor

She loved me.

The article was submitted after I walked away from her, and still, she loved me.

Loves me.

Present tense.

After reading said article, I took a trip I knew I had to take. I couldn't go home and crawl into a bed where Aaliyah hadn't been any longer. I needed help from someone bigger than me, bigger than the doctors, bigger than life.

"Hi there," I breathed out, lowering myself down in front of Grant's tombstone. "I know we've only met briefly, but I know how much you mean to Aaliyah, so I figured I should give this conversation a go. Um, she's not doing too well, Grant," I said, sniffling as the words left my mouth. Speaking them out loud made it even more real that Aaliyah was suffering. "Our girl's not in good shape. And I'm fucking terrified. She doesn't want me near her. She doesn't want anything to do with me, and I can't blame her. I knew how much it hurt her to have people walk away, and I was a coward the moment things got hard. The moment things were tough, I was a chickenshit. I can't take that back, and I can't change the way I behaved but, you gotta believe me, Grant. I'm sorry for what I did."

I brushed my thumb against the bridge of my nose. "And I know you don't owe me any favors, and I give you the right to hate me as much as she hates me. But here I am...because I need your help. You're the closest thing to a father figure that Aaliyah has, so I am here to ask you something very important. You see, once this is over, once Aaliyah comes out on the other side of this, I'm going to ask her to be my wife. I have no doubt that she's the woman I want beside me for the rest of our time on this planet. No matter how long that might be. Which means I need her to come out of this, Grant. Even if she hates me for a while, I'm not quitting on this. I'm not quitting on us. I'm staying. Do you hear me? Even when I'm scared, I'm staying.

"So I need your help. I know you probably miss her, but I need you to hold off for a bit, okay? This is me asking you permission for her hand in marriage. I want to marry her, Grant, so I'm begging you, please..." I took a deep breath as I kneeled in prayer. I placed my hand against the engraved stone and whispered as the winds brushed against my skin, as tears fell down my eyes, as every part of me began to tremble in fear. "Please, Grant...Please..." I cleared my throat, and softly said, "Please don't take her yet."

After I finished my conversation with Grant, I headed to my car, where Luis was waiting to drive me home.

"You okay, Connor?" he asked me.

"No," I replied.

I'd never be okay if she wasn't.

Before he could reply, my phone began ringing and Damian's name flashed on the screen. Within seconds, I answered. "Hey, what's up?"

"You need to get back to the hospital, Connor. Fast."

I swore Luis could've driven faster, but he did the best he could. My mind couldn't stop the panic from what was happening to Aaliyah. Damian sounded nervous on the phone. Had things become worse? Was she slipping away? Was I losing her?

Please, don't let me lose her. Not like this. Not now.

I darted out of the back seat of the car and straight toward the hospital doors without even closing the door behind me. I couldn't waste a second more not knowing about Aaliyah's condition.

The second I hit the lobby, Damian was waiting for me. He stood up from a chair and walked in my direction.

"What is it? What's happening? Is she okay? Is she...?" I swallowed hard as tears burned at the back of my eyes. "Did she...?"

Die? Was she gone? Fuck, I couldn't breathe. If she was gone...if she was no longer...

"Dude. Calm down. Relax." Damian placed his hands against my shoulders and locked his dark eyes with mine. Then the corner of his mouth twitched and it turned up into a grin. "They found one."

"What?"

"They found Aaliyah a heart."

FORTY-THREE

Aaliyah

A HEART.

A heart for me.

Damian was there when Dr. Erickson told me the news. I was glad, too because I needed a hand to hold, and Damian was quick to offer me his.

I always thought when I'd find out there was a heart for me, I'd feel an overwhelming amount of joy, but I felt indescribable guilt. Guilt that someone had to lose their life for mine to continue. That there were people now grieving the loss of their loved one. That the source of their despair was my triumph.

I felt ill from it all. As if I was cheating death. It all didn't seem fair.

"Circle of life," Damian said, still holding my hand. He said it so calmly as if he could tell the places my mind was spiraling. "Every beginning has an end, and every ending begins again. This is a good thing, Aaliyah. This is good."

I nodded my head as Dr. Erickson walked me through everything that was happening. He explained how the family was saying their final goodbyes, and that after they were taken off life support, his team would move full speed ahead to prep me for surgery. And within a few hours, I'd have a new heart.

It all felt surreal, as if I were floating in a dream that was leading me to a future I started to doubt I'd ever have a shot at.

Damian excused himself for a while as Dr. Erickson kept explaining the next steps to me. When he finished, I was left alone for a moment to sit and think about everything that was happening. I thought about what it meant for me to get this heart, what it meant for another family to lose said heart. Life was complicated in ways I'd never be able to understand.

There was a knock at my door, and I was surprised when I looked up to see Damian standing there with Connor beside him.

I sat up a bit in my bed and tilted my head in confusion. "What are you doing here?" I asked Connor, then I looked at Damian. "You told him?"

"I had to," he confessed. "He's my brother." He patted Connor on the back and nodded once. "I'll let the two of you talk."

As Damian left the room, Connor stepped inside.

"Hi," he whispered.

"Hi," I replied, uncomfortable with how comfortable he made me. I should've hated him. I should've told him to leave. I should've pushed him away, but instead, I stayed quiet, waiting for him to speak. Waiting to see what he had to say.

He cleared his throat. "You're getting a new heart."

"Yes."

"That's amazing."

I stayed quiet.

He moved in closer.

The machines beeped more.

He took a step back.

"Listen, I don't want to add any more stress to your life, Aaliyah. I get it, you hate me. I don't blame you. For the past few weeks, I've hated myself more than ever before, but please, Aaliyah...let me stay tonight. You're going into surgery soon, and I can't be anywhere else but here. I don't even have to talk to you. I won't even look at you if you don't want me to. If you tell me to stare into that corner, I'll stare all fucking night, but I can't leave you, okay?

"I can't leave you in case something goes wrong, in case the surgery doesn't work, and, God forbid, in case you end up leaving me...so please, Aaliyah. Please? Please let me stay tonight because the idea of walking away now burns my entire being. Please, Red...please..." He closed his eyes for a moment and when he reopened them, tears began streaming down his cheeks. He pushed his tongue into his cheek as his body began to tremble. As his whole existence began to crumble right there before my eyes. "Please let me stay."

He stood there completely broken. He showed me his hurts and laid them there to bleed in the open. I saw his fear, I saw his panic, but mostly I saw his love. Love didn't only show its face during happiness. It didn't skip by only during the sunshine. No. Sometimes—most of the time—love was a storm at war.

Love explored the world during the darkness. It crawled through pain, fought through combats, and hit rock bottom with a million battle scars. Love wasn't only the rainbows. Love sparked in the lightning and screamed during the thunder. In that very moment, love rained down over Connor, and his love was being directed straight toward me. Raw. Unleashed. True.

I shifted around in my hospital bed and stared down at my hands.

I thought about it, too. If I didn't make it out of the surgery. If the heart transplant didn't work. If the sand of my life ran out. If I never saw him again. If our last exchange was one filled with me asking him to leave.

When all I ever wanted was for him to stay.

"Will you read?" I spoke softly, looking his way. "Will you read the comic book to me?"

He followed my glance to the side table where a stack of comic books sat that Damian had dropped off for me.

"Yes," he said without a second of hesitation. "Can I pull my chair up close to you?"

"Yes," I said without a second of hesitation.

I wanted him close.

I needed him close.

I missed his closeness.

He grabbed one of the comic books and dragged a chair over to me.

He began reading to me, and I fell asleep to his words. When I awakened during the night, I found his head resting against the edge of the bed as he slept. His hand was wrapped around something as he rested his arm in his lap. I reached down to unwrap whatever it was that he had in his grip, and my emotions overtook me as I stared down at a handful of quarters.

Before long, I fell back asleep. I was awakened again, this time by a nurse. Connor was no longer beside me, but the quarters rested against my lap. I glanced around, and I was stunned to find my room covered in Post-it Notes. They covered all the walls and the railings of the bed. The television had them all over, leaving me floored.

I picked up one next to me, and I recognized Connor's handwriting right away.

I wish for more time with Aaliyah.

I read another.

More time with Red.

I wish I could marry her.

I wish I could kiss her.

I wish for one more minute with her.

I wish for her healing.

There had to be hundreds of wishes he'd made, scattered around the room. Hundreds of tiny Post-its with his words that went straight to my heart.

"Well, good morning, sunshine," a nurse said, walking into the room. "I see you saw your love letters awaiting you. That boy showing up every day must really love you a lot."

I shook my head. "No. Damian is just a friend."

"Oh, no. I don't mean him. I mean Connor. The guy who's been sitting outside in the lobby every single day. The staff are calling him the modern-day Romeo. He said he knew you probably wouldn't want to see him, but he's waited outside the whole time. Then when you'd fall asleep at night, he'd come in and quietly sit with you. Really sweet if you ask me."

Her words stunned me. He'd been there every day? It had been over twenty-five days of me being in the hospital. How could he possibly wait that long without me giving him any signs that I'd give him another chance?

When it came time for me to be wheeled to surgery, the nurses told me that I had a crew waiting to wave me off down the hallway. As I turned to wave toward Damian, my damaged heart started beating faster as I looked down and saw the bluest of blue eyes staring back at me. He stayed.

Who knew that even broken hearts could still beat for love?

"I love you," I mouthed, staring straight into his eyes. I had to say the words. I had to let him know that no matter what, I loved him. Because outside of all of the bullshit, outside of our human dramatics, I knew it to be true that he was the lights for me. He was the eastern lights that shone over me for a short period of time and in such a vibrant way reminding me that I wasn't alone. He was the light that touched my darkness, and for that, he'd be awarded a forever kind of love.

I said a prayer before the surgery. I didn't know to who. To God, to the universe, to aliens. I said a prayer to whatever it was that was out there, knowing that all I needed to do was stay a little longer for Connor. So we could fight. So we could scream. So we could make up. So we could fall deeper into whatever it was that we were on the tip of discovering.

Tears found me as Connor parted his mouth and whispered, "I love you, more."

FORTY-FOUR

Aaliyah

PUMP, *PUMP.*
Pump, pump.
Pump, pump…

My chest rose and fell.

I felt them. I felt the heartbeats. Heartbeats that were mine, but not exactly mine.

Borrowed time. A promise for another tomorrow. A blessing I wasn't certain I deserved, but I knew I'd never take it for granted.

Thank you, William.

The transplant went extremely well, and I was stunned at how little pain I felt afterward.

I had to stay in the hospital for a few weeks after, but soon enough, I was released and able to go back to my apartment. Damian was there by my side every single day, organizing my medicine and helping me every step of the way. Everything was going well with recovery, but even though I had a new heart, and it was beating, it didn't take away the sadness that sat inside me. There was still so much trauma I had to work through outside of recovery—Marie, for instance.

Plus, I'd missed Connor, yet I knew it wasn't time for me to reach out to him just yet. I needed to fully recover, to know that I was going to be okay before I could show up to him and tell him all of my feelings.

So when my doorbell rang, and I saw it was him standing downstairs with a bouquet, I was quite surprised. I headed downstairs and opened the door for him.

"Hi," I said, crossing my arms across my body as the chilled autumn air pushed past me.

"Hi," he replied, his voice low. "I know you probably don't want to see me right now, and I get that, Aaliyah, but I needed to see you. I need to see that you're doing okay, that you're healing…that you're here. So, I'm sorry, but I needed to stop by."

"It's okay."

He frowned. "It's not. None of what happened between us is okay. I made a million mistakes. I knew nothing about love, nothing of heartbreak, nothing, Aaliyah. I knew nothing about love until I met you. You deserve everything, and I never want you to be unhappy because of me. But…I just want to say this."

"Connor…"

"Please, Aaliyah. I'll leave you alone after this, I swear, but I need you to know my truth."

My eyes fell to the ground for a moment before I looked back up at him and nodded, giving him permission to continue.

"You changed me. You awakened parts of my soul that I didn't know were sleeping. I realized that it's not love or commitment that I'm afraid of. I'm afraid of death. I'm afraid of losing the things that I care about more than anything. I spent most of my childhood paranoid about waking up one morning and finding my mother dead. To this day, I struggle with the fact that the cancer might come back and be more intense than ever before. I'm fucking terrified of losing her, losing you.

"I'm scared of the unknown. I'm scared of going back to living in that place where I witness the people I love hurting, and I cannot do anything to take that pain away. I'm scared, Lia…I'm scared."

"I understand all of that, truly. But even with my transplant, there's a chance my body could reject the heart. There's still so much unknown about how my life will go, and I can't take away your fear, Connor."

"I'm not asking you to do that. I'm asking you to allow me to be afraid but still let me stay. Because the idea of not having you in my life at all is scarier than any what-if. Do I want to grow old with you? Yes. Do I want to count all of your gray hairs and mock you about it years from now? Absolutely. Do I want to fall in love with all of your wrinkles? One hundred percent. But if all I get is here and now, I want it, Red. I want this, you and me, at this very moment. I want every moment that God will give me to be yours.

"So this is me asking, begging for you to give me another shot. I won't be perfect, but I won't run. Even when I'm scared, I'll stay. Even when I feel like the world is slipping away, I'll stay. If I had to live forever, I'd like to live forever with you. But if I'd only had today, I'd like to sit on top of a rooftop and stare out at the eastern lights with you. It doesn't matter how many days, weeks, or years we have, I'm in. Be it today or forever, I only want you."

I bit my bottom lip, my nerves shook from his words. "Do you want to see my new place?"

Confusion flashed over his face, but he didn't turn down the invitation. I walked him upstairs, and when I opened the door, his eyes lit up when he looked around the place. There were hundreds of Post-it Notes that I'd been filling out over the past few weeks because I was hoping for this very moment. I was hoping for the day he'd come back to me.

I grabbed a Post-it and held it out to him.

I wish for Connor to come back to me.

"See?" I whispered, moving in closer to him. I closed my eyes as he wrapped his arms around me and rested his forehead against mine. "I wished for you, too."

In life, we weren't guaranteed forever. We were promised only now. So, I made it a point to live in the moment, in the now because there was nothing else. There was no yesterday, there was no tomorrow, only that moment. If I only had one hour, one minute, one second, I was going to make it count. I was going to spend the remainder of my time sitting in love, with him, with us, with our flashes of love.

FORTY-FIVE

Connor

I'D SPENT EVERY MOMENT AT AALIYAH'S APARTMENT SINCE SHE'D invited me back into her life. I promised myself, and her, that I'd never take our love for granted. That I'd be there day and night, no matter how scared I became. And truthfully? I was still terrified, but I was learning quickly that being scared was okay if you were brave enough to face those fears.

Each day, Aaliyah reminded me why I was facing my fears. I tackled them for her smile. For her laugh. For her love. If I was able to love her, then nothing would scare me away ever again.

"Go to work." Aaliyah smirked as she pressed her lips against my forehead. My head had been resting against her chest gently, avoiding her incisions. Each morning, I loved to listen to her heartbeats. Each night, I did the same.

"But I like it here more," I muttered, snuggling up against her.

"That's the fifth time Damian had called you," she said, pushing herself up to a sitting position. She cringed a little, and I became more alert. She was still a bit sore from surgery, but she was a trooper. I worried more than she did. I didn't see that changing anytime soon. Maybe that was what love was, sometimes—worrying about the things you loved the most.

I groaned.

She laughed and kissed my lips. "You are going to have to get back to reality at some point, Connor. You can't stay here with me all the time."

"Says who?"

"Says me. You have a dream to go catch."

"I've already caught her," I said, pulling her into me so now she was sitting in my lap.

"Don't be corny." She snickered, trailing kisses down my chin. "I mean it. You have a whole company to run. Go get showered and get to work. I'll be here when you come home."

Home.

The place wherever she had been.

I reluctantly listened to her demands and pulled myself together to head to my office. Damian was quick to chew my ass out for not being around, but a big part of me knew he understood.

"Listen, I know you just got all happy and shit, which, congratulations by the way, I'm glad you both pulled your heads out of your asses, but I couldn't keep this to myself much longer," Damian said, dropping a packet on my desk.

Instant unease hit me. The last time he dropped a packet on my desk, it told me that Marie was Aaliyah's mother, and well, needless to say, Aaliyah was still processing that disaster.

"What is this?"

"Walter Rollsfield's grave dig. I know you didn't tell me to go digging on him, but after the shit I found out about his wife, I knew I had to. I'm pissed I didn't do it sooner. We could've avoided all of this shit."

I opened the files, and the wave of nausea that hit me made me almost pass out. Damian had gathered old emails from Walter to other clients of his. Contracts. New properties that he'd bought under another business name.

My properties.

Walter Rollsfield bought every property that I'd brought to him for my passion project, and he was secretly planning to turn them all into luxury condominiums. Every. Single. One.

"Turns out the asshole was the one getting in the way of all of your hard work. Every single location he swept up to make a profit for himself. Dude…he sold you out. I wouldn't be shocked if the Queens property fell through sooner or later, too."

Why would he do that to me? From the jump, I looked toward Walter as a father figure. He'd taught me the ins and outs of business. He invested in me, in my dreams. Why would he go through all of that just to steal from me? To lie and cheat. To take something that I loved, something I truly believed in, and take it for himself.

Hell, he'd stood beside me flabbergasted and angered by the fact that the deals kept falling through! Was that all an act? Was I some kind of pawn in some twisted game of chess he'd been playing?

I trusted him.

I trusted him more than I'd trusted anyone else in the business. The whole time, I sat stunned by how he could raise such a monster son, when in reality, Jason had been mirroring his own father.

Right after I read through everything, I headed over to Walter's office. His secretary was quick to tell me he was in the middle of a meeting, but I didn't give a shit. I barged right into his conference room, not giving a damn what I was interrupting.

The moment I flung the door open, a room of about ten gentlemen turned to look my way. At the head of the table sat Walter. He narrowed his eyes at me, baffled.

"Connor, what are you doing here?"

"Is it true?" I barked, my chest rising and falling hard as I stared into a set of eyes that I'd trusted for so many years.

Walter laughed nervously, shaking his head. "I'm in the middle of a meeting. Maybe later will be a better time to talk, son—"

"Don't call me son," I hissed. "Is it true you bought all of the apartment buildings that supposedly fell through for me?"

Walter grimaced, and he cleared his throat. He looked at the gentlemen sitting around him and pushed out a fake grin. "I'm sorry, everyone. If you will excuse me for a moment, I need to handle this conversation in my office," he said as he stood up and marched past me. "I will be back in no time."

He headed for his office, and I followed him, staying right on his heels. The moment we were inside, he slammed his door shut and turned to me, fuming. "Are you insane, boy? Do you know how important that meeting is to me?"

"Do you know how important those buildings were to me?!" I echoed as rage shot throughout my entire system. The more I stared at the asshole, the more irritated I grew.

He walked over to his bar and released the longest sigh as he began pouring himself a glass of whiskey. "Truly, Connor, I cannot believe you are coming to me with this bullshit. After everything I've done for you."

"I've done plenty for you, too, Walter," I said. "Taking on Jason, for instance."

"If you think you've done anything for me, you must be kidding yourself. I made you, little boy. Without me and my investments early on, Roe Real Estate wouldn't exist. A warning—don't bite the hand that feeds you." He walked around to his desk, pulled out his chair, and sat. He was acting as calm as a clam as if he hadn't ruined my dreams.

"You screwed me over and pretended it was someone else."

"Between you and me, I'm shocked it took you this long to realize what had been going on. All the clues were there. But you know what they say, you can lead a horse to water, but you can't make them drink."

"Why would you do this?"

"Isn't it obvious? Because I love money. Don't get me wrong, the properties you discovered are outstanding. They are going to make great homes for very wealthy people down the line. Which, in turn, would make me very wealthy. It's a win-win." He sipped at his whiskey and then paused. "Well, I guess it's a lose-lose for you. But hell, I'm happy."

"You son of a bitch," I sneered, wanting nothing more than to slam my fist into his face. His smugness was driving me insane. "You lied to me about everything."

"Yeah, well, welcome to the real world. People fucking lie to get what they want. You really thought I made it this far in life with honesty? Truthfully, you've helped me a lot. I'll send you a thank-you check after my profits start rolling in."

"I want nothing to do with you. I want nothing else from you. I'm done with you. Do you hear me, Walter? We are finished."

"Yeah, well, I wish it was that easy, but you see, there're something called contracts that keep you from walking away. When you signed to work with me, I was given forty percent of Roe Real Estate. So even if you're mad, we are still business partners."

"I still own a majority. I'll work like hell to get rid of you."

"Oh, no." He shook his head in disappointment. "You didn't read the small print of Jason's contract, did you? Ah, the young and naïve always forget to read the small print. When you signed over the West Coast property, you gave Jason twenty percent of the company. Which means you only have thirty percent. So it looks like majority of Roe Real Estates belongs to the Rollfields. Tough break, kid. Really."

"The contract only stays solid if Jason remains in the position for a year," I told him.

"Yes, and he will. I have a fat check waiting for him after he completes his year working there, and then he will sign his shares over to me, making me the majority owner of the company. Plus, Jason will now definitely stay at the position, knowing you were fucking his girl. He's petty that way. He'll hit you where it hurts—in his wallet. So, let's have you stay in your lane. I don't want to end up firing you, son, but don't think that I won't."

"This was your plan the whole time, wasn't it? You planned to take over my business all those years ago. You were using me."

"Now you're catching on. You didn't truly think that I believed in your little dreams, did you? You had a charming face and personality that I knew people would eat up. You were the puppet, and thank you for making it so easy to pull your strings. Come on, Connor. You didn't truly think that low-income luxury properties would be a thing, did you? That's a joke of a concept. No one would touch that with an eight-foot pole."

"I looked up to you. You were like a father figure to me," I confessed, feeling idiotic.

"Ding, ding, ding! There it is, folks! The secret to this whole game. The moment you told me about how your father walked out on you, I knew that was my way in. Sorry if you took it personal, kid. It's just business."

Every part of me felt defeated.

Everything that man had done for me in the past was simply to stuff his own pockets. I felt abused, used, and he had no problem destroying my life.

Everything I'd built, everything I'd hoped to build, was coming crashing down around me. And there was nothing I could do about it because I signed my soul away to the devil who appeared as my guardian angel.

"He can't legally do that, right? There's no way that's legal," Aaliyah said as we sat on her couch. I went straight to her place after my conversation with Walter. I felt like a damn idiot. How had I been so blind to the truth that was right in front of me? I spent so much time thinking Walter was a saint, someone who saw a young kid and believed in them and their stupid dreams. In reality, all he saw was a way for him to make a profit.

"Even if it wasn't legal, I have a feeling he'd get away with it. This is what he does—he gets away with shit and profits from it. I doubt I'm the first person he'd done that with, and I doubt I'd be the last."

"I hate him." She sighed, moving in closer to me. She rested her head on my shoulder.

"Me too," I replied. "I can't believe he tricked me for this long. If only I would've had Damian look into him sooner…"

"This isn't your fault, Connor. Walter Rollsfield is a pathological liar. There is no way you could've known. I didn't know about Marie, either. They both presented themselves as something they weren't to get what they wanted. Honestly, I think their whole relationship is built on lies. They can't be honest with each other because they are far from honest with themselves. It's actually sad the lives they live. We should count our blessings that we found out at all. I'm sure there are still people who think very highly of the assholes."

I sighed and rested my head on top of hers. "What am I going to do now? I cannot, in good conscience, stay in business with him. I'll have to hand Roe Real Estate over to him."

"Well." She laced her fingers with mine and held me close. "If it comes down to starting over, we'll start over together. You're not in this alone, Connor. You built yourself a name over the past year from the ground up. We'll do it again. But no matter what, I'm here to build with you."

"Thank you, Red," I whispered, moving to brush my lips against hers.

"Always, Cap."

Later on, we moved to the bedroom, and she fell asleep before me. I rested my head against her chest, listening to her heartbeats. My favorite song, my favorite lullaby. I had no clue how everything was going to be okay, but as long her heart kept beating, I knew no matter what, we'd figure out how to face the world together.

FORTY-SIX

Aaliyah

"**A**ALIYAH, WHAT ARE YOU DOING HERE?" MARIE ASKED AS I stood on her front steps. "Are you okay? Is it your heart…?"

I hadn't seen her since she appeared at the hospital. I haven't even digested the information that she was my biological mother completely, but I wasn't standing in front of her for me. I was standing there for Connor.

"I'm fine," I coldly stand, wrapping my arms around my body. "Can I come in?"

"Yes, of course."

She stepped to the side, allowing a pathway for me, and I walked into her home. Over the past few years, I'd spent a lot of time inside those walls. I dreamed of all of the family gatherings we'd share together in this home. I thought about all the holidays we'd have together. Funny how it was best sometimes when dreams didn't come true.

If I would've ended up marrying Jason, my world would've ended up being a true tragedy.

"Can I get you something to drink? Water? Tea?" she offered. Her hands were shaking. Clearly her nerves were eating at her. A part of me felt a flash of guilt, but I couldn't feel bad about her being uncomfortable. I needed her to be uncomfortable for what I was about to request of her.

"No. I'm fine."

She fiddled with her fingers and pushed out a smile. "I didn't know if I'd be able to speak to you again after the last time. And after Damian took over my position, I wasn't allowed to see you."

"Of course, you weren't. Only friends and family were allowed."

That stung her.

"Well, what did you want to speak about? Do you want to continue our conversation?" she asked.

"No. Not now. I'm not here for me. I'm here for Connor."

"Connor? What does he have to do with anything?"

"He has everything to do with this. Walter is threatening to take over Roe Real Estate, and I need you to stop him."

"What?

"Don't play dumb, Marie. We know everything. Walter told Connor about how he was planning to take over the company and buy Connor out down the line. I need you to tell him not to do it."

"I'm sorry, Aaliyah, I have no clue—"

"I never asked you for anything," I cut in. "I never asked for anything, and you used me to get what you wanted these past few years. So you owe me. I need you to do this for me, Marie."

"Wait. How would Walter be able to take his company? None of this makes sense to me."

She looked completely stunned by the situation at hand, but I couldn't tell if she were just acting surprised. That was the thing about catching people in lies—once they told the truth, you'd always doubt it.

"Is he here right now?" I asked.

"Yes. He's in his office. I can't believe that he'd do that to Connor, though. Even with everything that happened between you and Connor and Jason, I can't believe that Walter would do this."

"How well do you know your husband?" I asked.

There was a hesitation in her eyes as I asked her the question. She parted her lips to speak and paused for a moment before she cleared her throat and hollered, "Walter. Can you meet me in the living room?"

"Woman, you know I don't like you hollering in the house like that. What is this about?" Walter grumbled, walking into the living room. The moment he saw me, his eyes narrowed. "Aaliyah. What are you doing here?"

"Trying to settle an issue," I explained.

Marie turned to Walter and stared at him, seemingly baffled. "Is it true you are trying to take over Connor's business?"

Walter's thick eyebrows furrowed. "You called me in for this nonsense? I don't have time for this, Marie."

Her mouth dropped, stunned. "Why would you do that? Why would you try to take something that boy created?"

"I created him. Anything he has is because of me, which gives me the right to take it away, too."

"You didn't create him," I snapped toward him. "Connor created everything about Roe Real Estate. You simply profited from him being good at what he did."

"He might have been good, but I'm better, little girl. And honestly, I don't even know why you are here having this conversation, seeing how it has nothing to do with you."

"It has everything to do with me. I love him, and I am here to fight for him."

Walter rolled his eyes. "You love him for now. Wait until I take everything from him. You think I don't know what kind of woman you are? You're a poor girl who falls for rich men to find an easy way out of life."

"That's not true, Walter. You know Aaliyah's a good woman," Marie said, backing me up.

"I thought that before she was so quick to jump into bed with another man after my son," he spat out.

"He stood me up on my wedding day! After cheating on me God knows how many times. And somehow, you are making me the bad person for falling in love with a man who treated me right?"

"He couldn't have treated you that well if he only wanted you after you had a new heart," he said coldly.

"Walter!" Marie cried, but I didn't let his words anywhere near my emotions. I knew he was simply a cruel man who did and said cruel things.

He waved her off. "Oh, save the hysterics, Marie. You don't need to keep acting shocked by anything I'm saying. You knew who I was when you married me. Which is why you thought you had to keep the fact that Aaliyah was your daughter a secret."

Just like that, the air was knocked out of Marie's lungs as she stumbled backward. "You knew?"

"You really think I'm an idiot and couldn't put two and two together? I allowed it because I figured it could've been good to show our knucklehead son in a good light and marrying Aaliyah would've done that. I weighed the pros and cons of the situation and came to realize that it was the right business move to make."

"You're an evil man," I said as my hatred built for him each passing second.

"Yes, well, at least I didn't leave my daughter at a fire station in order to stay rich," he said, rolling his sleeves up. "Are we done here?"

Marie had tears of horror rolling down her cheeks, and a part of me wanted to comfort her. But then again, she knew who she married. She knew who she crawled into bed beside each night. She made her bed, and now she had to decide for herself if she was going to sleep in it or move along on her own.

"We aren't exactly done yet." I pulled out my cell phone. I made a quick call and when the person on the other line picked up, I said, "Hey, yeah. It didn't work out, so you can come in."

Within seconds, Damian walked into the house without knocking and came over to me holding a stack of paperwork in his hands.

"What's the meaning of this?" Walter asked, his brows lowered. If he should've been intimidated by anyone in the world, it was Damian. Connor bathed in kindness and love. But Damian? He could kill a person solely with a look.

"Just a bit of good cop, bad cop," I explained. "You should've really worked with me—I was the good cop."

"And I'm the bad," Damian said, dropping the packet on the coffee table.

"You really think I should be afraid of you and your tough-guy act? You're a child. Nothing you can do..." Walter picked up the files, and when he opened them, he paused his words. "Where the hell did you get this?"

"I'm the grave digger," Damian calmly stated. "I dig shit up."

"We are going to need you to do is sign all of Roe Real Estate over to Connor. You're going to give him total control over it all, and you aren't going to try to cheat him out of anything," I told him.

"Otherwise, I'm sure the FBI would be interested in your whole money laundering issue," Damian said.

"Money laundering?!" Marie gasped. It was becoming clearer and clearer that she knew nothing about what was going on with Walter and the life he seemed to be living behind her back.

Walter looked devastated by the fact that Damian caught him in a handful of scandals, some that would've easily landed him in prison for a very long time. Luckily, we didn't want to destroy him. All we wanted was for Connor to have everything he worked so hard for.

Walter grumbled a bit and paced as he flipped through the pages. Then, he looked over to me. "I'll have my team draw up the contracts to have everything transferred over to Connor."

"Including the Queens property," I said, knowing that Connor deserved the location that he'd fell in love with for his dream to come true.

"Fine," Walter muttered, unamused.

"And one hundred million dollars for him to invest into said property," Damian stated.

I tried not to react to such a high demand as Walter's eyes bugged out.

"That's ridiculous!" he shouted.

"Page five. Do you really want that coming out, Walty-Walt?" Damian dryly asked.

Walter flipped to page five. The look of shock hit him hard as he closed the packet. "Fine. Deal."

Damian smiled. He actually smiled a big, bold grin. "It was great doing business with you, Rollsfield. I hope you have a good, fucked-up life. Come on, Aaliyah, let's hit it."

As we turned to leave, my eyes locked with Marie's for a moment. I saw the sadness in her eyes. My heart tugged a bit, but I wasn't ready to deal with what that tugging sensation stood for. I wasn't ready to deal with her hurts while I was still licking the wounds of mine.

Damian and I stepped outside, and I looked at him, a bit confused. "What was on page five?"

"Let's just say it involved his pool boy in the Hamptons and plastic hot dogs."

Well then. I'd rather not know any more details.

FORTY-SEVEN

Connor

"HOLY SHIT." I STARED AT MY LAPTOP AS AALIYAH SAT beside me with hers in her lap. We'd both spent our Saturday in pajamas, playing catch up on all of the work we'd been falling behind on. When a certain email landed in my inbox, I felt as if I were seeing things.

"What is it?"

"Walter Rollsfield… He's giving me his shares of the company. He's also taking the West Coast property back from Jason and shifting it to my name."

"Oh? Wow. That's amazing," Aaliyah said, shutting her laptop and moving in toward me. "Is that all he said?"

"No, actually. He's also leaving me the Queens property and giving me one hundred million dollars to invest in it."

"Whoa! That's wild!" Aaliyah said a bit too excitedly.

I narrowed my eyes. "What did you do?"

"Who me?"

"Yes, you. Why do I get the feeling you're keeping something from

"Damian and I might've gone ahead and shook Walter up a bit and threatened him."

"Shook him up? What are you two? Leaders of the mafia?"

"No, silly. I was the good cop, and Damian was the bad cop. We ruffled some feathers and got what we needed—what you deserved."

I sat there a bit stunned by what she and Damian had done for me. I placed my laptop down before reaching around her waist and pulling her onto my lap. I loved how she fit against me, as if she was always meant to be there.

"You're too good for me," I whispered, resting my forehead against hers.

"I think I'm just right," she disagreed.

"This means more to me than you'll ever know, Aaliyah. You've saved my career. But more than that, you saved me from a lonely existence."

"I love you."

"I love you more." I kissed her lightly, grazing my teeth against her bottom lip. "Though, I am kind of upset that you played cops without me."

"I even bought handcuffs in case Walter would've acted out," she joked. "If you want, you and I can play good cop bad cop tonight."

"Oh, yeah?"

"Yeah." She pointed her fingers toward me as a pretend gun. "Stick them up!" I slightly grind my hips against hers, and I watched as bashfulness hit her cheeks. "That's not exactly what I thought you'd be sticking up."

"Can you blame me? I miss feeling myself inside you," I muttered. I understood how important it was for Aaliyah to fully heal, and how she couldn't partake in any intense activities for a while. Which meant our sex life had been put on hold. But I missed tasting her, pushing myself deep inside her, listening to her moan my name.

She bit her bottom lip and slowly began to grind against my cock. "How much do you miss me?"

I groaned in pleasure. Damn, that felt good. "So much."

She leaned in and slowly trailed her tongue across my bottom lip before sucking it gently. "How much do you want me?"

Shit... "So much."

"How slow can you take it with me? To make sure I don't overexert myself?"

"Baby...trust me, I'll do all the work. All you have to do is let me have my way with you. All you have to do is say go."

She wrapped her fingers around her T-shirt and pulled it over her head. Her beautiful bare breasts sat in front of my face, making my cock throb even more. My eyes fell to the beautiful scar developing against her skin. That scar meant everything to me. It meant more moments like the one we currently shared. It meant more moments of love. More moments of laughter. More favorite memories to collect.

More time.

Time was such an odd concept, how it came and went. Each second passing, each minute evaporating. If I had any magic, I'd love to be able to freeze time, so I could enjoy my favorite moments a little bit more.

But that wasn't how time worked. It kept ticking by, but I learned that was okay. Every moment that passed was a blessing because many never had the chance to witness them. I was thankful for being given a few extra moments of time to spend with Aaliyah. Each second mattered. I wouldn't waste a single one.

I led her to the bedroom that night and lay her down. I undressed her bottom half as my hands roamed over her breasts. I kissed every inch of her, going slowly, being gentle every step of the way.

I made love to my best friend that night.

And I wasn't afraid to take my time.

We rose the next morning before the sun and did what we'd grown accustomed to doing on Sunday mornings. We packed a picnic and headed off to go visit Grant. Every Sunday since Aaliyah and I came back together, we'd enjoy our Sundays with Grant. We'd sit and laugh and read the comics as the sun kissed our skin.

There was nothing I loved more than watching the sunrises with Aaliyah, other than watching the sunset with her in my arms.

I felt like I owed Grant the world for not taking Aaliyah away from me too soon, and I'd spend the rest of my life thanking him for that very fact.

I held Captain America's book in my hand as I read out loud. Aaliyah sat completely wrapped up in the story. "It was at that very moment that Captain knew he'd discovered forever when Little Red Riding Hood showed up in his world," I said, making Aaliyah laughed.

"What?"

I kept reading. "Because Captain realized that the secret to life wasn't having powers. The secret to life was having love. Love was the greatest superpower any person could've ever had. So with that, Captain got down on one knee." I closed the comic and smiled as I reached into my back pocket and pulled out a ring.

"Connor," Aaliyah whispered, stunned as she stared at the diamond.

"You are everything good in the world, Aaliyah Winters. You are heaven on Earth and my very best friend. So if you would do me the favor of becoming my wife, I'd really appreciate that a lot. Because it turns out I need more than flashes of love. I need your full-time love because you make me whole. Your love is my destiny. Will you marry me, Red?"

Her lips pressed against mine within seconds but not before she whispered, "Yes."

With one single word, my life became that much brighter.

With one word, I was complete.

FORTY-EIGHT

Aaliyah

IT WAS DECEMBER WHEN I FOUND THE COURAGE TO CALL MARIE.
The snowflakes fell softly overhead and melted seconds after they hit the streets of the Upper East Side. The past few months had been a blur of me being in recovery and falling deeper in love with Connor. Falling more in love with myself. If I'd learned anything over the past year, it was that loving oneself was truly the best act of rebellion anyone could partake in.

I wasn't perfect. I still had flaws. Sometimes I judged others; sometimes I judged myself. I nitpicked at my scars, and at times, I hated the number sitting against the scale. Yet the greatest discovery of self-love was realizing you didn't have to be perfect in order to be worthy of love, of respect, of the ability to grow each and every day.

The truest form of authentic love began when one could look in the mirror, see the flaws, and still accept yourself as a full being who deserved the highest level of happiness.

I knew it was important to work on myself before I could face my past. I had to create boundaries strong enough to keep me from allow-

We planned to meet at our favorite coffee shop.

"Are you sure you don't want me to come in with you?" Connor asked as we sat in the back of his car.

I gave him a lopsided smile. "Yeah. This is something I have to do on my own. But can you wait for me? I'm not sure how this conversation will go or if I'll be in and out. But…"

"I'll be right here. I'll wait for however long it takes."

My lips landed against his, and his kiss gave me an extra dash of courage. That was what Connor's love did for me. It made me stronger every single day.

I climbed out of the car, allowing the snow to sweep against my cheeks as I tightened the belt on my wool coat. Marie was sitting inside the coffee shop already, staring down at her hands which were wrapped around a cup of coffee.

As I pushed the shop's door open, a bell dinged overhead, noting my arrival. Marie instantly looked toward me, her eyes filled with pain.

Those eyes.

How didn't I notice before how much they looked like mine?

Her eyes, and nose, and the slight dimple in her chin.

A wave of nausea hit me, but I didn't run away. I allowed myself to feel the discomfort because no feelings were unwarranted.

"Hi," she breathed out, going to stand.

"No, it's fine. Keep sitting," I said, sliding into the chair across from her.

She eased back down and returned her hands to her coffee cup. "I was going to order you a drink, but then again, I wasn't certain you were going to show."

"It's fine. I don't need anything."

"I was surprised when you messaged me about meeting."

"Yeah. Sorry it took so long. I needed time."

"I get it, Aaliyah, I do. I'm just happy that you called. I know you probably think the worst things about me. And I know my reasoning doesn't seem to make sense, but—"

"Are you still with him? With Walter?"

Her eyes flashed with guilt. That was her answer. No words were needed.

"Now, I know it probably seems pathetic..." she started to explain.

"He's a monster."

"I can see why you'd think that, but...I mean, he..." She took a deep inhalation and released it slowly. "He's all I've ever truly known."

"Make a new story. Learn something else."

"It's not that easy."

"I didn't say it was easy, but it's always worth it." Over the past few weeks, I thought about what I'd ask her. I thought about the questions that I'd have, the pain that I believed she could make dissipate with her replies, the missing pieces of my soul that maybe she could've filled. But as I sat in front of her, I realized our conversation wasn't about me. It was about her.

I'd already figured out how to love myself. Marie didn't even know where to start. It turned out self-love wasn't given to every individual by a certain age. Some people died without ever discovering themselves. Some individuals never were able to stare at their reflections and know that they were loved.

That thought alone made me sad because I knew with a few different choices in my life, I could've been her. That could've been me. I was no better than any other person who didn't know how to love themselves.

"I forgive you," I whispered. "For your choices you made. For giving me up. For scheming to bring me back into your life. For the lies, the scandal. I forgive you."

Her eyes flashed with hope as she reached across the table, placing her hands over mine. "You have no clue how much that means to me. Aaliyah, this is it. This can be a new start for you and me. We can—"

"No." I slowly pulled my hands away from her. "You misunderstood. I forgive you, Marie. But that doesn't mean I can open myself up to having you in my life."

Forgiving someone didn't mean you had to invite them back into your world. Sometimes forgiving meant finally letting them go. Forgiveness meant cutting the final cord of one's connection to your soul.

"I hope you find happiness, Marie. I do. I hope you start your journey to loving yourself. I hope you have more good days than bad, and

I hope you laugh. I hope you find joy in the darkness. And I hope you leave him because even though you've hurt me, that doesn't mean you deserve to be hurt, too. If you allow it, Walter will hurt you until the day you die."

"Maybe I deserve that." She lowered her head and stared at her hands.

I placed mine against hers. "No one deserves that."

She looked at me with tears in her eyes. "I've made so many mistakes in my life."

"That's okay. Begin again now. Can I ask why you stay with a man like him?"

"At one point, he was my everything. I was just waiting for him to come back to me… To be the man I thought he'd always been. I'm waiting for something that I know was probably always a lie."

"Find your ugly truths," I said, thinking about the conversation Connor had with me months ago. "It's better to sit with the ugly truths than bathe in the beautiful lies."

She gave me a halfway grin before wiping the tears from her eyes. "I'm sorry, Aaliyah, for everything. For hurting you. For leaving you. For all the bad choices I've made."

I smiled. "Thank you for that." I glanced toward the front window, where Connor's car was still waiting. "I should probably get going…"

"He proposed to you," she mentioned, staring down at the ring on my finger.

"Yes. A few months ago."

"Congratulations. He's a good one."

"Yes. He is." I stood up from the table. "I wish you the best, Marie."

"I wish you the same."

I turned to begin walking away and paused when I heard Marie call out my name. I looked back to see her standing with trembling hands.

"Cole was a good man. A powerful musician who loved the written word. He smiled like the sun and loved like the moonbeams. He laughed like you, tossing his head back in full chuckles. You have his nose and his Cupid's bow. He loved trying new things, and I know for a fact that if he knew you existed, he would've never let you go." Her lips parted as tears began falling down her cheeks. "At Your Best, You Are

Loved," she said, making me raise an eyebrow, confused by her words. "It was the song Cole was playing as I walked into the jazz bar that first night. There's a version by The Isley Brothers, but the version I knew was by—"

"Aaliyah," I muttered, feeling a wave of emotions. I'd listened to that song a million times, wondering if it was crafted for me.

She swallowed hard and nodded. "At your best, Aaliyah, you are loved."

I could count the number of facts I knew about my mother on multiple hands. She wore Chanel No. 5 and liked her coffee black. She loved to read, and when she smiled, you'd see all of her teeth. I'd gotten my eyes from her and my ears. She named me after the gone-too-soon musician Aaliyah, who I listened to throughout my teenage years. She dedicated "At Your Best, You Are Loved" to me.

My mother loved brunch, and hated peas—like me. She cried during commercials, and ate a salad with every meal. She couldn't stand Brussels sprouts, and the way she loved? She probably loved so much it hurt her. She gave her love to people who didn't deserve it. She was flawed—like all humans.

She had tight coils of hair dipped in black ink. Her laugh was infectious, the kind that made others chuckle just from the enjoyment of her sounds. She danced, too—poorly, like me, but oh, how her body swayed. And she was sad. Maybe sadder than most. Maybe lonelier, too.

I hugged her. I pulled her into me and held on tight. She held me back, and as she began to cry into my shoulder, I held her some more. I knew once I let go, we'd probably never speak again. I'd move on with my life, and she'd hopefully begin to discover her own.

So I held on a little longer because I wasn't completely ready to let her go.

"Thank you, Aaliyah," she whispered.

"You matter," I softly said back. "You matter, Marie."

I said the words I'd wished someone would've said to me when I was a child. I said the words I'd craved when I was sitting in the realm of loneliness. I gave her the words that she was never able to give to me. Then I let her go.

I walked back to the car where Connor hopped out and opened

the door for me. He looked at me with concern in his eyes. The care he showed me made the cracked pieces of my soul begin to heal again.

He didn't say a word, but he wrapped his arms around me as the snow fell overhead. He knew I needed the comfort, and he delivered it without question. When we arrived home, I still felt a bit emotional.

I hadn't spoken to Connor about the conversation I held with Marie, and I didn't think I had to share all of the details. Not yet, at least. I needed to sit in them a bit on my own, but I placed the song "At Your Best (You Are Loved)" on his living room speakers. The music filled the penthouse, and I stood up from the couch. I closed my eyes and began swaying back and forth alone.

Tears began to fall down my cheeks as I moved to the song. My emotions of the day started to catch up to me, and before I could crumple, before the ache in my chest could grow too large to handle, Connor caught me. He pulled me into his arms and began slow dancing with me. He didn't ask questions. He simply swayed his body with mine.

He slow danced to a song that he didn't even know the backstory to. I lay my head against his shoulder as the tears fell freely.

"Feel it all, Aaliyah, you are safe here," he said, holding me close to his body. The song played on a loop, and we kept dancing throughout the night. His lips fell against my forehead, and he whispered, "At your best, you are loved."

He healed me by simply existing in my world. He was my person.

My lover.

My friend.

My family.

And at his best, he was loved.

EPILOGUE

Connor

One Year Later

SHE WAS NERVOUS, AND I COULDN'T BLAME HER. IT WAS A BIG day for her, and her anxiety was warranted. Hell, I was an emotional wreck. I couldn't imagine how Aaliyah was feeling.

We sat inside of the conference room at Roe Real Estate, waiting for the group to arrive.

"Do you think this is stupid?" Aaliyah asked, holding a huge teddy bear in her arms. "Oh gosh, this is so stupid."

"It's perfect," I told her for the fifty millionth time.

She rubbed her sweaty palms against my pants, and I didn't mind it one bit.

"Hey, they're here," Damian said as he popped his head into the room. After he announced the arrival, a group of around thirteen people walked into the room. One wife, six adults, and six grandchildren.

For the longest time, Aaliyah went back and forth about meeting the donor's family. She was terrified that they'd resent her, and be angry that she was able to live, while they loss their loved one, but after going through the lengthy process of writing one another through the donor program, which protected individual's privacy, Aaliyah and the donor's family decided they'd like to meet in person.

The donor's name was William Brick, and he was loved.

The moment his family entered the room, there was nothing but an outpouring of appreciation.

William's wife, Addie, cried instantly, pulling Aaliyah into a hug, which made her cry, too. And hell, I started to tear up from the interaction. It didn't take long for us all to be an emotional mess.

"Oh, my goodness, you're so young," Addie said, placing her hands against Aaliyah's cheeks. "This is good. This is so good."

Aaliyah smiled and laughed nervously. "I was scared to meet you all."

"I understand, but we are just thankful that you did. The fact that we get to see someone surviving and thriving because of our loved one, well, if that isn't magic, then I don't know what is."

"Please, everyone, take a seat," I said, gesturing to the chairs surrounding the table. We all sat and laughed as our nerves skyrocketed through the room. Aaliyah began telling her story about how she came into needing a heart transplant, and then Addie and her family shared stories of William.

Aaliyah and I wanted to know them all, too. They told us about his service in the military. They told us about his bad taste in music and movies. About his goofy impersonations.

"He could do a perfect Jim Carrey impersonation like no other," his daughter, Becca, said, holding her son in her lap. She chuckled at the memory. "I remember being a kid, and whenever I'd get pissed at him, he'd do the Ace Ventura impression and force me to laugh."

"That was our Grant, though." Addie nodded. "He was the light in every room."

"I'm sorry, what did you just say?" Aaliyah asked, sitting up a bit in her chair. "Did you say Grant?"

"Oh, yeah. It was William's middle name. Most people called him Will, but the family called him Grant. I'd been calling him that since the day we'd met."

Aaliyah looked toward me, with stars in her eyes, and I felt it, too. The overwhelming love that our Grant was sending our way. I squeezed her hand under the table, and she squeezed mine back.

"Well, I don't want to keep you all for too long, but I have this gift for you. Well, we have thirteen of them, to be exact, in the other room. But here it is," Aaliyah said, standing from the table and walking over to Addie with the teddy bear in her hands.

She handed it over, and Addie looked a bit confused. "Well, thank you, sweetheart," she said still a bit stumped.

"Squeeze it," Aaliyah said, nodding in her direction.

Addie did as she was told, and within seconds, tears began flowing from her eyes as the sound of William's heartbeats began to be heard from the teddy bear.

"Is it...?" Addie asked, her voice cracking.

"Yes. I figured you all deserved to have him with you in some way, shape, or form," Aaliyah explained.

Dammit, who was cutting the onions?

By the end of the visit, everyone was in tears, but they were tears of love, of gratitude, of peace. After the family left, I stood in the office, pleased with how everything went during the conversation with the family.

Aaliyah walked over to me and fell into my arms. "His name was Grant," she beamed.

"Because of course it was." I laughed. I glanced down at my watch and stood up straight. "Oh shit, we gotta get going. It's already noon, and we can't be late. It is, after all, our wedding day."

We didn't start our day like most couples on their wedding day, and we were all right with that because we weren't like most couples. We were our own story, our own adventure, our own happily ever after.

We headed from my office to the place where all of the magic began—Oscar's Bar. A few years ago, I was a superhero, and she was a lady dressed in red. She was looking for an escape, and I was looking for her without even knowing it.

Oscar's was decked out with decorations, thanks to my mother and my small-town village, who all came up to New York to celebrate Aaliyah and me. The moment we walked inside, Jax and Damian grabbed me to take me to the men's room to get ready, and Mom and Kennedy pulled Aaliyah over to the ladies' room.

"You're late," Jax said, handing me my outfit that was hanging on one of the bathroom stalls. "You shouldn't have been late today."

"It's not like the show could go on without me," I said, unbuckling my pants and sliding out of them to toss on my wedding outfit. "But before we get things going, how about a joke?"

Jax and Damian groaned in unison.

Look at me, getting two grumpy best friends. I wouldn't have it any other way.

"A superhero walks into a bar and marries a woman dressed in red. And they lived happily ever after," I said.

Jax narrowed his eyes. "Are you being extremely corny right now?"

"I'm being extremely corny right now. I love her, Jax."

"Shit. I'd hope so, seeing as how I paid an arm and a leg to fly up here for this wedding. Do you know how expensive direct flights are? This shit is wild."

I laughed. "Yes, well, I would say I'd pay you back for the flight, but I'm not going to."

"Why doesn't that surprise me." He arched an eyebrow. "Are you really wearing that?"

"He's really wearing that," Damian said dryly, looking at me as I slipped into my outfit.

My Captain America costume.

Still fit like a glove.

A very, very tight glove, but a glove nonetheless.

"What? I think it looks good? And what else would I wear to a wedding on Halloween night?"

"I can see the complete outline of your balls," he said, unamused.

"Wouldn't be the first time you've seen them, am I right?" I joked, nudging him in the arm.

Jax shot a look at Damian. "I've never seen this dude's balls before."

"I know. Connor's just weird as fuck."

"But for some reason, you two still love me." I smirked.

"We feel sorry for you and your mental illness. We'd be bad people if we abandoned you," Jax said, patting me on the back.

I took a deep breath, feeling the nerves of the whole situation hitting me. I was really about to do this. I was about to marry my best friend.

"Any words of advice for a nervous groom?" I asked Jax. "I mean, you've been with Kennedy for years now. What wise words do you have for me and my marriage?"

"You're wrong," he said without thought. "Whatever the situation, even if you're right—you're wrong."

Before I could reply, Kennedy popped her head into the bathroom. "Jax, I need the diapers, and they weren't where you said they'd be."

"Did you check behind the bar like I mentioned?" he asked.

She sighed. "You didn't say behind the bar."

"I did say..." Jax paused. He looked at me, and then he turned to his wife and gave a big, fake smile. "You're right. I didn't say that. I'm wrong."

She nodded. "Of course, I'm right. I'm always right. Now come help me. Trevor's diaper exploded all over the place."

Jax smirked at me and shrugged. "See, kid? You're wrong. Just remember that, and you'll be fine. I'll be back."

He walked out of the bathroom, leaving me with Damian, who seemed even quieter than his norm. He was holding a piece of paper in his hands as his brows stayed lowered.

"What's going on, buddy? You okay?" I asked, walking over to him.

He grimaced, folded the piece of paper, and slid it back into his pocket. "It's nothing."

"You can't lie to your brother on his wedding day," I warned.

"I'm not trying to bring down the mood."

"The mood can be brought down for a moment, then we'll turn it back up. What's going on?"

He sighed and handed me the letter. "It's from my father. Well, it was sent on his behalf. He's been in California all this time. He's known where I've been my whole life. I guess he recently croaked. But, before he died, he wrote me that note. The funeral is next week."

"Holy shit." I read the letter, stunned. His father's name was Kevin Michaels, and he'd invited Damian to California to find the answers that Damian had been searching for his whole life, the missing pieces to his story.

"Are you going out there?" I asked.

"I feel like I need to, but I don't know how long I'd be out there. I don't know how long it will take me to get the answers I want. The answers I fucking deserve."

"Yeah. I get that."

"I don't even know what I'd do for work. I can't go out there wasting time and money looking for pieces of my fucked-up story."

"Unless you had a West Coast real estate company to run, that is."

He turned my way and cocked an eyebrow. "What?"

"Our West Coast property had been down since the situation with Jason and Walter. I'd been holding off reopening until we had the right person to run it. It makes me feel stupid that I've taken this long to realize that the right person has always been you."

Damian's brows knitted together, and he frowned. "You don't have to do me any favors, Connor."

"Yes, I do. That's what family does. We look out for each other. Go out there and find your answers, Damian. You deserve to know your history."

He sniffled a bit, and that was the closest I'd ever seen Damian get to crying. "Knock, knock," he said.

I smirked. "Who's there?"

"You." He shrugged. "You're there. You've been there for me since you showed up, and I don't think you know how much that means to me. You're the brother I always wanted." I felt myself on the brink of tears, and he rolled his eyes. "Don't make it weird, Connor."

"No, I mean, I'm not gonna cry."

"You're already crying."

"Well, you can't just say shit like that, Damian, and expect me not to cry, dammit! Can I hug you?"

"No."

"Can I say I love you without making you uncomfortable?"

"Probably not."

"All right then, I hate you."

He smirked. "I hate you, too."

I scratched at my beard. "But we do need to get together sometime and work on your punchlines. That was a very odd joke."

"I'll leave the joking to you, seeing how you're such a joke yourself."

I chuckled and nudged me. "See? That's a funny joke."

"I wasn't kidding. I think you're a joke."

I smiled and patted him on the back. "I love you, too."

He stood up taller, shaking off his emotions. "Enough about me. Let's get you married off, old man."

I pointed a stern finger at him. "Don't call me old man! Jax is an old man, not me!"

"Yeah. Whatever you say, old man."

The rooftop of Oscar's Bar was set up with chairs for our guests. There were sunflowers throughout the space—her favorite. There were bags of Cheetos resting in everyone's goodie bags—my favorite.

I stood at the altar with my best friends standing beside me. The sun had begun to set behind me, and that was her cue.

That was her sign to enter the space, in her beautiful red dress that made me fall in love with her all those years before. She stood tall with a bouquet of sunflowers and walked down an aisle sprinkled with quarters. Her skin shone as the light hit her, highlighting every beautiful inch of her being.

As she reached me, she passed her bouquet off to my mother, and then Aaliyah turned to face me.

I took her hands into mine because the idea of not touching her was too much for me.

"Hi," she whispered.

"Hi," I replied.

"Ready?"

"Ready."

She smiled at me, and I smiled back, feeling the warmth of her love radiating off her entire being.

My beginning, my middle, my end.

She took my last name that evening, and we danced the night away with our loved ones. We celebrated life. We celebrated the beginning of something magical. Something that would last forever.

After the evening came to an end, Aaliyah and I stayed on the rooftop for hours, waiting to witness the sunrise together. This time when the sun warmed our skin, I didn't let her go. This time, I was wise enough to hold onto her tighter. This time, I'd stay as long as possible. I didn't care if it were for hours, months, or years. I was completely invested in her, in our story, in every single adventure we had yet to deserve.

Every inch of me belonged to my Little Red Riding Hood, and every piece of her was mine.

For as long as we both shall live.

The end.